HAPPY
DREAMS

HAPPY DREAMS

JIA PINGWA

TRANSLATED BY **NICKY HARMAN**

Text copyright © 2007 Jia Pingwa
Translation copyright © 2017 Nicky Harman
All rights reserved.

Previously published as 《高兴》 by the People's Literature Publishing House in China in 2008. Translated from Chinese by Nicky Harman. First published in English by AmazonCrossing in 2017.

Published by AmazonCrossing, Seattle

www.apub.com

Amazon, the Amazon logo, and AmazonCrossing are trademarks of Amazon.com, Inc., or its affiliates.

ISBN-13: 9781611097429
ISBN-10: 1611097428

Cover design by Kimberly Glyder

Printed in the United States of America

HAPPY
DREAMS

1.

"Name?"

"Happy Liu."

"It says 'Hawa Liu' on your ID card. What's with this 'Happy Liu'?"

"I changed my name. Everyone calls me Happy Liu now."

"'Happy' are you, Hawa Liu?"

"You must call me Happy Liu, comrade!"

"Happy Liu!"

"Yes, sir!"

"Know why I'm handcuffing you?"

"Because I had my buddy's corpse with me?"

"And . . . ?"

"I shouldn't have been at the station with Wufu on my back."

"Well, if you know that, why did you do it?"

"He needed to go home."

"Home . . . ?"

"Freshwind Township, Shangzhou District."

"I'm asking about you!"

"Right here."

"Huh?"

"Xi'an."

"Xi'an?"

"Well, I should be from Xi'an."

"Tell the truth!"

"I am telling the truth."

"Then what do you mean by 'should be'?"

"I really should be, comrade, because . . ."

It was October 13, 2000, and we were standing on the east side of Xi'an Station Square, outside the barriers. The policeman was taking a statement from me. The wind was blowing hard, and leaves floated down from the gingkos, catalpas, and plane trees around the edge of the square, covering everything with brilliant reds and yellows.

The thing I most regret is not the bottle of *taibai* liquor, but the white rooster. Freshwind folk believe the spirit of someone who dies away from home has to make its way back. In case the spirit gets lost, you tie a white rooster to the body to guide it. The rooster I bought was supposed to help Wufu's spirit get home, but in the end, the bird messed up everything. It weighed two and a half pounds at the very most, but the woman insisted it was three pounds. I lost my temper.

"Bullshit! No way is that three pounds! I can always tell how much something weighs! Do you know what I want it for?" (Of course, I didn't tell her what I wanted it for.)

But she kept shouting. "Put it on the scales again! Go ahead and put it on the scales again!" So then the policeman trotted over to sort out the argument.

And he saw the bedroll tied with rope. "What's that?" He jabbed it with his baton. Lively Shi went as pale as if he'd smacked his face in a sack of ash. Then the stupid fucker opened his big mouth and said it was a side of pork, of all things.

"Pork? You wrap pork up in a quilt?" asked the policeman. He carried on poking, and the corner of the bedroll came undone. That was when that coward Lively showed his true colors. He dropped the *taibai* bottle and took off. The policeman immediately pounced on me and handcuffed one of my wrists to the flagpole.

"Would you be so good as to handcuff my left wrist instead?" I asked with a smile. I'd pulled a muscle in my right arm digging the trench.

This time, the baton jabbed me in the crotch. "Don't joke around!" So I didn't joke around.

Everything looked blurred, as if my eyes were gummed up with boogers. But I told myself to stay calm. The ink wouldn't come out of the policeman's pen, and he kept shaking it. The patch of pimples on his forehead flamed red. I tried to put my foot on a drifting plane-tree leaf but couldn't reach it. I'd never seen a young man with so many zits. Obviously not married yet and fierce as a young billy goat!

Click. A reporter was taking a photograph.

I took an instant dislike to her. She was done up like a little girl, with bangs down to her eyebrows, though she was clearly well into her thirties. I didn't notice her at first. When I did, I smoothed my hair, straightened my clothes, and presented my profile so she could take another picture. But the next day in the paper, they used the one where I was bent over as if I was giving a statement, and in front of me was the flower-patterned bedroll tied with rope. One of Wufu's feet was sticking out, and you could see his yellow rubber shoe stuffed with cotton wadding. Dammit, that picture was no better than a head-on mug shot, enough to make anyone look like a criminal. I have a prominent nose and a well-defined mouth, but she wouldn't take me in profile, the bitch.

No way did that photo look anything like me!

Once Wufu's body had been taken to the funeral parlor, they let me go. But I had to go back to the train station to wait for Wufu's wife, who was coming to deal with the funeral arrangements. The square in front of the station was full of people who'd seen the newspaper, and they pointed at me. "Look! That's the man who tried to carry a corpse onto the train! Hawa Liu!" I ignored them. Then they shouted, "Shangzhou husk-eater!" That was an insult to Shangzhou folk, so of course I paid

3

even less attention. (Where I come from, the land's so barren that there's not enough grain to last year-round. Come springtime, all there is to eat is a ground-up mixture of dried persimmons and toasted rice husks.)

I needed some time to think. Though Wufu's body had been taken to the funeral parlor, I felt his spirit must still be around here in the square, maybe perched on the traffic lights or sitting on the piles of roast chicken, hard-boiled duck eggs, bread, and bottles of mineral water on the street vendor's cart. The small of my back felt sore and tired now, and I pushed my hand against it. Then I had another thought: *How good a car is depends on its engine, not on its body, right? And like a car's engine, a kidney is fundamental to a human body, isn't it?* My flesh was from Freshwind, and I was Hawa Liu, but I'd sold my kidney to Xi'an, so that meant I really did belong in Xi'an. Yes, Xi'an! I was very satisfied that I'd worked this out. It made me feel sort of lonesome, but proud too. I held my head high and began to stride along. And each step proclaimed, *I'm not Hawa Liu. I'm not a Shangzhou husk-eater. I'm Happy Liu from Xi'an. Hap-py Liu!*

When I first met Meng Yichun, she said, "Happy Liu, you don't look like a peasant."

I disagreed. "I'll always be a peasant, like mutton always smells like mutton," I told her.

But she said she'd met a lot of men in Xi'an—officials, businessmen, and academics—and some of them were no more than peasants. Her words went right to my heart. I always thought I was different from the people around me, at least different from Wufu. It was hard to put this into words, but I knew I was destined for better things.

I can give you some examples. One, I'm really good at doing math in my head. When I had to do math problems as a little boy, I could give you the answers without having to work out the problems on paper first, even if they were three- or four-figure numbers. Of course, I had my own ways of doing them. Two, I'd walk thirty *li*, and go hungry too, to get to an opera in the County Town. Three, my clothes are old, it's true, but they're always clean. I don't have an iron, but I pour boiling water into my enamel mug and use the bottom to iron the wrinkles out of my pants. Four, I can play the *xiao*, the flute you hold vertically. Back in Freshwind, lots of people could play the fiddle, but only I played the flute. Five, if I have a problem, I don't tell anyone about it. If it gets really bad, I just laugh at myself, and that's it. Six, I hate foulmouthed people. What have you got against heaven, or your parents? What's the point of getting angry with them? The man who bought my kidney said it was going to a big company boss, so he had to check I didn't have any other diseases. Go ahead, I said. The only thing he found was hemorrhoids. Then he said I was mentally alert, but I'd let my body go a bit. I got annoyed at that, but I stayed polite, and when he was leaving, I gave him a basket of free-range pullets' eggs. Seven, I was born with upturned lips, so I'm happy by nature. Four years ago, when old Mother Wang was matchmaking for me, I played the flute for three days and three nights. Mother Wang said I had to build a new house, so, to raise the money, I sold my blood. I did this three times, until I heard that people from Dawanggou had caught hepatitis B from selling their blood, so I didn't do that again. I sold my kidney instead. I used the money to build the house, but then the girl went and married someone else. OK, so she married someone else. I still played the flute for three days and three nights, and then I went out and bought a pair of women's high-heeled leather shoes with pointed toes. *That girl was just a bunion!* I thought. *I'm going to marry a woman who wears high-heeled leather shoes with pointed toes!*

And of course, a woman who can wear high-heeled leather shoes with pointed toes must be from Xi'an.

It's hard to explain why I have such strong feelings for Xi'an, but after my kidney was transplanted into a Xi'an man, I kept dreaming about the city walls and the great wooden gates with studs on them as big as rice bowls, and the bell tower with its gilded roof. In my dreams, I was sitting on a white rock under a crooked pine outside the city walls.

5

When I arrived in Xi'an, the gates in the city walls and the bell tower were exactly as I'd seen them in my dreams, and outside the walls there really was a crooked pine tree with a white rock under it. And so I figured a few things out. There was a reason why I was never physically strong, not like Wufu, who could splash across a river waist deep in water with a load of firewood weighing a hundred and fifty pounds on his back. There was a reason why Wufu could eat ten pounds of cooked sweet potato in one sitting, but I burped acid after I'd eaten three pounds. There was a reason why dopey Wufu had married ages ago and had kids, whereas I was still a bachelor. And the reason was this: I was meant to be a city man, from Xi'an.

2.

I really did become a man from Xi'an. If human life can be divided into stages, then the way I see it is that my Freshwind stage was a messy heap of straw, scattering whenever the wind blew, and the next stage for me was city life.

I'd better explain about Wufu, hadn't I? Without leaving anything out. You see, I was fated to stick with Wufu, always, even though he was extremely ugly and extremely coarse. In the train station square, and then at the local police station, I kept saying that the pair of us were inextricably linked together. We must have sinned against each other in a previous existence, so that each of us owed something to the other in this life.

He was five years older than me, so in the normal way of things, he should have taken the lead, but actually it was the other way round; he tagged along behind me. Gem Han said I was nice to Wufu only because of his young missus, but that was insulting to me. Why would I fancy a woman with such big breasts and a butt as broad as a bamboo sieve? Mighty was surprised at my taste in women. He said that peasants were primitive in love and liked women with big breasts and hips because they were good for childbearing. Fine, then that just proved I was no peasant! Well, anyway, Wufu's wife gave birth to three sons, a trio of bandits, and Wufu had a terrible time feeding them. There wasn't much farmland around Freshwind, and after they'd built a railway here and a highway there in the 1990s, there was even less. Anyone who could went off to the city to get a laboring job. But Wufu was dumb, and no one wanted to take him along. So I took him under my wing. We stayed near the County Town first and did all sorts of work: building houses, digging graves, making sun-dried bricks, and building brick stoves. We hardly earned any money, and as soon as we got home, we had to turn around and go back again. Back and forth, back and forth, for years. Every time we went home, I'd say, "Wufu, while you're screwing your missus, all I ever get my leg over is the edge of the bed. It's not fair."

Wufu used to say, "What can I do?"

Once I said, "Don't go home. Stick around tonight." So Wufu spent the night drinking with me instead.

When I sold my kidney, no one in Freshwind knew except Wufu. "Keep your trap shut, you hear me, Wufu?" I told him.

"You can trust me," he said. "I was a Little Red Guard in the Cultural Revolution, and I stuck my Mao badge right into my chest, and now I'll do the same for you!" Then he got a safety pin and stuck it into his flesh, and the wound bled all over the place. I grabbed it off him, but it left him with a second scar on his chest.

Gem Han was the first to leave Freshwind for Xi'an. At first, we heard he was only scraping by, but then rumors came that he'd gotten mega-rich. With Han as the yeast, the Freshwind dough bubbled up, and quite a few people joined him in Xi'an. I tried to get Wufu excited about it. "Let's go too!" I said.

But he just said, "Here in the County Town, I fit in, everyone eats and dresses pretty much like me. But if I went to Xi'an, I'd stand out like a sore thumb. It'd scare the shit out of me."

I hated seeing Wufu shit-scared. It wasn't as if Xi'an people were man-eating tigers or had three heads. He was hopeless! I ignored him and sat down on the pavement for a smoke. There was a dog nearby, gnawing on a bone without a shred of meat on it. I kicked the dog away and threw the bone up onto the roof opposite.

Wufu looked at me doubtfully. "If we do go, can we come back again?"

"If I do well for myself, I'm certainly not coming back!"

Wufu looked shocked. "But you've just built a house with two rooms!"

"So what? If a new house keeps me in Freshwind, it's no better than a coffin!" As soon as the words were out of my mouth, I realized that going to Xi'an was a done deal. My kidney was calling me from Xi'an. I had to go!

Wufu said, "If you're really not coming back, then you'll leave me your new house, right?"

I was furious. "Yeah, and you can have these shoes too!" And I took one off and slapped him over the head with it. You slapped the guy, he just smiled at you. That was Wufu, all right. "Come on, you're getting me some noodle water!" I said.

We went to the noodle shop with our *ganmo*, dry flatbreads, so we could dunk them in the bowls of noodle water. But it was no good asking for the noodle water without buying any noodles, so when Wufu took along a clean bowl, I told him, "Just pick up someone else's dirty bowl." That way, the noodle seller would think we'd already eaten our noodles and she'd give us the hot water for free. Wufu was such an idiot, he never thought of stuff like that.

Once I asked Wufu, "Someone saves a person's life, and the person he saves then saves someone else. Of the two, if one had to die, which should it be?"

Wufu looked nonplussed. "Which?" he asked.

"The one who was saved shouldn't die," I told him.

"Why?"

I sighed and refused to tell him, just tapped his forehead with my flute. "Massage my neck for me!" He did it right away. His touch was

9

perfect, not too light and not too heavy, and he got the acupressure points too.

I never saved Wufu's life, but I needed him all the same. Not just because Wufu did what I told him, but because I'd already put a lot of effort, and money too, into looking after that dumbass.

"You're coming, Wufu," I said. "You're coming with me."

3.

Wufu and I arrived in Xi'an on March 10, 2000. Wufu was all keyed up the minute he got off the train. His mouth hung open, he went rigid, and he started to pour with sweat even though it was a cold day. The odd thing was that we were both wearing our best clothes, but we looked scruffy and dusty. And our hands suddenly looked really swarthy—how did that happen? Wufu hung on to my jacket and walked so close behind me that he was treading on my heels. I told him to let go, but then I was worried he might get lost.

"OK, Wufu," I said, "you walk in front. Just go the way I tell you to." There were block after block of buildings, big and small, fat and thin, poking up into the sky, and roads piled on top of one another, twisting and turning. Downtown was like an ant's nest, a hurly-burly of humans and cars, all mixed up together. Still, even though I couldn't see the sun, I had a rough idea of east and west, and where we were going. I tried to lighten the mood. "Wufu," I began, "an ox . . ."

I hadn't finished speaking before Wufu butted in. "Ox? What ox?"

He was really bugging me. "If the head of the ox is facing east," I said, "which way does the tail point?"

"West."

"Wrong! It points down."

Wufu thought hard, then said, "You're a smart guy, Hawa!"

Of course I am. I told him not to walk along with his arms squeezed against his ribs. "Relax! Swing them around! And stop lifting your feet up so high. People will think you're from the mountains if you walk like that. And pick the crumbs from between your teeth."

But Wufu just kept going on about how he wanted to piss. How he needed to go so bad, his piss was going to hit the ceiling. He was purple in the face from holding it in. When we finally found a WC, I saw he had a pocket sewn into his undershorts, with fifty yuan in it.

"The city's full of thieves!" he said. "It's a dog-eat-dog world here!"

We headed south, to a place called Fishpond Village. We needed Gem Han to set us up in Xi'an. As we arrived, we passed a man on the side of the road burning "ghost money" for his dead parents. There must have been ghosts around, and it seemed like they were messing with us: we went all around the village, but we couldn't find where Gem Han lived. Fishpond Village used to be in the countryside, but it had been swallowed up by the city, and the villagers, though they were still registered as farmers, had sold off their land and used the money to build rental properties. The buildings were three or four stories high, even six stories, but they weren't built of reinforced concrete, just bricks and concrete blocks piled one on top of another, and the lanes between them were narrow and dark.

"Will those buildings fall down?" Wufu asked.

I looked up at the spiderweb of electric cables overhead, crisscrossing the sky like a sieve. "That's dangerous."

"Good thing if they do fall down. They're peasants. How come they get to build all these houses?" said Wufu.

I aimed a kick at him to make him shut up.

We finally tracked down Gem Han. He didn't look anything like he used to; he had a buzz cut and wore leather shoes. He was astonished when we turned up, but he was happy to see us. He offered us a drink, got a bottle of wine out from under the bed, and then cursed because he couldn't get the cork out.

"I hate it when people give you wine but don't give you a bottle opener!"

He was obviously showing off, so I simply smiled. "Let's have tea," he said, and served us some. The whole time we were drinking it, he was on the phone. If it wasn't someone asking him out to dinner, it was someone else asking him to fix them up with a job.

"Hah!" he exclaimed. "I've turned into Freshwind's Xi'an office!"

"Ah well, you've made it, so now everyone else wants to get in on the act!" I said.

I meant it as a compliment, but he grumbled, "I'm not the goddamned emperor with a country to look after!"

I was about to casually spit on the floor, but I made myself swallow the gob of phlegm instead.

Gem Han inquired what we were going to do in Xi'an. "We're like tigers, hungry enough to eat the sky. We just don't know where to start," I told him. "We'll do whatever you tell us."

Wufu butted in. "You eat the meat. We'll be happy with the soup!"

Han said we could start as trash pickers.

Trash pickers? It never occurred to me I'd be picking trash in Xi'an! "I pick trash," Gem Han said. *Who're you kidding?* I thought. *You mean we can look like you if we pick trash?* But it was true, Gem Han was a trash picker.

Han told us that Xi'an was deep water, deep as an ocean, so deep it made your head swim when you first got here.

"Mine's swimming," said Wufu.

"Everyone comes to earn money, and the clever ones can turn the paper on the ground into cash. But if you don't make good, the paper on the ground's never going to be anything more than paper, even if you get down on your knees and pray to it."

"I get it," said Wufu.

"People come here from Freshwind with zero—no skills, no money. Do they expect to sell their asses?" said Han.

"What a thing to say!" said Wufu.

I told him not to talk so much.

Gem Han laughed and patted my shoulder. "You were right to come to me. Trash collection is the way to get started in Xi'an, and I wouldn't tell that to just anyone." Wufu's droopy eyes opened wide at that, but Han wouldn't let him get a word out. He simply got up and pushed Wufu into the armchair he'd been sitting in himself. Wufu sank right into its leather upholstery.

Then Han started to instruct us in the world of trash collection. He made it sound as complicated as the realms of Buddhist cosmology, and by the time he'd finished, I was an initiate. Trash pickers in Xi'an were a new social class, he explained, made up of folk from the countryside who came and settled all around the fringes of the city. It was not a tightly organized business, but there were regulations, and different territories, and five grades of people working in each territory.

Bottom of the heap, in the fifth grade, were the rookies, a sad bunch who had to spend their time lugging around a big laundry bag and a garbage-picker hook. They went from street to street, rifling through trash bins, or they crawled over the out-of-town garbage dumps. They were lonely souls, always hungry but grateful they weren't starving to death. The fourth grade had entered the trash-picking priesthood, so they were better off. With the right introductions, you could pull your cart or pedal your three-wheeler around the streets, but only on your allotted patch. You couldn't descend like locusts anywhere you wanted. You could pick up or buy stuff, and earn fifteen yuan a day, even twenty if you were lucky. Grade three trash pickers subcontracted a modern housing estate, so they were lucky, they didn't need to do street collections. If they were sharp-eyed, they'd spot when someone had a coal delivery or bought new furniture. They'd offer to lug it up the stairs, and they'd get the owner's trash in exchange, sometimes for free. They earned about twenty yuan a day too, but it was a steady income, and sometimes they could afford to buy good stuff, like an old TV, a radio, a sofa, a bedstead, or secondhand clothes. Grade two were the big guys, in charge of a large neighborhood. They controlled those in the fourth and fifth grades, who had to pay them regular kickbacks. Grade two guys were in charge of Xi'an's "city villages," which were densely populated and had all sorts of businesses within their boundaries. As long as they paid an annual bribe of 20,000 yuan to the city village's government chief, they were Kings of Trash on their particular patch. Gem Han had made it to second grade, but he wasn't going to rest there. He had hopes of becoming a Number One. There were four Number Ones in Xi'an: Wang in the north, Lu in the west, Liu in the south, and Li in the east. Everyone in town knew their surnames, and they all shared the same first name: Power. The four Powers all dressed in smart suits and had nice manners. Whenever they did the rounds collecting their dues from the trash pickers at each grade, they were all affable smiles, until someone stepped out of line or didn't pay up, and then they'd get beaten up or driven out by some unidentified thug. Of course, the Powers also had their responsibilities. If you had a problem, or the police stopped you, or the local thugs tried to extort money from you, then you had to take it up the grades, and the Powers would settle it.

Yup, I certainly admired Gem Han. He had a big broad face, dotted with gleaming pockmarks. When he went to use the toilet, I said to Wufu, "He's one tough guy. See how he stomps along!"

Wufu said, "Those pockmarks, they're because his family grew the worst crops in Freshwind . . ."

What Wufu didn't understand was that plates might not be as good as a bowl for water, but plates were what you needed for a feast. I told him to go and buy Han a packet of cigarettes.

Wufu hemmed and hawed, and eventually asked, "Which ones?"

"Lucky Cat!"

"Aren't they expensive?"

"We want expensive ones!"

Gem Han accepted the smokes coolly, not looking down his nose at them but not particularly pleased either. He changed into another pair of leather shoes, polishing them on a corner of the bedsheet, then took us to the east side of the village to rent a room. The lane was a long way from anywhere, and very narrow. The third building along, facing north, looked as though it was supposed to have had several stories but for some reason had been left as one story. There were two trash pickers already living downstairs, but on the roof a couple of brick-built rooms had been thrown up. Wufu and I got one each. It was not a great place to live, but, hey, it was cheap. The good thing was that there was a locust tree in front of the building, a big one, which shaded the yard and our rooms too. Then Han took us to rent a couple of carts. There were only two left, and one had no tires on the wheels, just a bit of old rubber tied around them. Wufu got that one, because he was stronger than me so he didn't mind pulling it. Then we bought hand scales from an old guy at a stall, and that was when I found out that these scales always under-weighed: a pound of trash only ever tipped the scales at eight-tenths of a pound. Finally, Han took us into town, making sure we noted landmarks we were passing, especially the names and signs on the shops where we turned corners. I was tired of listening to his instructions by the time we got to Prosper Street.

Prosper Street was a good name for our patch.

4.

Someone was planting a tree on Prosper Street. A square hole had been dug, and beside it lay a sapling, its side branches pruned off so all that was left was a trunk sticking out like an arm, and about as thick. My heart skipped a beat. I remembered my dream: I was sitting on a white stone under a crooked pine outside the city walls, and how I'd thought when I woke up that I could be a tree growing in the city. Was I this very tree?

"What tree is that?" I asked Wufu.

"An indigo bush."

"Good," I said.

"Good?"

"Yup. From now on, look after that tree!"

Wufu looked puzzled and acted dumb, his mouth gaping.

"Mouth!" I snapped.

He shut his mouth.

Prosper Street was in the southeast corner of Xi'an, about ten streets away from where we lived. It so happened that three days before we arrived, the old guy who picked the trash on this patch was knocked down while crossing the road and killed. That was what Gem Han told us. He said the old guy had it coming, and it was right that we were replacing him. I bought a bottle of liquor, sprinkled it on the road to placate his ghost, and said a little prayer, asking him not to hold it against us. Wufu couldn't understand why I was sprinkling liquor on the road—what a waste! I didn't say it out loud, but I was worried the story would spook Wufu. He couldn't ever screw up the courage to cross a road until all the cars were gone, and even then, he'd start running as if a pack of wolves were at his heels. Well, that couldn't be helped, Wufu was never going to be a city man.

Gem Han took us back to Prosper Street and left, without telling us how we were supposed to pick trash. Wufu started grumbling that he was starving. Wufu must have had worms—he was always starving! Around the corner was a little shop run by Shanxi folk who sold knife-cut noodles, and I ordered four bowls. Wufu wanted five, but I said no firmly: "They all come with minced meat on top of the noodles!" Wufu squatted on the bench, and you could see his shoes had holes. They were also filthy, and three flies had landed on them to wash their faces. "Wufu!" I said, and gestured for him to sit down properly.

Wufu ignored me, just complained that the saucer of red chili oil was empty. "Where's the chili oil, mister?" he shouted at the noodle-shop owner and smacked his lips. I tried to hush him up, but he shouted for more garlic. "Bring us a garlic bulb, mister!" I stopped eating, put my bowl down, and glared at him furiously. He was busy pushing the noodles into his mouth and shouting for two bowls of noodle water with his mouth full. Everyone in the shop looked at him, eyebrows raised.

"Haven't you ever eaten a meal out before?" I muttered.

He looked up at me, concerned. "Eat up, Hawa! It's good!"

We never got our noodle water, so Wufu had to be content with the tea they served every customer at the start of the meal. He took a slurp and swilled it around his mouth, making a noise like he was gargling, trying to swill bits of food from between his teeth. The noodle seller thought Wufu was about to spit it out on the floor, and he yelled for the waitress to bring a spittoon. But Wufu sucked in his cheeks and swallowed the tea in one gulp.

As soon as we left the noodle shop, I had a good laugh.

"What's up with you?" Wufu asked.

"Just remember," I told him, "next time you eat out, no squatting on the bench, no smacking your lips, no shouting about how good it is, no swilling tea around your mouth. And if you do rinse your mouth out, don't swallow it after!"

Wufu looked downcast at my strictures. "Did I make a fool of myself?" he asked.

"Yes, you sure did!"

By the time I got to the end of the list of things Wufu shouldn't do, he looked flummoxed. "But how am I supposed to enjoy my meal with so many rules?" Then he said, "I miss Moth," and he sat down on a stone block by the road, his face looking all frostbitten. Moth was his missus. Why on earth had I brought a wimp like this to Xi'an? I felt like saying, *You've only just gotten here, and you already want to go home? Off you go then!* But he wouldn't even be able to find his way out of the city. I felt sorry for him, and besides, there was no one but me willing to take him along.

I pulled him to his feet and said, "Wufu, look at me! Go on! Look at me!"

Wufu's eyes were like a dead fish's, dull as sludge. He held my gaze for less than ten seconds, then looked away.

"Look at me!" I repeated. "If you've got the courage to look at me, then you can face Xi'an! Stop acting so gloomy. It doesn't do you any favors! Wufu, I'm going to give myself a new name. Know what it's going to be?"

"A new name?" Wufu stared.

"Yup, it's going to be Happy!"

"Happy?"

"Happy Liu, that's what I'm called from now on. No more 'Hawa Liu.' If you call me that, I won't answer. I figure Happy's a good name." I was really pleased with it. In fact, I suggested that Wufu choose a new name too.

But Wufu said, "A name's just a name. Calling yourself 'Piglet' doesn't make you a piglet. What good's my name ever done me? I mean, 'Five Riches'!"

I told him that was because Wufu sounded too much like "No Riches." A name is very important, as I said to him. Take Prosper Street. It was such a lucky name, and it made me think about the names of countries like America, Germany, Britain, and France. In Chinese, they were written with characters that meant "beautiful," "virtuous," "heroic," and so on. No wonder they were powerful countries. Cambodia, Nepal, and Myanmar would never get rich, I said. Their names in Chinese meant "village," "mud," and "marsh"!

And I carried on, explaining to him that writing a name was like writing a charm, and saying a name aloud was like chanting a spell, it had the power to shape your destiny. My name in Freshwind was Hawa, so how could I be anything other than a peasant? How could I ever find a wife or be happy? I'd been wanting to change my name for a while, but Freshwind folk didn't appreciate stuff like that. Now that I was in Xi'an, it was another world. I was going to be happy, so I'd call myself Happy Liu. "The more I'm called 'Happy,' the happier I'll be, get it?"

Wufu didn't get it, and he wasn't going to change his name either. He was going to stick to "Wufu."

5.

As soon as I changed my name to Happy, a lot of happy things happened. The first few days picking trash, we took in fifteen yuan, but then that went up to seventeen or eighteen, and then I actually upped it to twenty yuan. The other trash pickers in Fishpond Village couldn't believe it.

Wufu's reaction was to say, "Well, you're a smart one, aren't you!"

The thing I found most incredible was that I only had to wish for something and it came true. For instance, we had to cook for ourselves, and we were about to buy a wok when we found one in the trash. True, one of the handles had broken off, but it didn't leak, and it held just about enough food for a meal for Wufu and me. Another time, Wufu was grumbling that using coal to cook with was too expensive, and I remembered that we burned wood in the mud-brick stoves we used at home. Xi'an folk never used firewood, and it was easy enough to pick up plenty. We simply had to roam around Fishpond every day when we got back from Prosper Street to gather enough kindling and branches. Then, Wufu's shoes were filthy, and they'd really had it. I told him we'd have to get him some decent secondhand ones, and the very next day, a pair turned up in the trash, rubber-soled too.

We settled down nicely. Wufu started cooking as soon as we got back from Prosper Street. He would steam a few dozen *ganmo* in a basket suspended from a wooden stick and boil up corn porridge at the same time, getting it just right, not too thin and not too thick, testing the consistency by dipping in a chopstick and watching the porridge slide off it in a thin stream. Most times, we ate it with a daikon radish that Wufu shredded and pickled. Wufu knew I loved fermented bean curd, and he bought a saucer of it for me. We sat there on our flat roof—a mouthful of shredded daikon, a mouthful of *ganmo*, then a slurp of the porridge. When Wufu finished, he would cross his left leg over his right and fart, then change his legs over and say, "Life's good, eh, Hawa?"

"What did you call me?"

"Happy! There aren't a lot of Freshwind folk living it up like we are!"

"You clean up the wok and bowls, and I'll play my flute." I always liked playing my flute when I was happy. Sometimes birds flew into our tree when I played. Playing the flute to bring the phoenix, I called it.

Wufu always said, "That's not a phoenix, it's a dusty gray sparrow." Wufu had no culture, he didn't know a thing about metaphor and imagination. If I saw a phoenix, then a phoenix it was, and the treetop was a cloud, a green cloud. The green cloud was home to mosquitoes and flies, and they were always pissing little droplets of water. I played and played, and the droplets got heavier, and more continuous, and I finally realized it was raining. Wufu was still scraping the wok. He wouldn't leave any leftover food, it all had to be eaten. His maxim was that anything could be wasted, but not food.

"If you carry on eating when you're full, isn't that wasteful too?" I said.

He said nothing for a moment, then asked, "What's today's date?"

"I'm not a woman," I told him. Women had periods, so they always knew what day of the month it was. We men only had a rough idea. We knew that when it was light, we went out to work and when it got dark, we came home, ate, and slept. We needed a calendar.

I said, "If it carries on raining, we'll have to stay in."

22

"Afraid of a bit of drizzle?" Wufu jibed, but then he smiled. He cut off a little piece of the bean curd, wrapped it in greaseproof paper, and stuck it in the inside pocket of my jacket.

We didn't walk from Fishpond to Prosper Street anymore because we now had a bicycle. We'd bought it off the gateman at some government offices for twenty yuan. It was a noisy old machine, except for the bell, which didn't make any noise. We rode one behind the other, and we could get from Fishpond to the trash depot at the northern end of Prosper Street in less than twenty minutes. I was good on a bike. I could ride without using my hands, but Wufu was too heavy for me to pedal, so he had to do the pedaling. Whenever we met a crowd of people, he used to shout, "Off! Off! Quick!" and I got pretty nimble at jumping off the back carrier.

The trash depot was run by a man who'd come from Henan, though he wasn't Henanese himself, only his wife was. He was as scrawny as a monkey, so that was what we called him. Wufu felt it was all wrong that a man that skinny should be running a trash depot.

"Drink?" offered Scrawny, taking a sip himself. Whenever he saw us, he always brought a small flask out of his inside jacket pocket. We said no. The threatened rain had not come, and there wasn't a breath of wind either.

"You don't seem to have a lot of energy this morning. Been spending the night with hookers?" said Scrawny.

"Happy Liu's having a nervous breakdown," Wufu said. It was true my nerves were strained. But dammit, I didn't think that qualified as a nervous breakdown. It was just that I happened not to have slept well the night before. Wufu's head only had to touch the pillow and he was dead to the world. I figured he must have been a pig in a former life. But I was kept awake by the birds twittering and shitting in the tree, and the woodlice crawling around the bottom of the walls. Then there was the din from the night market. Though you couldn't actually hear what people were saying, the noise got to me, like a scratchy wheat bristle. I tried to feel good about it, but simply feeling good about it made my head teem with thoughts, one image following another. *But why are they just in black and white and not color?* I wondered.

"Aren't you fussy!" said Scrawny.

Maybe I'm fussy, but so what? You think a trash picker can sleep anywhere? I thought. I took out a cigarette but didn't offer him one. In the sunshine, the smoke cast a yellow shadow on the ground. I couldn't help thinking that, of all the people smoking in the world, only I would notice that smoke cast a yellow shadow on the ground.

Scrawny was a bully and a coward. He started in on Wufu. "Hey, go get this bottle filled up!" Wufu hemmed and hawed, but eventually he went to the liquor shop at the end of the lane. After he returned with the bottle and gave it to Scrawny, we left the bike at the trash depot and took off with the carts we'd left there the night before for safekeeping. Wufu started bad-mouthing Scrawny. He said he'd asked around and found out that Scrawny had once been a trash picker too. But now that he was running the trash depot, he was giving the trash pickers a hard time. I said he was scum. Wufu said he was rolling in money. I said being scum had nothing to do with whether he was rich. We should be careful not to offend him, but we didn't need to ingratiate ourselves either. The next time he told Wufu to go buy him smokes and booze, Wufu should just play dumb. Wufu muttered that he'd only half filled the bottle and topped it off with water.

Our patch on Prosper Street consisted of the main street and ten lanes running east-west across it. I was in charge of the five lanes at the northern end, Wufu, the same at the southern end. Up and down we went all day. As Wufu said, it was like a donkey pulling a millstone—a short route but you covered a huge distance. He traced and retraced his steps dozens of times a day, until his legs and feet were swollen. He never collected as much as me, and he complained that city folk were even more skinflint than people in the country. Why wouldn't they throw out their old, broken stuff?

"Picking up trash isn't all about working hard or having a loud voice. It has a lot to do with luck, and luck comes when you're being positive," I told him.

"You need luck to pick up trash? How's that?" Wufu said, rubbing his ankles. They were all swollen, and when he pressed them, it left a dent in the flesh. Wufu didn't think that a positive attitude brought you luck.

The way I looked at it was this: my stomach was acting up and I had terrible insomnia, but I hadn't gotten sick. The thing was, every so often, I made sure to thank my innards. I thanked my remaining kidney for doing the work of two, and it responded to the encouragement and worked even harder, and I didn't get so much as a backache now. I thanked Prosper Street for keeping us in food and drink. If ever I made it big in Xi'an, then I'd build a skyscraper on Prosper Street to mark where it started, the way people built shrines to the revolution! Every time I got to my five lanes, I straightened my clothes, scraped the corners of my eyes clean, and made a little bow to the buildings and all the trees on either side. The morning sunlight turned the buildings at the northern end crimson and put a little sun in every one of those windows. There were flocks of sparrows in the trees, and they greeted me in chorus: "Happy, Happy, Happy!" Those sparrows were the first to call me Happy Liu. And it was very strange . . . Every day when I started work, I always picked up something I wanted, even though my patch was so small.

Lane Seven West had a tea shop on the corner of Prosper Street. An old man sat outside, dozing over a glass bottle full of cold tea, though I never saw him drink from it. He used to collect parking fees when people left their cars on the main road. He always looked like he was half-asleep, but as soon as you parked and were leaving, he was right there, money jar in hand, to collect the fee of three yuan. A lot of drivers thought they could get away with paying one yuan and telling him not to bother to write out the receipt, but he wasn't having that! Then they'd get angry, cough up the three yuan . . . and still refuse the receipt, but he'd tear it off his pad and throw it on the ground. He was good to me though. Whenever I passed, he always called me over to offer me a drink of water. "You're a good-looking young man!" he used to say.

"Is that so?"

"Why's a trash picker like you always got such a cheery smile pinned to your face?"

"My name's Happy Liu," I told him. "Happy by name, happy by nature." That made him happy too, and he tried to give me the glass bottle for my water. I refused, but he hung it on my cart anyway.

It was the kind of glass bottle the long-distance truck drivers used, and the taxi drivers, and now I had one too.

"Hey, you! Trash!" I heard a shout, and a fat woman waddled toward me, carrying a bundle of old newspapers. City women dolled themselves up when they were young, but then they let themselves go and went all doughy as they got older. She upended my scales and peered at them. "Everyone says street vendors' scales always under-weigh. Are yours accurate, Trash?"

I ignored her and lit a cigarette.

"Whatever are you smoking? It stinks!" she said.

I had a special way of smoking. I inhaled, but instead of swallowing it, I kept it in my mouth and blew out smoke rings. Wufu did it differently: he rolled his own cigarettes for starters, gulped down the smoke, then slowly let it out of his nostrils. That always made him cough. I never coughed, or got phlegm either.

I hefted her newspapers onto my scales, and she leaned over to read what it said. The arms of the scales were level, but she pushed the weight along and it dipped like an ox drinking water. "Fine," I said, "that's twenty-two pounds. At one yuan per pound, that makes twenty-two yuan."

I went to give her the money, but she objected. "Other people give one yuan thirty a pound. What do you mean, one yuan per pound?

26

One yuan thirty a pound times twenty-two pounds makes twenty-eight point six. Rounded up, that makes twenty-nine yuan. I run a grocery, you know. You can't cheat me."

Petty-bourgeois was this woman's middle name. In a great big city like this, how petty could you get? She obviously ran her store like that, nitpicking over every little thing.

"Well? I'm asking you a question, Trash!"

To hell with her questions, I wasn't taking her bundle of newspapers. I put it down. I was a trash picker, not trash. I started to pull my cart away and she followed, hollering at me, but I didn't stop. Once I got to the intersection, I had a good chuckle. I didn't have to bargain with anyone. Some people were always going to disrespect me. After all, I wasn't completely respectable. Of course, I wasn't going to be a trash picker for my whole life, but I couldn't expect people to know that just by looking at me. Most people didn't have that kind of vision. I felt like taking a look at the newly planted indigo bush on Prosper Street, so I strolled over there, pulling my cart. I got a nice rhythm going, not too fast, not too slow. If I got the pace right, then I didn't get tired, and I could look in store windows as I passed them. The stores were getting more and more fashionably "foreign." In other words, they were the sort of stores foreigners would go to. I thought the signage in foreign letters looked good, and the wine bottles in the shop windows were prettier than Chinese liquor bottles. The foreign girls in the ads were pretty too. But I soon discovered that some of the handwritten labels on the displays had spelling mistakes—even the character for "egg" was written wrong.

"Hey! Come out here!" I shouted at the shop assistant. "You've written 'egg' wrong!" The shop assistant looked out but clearly didn't agree. I insisted. I wrote the character correctly on the ground with a stick, but he just told me to get lost. So I did. But before I went, I wrote the character for "egg" correctly on the label.

6.

Gem Han never told me how many trash pickers there were in Xi'an. But I saw in the paper (an old sheet of newspaper the street vendor used to wrap up my baked sweet potato) that every day several hundred trucks ferried trash out of town. I was shocked, but I was excited too. The better the wheat harvest, the more straw there was. The richer the city became, the richer the trash pickings. As long as there was trash, we could establish ourselves in the city, and the more trash there was, the better our standard of living.

We trash pickers were not just a derivative of the trash, we really mattered. We were vital to the city. Imagine, if there were no sanitation workers and trash pickers, what would Xi'an be like?

Had anyone ever considered that before? I hadn't, before I started trash picking. So many things are overlooked in life. Like, everyone needs to breathe, if you don't, you die. But did anyone go around counting every breath in and every breath out, as if no one had ever breathed before?

I felt that newspaper article dignified me, so I folded it and put it inside my jacket. I thought I'd paste it up on the newspaper board in front of the Lane Five Hotel.

The first time I saw that hotel, I thought it was really strange. It was very tall, and hexagonally shaped. When country folk first come to town, they think those skyscrapers are wonderful, so they stand there, counting the stories on the buildings. I was no different, but I went further. I became fixated on figuring out what was good about each skyscraper. The third time I stood in front of this hotel, it dawned on me why it was situated the way it was—at a T-junction, with one corner touching the crossing of the "T," and the front entrance set at an angle to oncoming traffic. It was to get the best feng shui. Four old people were in front of the newspaper board, reading. They complained it gave them a crick in their necks, and they started to massage one another's. I told them, "Count the stories! Push your shoulders hard back, stretch your neck, start from the bottom, count up to the roof, and then count down again! Go on, count! Better now?"

The old folk thought counting floors was a funny kind of medicine. "Won't it turn us into peasants?"

"Hah! Past fifty, you're neither pretty nor ugly. Past sixty, you're neither man nor woman. When your neck hurts, you're neither city folk nor peasants, you're just someone with a crick in your neck!"

When I got to the hotel today, I didn't see the old folk. I guess they hadn't come out yet, so I quickly stuck my newspaper article on the board and pulled my cart over to a place where I could eat my fermented bean curd.

Inspired by Scrawny and his hip flask, I always had a bit of bean curd in the inside pocket of my jacket, wrapped in greaseproof paper along with a toothpick, so I could get it out and nibble when I wanted. I'd invented my own special way of eating it. You see, I got a bit of the bean curd on the toothpick and put it directly on my tongue, so it didn't touch my teeth. Then I wrinkled up my mouth and nose, drew the toothpick gently out, and savored the bean curd. Nothing better! Wufu objected that it didn't stop you being hungry or thirsty, it didn't even stop you wanting to piss or crap. But, hey, when a dog chewed a bone, it wasn't for the meat, it was to savor the taste. There was something not quite right about that analogy though. How about this instead:

everyone needs spiritual fulfillment, and fermented bean curd did it for me, like listening to music. Poor old Wufu, he didn't know anything about music . . .

I hoped that passersby would see me doing it, but all of a sudden, there was no one in the street. I looked up at the hotel: tenth floor, eleventh, twelfth . . . On the fifteenth floor, someone was pointing a mirror at me, the sun glinting off it and making a ray of light dance all over me, like a white butterfly. It was a girl, and she was smiling at me.

Why was she smiling at me? There were plenty of pretty women on the streets of Xi'an. They'd burst out of restaurants as I went by, three or four at a time, all of them over five foot six, beanpole-thin and long-legged, and dressed in bright colors. They walked along, arms linked, so I couldn't get by. I had to warn myself, *Calm down! Calm down!* But when they brushed past, my heart pounded and my palms sweated. I couldn't look them in the eyes, so I looked down at all those pairs of stiletto heels and the slender feet in them. Their second toes were always the longest. That meant lucky in marriage.

Wufu and I often talked about pretty women. As far as I was concerned, pretty women were celestial beings, on a level with successful politicians, philosophers, and artists. They congregated in the city, which was why the city was a good place to be.

But Wufu grunted, "No city girls are as good as the girls in Freshwind. Women should be fat, with big butts and breasts."

It was like playing your lute to a cow, talking to Wufu, and I shut up. All this time, I had an image of someone floating around in my head. Who was she? I didn't know her name, I just knew she worked at the hair and beauty salon on Lane One North off Prosper Street. I was always astonished how all those people who crowded through the streets by day completely vanished in the evening. (Those skyscrapers were like the wooden chests with hundreds of drawers that held ingredients in a Chinese medicine shop and reached all the way to the ceiling. Did people never get the wrong door?) The flocks of pretty women were enough to make you lose your head, but they were gone in a flash, as fleeting as beautiful clouds floating across the sky, ephemeral and forget-table. The one in the salon was different. She wasn't going anywhere. It was as if all those pretty women had been turned into one real woman, right there in the salon. She was tall and had slender, straight shoulders, and long legs that skipped along. She had freckles on her nose. Thanks to the freckles, I saw her not as a goddess, but as someone genuine, someone I could become genuinely fond of.

Just thinking of her made me act more refined. My head cleared and I felt much smarter, like when I wrote an essay at secondary school and used all the elegant phrases I'd learned.

The girl on the fifteenth floor was still smiling at me. She had a very round face, not like the slender woman in the salon. I smiled back, which was only polite.

"Happy Liu!" she shouted. "Happy Liu! Come on up! I've got a gas cooker I want to get rid of!" She knew my name! But I had to get through the lobby to go up to her room, and no way was the doorman going to let me in. This was a hotel, he told me. I said I knew it was a hotel, but someone had called me up to collect something they wanted to throw out.

"Look at your shoes," he said.

There was nothing wrong with my shoes. They were fine. I hadn't even worn the heels down. But I had some dirt on the soles from when I'd gone to the toilet. I squatted down and scraped it off with a stick. "Let me in please, comrade," I said.

"No."

"But I've wiped the soles of my shoes clean."

"No."

"You wouldn't be keeping me out because I'm a trash picker, would you?"

He cracked a smile at that and let me in, but I had to go barefoot. That was embarrassing, because my toenails needed clipping. Which was all Wufu's fault. The evening before, I tried to get him to go to the house opposite to borrow some scissors from old Fan, but he said, "Who's looking at your toes?" and he didn't go, and now I was seriously embarrassed. Also, this was the first time I'd been in a really fancy hotel. The revolving door was like a meat mincer and spun me round three times before I could get out. Old man Ma's son back in Freshwind was a driver for the Office of Commerce in the County Town. He told me the first time he came to Xi'an, he drove onto a circular overpass and went round and round for half an hour before he could find the exit ramp.

I got a bump on the head from hitting the glass door, but eventually I got inside. The stone-tiled floor was so highly polished, you could see yourself in it, and wherever I walked, I left a footprint. Across the lobby I went, up to the fifteenth floor, down again carrying the gas cooker, getting hot and sweaty . . . and the footprints were still there!

Those footprints came back to haunt my dreams. I was either running madly around Xi'an barefoot, or running and running until I suddenly discovered I had no shoes on. Hell, my shoes! Where were my shoes?

That morning, after I got the gas cooker, I didn't go out picking any more trash. I was too worried about whether the cleaners had wiped my footprints off the lobby floor.

Toward evening, Wufu pulled his cart over to Lane Ten, where I was. He had a stewed phoenix claw in a plastic bag. "Chicken feet in Xi'an soy paste are really good," he said, giving it to me.

"They're phoenix claws, not chicken feet," I said.

"Of course they're chicken feet. Why do you want to give them such a fancy name?"

"'Cuz that's what they call them in the city. They're phoenix claws to me!"

"Whatever. Anyway, I bought two. I could easily eat twenty, but I've left one for you."

Wufu was so good-hearted, I was more than happy to tear it in half and give him back the other half. "Since you came to Xi'an, have you written 'Wufu was here' on a tree, say, or on a wall?" I asked.

"No."

"So where have you been then?"

"Just to Prosper Street."

Chatting with Wufu got kind of dull, so I told him all about leaving my footprints on the floor of the hotel lobby. It was such a luxury establishment, those footprints must surely have gone off on their own, exploring every corner of the lobby, then out of the hotel and up and down all the streets and lanes, as far as the city wall and up to the golden roof of the bell tower. As I talked, my eyes were full of those footprints, marching neatly along like soldiers. Wufu put his hand on my forehead. "Do you have a temperature, Happy?"

I batted his hand away, pissed off. "This is all in my imagination, get it? You should imagine stuff too. The more cramped your surroundings, the more you should imagine stuff. Imagination gives you wings like a bird, so you can fly."

Wufu still didn't understand, but I must have gotten him going, like how you start to stutter when you talk to a stutterer, or you yawn and everyone around you yawns too, because he suddenly took a deep breath, ran at the newly whitewashed wall in front of us, and with a flying leap landed a footprint on it. Heavens, he could certainly kick high. His footprint landed almost five feet above the ground. It was nice and clear, and there was a spattering of mud around it, so it looked as if it had been spray-painted on. "I've left a footprint too!" he said. Xi'an's Street Conditions Observation Unit had just started a Keep the City Clean campaign, and if their patrol had gotten wind of someone dirtying a nice white wall, they would have definitely issued a fine. But I didn't tell Wufu off, just took a quick look around. Luckily there was no one there, so I grabbed Wufu and we ran off. We ran till we were so parched we needed a drink, but there was no water left in my bottle.

"Is there a water faucet around?" Wufu asked.

"We'll buy a bottle of mineral water," I said. The water I bought was sweet, as if someone had put sugar in it. When we'd finished it, I scrunched up the plastic bottle and tossed it merrily into the air, but it hit the lamppost, making the dog standing under it bark furiously.

The dogs in Xi'an were all pets, and they didn't bite. But you had to be careful not to piss off their owners. I got worried someone might pop out from somewhere and say we were hitting her dog, but no one appeared, and Wufu and I quieted down.

We'd gone from being overexcited to feeling really flat. Wufu started rooting around in the waistband of his pants, brought something out, pinched it between finger and thumb, and dropped it on the ground. "And there I was, thinking it was a louse!"

I bent down to look. It obviously was a louse. "And there I was, thinking it wasn't!"

Wufu went red in the face and muttered, "How come I've got lice?"

"Don't go rooting around in your pants, showing people you brought lice to the city. Go straight home and take them off, then pour boiling water on them!" I quit being stern and eased up on him. "How come you picked so little trash today?" I looked at his cart. He said he'd seen a shop taking a delivery of goods and figured if he helped them unload, then they'd sell the packing boxes to him. So he started to help them. But he didn't recognize that some of the goods were sausages, since no one ate them in Freshwind. He thought they were carrots, though he wondered why they wasted so much plastic on wrapping them. So he put the sausage packets in with the vegetables. When the boss checked, she couldn't find the sausages anywhere. When she saw they were in with the vegetables, she asked who'd put them there.

"I did," said Wufu.

"You fucking idiot!" she yelled. "Or were you trying to slip them into the packing boxes and swipe them?"

"Am I 'a fucking idiot'?" Wufu asked. "I really didn't know they were sausages."

I thought of getting stuck in the revolving door at the hotel. "They're the fucking idiots! We're not less intelligent than they are, we've just seen less!" Wufu tore a corner off the old newspaper in his cart and deftly rolled himself a cigarette. He was more addicted to his smokes than I was, but he couldn't bring himself to buy cigarette papers and always rolled his own. "Just keep your eyes peeled from now on," I said. "And less talking!" Wufu dragged deeply on his roll-up.

About three hundred feet away from us was the entrance to an apartment building. On its front lawn were three cedars, their branches rising in serried ranks like multistoried pagodas, the lawn underneath emerald green. The blades of grass danced merrily in the breeze. "Talking less doesn't mean going around feeling sorry for yourself," I said. "Don't put yourself down. Look at that grass. It's stubby compared to the tree, but it doesn't feel inferior."

Wufu was still dragging on his cigarette.

"I'm talking to you. Aren't you going to say anything?"

"I can't say anything," Wufu said. "If I talk, the cigarette will go out."

I said nothing, and he said nothing. We both said nothing.

Three kids came down the lane, wearing baggy jeans, with bags slung over their shoulders and messy, bleached hair. They were bouncing along like their boots had springs in the soles. You often saw kids like this on the street. Sometimes they'd start dancing, hopping up and down like injured insects. I'm telling you, they looked like they were going to start jumping now, their legs bending and twisting like braided dough sticks as they walked along, but they didn't stop, just went into the apartment complex. A car roared by. Then another car came from the opposite direction. The license plate was 8888. City folk love their eights, because the word sounds like the word for getting rich, so four eights means four riches. A big businessman, for sure. An old woman was leading an old man across the main road, the man trailing his back foot close behind his front one. Three steps, four steps, and then they stopped in their tracks, like two shriveled-up trees. A drunken crowd tumbled out of a bar across the way and sat down on the pavement, alternately swearing at passersby and bursting into fits of laughter. A girl came by, walking gracefully with a dog in her arms, to a chorus of catcalls from the drunks.

A truck swerved into the lane from Prosper Street, its horn blaring. I thought it was a fire engine, but where was the fire? We craned our necks and watched. Then the truck suddenly shot out a jet of water, drenching us. We yelled, but the truck didn't stop, just shot by, still spurting water.

"It's the sprinkler truck," I said.

"Why's it sprinkling me?" Wufu said.

No one was paying any attention to us two sodden wretches. Suddenly I laughed. "It's nice and cool!"

Wufu looked at me. "Nice and cool!" he echoed.

He got to his feet. "Where are you going?" I asked. He said nothing, simply went over to the lamppost, picked up the plastic water bottle we'd thrown away, and put it back in his cart.

7.

In Freshwind, you always knew when it was dinnertime: smoke puffed from every chimney and billowed down the village streets. You could hear shouting and arguing and lots of colorful swearing from every household, and chickens clucked and dogs barked. In the city, you knew the time only from a wristwatch. But Wufu and I didn't have wristwatches, and the post office building with its big clock tower was a long way from Prosper Street, so you might go a whole day feeling that the sun's rays hadn't moved, that nothing had moved, and then all of a sudden it would be evening, and the rivers flooded. You see, I saw the street as a river, with the cars and the people as its water. Come evening in Xi'an, all the rivers became surging torrents as everyone left for home from factories, schools, and government offices. It often got so bad that we couldn't get across with our carts. Wufu would look at me from one side of the street, and I'd look back at him, and he would sit down on the pavement, take his shoes off, and give his feet a rest.

In the evenings, clouds emerged in the skies above Xi'an, drifting like tufts of cotton wool. Then the white cotton wool turned red, and the layers of cloud billowed outward and turned into countless roses that lay scattered all over the sky. Office workers had no time to admire the wondrous sight, they were in too much of a hurry to get home, and cars and pedestrians were jammed together so tightly that they were in danger of bumping into someone or being bumped into. Only Wufu and I had time to look at the sky, though Wufu just took one look and grumbled that the day was too short, so the only person who truly admired the sky was me.

This was something to be proud of, I figured. I could look at a scarred old wall and see in the markings there people, bugs and fish, birds and flowers. I could look at the branches on a tree and see which were cozying up and which were fighting. Looking at those roses all over the sky, so fresh and delicate, I suddenly found that woman from the beauty salon popping into my head. Why did the clouds remind me of her? It was strange, and scary too. *Hey, Happy Liu, stay away from her! What the eye doesn't see, the heart doesn't fret over. Take a detour!* And I took a detour and didn't go down her lane.

Wufu and I had to make our separate ways to the trash depot to sell our pickings. I dropped by the place under the circular overpass. This was where Wufu and I sorted and bundled what we'd collected every day before we continued on to the depot. No one ever came here, and it was quiet. The idea was that whoever got there first started sorting the stuff and then waited for the other to turn up. But if Wufu got there first, he liked to take a snooze, mouth agape, dribbling saliva. He could even sleep on a bare rock. Once, something funny happened: a taxi driver parked there to piss, saw Wufu, and mistook him for a corpse. He rushed off to report it to the police, making a huge fuss, but when they turned up, Wufu was sitting up. The police gave him a furious chewing-out. Today I got here first, and the ground was covered in puddles of piss and piles of crap. I'd written a clear notice on the bridge piers, "No pissing or shitting here," but the taxi drivers still used the place as a WC. I swore, pronouncing carefully, "Fuck . . . your . . . mother."

I couldn't speak standard Chinese, only the Freshwind dialect. Some Xi'an folk, when I was weighing their trash, made fun of my accent, so I swore I'd learn to speak standard Chinese. But when I tried it, I sounded funny to me, so I stopped. Standard Chinese was for standard people. Chairman Mao didn't speak it, he spoke the Hunan dialect, so I'd speak the Freshwind dialect. There was no one around me to hear right now, so I shouted Freshwind swearwords, using my best standard accent. It made me laugh. I had a sense of humor, Wufu knew that. Anyway, I decided not to do any more sorting or bundling. I picked up a clod of earth, and after the words "No pissing or shitting here," I added "or your tool will be confiscated." I felt pleased with myself.

At the depot, Scrawny weighed what I'd brought and then took out his flask for a swig. "Dammit, where's it all gone?" he exclaimed, but I ignored the hint. I picked up a twig and poked it in my ear, which tickled.

Scrawny's missus came to pay me, counting out the one- and two-yuan bills three times. Scrawny groped her breast. She jerked away and said, "Happy Liu's here!"

"I don't care if the mayor's here! I can grope anything if it's mine!"

I didn't care either. He could grope all he liked, those fat boobs of hers turned me off. As she passed me the money, she gave me a flirty look. "You haven't picked much today. Been goofing off, have you?"

"If I haven't got much, it's because Xi'an's a clean city!"

Scrawny said, "Huh! We're all flies! If Xi'an's suddenly clean, there'll be no crap for us to feed on!"

"Speak for yourself!" I said.

I leaned my cart against the wall of the compound and pumped up our bicycle tires. Scrawny told me that from now on, he was charging us one yuan every time we wanted to use the pump. Without a word, I gave him a two-yuan note. He scratched around for one yuan in change. "Forget it," I said. Then I let the tires down and pumped them up a second time.

I wasn't angry. What was there to be angry about? In fact, I felt pleased that I'd made my point so cleverly. Wufu turned into the compound, pulling his cartful of trash behind him and limping. Even from a few hundred feet away, I could see he was wearing a pair of leather shoes. Where had he gotten them from? The shoes had a bit of a heel on them, which made him taller, made his butt stick out, and gave him bowed legs, like a thief. "Why didn't you wait for me under the overpass?" he asked.

"Did you see anything under the overpass?" Surely he must have read my notice, "or your tool will be confiscated," and been full of admiration for my wit and humor. But he said he'd only seen a pile of crap. "What else?"

"Another pile of crap."

Wufu had brought even less trash than me. Most of it was toilet paper, soiled with crap and menstrual blood. Hordes of flies had chased the toilet paper here, but luckily we could leave those with Scrawny too.

We set off back to Fishpond on the bicycle, with Wufu pedaling as usual. He was full of complaints that he hadn't picked much because the gateman at the Lane Five apartment complex wouldn't let him in, and then another trash picker came out, pulling a cart piled high with trash. "Gem Han said it was mine. How did that greedy locust land on my patch?"

I didn't know the answer to that because I hadn't seen what'd happened. The buildings around us were fading from sight in the twilight, making them look a little like the mountain ranges behind Freshwind Township. Suddenly, all the streetlights came on, and the serried ranks of skyscrapers lit up too. There were so many lights, it was hard to tell where they ended and the stars began. Neon flickered in brilliant colors on the really fancy buildings, while the older blocks and the ones under scaffolding were dark and unlit. Everywhere the lights created fantastic, glittering shapes that changed as they flashed on and off, as if there were monsters living inside. The streets felt menacing, different from daytime, the cars transformed into roaming wild beasts, leopards and tigers, the people like brightly colored birds. As I stared and stared, a bunch of girls appeared like ringed pheasants with their dazzling clothes, weird hairstyles, and exaggerated, surreal ways of talking and moving.

"I feel dizzy, I can't help it," Wufu said.

I was quite happy to feel dizzy, because I was being dazzled. "Look how short that miniskirt is! Her legs look like white daikon radishes!" I said.

Wufu turned to look. "Which one?"

"Watch the road!" I told him, and turned his head to face forward again. "I can look, but not you!" The back of Wufu's jacket was soaked in sweat, and he pedaled slower and slower. We passed a market, where stall-holders had almost finished packing up, though they were still shouting, "Packing up time! Everything's cheap!"

"How cheap?" called Wufu, still pedaling.

"Two pounds of cabbage for one yuan, tomatoes three yuan a pound!"

"That's not cheap!" Wufu said. But I made him stop anyway so I could go in, because I knew the stall-holders discarded any leftover green leaves when they packed up.

It never ceased to astonish me that city folk wouldn't eat the outer leaves of celery, only the hearts. They threw perfectly good leaves away! I was in luck. I got three enormous bundles for fifty cents, one of celery leaves and two of cabbage leaves. The cabbage was lacy with insect holes, but that only proved that the cabbages hadn't had pesticides on them. And I got a big pumpkin, for twenty cents. It was superb too. We Freshwind folk like our pumpkins well matured and yellow, with an ashlike powder on the skin that you can't scrape off with your fingernail. City folk only ate them young. Idiots! Gourmets they might be, but they were no judge of pumpkins.

I returned with the vegetables, and Wufu said, "How much did that cost?"

"Seventy cents."

"Pricey!" Wufu gave the lamppost a kick.

"Well, think how much electricity a lightbulb eats in a night. Isn't that more expensive?"

He said nothing. He was clutching five yuan in his hand, all small bills, filthy and soft. He was about to give me thirty-five cents, because we split food costs.

"Forget it!" I said.

"Hawa!" he protested.

"Say that again?"

"OK, Happy!" He began again. "Happy, have I been ripped off? That fat guy with the roving, yellow eyeballs, I had my suspicions about him. He sold me forty-eight pounds of cardboard for four yuan. Is that right?"

Though I got it immediately, I worked it out for him: "It's eight cents a pound, so eighty cents for ten pounds, so four yuan for fifty pounds. Wufu, if you can't do the math right, you're pathetically ignorant, you know that? You paid the man for two pounds you didn't get."

"Oh, did I?" he said. Then he smiled and sniffed at the cash in his hand. "They smell of mutton. That yellow-eyed fucker had *paomo* soup for lunch." Then he said, "Happy, who do you think's dearest to me in this world?"

"Your missus?"

"No, Chairman Mao!"

That was because banknotes had Chairman Mao's head printed on them. He kissed them, then kissed them again, then gave them all to me. Apart from some small change he kept on him to buy trash every day, he gave me all his earnings. There were no holes to hide money anywhere in my room, but I took out a brick that supported the bed and stashed the money behind it, tucked into two greaseproof paper bags, one with my money, one with Wufu's. His had a sheet of paper folded in it too, recording all the money he'd given me, and when. He wanted to give me his profits from today, but I was worried about getting the money mixed up. I was looking after his money, so I had a responsibility to him, that was my motto. I told him to hang on to it until we got home, so he tucked the notes inside his shoe.

"You found a pair of leather shoes?" I said.

"What am I, a moneybags? They were a present. An old woman gave them to me."

"She really gave you leather shoes?"

"Yes, really. She said they were her son's. Maybe he got a new pair, or maybe he died. They're good shoes, just a bit small, so they pinch."

I told him, "Take them off! Why are you wearing leather shoes? You're not a leather shoes man! You're a country bumpkin! People will think you stole them!" Wufu's toes were squeezed so tight, they'd swollen up like red radishes. My feet were narrower than Wufu's, and the shoes fit me nicely. The first owner might have had me in mind when he bought them. Just think, I'd planned to wear a new pair of shoes when we came to Xi'an, but in all the rush and scramble, I'd left them behind. These were obviously meant for me, weren't they? I stood up in them, put my weight on the ground, and took a few steps. "They don't hurt me."

8.

We got to our building in Fishpond. Obviously, the developers had left without bothering to finish it, so I dubbed it "Leftover House," a name even Wufu could understand. Actually, I liked to put a different spin on it: *You never know, one day we could make big money, and then this won't be Leftover House anymore, it'll be a shrine to our success, just like Yan'an is the shrine of the Communist Revolution.* I kept those thoughts to myself.

I walked across the yard to the door, looking back at my footprints on the ground. My toes pointed outward when I walked, but the prints were clear enough. "I hope it doesn't rain tonight," I said. I meant I didn't want the rain to wash my footprints away. But Wufu figured it was very stuffy and we needed rain. I got annoyed and ignored him.

We fixed our meal together. I had a sudden longing for noodles. We had no chopping board, so we normally just mixed the dough and pinched it off in lumps and cooked those up in a soup. But tonight I said I was going to roll out some dough for noodles. I took the bed quilt off, wiped down the rush matting underneath, and rolled out the dough into a sheet as big as a fan. Wufu was as happy as if it were New Year. He said he'd been wanting noodles too. "Long, thin ones or wide ones?" I asked.

"As you like."

What kind of noodles were "as you like"? You had to be fussy about your food! I certainly was. I didn't like noodles served with minced meat or chili oil. I liked "porridge noodles," boiled in the wok, the noodle water thickened with corn flour, and vegetables added. And they weren't simple to make. You had to get the size and shape of the noodles the same, a finger wide, no more than four fingers long, not too thin, but not too thick either. The water had to come to a rolling boil as you put them in to cook, so the noodles swelled up. Then you made a paste with cold water and flour—it had to be corn flour—mixed it quickly into a smooth porridge with no lumps, and slid it down the side of the wok, stirring all the time so the porridge didn't stick to the noodles. Then the vegetables went in. You didn't chop them with a knife, just pulled them apart with your fingers. A soup like this had to be properly seasoned. "A bit more salt," I told Wufu, "some finely chopped onion, and coriander, we need that, and some pounded garlic . . . Dribble on some chili oil, add some vinegar, plain vinegar is best. And if there's any leek-flower paste, that gives the flavor some bite."

"You're absolutely right," said Wufu, "but all we have is salt."

"Don't be so defeatist," I said to him. And I couldn't resist giving him a little sermon on the power of imagination. So we didn't have onion or chili or garlic? That didn't matter—we could imagine them! Everyone could imagine! There was a slogan from Chairman Mao's Great Leap Forward: "The bolder we are, the more we can wrest from the land." We'd thought ourselves to Xi'an, and now we were Xi'an folk. We'd think our food delicious, and it would taste delicious. Our wishes would come true.

The food was ready. We thought about our work as we ate, and we thought about money too. What was a trash picker? An environmental protection officer! I'd seen the mayor's speech in the papers, where he said he wanted to make Xi'an into a fine, big city, and that the only way to do that was to pay attention to every detail. Trash collection was one of those details. We might not make much money, but we were still doing better than Freshwind farmers. The yield from a small field earned you only eighteen yuan, and you could earn seventeen or eighteen yuan in a day here. And that seventeen or eighteen yuan was ready money, cash in hand. There was no comparison with making ready money every day. "Eat up!" I said, then added, "Don't stick your face in your bowl. You're not a pig! Easy does it! You don't have a wolf snapping at your heels!"

I had two bowls, then half a bowl more, and I was full. Then I stashed away the money I'd earned that day behind the brick under the bed, along with Wufu's money. "Wufu, they always say you need something precious to give a house good feng shui. Some people get antiques, some people buy stone lions, some people get a Daoist priest to write charms, but for us, it's money! There's nothing more precious than money. That's what we need to keep those evil spirits at bay. From now on, we're going to put forth shoots here. So what if we're peasants? Everyone in the city was a peasant only three or four generations back. You remember the couplets over the Lord Guan Temple back home? 'Anyone can become a hero like the legendary Yao and Shun. The most prized virtue is standing on your own two feet,' and 'Generals and premiers are made, not born. I view everyone the same.' Get it?"

Wufu finished first one bowl, then another, then another. Then he said, "No." There was enough left in the wok for one more bowl. I tipped it into a basin and said, "We can finish that tomorrow."

"It'll have spoiled by tomorrow," Wufu said. "Why don't I finish it now?"

And he did. Then he slumped to the floor, his neck rigid, his eyes red and glassy.

"Get up, Wufu!" I said. "It's got to go around in your belly, otherwise you'll never sleep with the amount you forced down!"

Wufu half got up, then sat down again and waved me away. "Don't talk to me," he said. "I can't talk right now. Your food was so good. If I talk, I'll puke it all up."

"OK, sit quietly, and listen while I talk." And I started to bad-mouth the Freshwind folk who'd stayed behind. "What have they got going for them? They used to put us down for not having a skill, but all they know is how to be carpenters or bricklayers. They say our work's not technical, but are they doing anything technical? They work their asses off from dawn till dusk, and the most they can earn for all that work is five yuan a day! We have it good. We earn our money, and we can go window-shopping! Ask any of the Freshwind folk how many of them have seen the golden dome of the bell tower. If you told them city WCs are all made of porcelain, they wouldn't believe you! Before you came to Xi'an, even the Freshwind Township people wouldn't pass the time of day with you. They assumed they'd be wasting their time talking to you, it was beneath their dignity! But I bet in a year and a half, if you go back to Freshwind, the houses will look really shabby, potholes in the side streets will send you flying head over heels, and as soon as villagers open their mouths, you'll realize how ignorant and uneducated they are!

"Come on, gimme a smile! Tell me something interesting that happened to you today. You said there was a trash picker coming out of the Lane Five apartment complex. That must be a scam the gateman's pulling. You'd better think of a way to bribe him. That's how the world works. As you go up in the world, you have to be more careful. If you don't puff yourself up a bit, you'll get bullied by every Tom, Dick, and Harry, like that gateman. How to bribe him? Well, you don't need me to tell you how to do that. Try smiling at him, and if you can't afford a pack of smokes, try giving him one. You could nip into the boiler house and fill his jar with hot water, or maybe sweep the entrance to the compound? Human relationships are not about the big things, they're about the details. The Communist Party and the Kuomintang fought for years, but when Chairman Mao met Chiang Kai-shek, they shook hands and sat down to a meal. That man Li in Freshwind, didn't he have it in for you because of a cigarette? You gave one to someone else but not to him, and he thought you were putting him down? Is your stomach settled now, Wufu? Go wash your clothes. They stink to high heaven. We pick trash. We don't want people thinking we are trash. Maybe the gateman wouldn't let you into the compound because you're so grubby, you spoil the view."

I tried to pull Wufu to his feet. He burped and tried to cover his mouth, but all his food shot out anyway. All those noodles that looked so good in the wok and in the bowl looked disgusting on the floor. A strand of noodle stuck to my knee.

Wufu looked embarrassed. He was also furious with himself for wasting food. Although he didn't want to, he had to wash everything, including my pants. While he was doing the wash, he asked me to play my flute, but I refused. I just tidied my room.

9.

I liked things to be clean. In Freshwind, if I went to someone's house and his missus was pretty, even if the place was a terrible mess and there was nowhere to put your feet, it felt cozy and sexy. But if the wife was ugly and the place was a mess, it turned me off. Wufu was a man, a very ugly one at that, and his room was as mucky as a pigsty. I'd told him off time and again, but he never changed. It pissed me off so much that I tried never to go in there. Now, I swept my floor, and wiped down the bed and the door. I picked up the stove—an old metal drum with a hole in the side for the fuel and a top opening for the wok to sit on—and shifted it from behind the door to under the window. The bed had been against the east wall, and I moved it against the west wall. I had a few clothes drying on a wire strung across the window, but they blocked half the light, so I took it down and strung it between the bedposts instead. I put the bag of flour on the west side of the cooker, so it balanced out the vegetable basket on the east side. I put the shoes under my bed, heels inside, toes pointing out. I remembered I'd found a broken mirror a couple of days ago. It had a design of a lucky magpie perched on a plum branch on it, but all that was left was a triangular fragment with the plum tree branch, and just the tail of the magpie. Where was it? I couldn't find that piece of mirror anywhere.

"Have you seen the mirror?" I asked Wufu.

"You mean that bit of glass?" He jerked his chin in the direction of his room. He'd made a big puddle of water by the door when he was washing his clothes.

Sure enough, there it was. "I was using it to peel potatoes this morning," Wufu said.

"It's not a bit of glass—it's a mirror!" I put it back on my window ledge. But I figured it might get knocked off, so I wedged it between three nails on the wall. It was right opposite the bed, a good position. I could see myself as soon as I got out of bed. Wufu's mind was focused on food while he washed his clothes. "The porridge noodles would have tasted even better with some soybeans. We always have plenty of those at home. Why didn't I think to bring a bag of beans with me?"

I was still annoyed and ignored him.

"Are you angry, Happy? It was just a bit of broken mirror. You're not a woman—what do you need a mirror for?"

"There's a woman in this mirror!"

Wufu came running in, waving dripping hands, to look in the mirror. He couldn't see a woman, just his own swarthy face. He said, "I hate looking at myself."

I told him to look again. He said he could see the bed behind him, and above the bed, a pair of women's pointed-toe high heels. Sitting on a shelf I'd tacked up, they were gleaming in the light.

I'd bought this pair of high heels after my marriage plans went down the tubes in Freshwind, and I'd brought them to Xi'an wrapped up in my bedroll. Wufu knew all this, but he kept telling me to sell them. "A pair of heels won't bring you a wife. All it'll do is attract thieves!"

"You've put them in the place of honor, like a portrait of Chairman Mao!" he said scornfully.

"Go and wash your clothes!" I had a new idea. In this life, everything you got brought something else along in its wake. For instance, if you got a teapot, you had to get four teacups too, and then you had to get a table to put them on, and that meant you needed stools . . . That was an interesting analogy, but it wasn't quite right. Here's another one: there were a few families I knew back home in which the wife didn't get pregnant for years after they got married, but when they adopted a baby, she got pregnant the very next year. So, the pair of leather shoes I got today must have been drawn to me by those high heels, and if I wore them, maybe I'd find someone to wear that pair of high heels?

I didn't bother telling all this to Wufu. Ideas like this were much too high-flown for him to understand. But they certainly stirred me up. I couldn't tell him that my girl was going to come dancing in at any moment, so I played my flute instead. It was a slow, sobbing melody that expressed my yearning but also a sense of pride.

Suddenly Wufu came tiptoeing in. "He's listening from downstairs!" There were two rooms, one on each side of the entrance. The east side was occupied by a fellow trash picker, a man called Eight Huang. I didn't know him too well yet. I felt I should keep him under observation for a while, and after that we could live in peace and harmony—as the saying goes, a good neighbor is more useful than a distant relative. But Wufu and Eight were best buddies right away. Wufu told me the Cantonese were all loaded, and the way they said "Eight" made it sound like "bucks," so we should call him Big Bucks Huang. Bullshit, he was just Eight Huang to me. He was a hefty guy with tree trunks for arms and legs, and he suffered from vitiligo. It gave him a funny white patch on his face, which spread over the bridge of his nose like a dusting of flour. Anyway, knowing he was listening didn't bother me. People were drawn to my flute like iron filings to a magnet and, after all, flutes were meant to be heard, so I simply nodded and kept playing.

Wufu emptied his dirty clothes water into the yard below. From down below, Eight shouted up, "Hey! You've soaked me!"

"What are you up to down there?" Wufu shouted back.

"Listening to the flute."

"Not allowed," Wufu said.

"Why shouldn't I listen?"

"Then get your money out!" Wufu yelled rudely. That made Eight angry. He went back inside, and we heard his door slam. I carried on playing. Wufu told me to keep the sound down so Eight couldn't hear. Then we heard Eight's door slam again, and he came up the steps, carrying a wicker basket.

"I've been frying bits of cured meat downstairs. You must have smelled it," he said. I took the flute away from my mouth. It was just a bamboo tube, and I rapped the stair posts with it.

"Don't pay any attention to Wufu," I said. "Some things you can own and some you can't. Does anyone own the wind? Does anyone own the moon? If you like music, Eight, can you tell me what tune I was playing?"

"I couldn't make it out," said Eight, "I just thought it was pretty."

Wufu sucked in his teeth and squinted sideways at Eight, but Eight was right: the birds in the trees sing sweetly, but no one knows what they're saying.

"Have an apple!" Eight said. "I've brought some up for you!" And he put down the basket. It really did have apples in it, but half of them were bad. The rest were as small and wrinkled as an old man's balls. According to Eight, he'd been to a fruit store to collect some cardboard boxes and helped clean up while he was there. The owner hadn't sold him the boxes but had paid him for his help in apples. "Fuck it," said Eight. "I spent half the day there, just for these apples. I'm telling you, I'm crooked, but these city folk, they're crookeder than me!"

I picked them over and chose one, but Wufu was a little embarrassed and refused to take one. "Come on, have one! No point just drooling over them!"

"Then I'll taste one," Wufu said. He picked a bad one from the basket, bit off the bad bit, and spat it out.

"Take a good one," I said.

"Oh no, I can't take a good one first, or the bad ones will go so bad, you won't be able to eat them."

"But if you start with the bad ones, they'll all be bad by the time you get to them. Take a good one!" I said.

But Wufu said, "That's not the right way to live!"

We were touched by Eight's gift. Wufu divided them up, leaving most of them to me, and we put them in our rooms. "Every time I eat one, I'll remember your kindness," said Wufu. He reached out and touched the bridge of Eight's nose. "Does it hurt?"

"No, it doesn't hurt, it doesn't itch, and it's not infectious," said Eight.

"It looks nice," said Wufu.

"That's as may be," said Eight, "but I can't see it."

I laughed. "Eight, I can tell you're destined to be a county magistrate."

"Me? A magistrate? There was a guy from my village—he shared a birthday, the very same day, month, and year, with me—who ended up as county head, but I just came to Xi'an to be a trash picker."

"Blame the vitiligo," I said. "In operas, a patch of white on the nose is clown makeup, and the vitiligo's given you a white patch like a clown, so you could never be a real-life county magistrate!"

I was joking, but Eight's face fell. I wished I hadn't said it. I couldn't think how to make him feel better, and I was afraid of making things worse.

When you've accepted a present from someone, you must say good things about them. In the end, Wufu said, "Well, at least you can say you've got a magistrate's face."

"You're telling me my face isn't ugly?"

"That's right, it's not."

"So there's nowhere I can't go with it?"

"Of course not!" Wufu said. At that moment there was a loud explosion, followed by more bangs, like a distant roll of thunder. Startled, we went outside to look. To the northwest, the night sky was all red with a huge fireworks display.

"Is today Sunday?" Eight said.

"Yup, so what?" Wufu said.

"Don't you know?"

"Know what?"

"Hibiscus Garden has fireworks every Sunday night."

It all goes to show you should never judge by appearances. Eight Huang actually knew Hibiscus Garden. Hibiscus Garden was a brand-new park in Xi'an, built in the style of the Tang dynasty. It cost 1.3 billion yuan to build, and, according to the billboards in the streets, it was meant to show just how rich and flourishing the city was today. I knew all that, but I'd never been there. And Wufu never paid any attention to billboards, so he didn't know anything about it, and he certainly hadn't been.

"If you haven't been to Hibiscus Garden, then you haven't lived in Xi'an," Eight said.

"Who says I haven't been? I was just testing you!" Wufu said.

"So you know it cost one point three billion?" Eight asked.

"Any idiot knows that!" Wufu said. I suppressed a smile and concentrated on the glittering sky.

Eight and Wufu started talking about how much 1.3 billion was. If it was all in hundred-yuan notes and you spread them out in the streets, every street and lane in the city would be covered with them. And, heavens! If you tried to count them up—but no one could count that much money. They got more and more animated, and then somehow drifted ever so naturally on to other topics. The bugs in the trees started pissing on us. I was worried that if the stuff hit my face, it would give me freckles or moles. I wiped my face with my hands, then put my fingers to my nose, but there was no smell. Eight and Wufu had gotten into a debate about what was the heaviest thing on earth. They agreed on two things: the first was grain. For instance, if you compared a bag of wheat and a bag of dirt of the same size, the wheat would be heavier. The second was bank bills—weigh a pile of money and a pile of plain white paper, and the money would be heavier. As Eight put it, "A million yuan in bundled-up bank bills could crush someone to death."

"Wrong!" said Wufu. "I'd be crushed to death by half a million! I'd let money crush me anytime!"

I didn't want to dampen their enthusiasm, or get into an argument, so I went back to my room, took off my new shoes, spat on them, and gave them a wipe. As I admired the bright shine, I noticed two ants carrying a tiny crumb as they emerged from under the scrap of cardboard that we were using to dry the *ganmo*. They were black ants, with round heads and slender waists, so slender it looked as though they were joined with cotton thread. So where were their bellies? The front ant was dragging the crumb in its mouth. The back ant was pushing with its front claws, its hind claws straining against the floor and trembling slightly. You couldn't see them sweating, or hear them panting, but you could see how much effort the endeavor cost them. I felt so sorry for them, I bent down, picked up the bit of bread, and put it by the ant hole at the bottom of the wall. But that terrified them, and they scurried away.

Hibiscus Garden's fireworks ended, and the din from the Fishpond night market hovered over us again like a pall of dust. I could hear Wufu and Eight arguing amicably on the rooftop. They sounded like old friends.

"Did Gem Han introduce you two?" Eight asked.

"No, we're from the same village, but I'm older. That makes me his senior, so in the village he'd have to call me 'Uncle.'"

"Gem Han said you're both from Freshwind Township in Shangzhou, right?"

55

"Freshwind Township's sweet potatoes are good. They taste like chestnuts when they're dried."

"Do you still cook ground persimmon and rice husks there?"

"It's a lifesaver in the early spring when the grain runs out."

"Is it true it stops you up, and you have to dig your crap out with a key?"

"Who said that?"

"Power Liu."

"You know Power Liu?"

"It was Power Liu who introduced me to Gem Han."

"Show-off! How could you know Power Liu? If you did, he'd have given you a job like Han's!"

"No, I'll head back home at the end of the year."

"You'll have earned enough?"

"You can never earn enough!"

"So why? You miss your wife?"

There was a pause, then I caught, ". . . scared of having a missus . . . I hate . . ."

"Who? Your missus?"

"The village head!"

Their voices sank lower, then fell silent. Why did Eight have to say stuff like that, of all things? Wufu was just like Pigsy in the classic novel *Journey to the West*: he kept hankering after his home village. Talk like this was sapping his morale, and I was beginning to get angry. I said loudly, "Aren't you two ever going to stop the chitchat?" As luck would have it, I'd hardly finished speaking when the lights went out.

"Why have the lights gone out?" Wufu said. "Has a fuse blown?"

"All the lane lights are out. It's a power cut," Eight said. We'd had a few power cuts in Fishpond. The city's neon lights were on all night, and we got the power cuts here, on the edge of town. Our needs were being sacrificed so the city center could stay lit up all night? Eight swore.

"Fuck! Why cut the power just now? They must have known we were talking."

"Go to sleep," I said.

"How can I sleep in pitch blackness?" Eight said.

"When you shut your eyes, it's dark anyway, isn't it? Go to sleep," I said. And so we slept, and the day came to a close.

10.

Wufu always quoted me as the authority on everything when he was with Eight. He said I had a mole on the sole of one foot, near the heel. According to the old saying, that meant I was born to be a leader of men. He said I had the stomach of an ox, and as I chewed my cud, all these great schemes came out. He said I had a photographic memory, that I could speed-read a newspaper, remember all the phone numbers of recruitment agencies, and shop rental agencies and marriage bureaus. I once said to Wufu that if Gem Han were a fish, he would definitely be a shark, and if he were a politico, he'd act like the boss and would never be anyone's assistant. Wufu used to make the same comparisons about me, adding, "You won't get me toeing the line for anyone, except Happy Liu!" I could hear him mouthing off to Eight, but I just let him continue. I figured every community needs an authority figure, and it was right that Wufu and Eight should recognize the need for a leader.

Early one morning, Wufu and Eight were in the shit-house taking a piss. They both stood a long way off from the hole, sticking their butts out so the spurts didn't hit the wall. Their piss scattered the piles of maggots with the force of a water cannon. Eight asked Wufu if he'd had any dreams, and Wufu said, yes, but he forgot what they were about as soon as he'd woken up.

"I haven't forgotten mine," said Eight. "There was this city chick prancing along in high heels till one of her heels broke, and I sat her on my cart and asked her why she wasn't wearing a red blouse. When I woke up, I remembered that dreams don't come in color."

"That's horseshit!" said Wufu. "Happy dreams in color!" Wufu gave Eight a bunch of examples about me, like how we'd once wanted to go to a film, but we didn't want to buy tickets. Wufu didn't dare go in, but I simply swaggered past the ticket collector, even patting the ticket collector on his big belly as I went by. Like, when we fell off the bike going down a slope, he'd immediately scrambled to his feet, but I told him, "Take your time, look around and see if there's anything worth picking up before you get up." And, sure enough, we found a coin, a five-cent piece! "When people like us pull our carts through the streets, we notice things like an empty plastic bottle here or a garbage bag there, but Happy Liu notices everything: what stores are on that street, what they sell, and whether the shop owners are tall or short, fat or thin. You'd better not get on the wrong side of Happy Liu!" Wufu looked extremely serious.

"I'm not going to get on the wrong side of him, or of you!" said Eight. Wufu was delighted. As usual, whenever he was cheerful, he lit up a cigarette. Then he took the sodden roll-up out of his mouth and offered it to Eight. Eight didn't smoke, but he could hardly turn down such a mark of favor, so he finished it. But it didn't agree with him, and I heard retching noises as he puked.

I told Wufu off for being nasty to Eight, but Wufu just laughed till his eyes were narrow slits. "What a dope! Just one smoke and he's puking!"

Anyway, Eight didn't go out picking that day, and Wufu stayed behind to look after him. By the afternoon, Eight felt better, but when he thanked Wufu, all he got in response was, "I took all day off work, so you owe me twenty yuan!"

"When did you ever earn twenty yuan in a day?"

"Well, if I don't earn twenty, at least I get ten. Give me ten, OK?"

"I had last night's dumplings for breakfast, and I puked them all up, and that's six yuans' worth."

"OK, I'll settle for four," said Wufu. But Eight wasn't about to give him anything, so Wufu started rifling through his pockets. Eight was stronger than Wufu, but he gave up the struggle when Wufu tickled him under his arms. Not that it did Wufu any good, there was nothing in Eight's pockets.

"I don't have any money, but I'll give you a hand," said Eight.

What did Wufu need a hand with? He racked his brain, then remembered the gateman at the Lane Five apartment complex. He told Eight, and they cooked up a scheme for revenge. They looked very pleased with themselves.

The next day around noon, Eight pulled his cart over to Prosper Street, and he and Wufu went off to Lane Five. Eight never went anywhere without wearing a green safety helmet. He said that ten years ago he was doing blasting work building a reservoir, and he got so used to the helmet that he couldn't take it off now. Wufu just joked that it was Eight's fault the village head was screwing Eight's wife. He'd put the cuckold's green hat on himself.

Eight was furious. "Fuck that!"

"Are you swearing at me?" said Wufu.

"I'm swearing at the whole city. If it wasn't for Xi'an, would I leave my wife alone at home?"

"Didn't you tell her you were coming to town to earn money for her?" Wufu asked.

"What fucking money have I ever earned?" Eight said. "The city's full of rich folk, with their cars, their gold chains, their credit cards, and their bottles of Maotai. They're rolling in it, but they still suck up more, like they're sweeping up dead leaves. Money's a snobby bastard. It only goes to people who already have it."

"Then take off that green hat," Wufu said.

"I'll get a headache if I don't wear it."

Wufu smirked.

"Don't laugh at me, Wufu. Can you swear, with your hand over your heart, that your wife isn't messing around while you're away?"

Now it was Wufu who was furious. "Get lost! Go on. I don't need you to get me past the gateman!" And he turned on his heel and left.

Eight wasn't fazed. "So you can say that about me, but I can't say that about you? Can't you take a joke?" And then they were friends again.

When Eight and Wufu arrived at the Lane Five apartment complex, they were scared to go straight up to the gate, so they stood behind a tree on the other side of the road to keep an eye on it. Sure enough, a three-wheeler came out. Along with a big basket of vegetables, the man pedaling it had three big bundles of newspaper and some old plastic tubing. He stopped at the gate and handed over some vegetables to the gateman. Wufu pondered for a long time before it dawned on him that the man wasn't letting him, Wufu, in because he wanted the greens the vegetable hawker was paying him off with. "Bastard!" he exclaimed.

Eight figured they should stop the vegetable hawker and rough him up. That way he'd be too scared to pick trash. Wufu was doubtful. "Should a trash picker beat up another trash picker?"

"He's not a real trash picker. Why shouldn't we beat him up?" Eight said.

By this time, the vegetable hawker and his three-wheeler were a long way off. Meanwhile, the gateman was sitting on a stool, picking over his garlic chives and singing a line from a Qinqiang folk opera. "As the king, I take my seat on . . ."

Eight swore. "Fucking warbler! I've got a good eye. I'm going to throw a stone at him and then take off."

Wufu didn't like the sound of that. "A stone doesn't have eyes. If you hit him on the head and knock him down, then it's nothing on me. You threw that stone!"

"I know what!" Eight exclaimed.

"What?"

Eight muttered something to Wufu, who said, "Fine, you go buy it."

"You mean, I'm doing something for you and I have to pay for it too!" Eight grumbled.

"I've got a headache," Wufu said. "I really have. You go buy it. I'll buy you a melon." And he sketched its size in the air, as big as a basin. By the time Eight returned with a tube of compound glue, however, Wufu was annoyed with himself for having made such a grand gesture.

They stood watching the gate opposite. The gateman picked up his greens and went into the gatehouse. Wufu coughed. Eight bounded over, smeared glue all over the stool, then hightailed it back across the street.

Their patience was rewarded: the man came out of the gatehouse and plunked himself down on the stool, still singing. "As the king, I take my seat on . . ." He must have felt something wasn't right, because he stuck his finger under his butt, then jumped to his feet with the stool hanging from his pants. He gave it a sharp tug, and the seat of his pants ripped.

Having got his revenge on the gateman, Wufu kept his word and bought Eight a watermelon. The melons were grown under glass, and they cost an arm and a leg, so Wufu could afford only a small one no bigger than a soccer ball. He insisted on taking it back to Leftover House so I could have some too.

When I returned, Eight was sweeping the steps, and Wufu had his head under the faucet. "Have you been getting overheated, Wufu?" I asked. According to Chinese medicine, your body overheats if you're run-down. We all dreaded getting sick. Sometimes Wufu got constipated, and it gave him a toothache and a headache. I knew he was anxious and homesick, and that made him overheat, but he just bought himself a couple of painkillers and refused to see a doctor. He figured they were all quacks. He used to get me to bleed him, to make a cut between his eyebrows with a bit of broken pottery, or use a suction cup on him. Or he put his head under cold water.

"I've had a splitting headache all afternoon, but it's better now," he said. I grunted, took off my shoes, and rested my feet. "Do you know a cure?" he asked.

"I could bleed you between the eyes again, I guess."

"No, I want to know what there is besides bleeding or the suction cup or cold water."

Maybe I was used to answering Wufu's questions, or maybe I just liked playing teacher. Whatever it was, I coughed, cleared my throat, and told Eight to stop sweeping and come listen. "The thing is with you two," I began, "if it's not a headache, it's a toothache, or you start chatting for the sake of it and get into a shouting match. You know why that is? It's not the two of you arguing, it's your livers arguing—they get all fired up. You know what can cure that? First, you need to calm your heart, because with a calm heart, your spirit can relax. Second, do some good deeds. Third . . ."

But I hadn't gotten to telling them what the third was before Wufu butted in. "Some things really piss you off, other things can cure you!" I had no idea what he was talking about. Then they looked at each other and guffawed with laughter.

"Be serious!" I said.

"But you can't be serious about this!" said Wufu. And they told me how they'd taken their revenge on the gateman, interrupting each other the whole time. When they'd finished their tale, Wufu gave a thumbs-up. "What d'you think, eh?"

So that was what had been going on. I didn't like the way they'd taken their revenge on the gateman, and I certainly couldn't let them embarrass me like that. I cocked my little finger at them and spat on it. "Two wrongs don't make a right!"

They were taken aback. It was like my reaction was a bucket of cold water thrown in their faces, but they couldn't deny I was right. They hemmed and hawed for a bit, then Wufu came out with, "Just getting back at him."

"And now you've got back at him, you're even less likely to get into the apartment complex!"

"So what?" said Wufu.

"Crap! Did you come to Xi'an to earn money picking trash or to score points off gatemen? So you don't like money, huh, Wufu? Because when you got mad at the gateman, you were getting mad at money!"

Poor Wufu seemed to be shriveling up before my eyes. Looking terribly sheepish, he asked, "What should I do?"

"Include me next time. Don't go behind my back."

"I didn't want to go behind your back. I just thought there might be a scuffle. Eight and me, we can keep our end up, but you can't fight, and you can't take a beating either."

"Was Chairman Mao a military strategist?" I asked.

"What?" Wufu was nonplussed.

"Chairman Mao never carried a gun in his life! Didn't you know that?"

Of course, Wufu had seen plenty of films about Chairman Mao in the war, so he knew quite well that he never carried a gun, but he had no idea why I'd suddenly brought up the Chairman. He started burbling away like rice porridge in a stew pot, about the gateman treating him badly and if I didn't let him get his revenge, how could he get into the apartment complex, and was I going to get him in? I refused to be drawn into an argument. "Off you go, get my cloth shoes for me," I told him.

Wufu said to Eight, "You go get them!" So Eight went upstairs, brought me my slippers, and took my leather shoes back up.

We started in on the watermelon. When we were out earning money, we could forget about food, and it worked the other way around too. Eight gestured at the watermelon. "Eat up and shut up!"

"Eat up and shut up!" Wufu and I echoed. So we did. Wufu was proud of himself for buying the watermelon. He got the knife and carved it into three uneven slices. Then, to even them up, he carved a bit off the biggest piece and stuffed it in his mouth. That wasn't enough, so he carved a bit off another, looked at it, and stuffed that in his mouth too.

Eight was annoyed. "A greedy official's got nothing on you! If you cut any more, you'll have had the whole thing!" He grabbed a piece for himself and didn't spit the seeds out, just swilled the melon around in his mouth noisily and gulped it down. Then he stared stupidly as Wufu ate his, licking it and making it last a long, long time.

"City melons are so much sweeter than country watermelons," Wufu said.

I said, "You're not telling me they grow them on concrete slabs here?"

That annoyed him and he shut up.

11.

The city streets were so full of willow fluff, it was like a snowstorm. I chased a bit of fluff as far as Lane Nine. Lane Nine and Lane Ten started as one street and then forked. There was a small park at the fork, with trees and flowers and exercise equipment—parallel and single bars, see-saws, and a treadmill. The willow fluff lay in piles on the ground, rising into the air as people scuffed through it.

I pulled my cart into the park from Lane Nine and turned to go out onto Lane Ten. The piece of fluff I'd been following had disappeared. On Lane Ten I picked up three bundles of old magazines and some old wire in a bag. On the sixth floor of the building opposite, someone was flying homing pigeons. The pigeons wheeled overhead in repeating ellipses, gliding as they turned corners, then flapping wings that glinted silver in the sunlight on the straightaways. I whistled to them, but they didn't come down.

I'd nearly picked enough trash for the day, and I had time to admire the birds. I remembered something from a book I'd read in secondary school: "Birds glide through the air, fish glide through the water." Pigeons and fish, they were the same. In water, a fish's wings were called fins; in the air, a bird's fins were wings. What a poetic thought! As I watched, a dog barked at the pigeons. I realized it was lunchtime.

I didn't have much of an appetite, but somehow rice appealed. We hadn't had any rice in ages. Instead, what we usually did for lunch was bring along some *ganmo* from breakfast to keep us going, or spend four yuan on a big bowl of pulled noodles. The big noodle bowls were called "sea bowls" in Xi'an. That just showed how city folk have big mouths and small minds. No matter how big a bowl was, you could never describe it as holding the sea! Anyway, if I did have rice, I wanted Wufu to share the rice with me, so I went down to the south end of Prosper Street looking for him, and found him sitting beside the water faucet and trough in Lane Two.

Lane Two hadn't been developed yet. There were just a few office buildings, and the rest was all old-style courtyards of single-story houses. They had no running water and had to use standpipes in the lane. By lunchtime, the residents with their water containers on wheels had all gone, and Wufu was sitting there, gnawing on a *ganmo* and drinking from the faucet. He was sitting on the edge of the tub with his back to me, unaware that I was standing behind him and chewing on his bread as if he couldn't get it down his throat. He stretched his neck and patted his chest, then gulped some water and sighed gustily. We'd left Fishpond Village that morning without taking any food with us, so he must have sneaked a few of the musty *ganmo* we'd laid out to dry on the rooftop. But we had agreed that we'd keep those for a rainy day when we weren't working. And he'd just nabbed them to save himself from spending money on lunch. I was pissed off. "Wufu!" I said. He turned his head and looked at me, a lump of *ganmo* bulging in his cheek. He tried to swallow but couldn't, so he spat it into his hand instead. He looked so embarrassed that I didn't have the heart to tell him off. I wished I'd just tiptoed away. I pretended I hadn't seen anything and bent my head to drink, to give him time to put the *ganmo* in his pocket. "Thirsty work!" I said.

"Certainly is!" he agreed. "They put chalk in the water here. It doesn't taste as good as the water in Freshwind." Back to normal, he got up to pat a bit of grit off my shoulder. It was stuck and wouldn't come off. He spat on his hand and wiped it.

"You haven't had lunch, have you?" I said.

"No."

"What'll we eat? It's on me today."

"A bowl of noodles? Then we can make a proper meal when we get back."

"No way, that's not good enough. Let's go and have rice, with fried vegetables!"

We went to an eatery and ordered four bowls of rice, a dish of shredded potato, and another of stewed spicy bean curd, with a big bowl of egg-drop soup to wash it all down. Looking at this extravagance, Wufu asked, "Is it your birthday today?"

I wanted to hit him. "No! It's the UN secretary-general's birthday!"

Wufu looked puzzled. "UN? What country's that?" I was half-annoyed, half-amused, but then I suddenly felt sad. So I ordered another dish, salted pork strips. It was really good.

"Enjoyed your meal, did you?" the owner asked.

"Very nice, though the bean curd could have been better."

"Well, of course it's never as good as meat," the owner said.

"It was too soft. You couldn't pick it up with the chopsticks," I said.

"But bean curd is always soft!" the owner said.

"Where I come from, you can hang it from the hook of a balance scale!" I said.

"If you can eat it where you come from, then what are you doing here?" the owner said.

There I was, trying to make a helpful suggestion, and the guy turned nasty. Wufu stood up, ready to punch him, or at least settle the bill and go, but I stopped him. We were in no hurry. I sat where I was and worked on my teeth with a toothpick, not that there was anything in my teeth. Wufu did the same. Suddenly he said, "When you said Chairman Mao never carried a gun, is that because you've thought of a way to deal with the gateman?"

Why was he still on about that? "It's finally dawned on you, has it?" I said.

"I figured it out at lunchtime the next day," said Wufu, and laughed, very pleased with himself. Then he put his hand over his mouth, turned away from the window, and made me do the same.

"Scrawny's next door, buying booze. If he sees us, he'll make us pay for it," he whispered. I shot a quick glance out of the window, and there was Scrawny standing at the door of the liquor store. A small place, only one room wide and squeezed between two eateries, the liquor store sold soy sauce, vinegar, smokes, and booze, either in bottles or from the barrel.

The owner, a Henanese man, had a towel slung over his shoulder, which he used to wipe the sweat off his face, then to wipe the glass counter. He did a roaring trade in booze. People were always going in to buy shots, standing at the counter to swig it from black ceramic cups, then staggering out again. Some people took their cups in and sat there drinking all day, cracking jokes with the owner. He seemed to like listening to their stories. One morning, I was pulling my cart along and caught the good, nose-twitching smell of liquor as I passed the store.

"Come and have a drink, Happy Liu," the owner called out.

"I can't drink. It goes straight to my head," I said.

"You can't drink? And you with a red nose like that? Haven't you got the money? If you're broke, just tell me a funny story and I'll serve you a cup for free."

You think I'm that desperate for a drink? Huh! I turned and left. Every time I passed that liquor store after that, I always looked away.

Scrawny was always bragging to Wufu and me about how the liquor store owner was his buddy, because although Scrawny was from Hebei, his missus was from the same village as the owner, and when Scrawny married, he'd had to move in with his wife's family. Because the liquor store owner was one generation senior, strictly speaking, Scrawny should have addressed him as "Uncle." But, he declared, "I never have done! Never!" We were sitting by the window in the restaurant, so we didn't dare turn around or utter a squeak, just waited for him to buy his booze and leave. But he didn't. He stood there forever, laughing and joking with the owner. The owner told him he'd maxed out on his credit and had to pay.

"What are you worried about?" said Scrawny. "I'm not about to kick the bucket, and besides, I've got the trash depot, and two sons, and when they grow up, who knows, they might head up a liquor factory!"

"You're no different from your dad, old Nine Pounds, coming over from Hebei and crapping in our water. You think you can get something for nothing!"

"Leave my dad out of this, and give me another bag of melon seeds, Five Spice brand."

"I don't have Five Spice brand. Only Nine Spice brand."

"And where are they made?"

"In Henan."

"I don't want anything made in Henan. Their stuff's all fake."

"If you don't watch out, you'll feel a brick on your head! And those two kids your missus gave you, are they fake too?"

Scrawny just laughed.

As soon as he was gone, we could leave the eatery. Outside, the willow fluff in the air stuck to Wufu's matted locks.

"Do you think Scrawny's dad was called Nine Pounds because that was how much he weighed when he was born?" Wufu asked.

"Maybe."

"Scrawny must only have weighed a couple of pounds when he was born! What a pair, the father a tiger, the son a rat."

We started to laugh, but our laughs turned into yawns. "That meal's made me sleepy," I said. "I'm going to the Lane Nine park for a snooze on the stone benches."

Wufu came with me, but when we got there, he said, "I'm not going to sleep, or I won't wake up till it's dark. I'm off to do a few more lanes."

"We've picked a lot today, take it easy."

"You got to dig deep if you're digging for gold."

"This city's our rice jar . . ."

"What rice jar?" Wufu was nonplussed, again. What I meant was that the city always had trash, and if there was trash, we'd never starve. Like if you had jars of rice and flour at home, and you felt like a meal, all you had to do was scoop a bowlful from the pot. And now it was time for a snooze. City folk could enjoy life, why shouldn't we?

Just then, a three-wheeler creaked and groaned along the lane, a vegetable basket and three sacks of empty beer bottles in its trailer. Wufu, who had just slung the belt harness of his cart around his shoulder, gawked after it. Then he raised one foot and gave a nearby concrete post a good kick. The post didn't move, and all that happened was that he yelped with pain and doubled over. I went over to look. He took off his shoe, and I saw he'd split the nail on his left big toe. He swore furiously.

"What happened?" I said.

"Can't you see? It's that baldy who's been picking trash from the Lane Five apartment complex!"

Then I saw the guy. He had a face like a wax gourd and so little hair that it looked like wisps of sogon grass.

I coughed and went up to him. I'm telling you, I expected that he'd flee as soon as he saw the expression on my face, but to my surprise, he jumped off his three-wheeler and smiled at me. I could hardly not smile back, could I? So I did.

"Comrade," said Baldy, "is there a trash depot around here?"

"No!" said Wufu.

I shut him up and said, "Are you selling trash? I'll take you there."

"That's good of you." Baldy sounded surprised.

"It's only on account of Liu Bei," I said.

"Who's Liu Bei?"

"The warlord from the *Romance of the Three Kingdoms*—don't you know?" I said. Actually, it was divine inspiration that made me think of Liu Bei. Every trade has its patron saints, carpenters, pharmacists, thieves, they all do. Even brothel keepers and hookers have Pigsy from the novel *Journey to the West*. And I remembered that Liu Bei had once been a hawker of straw shoes and trash, so why shouldn't he be our patron saint? So that's what I told him.

"I never heard that before!" said Baldy.

Wufu had never heard that either, and cast an admiring glance in my direction. But he still objected to my taking Baldy to the depot. He tugged on my collar angrily. "While you're going on about Liu Bei, here's another horse with its muzzle in the trough, and if you don't chase it away, you're helping it!" He was about to go off in a huff to Lane Five, but I stopped him and made him follow me.

At the corner, a few blocks from the depot, I said to Baldy, "It's past that compound, but normally they only take scrap metal. You'll have to go and ask if they take empty bottles. Just watch out for the owner. He has a foul temper, and he has a wolfhound too. Don't barge in without asking. Instead, stand outside the gate and shout his son's name, and he'll come out. His son's called Nine Pounds."

"That's a lucky name!" Baldy said, and off he went to the depot compound.

Wufu still looked sour. In Baldy's absence, he sneaked an empty beer bottle from the three-wheeler and put it on his cart.

"Stealing a beer bottle's going to make you rich, is it?"

"I'm not as high-minded as you, Mr. Good Samaritan."

"There's a time to be high-minded and a time to be low-minded. And I can be very low-minded!"

Wufu couldn't figure out what I was saying, so he just hunkered down and rolled himself a cigarette. "I'd love to stick an awl into those tires," he said.

"Go for it! I'll watch you." But Wufu didn't move. "Those bottles are all yours. I don't want a single one," I told him.

"What do you mean? You're going to let me take them all?"

I shushed him, because Baldy was outside the depot gate, shouting, "Nine Pounds! Nine Pounds!" There was no sound from inside. "Nine Pounds! Nine Pounds!" he shouted again. The gate banged open, and out came Scrawny, an evil look on his face.

"What are you shouting? Eh? Eh?"

"Are you deaf? I'm shouting for your son, Nine Pounds!"

"Pah!" Scrawny spat, and a gob of phlegm dribbled down the front of Baldy's jacket.

"I want to sell some beer bottles," Baldy said.

"Go sell your mother's pussy! Scram!"

Looking pale and shaken, Baldy came back, mumbling, "Has he been eating dynamite?"

"Maybe he's in a bad mood because he's fallen out with his missus," I said comfortingly. "Haven't you ever worked in an office where the boss is in a bad mood? If you pick that moment to ask him to sign off on something, of course he's not going to!"

"When would I have worked in an office?" said Baldy.

"Never mind. You could always go and sell your bottles somewhere else . . ."

Baldy was touched at my concern. He confessed he wasn't really a trash picker, he was a vegetable hawker. Once in a while he'd pick up some trash, take it back to where he lived, and sell it at the depot there. He was only here today because he had something urgent to do around here. It was all panning out just as I'd planned. "If a man's got to take a piss, he can't hold it in," I said. "If you've got something urgent to attend to, we can take these bottles off your hands, but you'll have to take a bit less for them. Ten cents each."

Baldy unloaded his sack and sold the lot to Wufu.

As we counted them, Baldy and I started talking. If life was hard for a trash picker, it was even harder for a vegetable hawker. He was up early and in bed late, and never got a proper night's sleep. He had to shout himself red in the face, bargaining the peasants down, and had to keep the tax officers at arm's length, and then take all that back talk from his customers. Everyone in the city seemed to be trying to get one over on him.

"And now I've gotten one over on you," I said.

"No, you're a good man," said Baldy. He pedaled off, head held high. He was tall and skinny and, with his pant legs tied with string so they didn't get tangled in the spokes, his legs looked like sticks. He leaned into the wind, his few wisps of hair blowing like the sogon grass on my father's grave in winter.

Wufu sold the beer bottles to Scrawny and cleared seven yuan forty for them. He tried to give me four, but I refused. He stuffed them in my pocket, but I pulled away and my pocket tore. I glared at him and absolutely refused to take the cash.

Wufu looked at me doubtfully. "Then I'll buy you a pack of smokes," he said.

12.

Wufu went off to buy the cigarettes and didn't come back for ages. When I went looking for him, I found him bent over with his butt in the air, rifling through a trash can. He'd already pulled out three sheets of cardboard, which he'd anchored between his legs. Then he pulled out an old stiff-brimmed cotton hat, the sort that tourists wear, slapped it against his knee to knock the dust off it, and carried on looking. "SCOUT patrol!" I shouted. Wufu turned and fled, knocking over the trash can in the process.

The SCOUT patrols, more properly known as Street Condition Observation Units, were part of the Urban Administrative and Law Enforcement Bureau. In Xi'an, they were the trash pickers' mortal enemies. We hated them the way drivers hated the traffic police, and storekeepers feared the tax officers. Anyone who read the newspapers carefully would have seen daily articles about this or that SCOUT patrol cracking down on vendors' stalls, or coming under attack themselves. Patrols didn't wear uniforms. They were really just riffraff, but they considered themselves "officers" the minute they put that yellow band on their left arm. They swaggered around, three or four or five together, armed not with truncheons, but with chains for locking up bikes, shouting through loudspeakers as they did so. You could hear their rasping shouts, but you couldn't make out what they were saying. They spent a lot of time skulking in corners watching, and as soon as they caught you out committing some offense, they'd pop up out of a crack in the ground. Once, Wufu was pulling his cart along and the twine around his bundle of wastepaper broke, scattering the paper all over the road. The SCOUT patrol fined him five yuan for that. Eight was fined twenty yuan for pulling his cart along the main street, because trash carts were allowed only in the side lanes. Eventually, by arguing that it was too early for him to have collected any trash, he managed to persuade them to let him off with a letter of self-criticism. That was all very well, but Eight could only write a few characters, so he had to waylay some children on their way to primary school and get them to write the letter for him. They let him go after that, but he'd lost a whole morning of work. I'd been fined too. I once went to the post office to transfer Wufu's money home for him. I had a bad sore throat and a cough that day, and I stood outside, coughing away. I could see a man had his eye on me, and I thought, *What are you looking at? Haven't you ever had a cough?* I coughed up a gob of phlegm, and he came over. "Have you got a cough?"

"I've got a bad throat."

"You'd better see a doctor," he said, and gave me a slip of paper.

"Thanks."

"Look at the paper," he said. So I did. It was a fine for five yuan.

"What's all this about?" I asked. He fished around in his pocket, pulled out a yellow armband, and put it on. I stayed perfectly calm and said, "You're supposed to wear your armband on your left arm. Why did you have it in your pocket? Is it your duty to remind citizens to uphold standards of cleanliness? Or to entrap them into committing an offense and then fine them?"

He laughed awkwardly.

"You should take your job more seriously!" I said. "Which team are you on, and who's your supervisor?"

"And you are . . . ?" he asked.

I didn't answer, saying just, "I never believed you were simply a 'concerned citizen.' So I spat just to see what would happen and, sure enough, you pulled your armband out of your pocket!"

He looked flustered and started to grovel, promising to wear his armband in the future. As I turned to go, he said, "Have a good day, Mr. Cadre!"

He thought I was a government cadre! Interesting . . . I looked around and asked, "How did you know I was a cadre?"

"Because you turn your toes out when you walk, so I figured you must be one, but your belly isn't big enough, so then I figured I was wrong. But you really are one!"

Fancy being mistaken for a cadre, even once, I thought. After that, I didn't try to correct my duck feet, but there was nothing I could do about my belly. Even eating another half bowl every meal didn't make it any bigger.

Wufu hadn't run more than a few steps before he got suspicious, figured it was me, and stomped back. "You scared the life out of me!"

I made him set the bin upright and put the trash into it again. "Did you buy the smokes?"

"In my pocket."

I reached out, then grabbed his hat off his head instead and tossed it into the garbage. "What's that nasty thing you're wearing? Wipe the sweat off your face!"

"I sweat a lot," said Wufu. That was true. He only had to walk a dozen paces and the back of his neck was running with it. And his face would be covered in sweat whenever he ate, steam rising from his head. Freshwind folk have a saying, "The rich are greasy and the poor are sweaty." Rich folk always have soft, greased-down hair while poor folk go bare-chested all summer and you hear them exclaiming, "Hot, it's so hot! And all I have left to shed is my skin!" Wufu was resigned to sweating a lot, but there was one thing he was secretly very proud of: his naturally curly hair. Freshwind folks all assumed a female ancestor of his must have been raped by a Tartar, and they called him rude names like "Pekinese." But when we got to Xi'an, we saw tons of people who had curly hair because they'd had it permed, so Wufu stopped shaving his head. The first time Eight saw him, he thought that Wufu had had a perm. He tried to ruffle Wufu's hair, which made Wufu furious. "Hands off! You don't touch a man's hair like that!" Still, I couldn't get used to all those curls.

"Why don't you go get your head shaved!" I said. His hair was quite long by now, and matted and dirty.

"It's not long," he said. He tried to look at himself in a shop's glass door, but the door was open and he couldn't see anything.

"You'd better shave it before I take you to see the gateman," I said. I'd already told him there was no difference in how intelligent city folk and country folk were. The only difference between them was how much life experience they'd had. But you had to admit that apart from me, or people like me, you could tell city folk from country folk by how they looked. Wufu had such a dopey face, it was obvious he was a peasant, so his naturally curly hair struck people as funny. They might think it was permed, but a peasant with a perm didn't look like a German shepherd. He looked like a mutt dressed up as a German shepherd. "If you go around looking so dirt-poor and messy, you'll turn people off and they won't want anything to do with you," I warned him. "Not that I'm jealous of your curls. I'm just trying to help you sort things out with the gateman."

So Wufu went to the barber and had his head shaved, and off we went to the Lane Five apartment complex.

The gateman was certainly grim-faced—his mouth was so beaky, you wondered how he even managed to drink. He was dozing on his stool by the gate, but as soon as he heard footsteps, he opened his eyes and said fiercely, "Hey, what do you think you're up to?"

I wasn't afraid of him. No matter how fierce he was, he was only human. I smiled and offered him a pack of cigarettes, and we had the following conversation. It was blunt and to the point.

Gateman, to Happy: "Who are you?"

Me: "I'm his bro."

Man: "How can you have a bro like that?"

Me: "He's just a bit dark."

Man: "You can say that again!"

Me: "And he's a bit slow on the uptake."

Man: "Soft in the head, is he?"

Me: "A bit."

Man: "Soft as mush by the looks of things!"

Me: "He doesn't know how to talk properly. If he offended you, I've come to apologize for him."

Man: "You're trying to get him into the apartment complex, right?"

Me: "Yes, sir, you've totally understood. He wants to go in and pick a bit of trash. Would you be so kind?"

Man: "That's the way to do things! But I don't know why your bro didn't say a word, just barged in as if he owned the place! What was he playing at? You don't run a red light when there's a traffic policeman on duty, do you? I'm a gateman, and I sit here, and he ignores me!"

Me: "He doesn't understand the rules."

"No education at all!" The gateman tore open the pack of cigarettes. "I don't smoke fake smokes." He sniffed one, rolled it between his fingers, then stuck it between his lips.

"Hurry up and light it for him," I told Wufu. The man inhaled deeply, shut his eyes and savored it, then snorted a dense cloud of smoke out through his nostrils.

"Whatever happened to your curly mop?" he asked Wufu.

"Shaved it."

"You look quite decent like that."

Actually, the gateman was easy enough to handle. He had his little powers, and all you had to do was allow him the pleasure of wielding them and bossing people around. The way big people got big was by conferring a bit of power on little people like the gateman—that earned them a good name. If you weren't any kind of official, or rich or good-looking, and you ignored him, he'd behave like a dog and rush up and bite you. I started to butter him up, telling him how important his gate duties were, how much responsibility he carried at keeping the riffraff out, and how he was the first defense against robbers and thieves. "In the old days, the Tang dynasty's General Yuchi Jingde was venerated as a gate guardian," I said. "Nowadays, you have to be politically aware and highly responsible to guard the gate."

"Exactly!" he said. "I've got the party's trust, and I'm dedicated to my work! In five years, not a single family has been burgled here."

I said things like, "I can see you're absolutely cut out for this job. You look so fearsome, even Mount Tai wouldn't stand in your way. Obviously, you've won their respect!"

"They treat me well here," he said. "All the officials smile at me when they pass. But there are some bad people too. There's a young woman in Building Three with a BMW! I don't know how she got hold of a car like that. She really gets me wound up, blasting her horn every time she comes back. But I turn a deaf ear. I make her wait three or four minutes before I open up the gate. What a way to behave!"

"Not good," I agreed.

"You and me, we see eye to eye."

I continued to flatter him so grossly, I nearly made myself laugh, but he lapped it all up. I could have called him Chairman Mao and he would have taken me seriously.

Finally, we came to an agreement: the gateman wouldn't let anyone else pick trash from now on, but Wufu had to give him a cut of any trash he collected inside. The cut worked as follows: five cents on every pound of old newspapers, two cents on plastic waste, eight cents on scrap metal, and one cent on every beer bottle.

"Shake on it then!" I ordered them. Wufu had big hands, and the gateman yelped in pain when they exchanged a handshake. That afternoon, Wufu got a huge haul of trash, including three coal stoves and four aluminum pans and bowls. As he left, the man called him over to the gatehouse, handed him a strip of sacking, and said, "Behind Building One, there's a shed with some old radiators. You can take three of them, wrap them in this." In the shed, Wufu found piles of iron pipes, steel rods, radiators, wire, and a collection of nuts of all sizes. Wufu took three radiators, then added three steel rods, and carried his bundle out of the shed. Then he dived back in for some nuts.

13.

From then on, Wufu went there to pick trash every day and got to know the gateman well. The man always used to say, "Hey, Wufu! Tell me about your home village."

Wufu couldn't string two straight sentences together, as the gateman knew perfectly well, so putting him down by bombarding him with questions was a fine form of amusement.

Gateman: "Is it true that the pick of the workforce has left Freshwind for the city?"

Wufu: "There's no workforce at all left in Freshwind. If someone dies, there's no one to carry the coffin to the grave."

Gateman: "What do the women do when they miss their menfolk? Do they use cucumbers? Do they do rumpy-pumpy with their fathers-in-law?"

Wufu: "What?"

Gateman: "Nothing. The National Coal Corporation's having a meeting in Xi'an right now. Why haven't you brought any girls from the countryside?"

Wufu: "If they're all in a meeting, what do they want girls for?"

Gateman: "Services. They have droves of them when there's a coal meeting, and the girls end up pissing black pee."

Wufu: "What did you have for lunch?"

Gateman: "Stop interrupting me, Wufu!"

Wufu: "I don't understand what you're talking about."

Gateman: "Wufu! Never mind that you're as black as coal yourself. You've got a bulging forehead and a bulge at the back of your skull too. If that was all, we'd let it go, but on top of that, you've got a hump on your back. If you only had the gift of gab, we could let that go too, but you can hardly string three sentences together! Are you married?"

Wufu: "Yup, with three kids."

Gateman: "All yours, are they?"

At that, Wufu finally lost it. He grabbed a beer bottle and smashed it against the side of the cart. Glass fragments went everywhere, and he was left holding the neck of the bottle in his hand. The gateman was taken aback. He hurriedly patted Wufu on the shoulder. "You look even uglier when you lose your temper. OK, OK, help yourself to some iron pipes from the shed."

Wufu filled a sack. He wound some wire around his waist and threw three thick steel rods over the compound wall. Then he left the apartment complex and retrieved the rods from the holly bush on the other side. "You thought you could get away with gabbing like that, you great bellows-mouth! Stupid asshole!"

Wufu's haul was more than mine nowadays. Every evening, he told Eight and me what he'd taken from the shed. He figured he could shift the entire contents of the shed in six months. The thought certainly livened him up. He flicked a finger at the bridge of Eight's nose and made him fetch some sheets of brown wrapping paper from the bundle Eight had stored in his room. Then he folded a paper wallet for Eight, and a bigger one for himself. I knew this was all for my benefit. He still coveted the real leather wallet I'd bought after I sold my blood, and what was a paper wallet compared to a leather one? I smiled wryly. Just then, old man Fan came to the door.

Fan owned a house opposite. He was our landlord's cousin, so we had to be polite to him. But whenever we greeted him, he simply harrumphed and ignored us. Once I was buying flour at the Fishpond

Village store, and I was five yuan short. He happened to be standing nearby, so I asked if he'd lend me the money. I made a point of saying I'd pay him back as soon as I got home. But he refused. "Why should I believe you? You trash pickers are here today, gone tomorrow." I had to go home, get more money, then return to the store for the flour. So when he turned up at our door, I went to the shit-house. Fan saw Wufu folding paper wallets. "You making them that big so you can use them for ghost money?" Wufu was so angry, he got to his feet and went to his room. Fan honked with laughter. "Can't you take a joke?" Then he shouted at me, "Happy Liu! You shitting a rope in there?"

"Happy Liu's a cut above the rest of us. His turds are as long as a butt-cleaning stick," said Eight.

I hung around in the shit-house, but he wouldn't leave, so finally I had to come out. "Are you looking for me, Mr. Fan?" I asked.

"So, your turds are as long as a butt-cleaning stick? You certainly must be a cut above the rest of us, Happy Liu!" Most of the time when he flattered me like this, it was because he wanted something from me.

"What's up?" I asked.

"Just a small thing." He offered me a cigarette. It turned out he kept a pig behind the house, and he wanted to sell it. There was a slaughterhouse next to the food market at the east end of Prosper Street, and he wanted us to bring back a cart tomorrow evening and take the pig there the following morning. "I was going to take it in a pickup truck," he said, "but it's broken down, and seeing as it's on your way, could you do it, Happy? It's only a small favor."

"Sure," I said. "Only a small favor."

The next evening, Wufu and I pulled our carts back to Fishpond Village, leaving the bike behind. Wufu was really pissed off. "A small favor? This is what he calls a small favor? Even if the pig's not heavy, it still means walking to Prosper Street instead of biking. How much time are we going to waste on that?" I told him to keep his trap shut. We couldn't afford to get on the wrong side of old man Fan. And the next morning, I hauled Fan's pig to the slaughterhouse on my cart, with Fan following along behind. Wufu was behaving completely different from the night before. He even offered Fan a lift on his cart. "Look at you! Quite the goody-goody!" I teased him.

"Well, you're pulling a pig, so I'd better pull one too!" he muttered. Then he thought I hadn't gotten the joke.

I said, "You're going to go to all that trouble, just to get in a dig at the old man!"

Pulling the pig and old Fan on our carts, we headed toward a street near the city wall. We were attracting quite a lot of attention, so I began to hum a tune. I imagined that we were back in ancient times, when Xi'an was the great capital city Chang'an, when there were no apartment blocks, only family courtyards, and no cars, only horses prancing along and pulling carriages. *I should have had a horse pulling my cart too*, I thought, and imagined I could hear the clip-clop of its hooves and the bells jingling on its harness making a fine sound. Once, when I was collecting newspapers, I found a book amongst them. I took it home and put it by my pillow to read. It turned out to be stories of old Chang'an. One was about a military governor who rode down the streets every day and, whenever he spotted a pretty woman, he hung his whip on the ring handle of her front door, and the family had to play host to him that night. I wouldn't do anything so outrageous if I had a whip . . . but I didn't want one, I reflected. I only wanted people who had trash to get rid of to hang a sign on their door so I didn't have to wander around looking. But we didn't live in ancient times, and I smiled at my ridiculous fancies.

As I smiled, the woman who ran the eatery in the lane smiled back. She was standing at the door, pulling in customers and calling to passersby. "Come and have dinner, sir! Come and eat, madam!"

Wufu said to me in a low voice, "Is she calling me 'sir'? Do I look like a businessman?"

The woman overheard him. "Of course you do!" she said. "Everyone's a sir or a madam nowadays, and everyone's making money! Come try our noodles. The flour's milled from wheat grown north of the Wei River, the vinegar's matured in Shanxi, the peppers are local, from Yao County. You won't know how good they are till you've tried them!"

We shook our heads and made to continue walking, but she stood in our way, going on about all the different kinds of noodles: in soup, in chili oil, with meat sauce, noodles as thick as sticks with chicken and hot pepper in a huge bowl. She even called into the shop, "Clear the tables and serve these three gentlemen noodle soup!"

By now, I was annoyed. "I said we're not eating, and that's that. This isn't drumming up business, it's harassment!"

The woman's expression immediately changed. "Who said I was talking to you? I was talking to the pig!"

What a thing to say! I patted the pig, and it started grunting. "What are you getting so excited about?" I said to it. "Got yourself a girlfriend in the city, have you?"

I was dead pleased with my witty repartee and felt quite cheerful. Still, by the time we'd sold the old man's pig, it was halfway to midday, and we hadn't even started picking trash. Wufu was full of grumbles. When the old guy who collected parking charges asked why we had no trash, Wufu reacted like he was his best buddy and treated him to a litany of complaints about old Fan. I pulled my cart away.

In my opinion, Wufu was wasting his time prattling about his worries to that old guy. He might look sympathetic and occasionally add a word or two, but I was willing to bet Wufu's ramblings were going in one ear and out the other.

Me, I wanted to live up to my name and be happy. That's not to say I wasn't annoyed, but everyone should have a bird singing inside them as well as a crow cawing. I passed the intersection where the newly planted indigo bush was. It reached upward, no thicker than someone's arm but already covered in leaf buds. I gave it my full attention and silently saluted it. Just then, firecrackers crackled in the distance where a small store was opening for business, and three or four guys ran past, carrying old-fashioned revolvers.

There were a bunch of guys in Xi'an who roamed the lanes and streets with antique revolvers in search of a wedding or a funeral, a birthday party for someone elderly or a celebration of a newborn's first month, or a store opening. Then they would let off a salvo of shots and cadge some money for livening up the event. I had a sudden vision of getting these guys to come and let off a salvo in honor of the indigo bush to celebrate its survival in the city. Bang, bang, bang! I heard in the distance. The firearms had arrived at the shop's opening ceremony.

"Great!" I said.

I heard an answering echo. "Great!" I looked around and saw a beggar approaching in the distance.

This beggar was so plump and fair-skinned that the very sight of him cheered me up. He'd been standing some distance away, on the corner by a liquor store, and I thought, *If your clothes were clean and your hair combed, you'd look quite respectable.* At first, he was walking normally, but then as soon as he went past the shop door, he began to stagger like he was lame. *You fake!* I watched him very carefully. He came up to me and held out his hand. There was a one-yuan bill lying in his palm. "A bit of charity, old sir!" he wheedled.

Old sir? Was I really that old? I ignored him, and bent down to pick up an empty pull-tab can from the side of the road. But instead of going away, he stood there with his hand outstretched, muttering, "Old sir, old sir! I'm talking to you, old sir!"

"I haven't got any money."

"You must have, in the pocket of your suit."

It was true I was wearing a suit, given to me by an old woman in Lane Ten. She was probably well educated because she sold me a bag of books. Before giving them to me, she tore the flyleaf out of each

volume. I could see an inscription: "To Mr. Wang Deming, in appreciation of your generous appraisal." I asked her who Wang Deming was.

She said it was her husband and that I looked just like her husband
when he was a young man. "How old are you? Maybe you're his reincarnation, but he was a section chief in the Cultural Bureau. How could
he have been reborn as a trash picker?"

Clearly batty. Still, I felt I had to take her arm and see her home
because of her age. "Which year did your husband die?" I asked her.

"Ten years ago."

So I exaggerated my age, told her I was forty, too old to be her rein-
carnated husband. If he had been a section chief in the Cultural Bureau
in his earthly life, then surely he'd have the same job in the hereafter.
When we got to her home, she got out her husband's suit and said, "Are
you brave enough to put this on?" If she had tried to give it to me, I
would have said no. But, when she put it like that, of course I was brave
enough, and I put it on. What was there to be afraid of? If her old man
was a ghost, then he was still a section chief ghost, an educated ghost.

I certainly impressed Wufu and Eight with that suit. They said it
fitted me like a good saddle fits a horse, and even if I had no money,
I looked as if I did. Certainly the beggar thought that. But I didn't, I
really didn't. I pulled out all my pockets to show him they were empty.

"How come you're broke?" he asked.

"I'm a trash picker," I said.

"Oh." Then he whacked his palm against mine and gripped my
hand. When he let go, there was the one yuan stuck to me. "That's for
you!" he said.

This beggar pitied me! What a blow to my pride! I felt my face
burning with shame. I threw the money on the ground and stamped
on it. "Scram!" I shouted. "Scram, you bastard!"

He was startled, then flew into a rage. His leg suddenly wasn't crip-
pled any longer, and he aimed a kick at my crotch. What the hell . . . ?
I had to teach the brute a lesson. I dodged, and he lost his balance and

went down on his backside. Then he came at me again, flinging his arms around me. His breath stank so badly, I almost choked. I pushed his face away from me, but he grabbed the collar of my suit jacket with one hand and wiped snot all over my shoulder with the other hand. How dare he dirty my suit! I headbutted him, catching him on his chin while protecting my suit, then headbutted him again, this time forehead to forehead, and saw stars.

"How dare you insult me like that!" I managed, even though I'd almost knocked myself out. There were still stars in front of my eyes, but I saw him stagger. His jaw seemed to be dislocated. He had one hand supporting it, the other clamped to his forehead. He gave a quick upper cut to the chin, and his jaw connected again. He could move it side to side, and he could speak. "Who are you?"

"Happy Liu," I said.

"And I am Lively Shi!" he introduced himself grandly. His name was actually Lively! I slapped him round the head. I wouldn't have done that if he hadn't been called Lively. But Lively and Happy seemed to make a good pair. I found that funny.

The security guard at the hotel saw me slap Lively and shouted, "Hey, what d'you think you're doing?" The man's uniform looked like a police uniform, and Lively took him for a policeman. The guard clearly took himself for a policeman too, and Lively Shi saw his chance to do some complaining. The man crooked his middle finger and motioned me over. "Why did you hit him?" he asked.

I knew I was at fault, but I had an exit strategy. Turning to Lively Shi, I said, "Did I hit you?"

"Yup."

I smiled. "Comrade Guard." I deliberately addressed him by his job title, to remind him that he might be in charge of security inside the hotel, but he was just the same as me outside it. "Comrade Guard, it was to try and make him see sense. This bro of mine has no idea how to behave. I thought a slap might clear his head, but he's still so confused, now he's complaining to you." I turned to Lively. "The hotel is full of officials and tourists, and big-nosed foreigners too. You could go begging anywhere, so why come here and shame the Chinese people?"

I could see the guard was touched by my fine words, and I was winning him over to my side. Lively Shi really was dumb. He started saying, "Begging isn't stealing. I can go where I like, and if I've got nothing to eat, why shouldn't I beg for something?"

That pissed the man off. "Get lost!" he roared.

Startled, Lively Shi set off down the street, but he hadn't gone more than a few dozen paces when he stopped and looked round. The guard shouted again, and Lively Shi set off at a run. The guard stamped his foot, and Lively ran out of the lane and disappeared. I straightened my suit and felt annoyed that one shoulder now had snot all over it. I wiped myself down, and continued to pull my cart up and down the lanes. "Ai-ya," I sighed. You couldn't help but find Lively Shi amusing. He had certainly made a quiet morning seem a lot less lonely and boring. Lively Shi was a dogfish. When the fish were droopy, you put a dogfish into the pond. A nip here and a nip there livened up the others in no time. I turned to look after him and felt bad. I shouldn't have goaded the guard into driving him away.

14.

Without Lively Shi, things certainly were less lively. I'd just reached a bend in the lane, still thinking I might go looking for him, when a woman banished the thought from my mind. She'd been standing in the middle of the lane for quite some time with a dog in her arms. The dog was licking her nose, and she was lavishing fond kisses on its forehead. In Freshwind, men didn't normally keep cats, and women didn't have dogs, because dogs were horny by nature and might lead a woman astray, and a cat might mistake a man's penis for a mouse. I was baffled by the fact that city women had dogs. This woman was standing in my way. I hesitated, not sure whether to stop or pull my cart to the side. But just then, she stepped aside to let me by. Well, at least she had nice manners. That made me feel good toward her. As I brushed past, the dog spoke to me, "Woof! Woof!" I didn't understand dog language, but it sounded harmless, like a naughty child. I turned around and woofed back.

"Becker! Becker!" the woman said, and pushed its head into her bosom. I found myself wondering why all pretty women were pretty in the same way, but ugly people like Wufu and Eight differed in their ugliness.

My shadow overlay the woman's shadow; then the two shadows separated as lightly as two sheets of paper torn from a notebook. I tell you, I walked on by as if I walked past a pretty woman every day. At which point, she spoke. "Hey!"

Was she talking to me or the dog? Becker—what a funny foreign name for a dog! There were plenty of pets in the city, both cats and dogs. I had my own pet—my cart was my pet, as well as the tool of my trade. Any implement could have a soul, and could be male or female, I figured. Was my cart male or female? Should I give it a nice name?

"Hey, hey!" she said again. I got a whiff of her perfume. It smelled strange.

"Are you talking to me?" I asked. The worst thing about trash picking is that there's hardly any talking. I can tell you now that for anyone from Freshwind, trash picking isn't heavy work. Even if your legs get so tired that they swell up every day, you can simply heat some water in the evening and soak your feet in a bowl. What made it unbearable for me was that, even though almost everyone from Lane Five to Lane Ten knew me, they only talked to me to bargain over the price of their trash or, if they had nothing better to do, to make fun of me. Mostly they ignored me, even though I knew quite well that they knew me, and had teased me about my Freshwind accent only the previous day. If I smiled and greeted them, they would walk past as if I weren't there. As if I were a leaf or a scrap of paper blowing down the street. If I squatted by the side of the road, I was a post. This woman had said, "Hey!" twice, but she didn't have any trash to get rid of, so what was she trying to tell me? If she was asking my opinion about the way she'd groomed her dog, I'd have said it looked good, of course. She'd dyed a couple of tufts on top of the dog's head, one green and one yellow, and it was wearing its own little suit, as if it was her child, or rather her man! If she asked me where I was from, I'd explain it to her slowly. I wouldn't feed her the old line, "from a beautiful and fertile place," because beautiful places were not usually fertile, and vice versa. Freshwind was definitely beautiful but not fertile, and that was why I'd turned my back on it to come to Xi'an.

What she actually said was, "How much for old newspapers?" So she was only selling trash! That deflated me. I still tried to spin out the conversation though. "Oh, do you want to sell some old newspapers? They're ten cents a pound. How many have you got? Do you get several different newspapers delivered at home?"

"Come to that building in a little while, Entrance Three, Floor Six, the door on the left." And she stalked away, leaving me standing there foolishly. My clothes seemed to be flapping loose on me, as if I'd suddenly shrunk. Luckily, there was no one around. I took out a cigarette but couldn't get my lighter to work. Should I go to her building? Why should I have to see her snooty expression again? *Ms. High-and-Mighty, your old newspapers aren't going to make my fortune. They can pile up in your house for all I care!* But maybe I was being unreasonable. How could I expect a decent conversation with a complete stranger? Why was I blaming her? I argued back and forth in my head, and finally picked up my balance scales and a sack and headed to her building, to Entrance Three, Floor Six.

A cat was slinking down the stairs, silent as a tiger. These beasts were solitary; they didn't talk to anyone. I was a beast too. It was the birds who couldn't stand silence, and they twittered the whole time.

The door was open, and the woman was piling bundles of newspapers out on the landing. It was obvious she didn't want me going inside. I could understand that. All the same, at some houses where I collected trash, they'd invite me in, shoes on and all, and give me a drink of water and even offer me a smoke. And then there were the houses where they made me take my shoes off and put on slippers, or plastic overshoes. This was the first time I'd been refused entry at all. Maybe she was wealthy and her family didn't let in strangers, in case they used the opportunity to check the place out and then come back to break in. Or maybe she was living on her own. Whatever, she wouldn't let me in. I never even got a peek through the door. I just looked down at the newspapers, tidied them up, and started stuffing them in the sack.

In amongst the papers was a photograph, about six inches square. It was of a man, handsome with sleekly combed hair. I took it out and said, "There's a photo here." I put it down by the door, but the woman kicked it back at me.

"Don't you want it?" I asked. The dog had changed into something casual, a checkered coat and a pair of sunglasses. The woman didn't look at me or say anything. I could tell that something had been going on, and that it hadn't been pleasant. I felt sorry for this woman. I put the photo in with the newspapers and filled the sack. I hooked it onto the scales, holding the scales up good and high, and did the addition on my fingers like a little kid, talking her through it every step of the way. Then I got my wallet out of my pants pocket, making sure she could see it was leather. As I paid her the money, I looked at the dog.

"That's a pretty dog!" I said. I wanted to flatter her, partly to cheer her up but also to show her I wasn't a complete ignoramus, I had culture. That way, she might act a bit friendlier. But she was an ice queen. She never uttered a word, simply took the money and slammed the door shut. It was a big slam and created such a draft that it lifted my hair. That really upset me. *What a bitch, so rude! Why take out your problems on me? You might be pretty, but there are plenty of prettier women out there. You might be rich, but I've been to plenty of big businessmen's villas collecting trash. Would you slam the door like that on me if I wasn't a trash picker?* I was really angry by now, grinding my teeth in fury, scarcely able to breathe.

Whenever I was angry, I always wanted to have a smoke or nibble some fermented bean curd. But when I got the paper bag out from my coat pocket, my fingers found the toothpick. An evil thought occurred to me: I jammed the toothpick into the keyhole, as hard as I could, so it broke off.

Then I went downstairs with the sack over my shoulder, wishing I could meet up with Lively Shi.

But he wasn't on the street below. I wasn't in the mood to go shouting for trash, so I just walked through Lanes Seven, Eight, Nine, and Ten. Lively Shi was still nowhere to be seen.

Oh, Lively, lovely Lively, where are you? As I searched for him, my indignation gradually ebbed. True, she wasn't a good woman, but if people disrespected me, it must have been because I wasn't worthy of respect. After all, I wasn't the mayor, or rolling in money, or even a registered city resident. She wouldn't treat me like that if I were. Who was I? Well, I wasn't just any old trash picker, I reminded myself, certainly not! That woman clearly had no insight. All she saw when she looked at me was a bit of junk to be gotten rid of. But I was a pearl! She was just showing her ignorance, and I felt sorry for her!

At that, I stopped feeling mad. You had to put up with toads croaking if you crossed a marsh. I wasn't going to sink to her level. I got mad because I was poor. It made you think too much. I shouldn't have jammed the toothpick in her door lock. That was the kind of thing that Wufu and Eight would do, not Happy Liu!

I started looking on alley walls, on bus stops, and on lampposts, trying to find a locksmith. Finally, amongst all the ads for STD clinics, deodorants, fake ID cards, and rooms to rent, I found a locksmith's phone number. I called from a public phone to tell them to go over to her building—Entrance Three, Floor Six, left-hand door—and fix the lock.

"Could you tell me your name, please?"

"Huang," I said. "Eight Huang."

"Have you notified the local police?"

"They'll be there soon," I said. "And don't keep them waiting. You don't want to get on the wrong side of the police."

"Wait downstairs," the locksmith said. "We'll be right there."

"No, I'm at work right now," I said. "Just go straight up. My wife's at home. She's locked inside." I didn't go to the depot that afternoon, and I didn't tell Wufu what I'd done either. I took my cart back to

Fishpond Village as quick as I could. I sat alone at Leftover House, feeling bored and leafing through the newspapers I'd collected. I could hear birds fluttering around outside, and I stuck my head out the door. The locust tree was full of birds, and more were arriving as I watched. They started up with a tremendous twittering and tweeting. I'd never seen so many in the tree before, though there were always some there. I was curious. Back in Freshwind, if birds came and nested in your tree or under your eaves, that was a sign of good luck. What was such a huge flock doing here? Holding a congress? I didn't dare go outside, or make any noise, in case it scared them away. The papers were full of news about Xi'an. Of course, it was old news by now, but it was new to me. There was a story about a laborer who had climbed into a crane at a construction site and threatened to kill himself because he hadn't been paid, and the mayor had gone there personally to try and talk him down. And one about the tallest new skyscraper in the northwest, which was owned by a man who had spent ten years mending shoes on the corner of that very same street. And one about someone who had broken into a house and murdered an occupant, then fled, and fifty thousand yuan was offered for any information about the culprit. And one about a confrontation between local residents and demolition crews on one street, blocking traffic for five hours. I read on, completely absorbed, annoyed that I'd been in Xi'an so long without buying a daily newspaper. *You make such a big deal about being an educated man, Happy Liu,* I berated myself, *and you're turning yourself into another Wufu or Eight!* I gazed out the window, at the sky that seemed suddenly so high and so blue. It dawned on me that the birds had stopped singing. Where were they? I went outside and found Eight perched in the tree.

"How long have you been back?"

"A while." He snapped off a twig.

"What are you doing?"

"I've been pulling out the birds' nests to use for kindling."

A nest as big as a bowl fell at my feet. That made me really mad. I shouted furiously at him, and Freshwind curses I'd all but forgotten came bursting out of my mouth: "Bastard! Son of a bitch! Motherfucker! You piece of filth a thief wouldn't steal and a wolf wouldn't eat! There's kindling all around you. Why the fuck are you pulling birds' nests out of the tree? Where are the birds going to sleep with no nests? Would you want to end up sleeping on the street?"

My outburst petrified Eight. He slid off his branch, scraping and scratching his belly. "So, you do know how to swear!"

"I could use a fistfight too!"

"Someone screwed you over when you were out today, did they?"

"What?" I said, so outraged I nearly choked. Eight was not Wufu, and he'd touched a sore spot. I wasn't going to hold back now! "Screwed me over?" I yelled, even angrier than before. "I'm not you! I'm not Wufu! Let me tell you, the person who screws me over hasn't been born yet! You're the one who's going to be screwed over, you piece of filth a thief wouldn't steal and a wolf wouldn't eat!"

"It's true," he admitted. "I got my scales broken. The motherfucker said I'd cheated him by fixing the scales. But everyone does that, everyone cheats everyone else in this city! The fucker went and broke my scales! I'm so dumb, I get browbeaten on the street, then I come back here and the birds bully me and shit on my head! Why shouldn't I pull their nests down?"

"I'm trying to teach you how to behave, and you're not listening," I said.

"OK, I'll obey," Eight said.

"It doesn't sound like obedience!"

"I've said I will, OK?"

I went to my room, and I watched as Eight climbed back into the tree and replaced the nest. Maybe I'd been a bit of a bully, but I couldn't forgive him. I wished Wufu would come back, then things would be all right again.

15.

Wufu came back with some playing cards. These were long, thin *huahua* cards, with pictures on them—it was a game the old folk played in the countryside, much simpler than poker. I was astonished to see them in the city. Whatever was a big fellow like Wufu doing with them? He brandished them in front of me. I said, "Go play with Eight. Leave me out of it." But Wufu didn't intend to play with them. He'd bought the pack for old Mrs. Wang in apartment complex seven on Lane Two. There were eight old women living there—their children had jobs in Xi'an, and they'd all moved into town after their husbands died—and when they had nothing else to do, they spent their time playing cards. Wufu saw that their cards were creased and worn, so when he'd sold his trash at the depot, he hunted up and down the lanes for a new pack and found these.

"Well, you're full of ideas today, Wufu! Helping out the ladies!" I said.

"I can help you out too," he said.

"How?"

"You've got to get me a pair of shoes in exchange!" he said. I didn't understand, but when I asked, he just smiled.

The next morning was hot and sunny again. Xi'an does have four seasons, but spring and autumn last no time at all, while summer and winter are really long. Not long after the willow fluff had all blown away, the weather started warming up, and jackets were uncomfortably hot. But I went on wearing my suit, and socks and shoes too. For three days now, Wufu had been going without socks and was wearing plastic sandals. Every time he went out, he'd hitch up his pant legs and stick his feet, shoes and all, under the faucet. "If you keep wearing socks, you'll get maggots in there!" he jeered.

"The hell you know! Socks keep my feet cool. It's like how the ice cream vendors keep a quilted cotton cover over their Popsicle boxes!"

It didn't matter how cutting I was, Wufu still laughed. "Go ahead and wear your socks! If I go barefoot in sandals, it'll only be more obvious that you're in socks and leather shoes!"

When we got to Prosper Street, Wufu wanted me to go with him to apartment complex number seven.

"Has the gateman been bullying you there too?" I asked.

"No, but you've got to come!" There was a fountain in the apartment complex courtyard, and sitting around its edge were half a dozen old ladies, all snowy-haired and with faces as wrinkled as walnuts. They were chatting away, and suddenly one started laughing so hard, her false teeth fell out. Wufu picked them up for her, then stooped to rinse the teeth in the fountain. There was a chorus of "Hello, Wufu!"

"Here I am, ladies!"

"Have you had your breakfast? Did you have noodles or *laobing*?"

"I had rice gruel this morning."

"Very digestible," they all agreed.

"I could digest a stone," said Wufu, and he got out the *huahua* cards.

The old women took a good look at them. "Lovely!" they said. "How much are they?"

"Nothing, they're a present for you."

"Such an ugly face but such a good heart!"

"Not such an ugly face either," said Wufu.

"No, no, of course not."

"Isn't Auntie Lu here?" asked Wufu.

"Oh, we nearly forgot. She sent a message for you to go to her house. She's waiting for you."

Wufu came over to me. "I'm off to Mrs. Lu's. Coming?"

"Do you spend every day gossiping with them?"

"Sure, they sit waiting for me every day."

He's better at this than me, I thought. I so wanted that woman with the lapdog to talk to me, and Wufu had all these old ladies hanging on his every word. "Who's Auntie Lu? Does she like a good gossip too?"

"Come with me," he said, "but make sure you call her 'Auntie.'"

We got to Building Three, and a window opened on the fourth floor above us. "Wufu!" called an old woman. When we got upstairs, she was standing in the doorway, so warm and welcoming, we might have been her grandsons. In we went, and she told us not to bother taking our shoes off. But I insisted anyway, and a younger woman brought us each a pair of slippers. The second woman was dark-skinned and fat, and she blushed when she saw me. Wufu introduced me. Mrs. Lu said, "Turn in a circle." I turned around. Then she said, "Walk." I walked a few steps. I didn't have a clue what was going on.

"Happy Liu's better-looking than me!" Wufu said.

"Right," Mrs. Lu said. We sat ourselves down, and I felt her eyes on me. "How old are you? Tell me about your family. Are you married? What? Why not? Is that because you're divorced, or have you never had a steady girlfriend? I expect the right person hasn't turned up in your life yet. When she does, then it will happen." She called, "Cuihua! When the tea's ready, you come and join the conversation!" I realized Cuihua must be the dark, fat woman.

"Are you her daughter?" I asked Cuihua.

"No, just from the same village."

"You still live there?"

"No, I live in Xi'an now."

Mrs. Lu began, "Cuihua is twenty-six, she's got a fine full-moon face, and a nice temperament too. She's been working as a housekeeper, but her boss had a car accident and is in a coma. Her boss's husband's taken up with another woman, so he bought his wife a one-bedroom apartment and left her in Cuihua's care. He told Cuihua that when his wife dies, she'll get the apartment. Cuihua's in luck—not many girls have their own apartment in Xi'an!" Cuihua looked embarrassed. She poured us more tea, then shut herself in the bedroom. Mrs. Lu started in on a litany of complaints about city food. The rice tasted of nothing, the flour tasted of nothing, and the eggs fried up pale. Scallions in the countryside were so strong that a single stalk would flavor a whole wok full of food. Here, the scallions were grown in greenhouses, and they didn't give off a good strong smell even if you cut up a whole bunch. Did we have any pickled vegetables, she asked. She'd put aside a jar of them, she could give us some. I hurriedly said we had plenty, thank you. "Dear me, dear me," she kept saying. Then she got to her feet and went into the bedroom where Cuihua had gone, calling Wufu in with her. There was a lot of muttering, then they all came out.

"I have to go," said Cuihua. I grabbed my chance to say our good-byes too.

"Well, isn't that good timing!" said Mrs. Lu. "You can both see Cuihua home."

When we got outside, Wufu said, "Why don't you take Cuihua home?"

That didn't feel right to me, so I stopped a cab for her. I paid the cabdriver, and she let me, as if I'd only done what was proper. She was a simple country girl. I said quietly, "Make sure to take note of the cab number in case anything happens." I expected her to say thank you, but she just looked at me and blushed.

After Cuihua had gone, Wufu said, "That was nice of you to pay her cab."

"Well, she's a woman," I said.

"Do you like her?"

"Sure."

"Then marry her!"

"What a dumb thing to say!"

"It's not dumb at all. I took you over there today so you could meet Cuihua. She was interested, so now it's up to you."

"Oh!" I said. So that's what was going on! Wufu was playing matchmaker.

"Are you up for it?" he asked.

"No."

"She's a fine woman, and she's got everything you need. Why don't you want to marry her?"

"She's got bunions."

"I never saw any bunions!" said Wufu.

"That's because all you looked at were her big ass and her big tits!"

"You're thirty-five years old—you can't afford to be picky!"

"I know I'm getting on, but if I can't get a leather jacket, then I'll go butt-naked."

Wufu was so upset, he nearly cried. He said all he'd wanted was to do something for me for a change. Mrs. Lu wanted him to marry Cuihua, but he was already married, so he thought he'd match me up with the girl instead.

"Hey, I'll treat you to mutton *paomo* for that," I said. I meant it. *Paomo* soup, thickened with bread, was a Xi'an specialty. Wufu and I had wanted to try it a few times, but it was always too expensive, so we never got it.

It was evening by now, and we were back in Fishpond Village. Wufu started to scrape some potatoes for dinner, but I said, "Come on, we're going out for mutton *paomo*."

"You really mean it?"

"I'm as good as my word," I said. Then I said to Eight, "You come too."

Eight was busy scraping his room door with a whisk he was dipping in water. Ever since he'd pulled down those nests, the birds had been getting back at him. Whenever he was out, they perched on the lintel and crapped. It was runny crap too, and it dribbled all down the door.

"How generous of you!" he said as he left off washing his door to go wash his face.

"What a freeloader!" Wufu said in disgust. "Let's stay home. We can make potato soup."

"But I've already washed my face!" Eight said.

"Come on, let's go! Wufu's just teasing you," I said.

"The food's good when someone else pays," Eight said.

"The food'll be very good," I said. "And there'll be an egg on top for each of us too."

There were three mutton *paomo* cafés in Fishpond Village. They were all crowded, and we went to the second one. As we were eating our dinner, I looked down and saw a particularly fine-shaped foot. It belonged to a woman squeezed up alongside us. She had one leg draped over the other, her foot sticking out at an angle. It was long and slender, as fair as jade, and clad in lightweight sandals. I could hardly tell her to put it away, but I couldn't take my eyes off it. This was unbearable. In the end, I ate only half my mutton *paomo* before heading home. I loved women's feet, maybe because I was too embarrassed to look a woman in the face, so instead I'd look down and find myself gazing at her feet. I looked down so much that it got to be a habit. I'd actually developed the ability to tell whether a woman's face was pretty or ugly, simply by looking at her feet. Walking down the street, if a pretty pair of feet came toward me, I'd feel a fleeting emotion. But to have a delicate foot dangling motionless right in front of my eyes, that was too much. *Get yourself out of here,* I told myself. *It's making you remember the girl in the beauty salon, and then you'll start looking gooey-eyed. And you can't do that here!*

Wufu and Eight couldn't understand what was wrong. "Why aren't you eating? The *paomo*'s delicious, and you've left half of it!"

I paid the bill and went home. I was trying to make sense of my feelings. I could hear the birds in the trees, as if they were saying, *Beauty salon! Beauty salon!* It's true, I hadn't been by the beauty salon in a very long time. In fact, I thought I'd forgotten the woman, but she was still hiding in a corner of my heart. I thought of Cuihua. Why had I flatly rejected her? If I hadn't come to the city, if I hadn't gotten that pair of high-heeled shoes, if I hadn't seen the woman in the beauty salon, I wouldn't have been so picky. But now I was Happy Liu, a man about town, and I had those shoes and I'd seen the beauty salon woman, and a whole load of other women's feet. Cuihua was definitely not the woman for Happy Liu.

I was glad that the match with that woman in Freshwind hadn't turned out. She was a fine-looking magpie back home, but in Xi'an, she'd only be a dowdy sparrow. If we'd married then, we might be divorced by now.

Did true love exist? Take a married man: if he met a girl who was as good in every way as his wife, but no better, and that girl tried to seduce him, he'd probably stay faithful to his wife. And the same if that girl had just a little more to offer. But if she had a lot more going for her, much more, how long would he resist temptation?

Was I a jerk? No, I was not. But a white daikon turns green when it grows out of the soil, water turns to ice when it gets cold, and the environment changes people. That has nothing to do with morality.

All these thoughts were going around in my head when Wufu and Eight came back. They were still talking about how mutton *paomo* soup was much nicer than knife-shaved noodles, no question. The mutton came back on you when you burped afterward. They asked me why I'd left half my food. Was I feeling ill? Or did paying the bill make me lose my appetite?

"The man of virtue pursues morality; ordinary folk fill their bellies," I said loftily.

"That's us, 'ordinary folk'!" they said. The birds in the trees gradually went quiet. I yawned and said I was turning in, but Wufu didn't want to go to bed and wouldn't let Eight sleep either. He'd eaten his bowl of *paomo* soup, and half of mine too, and his belly was full to bursting. He went over to the tree, pushed his belly against the trunk to settle his dinner, and persuaded Eight to stay up to talk to him. Eight spent half the night cursing everything about Xi'an and laughing his head off.

16.

About ten days later, I had just pulled my cart into Lane Eight at lunchtime when someone asked if I'd be willing to carry some goods for them. About a hundred small cartons, not heavy, and they needed to be brought back to a building on Lane Eight. After that, the man said he'd give me the empty boxes. "Where are they now?" I asked. "Pagoda Street," he said. I didn't know it. Then he said it was near an area called Weigongzhai. I knew that there was a post office there, which we used to send Wufu's money home. It wasn't far, so I went with him.

The guy had whiskers covering half his face, and some kid in the street stared at him and called out, "Don't you have a mouth, mister?" Beardy lifted his mustache and said, "What's this then? Your mother's fanny?" Quite a wit!

When we got to Weigongzhai, sure enough, there was a turnoff called Pagoda Street. Its entrance was packed with antiques and curio stalls, and crowded with people. The buildings were all simple one-story houses, spreading out over a jumble of narrow alleyways going in all directions. The little shops sold all kinds of chinaware, pottery jars, carved stones, engravings, and the most extraordinary curios. We threaded our way through a maze of streets to the store Beardy was headed for, and that was when I found out that I was going to be pulling about a hundred glazed pots in my cart. Beardy turned out to be an antiques collector. It also turned out that he and the store owner hadn't settled on a price for the pots yet, and there was a lot of haggling, with the seller upping the price of a jar from two thousand yuan to three thousand. I was enjoying this, but I was careful not to get involved. They either shouted at each other till they were red in the face or draped arms round each other's shoulders like best buddies. I kept my expression blank. I didn't want to make things worse. Finally, I said, "When you've settled everything, let me know. I'm going for a stroll."

I wandered into the store next door to have a look, and the owner popped out. "Are you looking for anything in particular?" I wasn't, so I left. I tried another store, but the owner asked the same question. So I left again and stood around in the alley, people-watching. There were men with beards, and others with long hair tied back in a ponytail. They had on all sorts of outfits too, some quite garish. I saw one gaunt-faced man with hair right down to his shoulders. If I hadn't seen his Adam's apple, I would have sworn it was a woman.

I overheard a conversation between two men. "What a lot of artists here today!" one said.

"Bullshit!" the other said. "They're not artists."

"They must be, got up like that!"

"Haven't you seen how country folk look more like city folk than city folk do when they come to town?"

That hit a little too close to home, and I felt myself flush. I glanced at the pair of them, but they weren't looking at me, they were talking about the man with shoulder-length hair. I hurriedly turned down another alley, wondering what to do next. Then I saw a pagoda round the back of the stores. It was a strangely shaped structure, rather delicate, thinner at its top and bottom, and fatter around the middle. I assumed the street had been named after the pagoda. Was that why the antiques market was here too?

I headed toward it, in search of peace and quiet. And that was my first acquaintance with the Chain-Bones Bodhisattva, the first of many visits I made. I had no inkling at the time that it was a providential discovery, that the bodhisattva was beckoning to me from somewhere beyond this world. I was just idly curious, and eager to show off how clever I was. I stood looking at the pagoda, but it wasn't anything special. The top had fallen in, and there were weeds growing out of it. A soap-pod tree had poked through the brickwork and snaked skyward. A bird was perched on the trunk. I whistled at it, but it ignored me. I tossed a pebble at it, but it fell short. The bird still ignored me. So I turned my back on it and looked at a stone tablet, the only one there. It was cracked, and you could see where it had been glued back together. I bent to see what it said. It was hard work getting through even the first line:

In times past, a woman from Weigongzhai, fair-skinned and beautiful, about twenty-four years old, walked the streets alone, and the youths of the town vied with one another to befriend her, and even to get her into bed. She turned none of them down.

"That's classical Chinese. Can you read it?" I heard a voice from behind me. Someone was sitting with his back to a low wall nearby, pots and old tiles laid out in front of him. He was polishing his pots with a piece of cloth, and hawking up phlegm. I half understood the inscription, because I'd done a bit of classical Chinese at school, though I'd forgotten it. It was coming back to me, but I was about to go until that comment needled me, so I squatted down and peered at the stone again. This was how the inscription continued:

. . . Some years later, she died, and all those friends were grief-stricken. Together they raised enough money for her funeral. Because she had no family, they buried her by the roadside. One day, during Dali's reign in the Tang dynasty, a foreign monk arrived from the Western Regions. He saw the

gravestone, sat with legs crossed in the lotus position, and lit incense. Then he said his prayers, circling the gravestone and uttering praises for many days. Seeing this, someone said to him, "This woman was a harlot. Anyone could be her husband. Her family cast her off, and that's why she's buried here. Why is a monk like you worshipping her?" The monk replied, "This woman was a great sage. She was merciful and charitable, and sacrificed herself for the world's desires. This is the so-called Chain-Bones Bodhisattva, and now that she has completed her business in this world, she has become a saint. If you do not believe me, then open the coffin and look." And so the onlookers dug up the coffin and found that every bone in her body was locked together, just as the monk had said. People were amazed. They all engaged in a period of fasting and then erected a pagoda dedicated to her.

I read it once, then read it again. The only bodhisattvas I'd known were Guan Yin the Merciful, the Bodhisattva of Awareness, the Buddhist Lord of Truth, and the Earth Store Bodhisattva. I'd never heard of the Chain-Bones Bodhisattva. Plus, I thought that all bodhisattvas were pure and holy, and here was one who'd been a hooker! How could purity and filth exist side by side?

Maybe I'd misunderstood the inscription. I was just taking a closer look when Beardy came rushing up, covered in sweat.

"Did you settle on a price?" I asked him.

"They took a zero off, but as soon as they realized the jars were worth something, they stuck the zero back on again!"

"Do you know anything about this pagoda?" I asked.

"I deal in antiques! Of course I do!"

"Then tell me how come the Chain-Bones Bodhisattva was a hooker."

He explained she was a reincarnation of Guan Yin, who had turned herself into a prostitute in order to deliver all living creatures from suffering.

"A Buddhist prostitute?" I was very curious and wanted to ask more, but Beardy was pushing me to get moving and load up the cart with his goods. I put the Chain-Bones Bodhisattva out of my mind.

I hauled the cart, piled high with cardboard boxes, all the way to Lane Eight, then hefted the boxes upstairs one by one to the sixth floor. I'd already made the trip forty-odd times when Wufu turned up.

"What's happened?" I asked.

"Let's get these boxes done first," he said. He was much stronger than I was and could carry two boxes at a time. In another dozen trips, we'd finished the load. I leaned against the wall, completely pooped. Both my legs were shaking, and the harder I tried to keep them still, the more they shook, rustling like leaves in my pants.

"What's up with my legs? Can you give them a quick rub?" I said to Wufu. But his arms were shaking just as badly. We slumped to the ground, gasping openmouthed like two stranded fish. When we'd both gotten our breath back, Wufu said, "City folk live so high off the ground, I can't see the point. How do they go up and down when they're old?"

"What a worrywart you are! When people are so old that they can't walk, even if they live on the ground floor, they don't go out!" I asked him again what was up, and he said he'd brought Cuihua to see me. I wondered sourly if it had anything to do with his matchmaking plans. He knew I wasn't interested in her, but even so, he should have told me the minute she arrived. Now I was sweaty and dirty from lugging boxes, in no shape to meet a woman.

"That's how a man should look! Anyway, you can look as messy as you like if you don't want her!" He ruffled my hair.

I slapped his hand away. "Well, I'm concerned about my image." I made him go look after her while I patted myself down, washed my hands and face, and smoked a cigarette. I thought about what I'd say to her and walked out onto the main road behind the building.

It turned out she'd come to ask me if I'd help her get her ID card back. Poor Cuihua, she'd been looking after a woman in a coma, day in, day out, just so she could get a one-bedroom apartment in the city. The woman was dead to the world, and Cuihua had no one to talk to from morning till night. She said she was worried that she'd turn into a mute herself before her patient departed this life. She longed for someone to knock at the door, but the only one who ever did was the master. When she'd started working there, he was kind, but then he started talking dirty and tried to grope her. That was too much. Just yesterday evening, he'd made her give the woman a sponge bath. She'd soaked two towels in hot water, wiped her down with one hand, then reached behind her for the second towel. Something else landed in her hand instead, his you-know-what. She was so angry, she gave it a good squeeze, and the master collapsed on the floor. He yelled at her, she yelled at him, and she packed her belongings and left. But he'd refused to give her ID card back and, without it, she couldn't look for another job.

"I didn't want to tell you all this," said Cuihua. "It's so humiliating. I thought I'd ask Wufu to take me, but he insisted I should get you to go with me."

I looked at Wufu, who said, "No way I can do it."

I swore. I wasn't swearing at Cuihua or at Wufu. I was cursing that bastard who employed her. *You lowlife scum, you're shacking up illegally with one woman, and you've got your snout in another pot before you've finished your bowlful! You think any migrant worker girl is easy pickings, do you?* So I agreed to go and ask him for her ID back. "He can't be allowed to get away with that, if there's any fairness left in this world! That shit! Let's give him a taste of his own medicine."

I was fired up with indignation by then. "Is he big?" I asked Cuihua.

"Not tall, but built like a bear," she said.

"A professor? An ordinary government official?"

"Neither. He bought a car, hires a driver, and runs it as a taxi service."

"I need to go back home to change."

"Why bother to change if he's not educated?" Wufu asked.

"Are you brainless? If he was educated, I wouldn't need to change. You could confront him bare-chested, and he'd wilt as soon as you opened your mouth! But a businessman is a harder nut to crack. If I go looking like this, he's not going to be intimidated."

We had to store the carts in the depot first, of course. Scrawny asked Wufu what was up, why we were packing up so early. Wufu was such a blabbermouth, he told Scrawny the whole story of the ID card. "That sounds almost as difficult as debt-recovery, which is the hardest thing ever," said Scrawny. "Could you do with an extra hand?"

"Like who?" said Wufu.

"Someone who specializes in debt recovery, of course!" said Scrawny. "Someone who doorsteps the debtor and threatens to cut his throat when he comes out of his house!"

"What a brute," said Wufu. "How much does he charge?"

"Ten percent of the debt," said Scrawny.

"And to get an ID card back?"

"Oh, several thousand."

"You're pulling my leg!" said Wufu. And his nose started bleeding. Wufu often got nosebleeds, especially in the summer. He put a ladleful of cold water into a bowl to wet his forehead, and plugged up his nostrils with cotton balls.

Scrawny was surprised. "A big strong fellow like you getting nosebleeds?"

"I've always had them. The herbalist says I'm hot-blooded. When I overheat, I bleed."

"What, like a woman? Once a month?"

Wufu snarled at him.

Back at Leftover House, I changed into my suit and leather shoes. Wufu stayed as he was. He said, "What's the point? I could put on imperial yellow court robes and I'd still be Wufu, especially with the cotton stuffed up my nose."

Cuihua was staring at me. "You look like a different person in your suit. Your face has gone fairer than mine."

"He's fairer-skinned under his clothes," said Wufu. I said nothing. We went out and I made Cuihua walk in front of me. I didn't want her checking me out.

When we got to the man's home, I acted like the big boss and sent Wufu up to see if he was there. If so, Wufu was to tell him that Section Chief Liu had something to discuss with him.

"You should make yourself even bigger, a bureau chief. I've never seen one of those!"

"I'm a section chief!" I said.

Off he went, armed with a stick he'd found in a garbage can. A minute later, he came down, and said, "The door was open. There was someone sitting there brewing some *gongfu* tea. I went closer, and he asked me what I was doing. I panicked and ran away."

"Fine, stay here. And make sure you keep quiet!"

I went upstairs with Cuihua. Sure enough, the door was open, and there was the man sipping his tea. When he saw Cuihua, he looked startled, then coughed and carried on drinking his tea. The cough told me he wasn't much of a tough guy. He obviously knew we hadn't come to join the tea party. He got to his feet and came to the door. "You looking for me?" he asked, scowling.

"That's right," I said, deliberately keeping it low-key. "Nice life you've got here, enjoying your tea all on your own!"

"It's my hobby," he said. He wasn't going to let us in. He stared at my hand, which I'd stuffed into my pants pocket so he couldn't tell what I had in it.

"I'm from Cuihua's hometown," I said. "Cuihua's quit working for you, so you can give her ID card back."

The apartment consisted of a small sitting room, with a doorway to the left and to the right. There was a mop leaning against the left-hand door and a small stool by the right-hand door. I could easily get my hands on either of them, I noted.

"That guy who just came up, is he with you?"

"That was Cuihua's cousin."

"He came for a fight, didn't he?"

"What makes you think that?"

"He had a stick in his hand."

"And carrying a stick means he was looking for a fight?"

"If you go out carrying a stick, yes, you're looking for a fight."

"You go out carrying your penis, does that mean you're going to rape someone?" I felt quite proud of that remark. I smiled, and he smiled back, baring his gums. He was ugly all right.

"Are you from the countryside too?"

"I work at a newspaper office."

He looked at me again, and I got worried. If he asked to see my ID card, that would let the cat out of the bag. I got a grip on myself and made my face expressionless. I took a cigarette out, lit up, and blew a smoke ring that floated upward. What a whopper that one was.

He looked less sure of himself and turned to Cuihua. "Be honest, now. Have I ever treated you badly?"

"Oh, you've been very good!" said Wufu.

At some point, Wufu had come up behind me. I stopped him right there. If we got the ID card back, there was no need to say anything more. "Cuihua's needed at home. She can't keep her job in the city. Just give her ID card back."

The man fished it out of his pocket, and Wufu snatched it, grabbed Cuihua's arm, and hustled her away. Wufu had been a bit too forceful, and the man shouted, "Hey!" He was about to launch himself at Wufu, but I stood in his way.

"Don't go getting on the wrong side of Wufu. He's got a temper like a mad bull!" I warned.

Wufu was at the head of the stairs with Cuihua and overheard. "You bet I'm a mad bull!" He pulled the cotton wool out of his nose, and it started bleeding again. He smeared the blood all over his face. The man stayed where he was.

I made a point of saying to Cuihua, "Say, 'Good-bye, Uncle' before you leave."

"Good-bye, Uncle," she said.

"Anything else?" I asked.

"Oh, the house keys," she said, pulling the key ring off her belt and slinging it through the door.

I said, "If you were paid more days than you worked, then you owe Uncle."

"I don't owe anything. I was paid for last month, and I worked nine days this month and haven't gotten anything for that."

Of course, I knew today was the ninth, and I'd guessed she hadn't been paid. "Better pay her the nine days," I said to the man. "Then she doesn't need to come back for it."

The man glowered and said nothing.

I tried again. "Once the sheep's sold, you don't need its rope anymore. Cuihua, how much do you get a month?"

"Three hundred yuan."

The man got out a hundred yuan.

"OK," I said. "Three hundred a month is a hundred every ten days, ten yuan a day." And I gave him ten yuan change from my own pocket.

Once we were out of the building, I relaxed and told Wufu how clever he'd been for smearing his blood all over his face. "You know I wasn't mad at you, right?" he said.

"I know."

Wufu was pretty pleased with himself, and started going on about Cuihua owing us a meal because she'd made a profit.

"Why does she owe us a meal?" I asked. "She left that job and hasn't got another one, and you're telling her she owes us?" To my surprise, Cuihua burst into tears. I had no idea how to help. I couldn't find her a job, or even put her up in Fishpond Village in the meantime. All I could do was have Wufu take her back to old Mrs. Lu's place on Lane Two.

Cuihua went, unwillingly. But she'd only gone ten paces before she came running back. She pulled an envelope out of a small cloth bag. "Happy Liu, I have nothing to give you as a thank-you. I looked after that woman for three years, and that's how it ended. It made me so angry, I took a packet of chili powder when I left. Here, you have it!"

Wufu and Cuihua hurried down the lane, and I opened the envelope. A sudden gust of wind blew the chili powder into my face. I choked, and my eyes streamed with tears.

17.

Almost a week went by. Wufu might have gone to Mrs. Lu's to see Cuihua, but I didn't, and I never mentioned the ID card incident again either. But Wufu started to tell the whole story to Eight, bragging about me being a hero who never lost his cool. Before he got to the part about me posing as a section chief, I told him fiercely to shut up. In no way had I been a hero. In fact, every time I thought about Cuihua and wondered if she was still in Xi'an and if so, what she was doing, I felt how powerless and heartless I'd been.

When you're feeling low, you sleep a lot. One day I woke and didn't feel like getting up, even though it was light outside. I could hear the rain pattering on the roof. Wufu called out to me twice, but I didn't answer. He came in and put his hand on my forehead.

"Is it raining?" I asked.

"Are you ill? Your forehead isn't hot. Yup, it's raining."

"That's good."

"If it's raining, we can't go out picking. What's good about that?"

"Let's go to Hibiscus Garden."

That cheered him up. Back in Freshwind, if an opera troupe ever visited, Wufu never missed a performance. He cheered when everyone else cheered; he pushed and shoved with the best of them; he didn't even care what they were singing; he simply loved the bustle and excitement. The lure of Hibiscus Garden to Wufu was that Eight had been there.

But when I said that we should get Eight to come with us because he knew the way, Wufu was adamant. "Eight's only been as far as the entrance gate. I want to visit the whole garden—that'll take Eight down a peg or two!"

On the way out, Wufu quietly sneaked a straw hat from Eight's windowsill. He made me put it on to stay dry. He got wet.

We kept asking the way, and finally arrived at the square outside the park. It was still raining, but there was a long line at the ticket kiosk. "How come there are so many other trash pickers?" said Wufu.

I stared at him. "Just because we're trash pickers doesn't mean all the other park visitors are trash pickers too! Don't pick your feet up so high when you walk. Let your arms hang straight."

He stood properly for a moment, but then picked up a piece of cardboard and held it over his head. I made him toss it away, and we stood in line. There were advertising billboards all around the square. Wufu said, "If the ads got so wet they dropped off, we'd get several cartloads from them."

"You're like a dog that's addicted to eating shit," I said. He didn't say anything else.

When we got to the ticket window, Wufu said, "Two tickets, please!"

"Fifty yuan each," the young man said.

Wufu's jaw dropped. "Fifty? It can't be!"

The young man—who could have been a girl, he was so fair-skinned—glanced at Wufu, then called, "Next!"

At that point, I was so upset that I pulled a hundred-yuan bill out of my pocket. "Give me two tickets! Two tickets!" But before I could push the bill through the ticket window, Wufu grabbed it and ran, sloshing through the mud, slipping, getting up again, and running on, leaving one shoe behind in the mud. There were guffaws of laughter as I pushed my way out of line, retrieved his shoe, and caught up with him in the square. "You're so embarrassing!" I yelled at him.

Wufu was really wound up, and bellowed back. "It's all right for you, you're a bachelor, but I've got a wife and kids. Why on earth would I spend fifty yuan to go around a park?"

"There's no need to yell." My voice wasn't as loud as Wufu's, but I managed to pacify him. Of course I knew that money didn't grow on trees, but once we'd gotten that far, it was like a toad propping up a table: you had to just grin and bear it. I assured Wufu that there was no way I was going to buy a ticket now, but we shouldn't have made a scene like that in front of so many people. He could have gotten us off the hook some other way. "Why on earth did you just grab the money and run? Don't you get that sometimes saving face is more important than money?"

Wufu had stopped swearing at me for throwing money around but was still bad-mouthing Hibiscus Garden. "Hunker down," I said. "Hunker down and have a smoke." I pulled him over and sat him down and handed him a cigarette to shut him up, because people were still looking at us. Wufu handed the cigarette back to me and rolled his own. By the time we'd finished smoking, we'd both calmed down. We had no idea what we were going to do. The rain was stopping, and a distant patch of gray cloud hung in the sky. "Let's have another smoke," I said. We smoked standing up. I never smoked much back in Freshwind, but my cravings for it had grown ever since arriving in Xi'an, and now I needed three in a row before I felt satisfied. The amount of smoke we were puffing out between us must have reached right up to the cloud now above our heads, or maybe the cloud was made up of a whole bunch of smokers' exhalations. Gongs and drums struck up inside the walls of Hibiscus Garden, and there was a sudden roar of applause. Wufu didn't look around. Nor did I.

"What d'you reckon is inside the park, Happy?" Wufu asked.

"How would I know? I haven't been in," I said.

"You know the township head's second uncle?"

"You mean the stonemason?"

"He's carved stone lions all his life. He even went to the Xi'an Zoo to take a good look at the real lions. But when he came home, he said that the lions in the zoo weren't much like lions."

"Uh-huh."

"I figure there must be just rock piles and trees in Hibiscus Garden, but we're from the mountains and I've seen tons of those."

"Maybe the ones in there are different from real trees and rocks."

"I didn't say that right," said Wufu. That was because he had no idea how to explain himself using a metaphor. I just decided that since he hadn't let me see Hibiscus Garden today, I'd wait till next time, and I'd go in for sure, and see how the rocks and trees there were different from other rocks and trees. Huh! I wouldn't take Wufu with me, I'd go alone, up and down every rock face. I'd even piss wherever I wanted if no one was around!

"What's there to look at? There's nothing to look at! I'm not going in to look!" said Wufu.

"Look at this money instead!" I pulled a bill from my pocket, not a hundred yuan, but ten, and examined the design on it.

Wufu took the hint, and hurriedly got my hundred-yuan bill out of his jacket pocket and handed it back to me. "You just reminded me."

"Take it," I said.

"What d'you mean? Why would I take your money?" And he slapped it on my arm, where it stuck.

Wufu and I never agreed about money, no matter how many times we talked about it. It made me happy to spend money. But Wufu was super stingy, though he said he wasn't and that he just liked money. He figured the richer someone was, the more they loved money, and the more they loved money, the richer they got. That might be, but Wufu loved money and he didn't have a bean. He knew quite well that money attracted money, but he hadn't figured out that people were different: there were those who didn't fight for anything, so they didn't get anything, and those who, the more they didn't want something, the more they got it. Like me.

I laughed and peeled the money off my sleeve. Then it occurred to me that this money had given Wufu and me a Hibiscus Garden story. This particular bill had been through so many hands, it must have been the cause of countless stories. All the most amazing happenings in the world were hidden in money.

I was still daydreaming when Wufu said he wanted to piss and hurried over to some bystanders to ask where the nearest public toilet was. When he got back, he was in a very good mood.

"Guess what?" he said. "They said they'd been all around Hibiscus Garden and it was boring as hell! You and I have just earned ourselves fifty yuan each today!"

"How d'you work that out?"

"Because we didn't go in!" he said.

I was annoyed. "Whatever . . . Anyway, did you piss?" He said no, and it was getting urgent.

Wufu and I had two criticisms of Xi'an: One, there weren't enough stars. Two, you could never find anywhere to piss or shit. I mean, there just weren't any public toilets. Wufu needed one badly now. He searched around but couldn't see one, so he searched for some holly bushes, but there weren't any of those either. "My bladder's going to burst!" he said, bent over double.

What a lot of issues the man had . . . I felt like ignoring him, but how could I? "Keep walking!" I commanded. In front of us was a large puddle of rainwater, and he made to go around it, but I put my foot in the hollow of his knee and he sat down in the puddle, so the water splashed all over his face.

"Hey!" he shouted.

"Your pants are already wet. Just stay where you are and piss," I said in a low voice. A couple of people standing nearby were so startled, they came over to help Wufu up, but he just sat there in the water, his eyes glazing over. Then he got to his feet, his trousers soaked and clinging to his legs.

"I'm fine," he told them. Of course, Wufu was overcome with admiration at the clever way I'd rescued him, but I had no intention of walking next to him if he stank of piss. I headed south out of the square and bumped into Lively Shi on a street corner. Hey, what a transformation! This wasn't the whining, limping beggar of old. He had turned into a musician, sitting on the sidewalk and playing a penny whistle, an enamel bowl in front of him.

That made me despise him more than ever, because he was bringing a fine profession into disrepute. Did he really think that tootling away would make people drop money into his bowl?

> We came from the grasslands to Tian'anmen
> Square
> We hold the golden goblet high and sing a
> song of praise.

He dropped the tune a few times, but I could still sing along, and I remembered all the words. Heavens, how long had it been since I heard one of those folk songs honoring Chairman Mao? The city's shops broadcast songs, but they were more like crooning than singing, and the phrasing was all wrong. Those singers either puffed and panted like buffalos, or sounded like they had asthma.

Lively spotted me, of course. He said, "Uh!" and the notes petered out with a sigh. He gave an embarrassed smile and said nothing.

Recently I'd had a couple of dreams about Lively Shi. In the latest one, I was sitting in some bushes in a little park with my steamed bun and soda. I had just put them down on the leaves and opened my greaseproof paper bag with its fermented bean curd. This was a celebratory lunch because I'd collected a sack of aluminum tubes. Then, suddenly, Lively Shi was standing in front of me.

"Are you still limping?" I joked.

"I don't limp!" he snapped. He had a sharp stone in his hand and looked like he might crack me over the head with it if I said anything more. Then he saw my steamed bun and spat on it. "Is that yours?"

"Yup."

"I've got hepatitis. I need to borrow this steamed bun."

"It's yours."

And he was off, crouching down and disappearing through the dew-covered bushes. The dewdrops fell, and the earth glittered in the sunshine.

Right now, Lively smiled awkwardly and even stuffed his straw hat back onto his head. Did he think that made him invisible? I wondered. I took his hat off his head. "So you play the whistle, do you?"

He looked at me suspiciously, ready to pack up and leave. "You don't play badly!" I said kindly, and he relaxed. He poked at the coins in the bowl in front of him and chuckled. "Ha-ha! Ha-ha-ha!"

Every cell in my body brightened up at the sound. "Not a bad penny whistle, eh?" I said, taking it out of his hand, giving it a rub, and playing "Moon Reflected on Second Spring." Lively was goggle-eyed with astonishment. *You never thought I could play, did you, you beggar!*

Lively was the first to applaud, and then bystanders followed suit. I sneaked a good look at them as I played. Then I shut my eyes, swayed my head, and let my thoughts wander. I remembered the month after the woman in Freshwind turned me down and how Wang Kui had married her instead. While the firecrackers popped and exploded outside their gate and everyone crowded into their compound to enjoy the wedding feast, I shut myself inside my house and played "Moon Reflected on Second Spring" on my flute all day. I'm proud to say that I, Happy Liu, have a musical soul. I only have to see a flute and I'm drawn to it like a cat to the smell of fish. It's always "Moon Reflected on Second Spring," and whenever I play, I forget everything else. I was certainly drawing the crowds and the applause today, and the coins, one yuan and fifty cents, piled up.

I stopped only when I saw Wufu waving at me. Lively tipped out the contents of the bowl and counted it. It was nearly twenty yuan, all told. "Brother Trash Picker!"

"Call me by my proper name."

"OK, Happy Liu, you've got quite a knack. Let's go halves. I'll give you ten yuan, all right?"

I grabbed Wufu and turned to leave.

"Why are we going? You just earned all that money for him!"

"That's right," I said.

Wufu spat angrily, and the spittle blew back in his face with the wind.

18.

Now that I'd done it once—or rather, Lively had shown me that I could—I took my flute along with me every time I went out trash picking. I carried it stuck down the back of my collar, the way scholars in plays carry their fans. I thought of the Han dynasty hero Han Xin who carried a sword on the street, though he wasn't even capable of killing a chicken, and who was eventually granted the title of grand general. And I, Happy Liu, stomped along, head held high, and no one dared taunt me now.

Instead of taunts, I got a thumbs-up from old Ironman as he brought me a bowl of meatball soup. "That was good! Very refined playing!" Ironman had a meatball soup stall on Lane Eight. His soup was full of flavor and one of my favorites. He'd been there ten years, and he'd seen plenty. The compliment came like a breath of wind, stirring the flag on my flagpole. I pondered his words as I ate my soup. Was it that I didn't look like a trash picker with my flute stuck down my collar? Or was it that I looked refined by comparison with rough old Wufu? I laid the flute down on the table and continued sipping the broth as quietly as I could, no slurping nowadays. I thought, *This is just an ordinary piece of bamboo, but it's got a bellyful of musical notes, all ready to emerge as soon as the holes are chiseled in it. Huh! Who says Freshwind folks are dead-eyed country bumpkins, only good for coolie labor? No way!*

There were four people eating next to me, government office workers by the look of them. They started discussing a new boss who'd just been transferred to their organization. Then they started asking each other, "How many generations have your family been city folk?" I figured that seeing me must have made them suddenly shift from the topic of their new boss to how long their families had lived in Xi'an. I kept very still and strained my ears to catch what they were saying. If there was any hint that they were making fun of me, I'd try and reason with them. But it turned out that they were almost all first-generation city folk. They had an enthusiastic discussion about the way newcomers always had plenty of facial hair, but by the third generation, it was much sparser. So that was why I had a lot of facial hair! As I lowered my face over the soup, I quickly ran my hand over my chin. I found it hard to get a clean shave every day—my stubble grew thick and bristly. They moved on to another theory: all city folk came from the countryside. If you weren't a newcomer yourself, then your parents certainly were, or their parents. No city families prospered for more than five generations at most. After that, they always left for the countryside again or were reduced to dire poverty in the city. In the last half century, there had been two complete turnovers of the urban population: One was after the Liberation in 1949, when the Eighth Route Army rabble arrived in the city, toting their guns, and became section chiefs and staff, departmental heads, bureau chiefs, and even mayors. The complex network they formed at all levels of society completely transformed the city. The second time was at the end of the seventies when the Cultural Revolution was over and economic reforms kicked in, and people with big money from all sorts of trades came to Xi'an: they had mines, haulage, and pharmaceutical companies; they built factories, housing developments, and supermarkets; they were financiers, insurance brokers, and suppliers of food, drink, and entertainment . . . and the city changed again. The city was like an impregnable army camp, and city folk were its soldiers, coming and going like water.

I was fascinated by their conversation. How I wished Wufu was here to listen too. When he left this morning, he said he'd have lunch with me here, but so far he hadn't shown up. Wufu always missed out on good things to eat, and good things to listen in on. I ordered a cold bottle of Ice Peak soda from Ironman. After a hotpot, I needed something cold to wash it down. Then I could carry on enjoying the lively talk at the next table. I felt so good, I belched three times.

As it turned out, Wufu was in the middle of his lunch in another restaurant, an even classier one than Ironman's. At least that was what he told me afterward. He said he'd been wandering through the lanes with his cart, when he bumped into a bunch of guys, led by a fat man whose belly was so big that his pants had slipped down and were hanging off his you-know-what. A man that shape must be a businessman, and it was best to keep out of his way, thought Wufu, but he smirked quietly to himself. *Big Belly, when did you last see your prick?* The men who followed Big Belly were swarthy and ill-dressed, like peasants who'd just come from the labor market and were headed for a job. Wufu felt an immediate affinity with them and stopped to get a better look. Maybe some of them were from Freshwind? To his disappointment, none of them were. They looked back at him. "Bro, how many days have you been in town?" one of the men asked in a friendly voice.

"Five years."

"Putting down roots?"

"You have to, to stay here five years!" said Wufu.

He was still preening himself at this barefaced lie when Big Belly said, "Trash, come eat with me."

"You're inviting me to a meal?" Wufu was astonished.

"You look like you could use a good meal. Come on!"

Wufu was suspicious. The city was full of swindlers, and it wasn't wise to speak to strangers. "I don't know you," he said.

"So what?" Big Belly said. "If you want a meal, come with me!"

Wufu was still doubtful but followed anyway. They ended up at a just-opened restaurant at the south end of Prosper Street. There were still a dozen baskets of fresh flowers from the opening ceremony placed around the restaurant entrance, and Wufu thought it looked very plush. He hardly dared enter, until Big Belly herded them all in like sheep, and sat them, four to a table, at six tables. Back in Freshwind, at any family celebration, any passerby would be pressed to come and join the feast. A lively party was an auspicious one, so Wufu assumed that this was a dinner to celebrate Big Belly's dad's birthday, or to celebrate a baby's first month of life. He was just about to offer his congratulations when it dawned on him that there was no old man or infant to be seen. Big Belly ordered three big bowls of rice per person, for each table, but no vegetables or meat, or starters either. Well, so be it. They weren't going to turn their noses up at white rice, and they could do without the rest. They all dolloped on some spicy sauce and mixed in the soy sauce, and wolfed it down. Many more customers arrived, but they took one look at their group and walked out again. Big Belly stood watching and puffing on his cigarette. "Still hungry?" he asked.

"No, thirsty!" they chorused.

Big Belly called a waitress over and told her to bring a basin of spinach vermicelli soup for each table. Once they had eaten and drunk their fill, Big Belly sent them all on their way. "Be outside tomorrow at noon if you want more to eat."

"Fine!" They got to their feet and clattered off. Wufu didn't dare leave, but when he saw the others going, he grabbed his cart and ran off too. When he got to a narrow lane, he stopped. This must be a dream! He slapped himself so hard on the face, it hurt. Had he really just had a free lunch?

Then Wufu came looking for me. I had finished my soda and was coming out of the hotpot eatery when I bumped into him. "Look at you, turning up right after I've finished my meal!"

"Did someone pay your bill?" he asked.

128

"Fat chance!"

"Someone sure as hell paid mine!" And he told me what had happened.

I couldn't believe things like that really happened.

"Come with me tomorrow," Wufu said.

"There's more to this than meets the eye," I said. I was absolutely right. When we arrived at the depot, Scrawny had some news for us. He was always full of news, a traffic accident at a crossroads on Prosper Street, a section chief throwing himself out of the window of such-and-such skyscraper, or some guy from the countryside turning up to ask if Scrawny had seen his missus—she'd come to the city three months ago and vanished without a trace. His news today was that someone had been trying to ruin a newly opened restaurant: Every day this man invited a bunch of migrant workers to a meal there. They filled up the tables, but he bought them only rice, no meat or vegetables. Finally, the owner had had enough and got some friends to beat up his enemy. They went too far and killed him. Wufu and I looked at each other in dismay.

"Were you there, Wufu?" Scrawny asked. "Someone said they saw a cart like yours outside."

Wufu hurriedly denied it. "No, I didn't go, and Happy didn't either."

"I believe that Happy didn't, but you were definitely there. I can see it on your face!"

"Look at my teeth," said Wufu, baring them. "There's not a grain of rice stuck in them."

When we'd sold our trash and left, Wufu said, "That was strange. How did he know I had a free lunch?" I said nothing. "Do you look more like a city man than I do?" Wufu asked.

I thought of Ironman's words and straightened my collar. "Probably."

Wufu sighed. "I said we should stay working in the County Town, but you wanted to come to Xi'an, and Xi'an is full of phoenixes who look down on us as chickens, black-boned chickens at that, black right to the bone." Wufu told me he'd been to an apartment once to collect trash and the householder wouldn't let him in, but he could see inside. "God, there was so much stuff! Huge cabinets, giant TVs, fridges, carpets, dinner tables covered in fancy cups for wine and coffee. The slippers were leather, and satin, with pearls stitched on them! They're human beings just like we are. How come city folk and country folk live so differently? I'd never dream of burgling a place like that—I wouldn't dare—but if I got in and there was no one around, I'd scrape my muddy shoes all over the carpets, and I'd spit a gob of phlegm into the coffee cups on the table. I would!"

I looked at Wufu and remembered that I'd jammed a toothpick into the door lock of the house where the woman with the little dog lived. I felt a lurch of anxiety, and my cheeks and ears burned.

"Pah!" Wufu spat, and the gob landed on a concrete bench on the sidewalk. A mantis had just dropped from the branch of a tree above and was crawling up the edge of the bench on its long, spindly legs. Wufu suddenly grabbed it and messed with it, until one leg came off.

"What are you doing?" I shouted, suddenly furious.

"What's up with you?" he shouted back.

I whacked him across the face with the side of my hand. "How would you like it if I tore your leg off?"

Ironman, the owner of the meatball soup eatery, once said to me, "You're the best laborer I've ever met. Country laborers are all brawn and no brain. They've made a huge contribution to building Xi'an, but they've made it a lawless city too. They rob, they steal, they cheat, they fight, they kill. Sewage manhole covers disappear, public telephones are wrecked, and street signs, street lighting, municipal trees, and flowers are vandalized. Most offenders caught by the police and the SCOUT patrols are migrant workers." That really hurt . . . as if I'd had an electric prod jabbed into me, but I spoke firmly. I told him I simply didn't agree with him, and we argued back and forth for a long time. And now I'd just gone and walloped Wufu in the face.

Wufu didn't answer back. Blood dribbled from the corner of his mouth and crawled down his chin like a worm. If he'd fought back or run away, then at least I would have felt like I'd gotten it out of my system. But he didn't move. He just looked at me as if waiting for another blow. I felt so bad.

"Does it hurt?"

"Yes . . . no."

I wished I hadn't done it. I never imagined getting that angry. I nearly told him to hit me back, I deserved it, but I didn't. I just said, "I'll never hit you again, Wufu. I only did it because I was so upset." What I meant was, when you're poor, your head's full of worries. When you're poor, if you see a bit of meat, you're so desperate, you'll even chew the bone. "We've come to Xi'an of our own accord, and we have to accept it as it is. It isn't as good as what we imagined, but it's nowhere near as bad as you make it out to be. We have to put up with it, there's no use complaining. It only makes it more difficult to have a good life here. We have to get Xi'an to accept us, Wufu. We have to believe we can live well here, and see things differently. For instance, if you see a tree by the road that's been blown over by the wind, think of it as our tree and go straighten it. Or if a fancy car stops in front of you, and people get out, dressed to the nines, you have to admire their shiny car, admire the way they shake hands and nod and smile, admire the way the woman walks, take a deep breath of her perfume . . ."

"I can't stand the smell of perfume," said Wufu. "It makes me dizzy."

I sighed. Wufu never listened to reason. I should just forget it. All my words went in one ear and out the other, I might as well be talking to myself. If wisdom meant anything, it meant thinking things through. Once you'd thought them through, little by little you applied that reasoning to your everyday life. I was excited by these ideas, they made me want to smile. So I did.

When I smiled, Wufu smiled too.

19.

The days went by, and Wufu managed to stay out of trouble. The two of us began to earn a good reputation on our Prosper Street patch. When there was no trash to pick, or I wanted a few moments' break, I would get out my flute and play. It gave the neighborhood folk a whole new level of respect for me, though they couldn't understand how a trash picker knew how to play, or why (because I wasn't looking for sympathy, or busking. I was simply doing it for my own enjoyment).

"Happy Liu! Seeing you makes me happy!"

"Everyone's happy!" I'd say.

"Play us a tune, Happy!"

I was always being asked for a tune. I usually complied, pulling the flute out from my back collar and wiping it on my belly. "I've got a bellyful of tunes. Which should I play?" And I'd strike up a few bars. The rumor in the lanes was that I had studied at the music conservatory, but that my family had fallen on hard times and I'd been forced into trash picking. Hah! It all added a bit of mystique to my image, and I didn't disabuse them. In the end, I even began to believe that I really had graduated from the conservatory and looked properly cultured.

One day, I went to an eatery to collect trash. In its backyard was a huge pile of empty beer bottles. The boss had upped the price he was asking because there were so many, three or four hundred. Normally, one bottle went for ten cents, but he wanted twelve.

"OK," I said, "but give me a full bowl of noodle water—I'm thirsty." He brought me the water, and I took a sip. It tasted like plain water, obviously from the first batch of noodles, so I asked him for the water from the second batch (the same water got used each time noodles were cooked).

"Hey, you've got fancy taste buds!" he said. I certainly did, and I wasn't going to accept just anything. There was an old guy sitting in the eatery who must have been the owner's dad because he looked like the younger man. He'd been watching his son, and now he said, "Give Happy Liu some second-batch noodle water!"

I smiled at him and asked, "How did you know my name, sir?"

The old guy said, "Because I've heard you playing the flute." The owner wasn't too happy, but when the second batch of noodles had been cooked, he brought me a bowl of the water. The old man shifted his stool to my table. "Noodle water is the best drink there is," he said. "And connoisseurs always go for second-batch water." I explained I liked my food well flavored. I found the first-batch water tasteless, that was why I asked for second-batch water. The old man said, "That shows you're from a noble family!"

"If I'm noble, what am I doing picking trash? Is that an insult or a compliment?"

"You're not a real trash picker," he said. "You may fool everyone else, but you can't fool me! OK, your clothes are shabby and your skin's coarse, but that's just a cover. I bet you're an educated man. I've heard about educated folk who pass themselves off as laborers so they can do research. Are you going to write a book about the lives of city trash pickers?"

I was astonished. Was that how the old man saw me? I didn't know how to respond. "Ah . . . what a fine beard you've got, Uncle!" I said.

He fingered it and said, "I bet I'm right!" I was flabbergasted. I had to get out of there. I went into the backyard and started stuffing the beer bottles into bags.

The old man was convinced he'd seen through my disguise. He told the waitresses, "They say you can't know the quality of a person by their pimples, but breeding will always show in a face. The old gentleman who came in a few days ago, he may not have looked like anything much, or been smartly dressed, but you could tell he wasn't an ordinary person from those shining dark eyes he had, and the way he held his cup between two fingers. Turned out he was a professor. Xi'an has a huge cultural heritage underground. You can't build the foundations of a house without digging up cultural relics, and that prof's in charge of verifying it all. People like that are careful . . . A wise man doesn't put himself above the rest of us!"

The old guy was sticking to his opinions, but he had a good heart. I was aware of the waitresses staring at me from the windows as I collected the beer bottles, but I carried on acting cool and calm, making my movements as graceful as I could, as if I was handling precious antiques, instead of beer bottles.

I filled one sack, then another. I was about to fill a third when I heard shouting outside the front door. There were always brawls and arguments in the street, usually cheered on by onlookers with nothing better to do. I paid no attention. Then it got louder, and I heard someone shouting, "You're both trash pickers. Why are you so different?" I picked up the sacks and went to the restaurant door. There was Wufu.

I finally figured out what was going on. Wufu must have picked a lot of trash and come looking for me much earlier than usual. He was pulling his cart down the lane, sticking to the curb, and a car had pulled in behind him, to let an oncoming truck pass. The car was stuck behind Wufu, the driver leaning on his horn because Wufu was going so slow. Wufu would have been happy to let the driver pass, but you weren't allowed to pull your cart onto the sidewalk, and in any case, it was crowded with people and bicycles. The driver was jammed up behind the cart, cursing Wufu, his head stuck out the window. "You're worse than a dog. Decent dogs don't block the roadway!" Wufu kept his cool and let the driver swear at him.

Then the restaurant owner came out carrying a bowl of dirty dishwater, and joined in. "You've got some nerve, pushing in front of a car. Are you going to pay for a paint job if you scratch it?"

Wufu got mad. "What do you want me to do? Fly? The car in front won't let me pass."

"Are you talking back?" the owner shouted. "You blind dog!"

"Same to you!" Wufu shouted. And the owner slung the whole bowl of dirty water over Wufu.

"What the hell's going on?" I said. Wufu caught sight of me, and tears rolled down his cheeks. He was trying to brush off bits of rice and vegetables stuck to him. "Leave that," I told him. "Let the owner wipe you down." The owner looked shit-scared when he heard me say that. He turned and squinted at me, and I kept my face expressionless.

The owner's dad came out and rapped his son over the head with a flyswatter. "What are you playing at? Don't you know who Happy Liu is?" He was keeping his voice down, but I could hear him and was grateful to the old man.

I waved my hand at the bystanders to tell them to scram, and said to the owner, "Go wipe that muck off him!" I kept my voice down too, but I meant exactly what I said.

"Wufu, why did you get in the way when I slung the water out?" the owner said as he cleaned him up.

Wufu didn't answer. He simply lifted a foot and said, "There's still muck on my shoe."

Instead of picking a strand of noodle off Wufu's shoe, the owner dropped the cloth and said to me, "How did someone like this get to be a trash picker?"

"And how did this respectable gent end up with a son like you?" I retorted.

The driver had stopped honking, and he rolled his window up, so I couldn't see his face clearly. The bystanders were all whispering to one another, no doubt curious as to how I'd got the better of the restaurant owner. The old guy was telling the restaurant staff, "Manners make a man, you mark my words!" Yes, that was how I'd got the better of the owner, with my manners. I made a point of not rushing off. With a laid-back air, I told the waiters to load the sacks with the empty beer bottles onto the cart.

"And make sure to pack them in properly. Pack the spaces between the bags—I don't want any bottles broken." Once that was done, I said to Wufu, "Pay the man thirty-six yuan." He did as I asked, and we pulled our carts away.

Wufu was off like a frightened rabbit. "Slow down!" I told him. "Slower!" When we got to the next turn, we stopped and I paid Wufu back. "You see, I wanted you to pay the owner, because I didn't want to be fiddling around counting out small change in front of him."

Wufu started swearing again, directing his colorful Freshwind curses at the restaurant owner. "Go drown in the river! Fall off a precipice! Get struck by lightning! I hope your family line dies out with you! I'm gonna rob your restaurant, beat you up, hold your head in the dishwater, shit and piss in your kitchen pots, and make you grovel on your knees to me!"

"Stop that filth!" I said.

"You want me to be clean inside, but can't I at least talk dirty?" he objected. I looked at him and felt tears well up. It was the first time I'd cried since I was a kid, and once I started, I couldn't stop; my tears spattered on the ground. Wufu was dumbstruck. "What's up, Happy? Is it because I don't do as you say? I'll stop swearing now, I will." The tears were still running down my face.

Afterward, when I'd calmed down, Wufu told me my tears were like a leaky faucet, and thick, like lacquer-tree sap. They slid down my face, leaving clear tear tracks behind. He told me he'd never dreamed that I could get so upset for him, and it scared the hell out of him.

He was wrong. I wouldn't cry for him, or anyone. I was grieving for myself. All those people were thinking I must not be a trash picker, but that was exactly what I was! I could get Cuihua's ID card back for her, I could stop Wufu from being humiliated, but only I knew whether my shoes pinched my feet.

I was convinced that I was a proper city man, but why did I always dream I was back in Freshwind, walking the fields? Then I thought of my kidney. It was part of some city man's body now, and that was enough for me: it made me a city man myself. But where was the man with my kidney? Was he my shadow, or was I his shadow? He might be the biggest boss in town, but I was a trash picker. It was like ceramic: Why did one piece go to make the oven range, while another piece ended up as a urinal?

"I need to find someone!" I said.

Wufu looked stupefied again. "Find someone?" he repeated. "Go ahead then! One day I'm going to find that restaurant owner and settle some scores with him!"

I looked up into the sky. A plane was flying overhead, trailing a long plume of smoke, like it was slicing the sky in two. I stopped crying, but back in Fishpond Village, I had a backache all that night.

20.

My back began to ache, for the first time since my kidney was removed. To stop the ache, I got into the habit of pressing my hand against it. Wufu thought I was striking a pose. "If you got a bit fatter," he said, "you could be Chairman Mao from the side." He was talking about the big picture of Mao in wartime standing in front of a cave house in Yan'an, on a billboard in Bell Tower Square. I made a special trip to look at it once. The great man was gazing into the far distance. I never did that. No matter what I was looking at, my gaze only reached a few dozen feet.

I asked Wufu, "Do you know where your stomach is?"

"No," he said.

"That's good."

"Why is that good?"

"It means it's doing its job well."

"Wasting food, more like it," he said.

I was about to tell him that it's bad when you become aware of where an organ is in your body, because it means it's sick. That's what had happened to my back. But Wufu didn't understand what I was talking about, he only wanted to pass on some gossip about Eight. On his trash-picking rounds, Eight had picked up an old bicycle, so old it was all rusted, and every day when he got back to Leftover House, he spent hours trying to fix it. Wufu figured that Eight had stolen the bike.

"Who would rip off such a battered old machine?" I said. "He must've seen us coming home on our bike and thought he'd like one of his own."

"Well, he should keep his eyes to himself."

"You laugh at people who are worse off than you, but you can't stand it when someone's better off than you either!" I admonished him. Just then, Eight called up to ask if I'd fix the chain for him, so I went downstairs.

After I'd worked on it for a while, I needed a wrench to tighten a nut. Wufu had found one when he was trash picking, so I told Eight to yell up to him. But Wufu turned a deaf ear and refused to answer.

"Call him a few names!" I told Eight. "That'll make him hear you."

"Wufu!" Eight shouted. "Got dog's fur stuffed in your ears?"

"Speak for yourself!" Wufu shouted immediately from upstairs, but he brought the wrench down. Then he tried to cadge three yuan off Eight in return.

"What do you want three yuan for? A bottle of beer?"

"I've got ninety-seven yuan. I want to round it up."

"Fuck you! I've got to lend you money for using your wrench once?" But he handed it over anyway, adding generously, "No need to pay it back."

"You're right about that!" said Wufu.

But Eight did have one condition. When we'd fixed the bike, he wanted Wufu to take him for a ride around Fishpond's lanes. Wufu was only too happy to oblige, and when the bike was ready, Eight got on the back and Wufu pedaled off around the village. When they'd gone, I washed my clothes in the yard. It was pitch-dark by the time I finished and they'd gotten back. Wufu had brought me a bowl of *hulatang* peppery beef soup in a plastic bag.

"Been twisting Eight's arm to buy you dinner?" I asked.

"A boss treated us."

"A boss treated you? Which boss?" I looked at him narrowly. "Last time you got a free meal, you almost got into trouble. And now you've done it again?"

"You think I don't remember? Ask Eight. It was Eight who got us treated to a meal!"

"Why don't you just say I paid and be done with it?" Eight said, then stomped off to his room and shut his door on us.

The look on Eight's face made me suspicious, and I got Wufu to tell me what had really happened. Apparently, they reached a lane at the northern end of Fishpond Village, and the trash pickers who rented rooms there were all sitting in their doorways, sorting their takes. There was a bunch of old plastic bags and sacks lying around, and the trash pickers told Wufu and Eight that they'd been to a big garbage dump at Dengjiapo, on the edge of town. Wufu and Eight, green with jealousy, asked where the Dengjiapo dump was. The man told them that there were fixers in town who charged tens of thousands for business tips, and if they wanted directions to Dengjiapo, they had to take him to a meal. So they asked him to an eatery on the edge of the village and agreed they'd buy him hotpot with rice noodles, only he asked for pepper soup, which was one yuan cheaper. The three of them had three bowls of soup each, and when they'd almost finished, the guy said to Eight, "You said it's on you, so you pay."

"We'll let the owner pay," said Eight, and took a matchbox with a few dead flies from his pocket. He put one into the spoonful of soup he had left, and started yelling, "Missus! Missus!"

"What's up?" the eatery owner asked, coming over to their table.

"What's this?" Eight asked. He picked the fly out of his soup with his chopsticks, put it on the table, and bashed it until he'd flattened its head. "We may not be very clean, but we don't eat flies!" he said fiercely. "It's making me feel sick!" And he made a big show of gagging, like he was going to throw up. The woman hurriedly swiped the fly onto the floor and apologized. "Sorry?" said Eight. "Is that all?"

"Please keep your voice down. There's no need to let other customers know."

Eight raised his voice. "There's a fly in my soup! Why shouldn't I say that? There's a fly in my soup!"

So the woman gave them their soup on the house, and Wufu made her throw in an extra bowl, which he brought back to me in a plastic bag.

"Eight has four dead flies in that matchbox," Wufu told me. "He must have had tons of free meals that way."

"Then take a page out of his book! Why don't you put two flies in while you're at it?"

"I'm not a blatant thief like Eight. Eat up while it's still hot."

"You think I'm so desperate for food?" And I stomped angrily up to my room.

I heard Wufu calling to Eight. "Hey, Eight! You conned this extra bowl of soup! Come and eat it! Happy's angry!"

"Well, that's what you get for shooting your mouth off!" said Eight. "I only told the truth."

"You're so fucking ready to snitch on people," said Eight.

A little while later, I heard Wufu's heavy footsteps coming upstairs, and he burst into my room. "Are you angry?" he asked. I ignored him. "I threw the pepper soup away," he said, sitting down in front of me. "I want to talk to you about something. I figure the Dengjiapo dump is a good place for trash picking. Why don't we go there first thing every morning, then go to Prosper Street? That way, we might make six or seven more yuan every day." I still said nothing. "Talk to me! I'm serious here!"

"I'm not going."

"Why not?"

"Because we've already got our own patch. Why bother to fight over more trash at the dump?"

"If it's too dirty for you, I'll go with Eight."

"Go to bed," I said.

He got up and headed for the door. "So, you won't be angry if I go with Eight?"

I couldn't stay angry with Wufu when he was like that. I almost called both of them in to find out what went on at the Dengjiapo dump, then changed my mind. I swept the floor, then got the high-heeled shoes down from the shelf and wiped the dust off them. Xi'an wasn't as clean as it looked. Even when I kept the doors and windows shut, it only took a couple of days for the shoes to get a layer of dust on them.

While I was fiddling with the shoes, Eight crept up the steps to see what was going on, and I heard him talking to Wufu in his room. "Is he really not going? Is he polishing that pair of heels because he's missing his missus?" I heard Eight ask.

"He hasn't got a missus!" scoffed Wufu.

"How come? Is he divorced?"

"Shut your trap! Or I'll shut it for you!"

I smiled inwardly, finished polishing one shoe, and started on the other. I set myself the task of polishing these high heels every evening, the same way young monks chanted the sutras and beat the wooden fish clappers in Buddhist temples. The rhythmic beating of the clappers helped them drive out thoughts and focus on mindfulness. I polished the shoes when my head was too full of thoughts, and focused my mind on the shoes. Not that it made me forget things though, in fact, it reminded me of everything I longed for.

After rubbing the shoes, I started rubbing the small of my back. Ouch, it was hurting again.

The next morning, Wufu and Eight had left for the Dengjiapo dump by the time I got up. They hadn't made breakfast, and the stove was cold. I made myself some breakfast and had two bowls. When they still weren't back, it suddenly dawned on me that I could use the time to take a ride around the city by myself.

As long as you didn't care about losing your dignity and were quick
off the mark and hardworking, you'd never starve as a trash picker in
the city, even if you were a total stranger here. You could earn ten times
what you got back in Freshwind. I had two reasons for not going to
the dump: one, I didn't see that we could earn much more by going
there; two, I cleared enough on the Prosper Street patch to get by. I'd
go sightseeing! I'd been here a long time, and all I knew was Fishpond
Village and Prosper Street.

I was going to do this right and get to know the city inside out.
Merciful Buddha, I might even bump into the guy I was looking for.
From early on, I'd learned that the difference between city folk and
country folk was not in their intelligence but in how much they'd seen
of life. I needed to see more of life. Take Wufu and Eight: they were
just caterpillars inching along the ground. But I was going to be a moth
and take wing.

I left the remaining food for Wufu, got on the bicycle, and went
for a ride. From then on, I did that every morning: rode into the city
when Wufu and Eight went to the dump. Wufu never understood, but
he didn't object either. When he returned from the dump, he and Eight
got on Eight's bicycle. Eight dropped him off at the Prosper Street trash
depot and then went on to his own street.

People who live in Xi'an are always talking enthusiastically about
the glories of bygone days. "Just look at the city walls . . . They're the
most complete city walls in the whole world. They're the outer edge of
the Ming city, which was only an eighth of the size it was two thousand
years ago in the Han and Tang dynasties. Back then, it was one of the
two greatest cities in the world, along with Rome, and people came
bearing tribute from all over the world!" Too bad I wasn't alive back
in the Han and Tang dynasties. Still, now I was off to figure out the
lay of the land, to look for the gated wards the city was divided into in
ancient times, all one hundred and eight of them. I had a huge sense
of purpose. I wasn't pedaling to pick trash or just meandering. I was

making a tour of inspection, and, hey, I was happy! I went to see the Big Wild Goose Pagoda, the Confucius Temple, the Town God Temple and the Great Xing Shan Temple, the ruins of the Daming Palace, and the Feng Qing Lake. Of course, I took in the new High-Tech Development Zone, the Shopping Mall Building, Finance Street, and the City Hall Plaza. I learned a secret: Xi'an street names largely followed ancient names, and they were good names. Somehow, it felt lucky to go looking for them, map in hand. There was Lucky Lane, Abundance Lane, Unending Street, Eternal Happiness Street, Virtue Lane, Broad Ford Lane, and Clear Sky Lane. You could really let your fancies take flight. Then there were the names that told you what went on in the streets in the olden days, such as Timber Market Street, Sheep Market Street, Charcoal Market Lane, Oil Lane, Flour Lane, Bamboo Market Street, Royal Coach Lane, Chariot Lane, and Martial Arts Lane. Too bad there wasn't a Trash Pickers Lane. Thirteen dynasties had made Xi'an their capital, and each dynasty must have had countless trash pickers, but there was no street that bore their name.

Maybe in the future, I thought as I stood in the street. I wanted a Trash Pickers Lane, or better still, a street named after me! Happy Lane.

21.

Leftover House was getting more and more cramped. Every day, Wufu and Eight brought more trash back from the Dengjiapo dump and heaped it in the yard or up on the rooftop. Even the stairs were piled high with cement bags, sun-parched or sodden and moldy. Come evening, they used to pick the stuff over, separating the paper and cardboard from the metal and plastics. Whatever the category, they had to have a certain amount of it before they could take it to the depot and sell it. In the meantime, they tied stuff into bundles with plastic twine or sandwiched piles between bits of wood, then weighed them down with bricks. Later, Wufu's room, Eight's room, and the roof of his cookhouse, the shit-house roof—all filled up too. Everywhere stank, and there were swarms of flies and mosquitoes.

What could I say? It was turning the place where we ate and slept into an unhygienic garbage dump, but I couldn't say that. Instead, I said, "The weather's getting hot. Mind you don't set the place on fire with everything so dry!" Finally, one morning they didn't go to the Dengjiapo dump. Instead, they took part of the trash to a depot on the west side of Fishpond Village.

"I need the bike this morning, Happy. It'll take several trips. Quit doing all that sightseeing and wait for me here. Otherwise, you'll have to hoof it on foot."

"Why would I go on foot when I can take a cab?"

"You do that! Even dogs get to ride in cabs here. Treat yourself to a ride—for us!" said Eight.

"Yup, spend a bit of money, why not?" said Wufu.

"Once I've sold off this stuff, I'm hiring a cab too. Two of them, one to ride in and one to follow behind me!" said Eight.

"Eight's got gambler's luck—yesterday morning at Dengjiapo, he picked up tons of cement bags! But all you're going to end up with, Happy, is a bellyful of hunger pangs."

"You can have your trash, I'm having the whole city!" That day I'd gone to Pagoda Street, I overheard the antiques collector telling Beardy, "A great collector collects with his eyes." Well, I was using my feet to take possession of this city. I was damned sure that lots of longtime residents hadn't been down every street and lane of Xi'an, but I, Happy Liu, could tell you where every single one was.

I walked to the head of the lane and hopped in a cab. This was great. In no time at all, we were on Chenghe Road, outside the South Gate, the sky rosy with morning clouds, the crenellations of the old wall towering over the trees of the city. What a beautiful sight. You could write a poem about it. I didn't. I simply said, "Ah! . . . Ah!" and draped my arm ostentatiously out the cab window. I thought about the mole on the sole of my foot, which meant I was a born leader, and imagined I wasn't a trash picker in a cab but a great leader in a stately convertible, inspecting the troops. I'd seen stuff like that in films. I could almost hear myself shout and the resounding answering shouts of the masses:

Greetings, comrades . . . !
Greetings to our leader . . . !
You have worked hard, comrades!
Not as hard as you, great leader!
You've caught the sun, comrades!

Dammit, I must have said the words aloud. The cabdriver slammed on the brakes. "What did you say?" he demanded.

"I said you've caught the sun!" I said.

"You've caught it, more like!" he said. He'd shattered my beautiful daydreams and I glared at him. He hurriedly changed his tune. "Do you want to get out here, comrade?"

"No!" I was furious.

"Please don't hang your arm out the window," he said. "It's dangerous. Now, where would you like to go?"

What a pain in the ass this guy was! I'd initially told him that I wanted him to drive me around, wherever he wanted. Now he was asking me again. Why was he blabbing on? Didn't he have enough people to talk to? Being lonely was no excuse for being annoying.

On impulse, I said, "The Chain-Bones Bodhisattva Pagoda!" I have no idea what made me think of that, but I repeated it. "The Chain-Bones Bodhisattva Pagoda."

"The Chain-Bones Bodhisattva Pagoda? Is there such a place?"

He was a cabdriver, but even he didn't know. I was really pleased with myself as I gave him directions. It was worth every cent of the fifty-five yuan I spent on the fare for the nearly two hours I spent looking at the scenery out the window. I was also watching for the man who'd received my transplanted kidney.

Back in Freshwind, there was a monk at the Shang Yuan Temple who used to tell me, "If you meet someone who's a complete stranger, but you feel you recognize them, or for some reason you feel drawn to them, mark my words, it's because they were a relative or friend in a former life. That's karma."

The man who had my kidney surely had a karmic bond with me. But I searched the faces of the passersby, and none of them looked familiar. We got to Pagoda Street. Over the entrance to the pagoda a couplet had been inscribed: "Enjoy life, don't spoil it by rushing around," and "Take a break before going after fame and fortune." What a fine couplet! I paid the cabdriver, and after taking another look at the great jumble of stalls selling curios and the delicate Chain-Bones Bodhisattva Pagoda, I sat on the edge of a flower planter at an intersection. While considering what to do next, I had a smoke.

I wondered about the Chain-Bones Bodhisattva Pagoda. Had it once been a monastery? Why had it been abandoned? Was it because it was dedicated to a Buddhist prostitute? Then why was it still there? I was startled from my reverie by a screech of brakes. And then I did something heroic—my most brag-worthy exploit in all my time in Xi'an, in fact.

There was a car, Shaanxi-registered, to be precise. In my view, you could view all cars as wild beasts, and this car was a leopard. It came racing from out of the lane, horn blaring, and hit a kid on a bike who was just crossing the main road. The car screeched to a halt, as I've said, and the driver opened the door to get out. Meanwhile, the kid had gotten to his feet, turned around, then sat down again. The driver took this to mean that the kid was OK, so he pulled his leg back into the car, shut the door, and restarted the engine. The kid wasn't bleeding, true, but the bike was totaled. Was this going to be a hit-and-run?

I rushed over. "Hey! Hey! Aren't you going to see if the kid has a concussion? And if his bike's still rideable?"

"Stand to the side!" said the driver. *Get lost* was what he meant, but they had a funny way of swearing at you in Xi'an, sort of refined-turned-vulgar. Well, I wasn't going to simply stand by and watch. I tugged at the car door, but it didn't open and he started to drive off. I was suddenly furious. I spat my cigarette out and threw myself on the car hood. It was covered in dust and someone had drawn a turtle, meaning "bastard," with their finger in the dust. I'm telling you, I thought the driver would have to stop when he saw me on the hood, but the car kept moving; he must have thought that I'd slip off. I gripped the windshield wipers and hung on tight. Was that bastard of a driver so mad he was trying to kill me? I yelled and shouted. Everyone on the street could see what was going on, and there were shouts of alarm. The car was picking up speed. Now I was so focused on staying put, clutching the windshield wipers for dear life, that I had no strength left for cursing. I couldn't feel my head or my legs anymore. I only had ten fingers and a belly: my fingers were claws and my belly a suction pad. I was breathing hard and fast. I tried to pull myself up, but I kept sliding down, my arms first bent, then straightening little by little. I wished my clothes would fill with wind and block the driver's view so he'd stop. But only the back of my jacket ballooned a little; the rest of my clothes were flattened underneath me. The car drove on for a long, long way, down one lane, then another, and I couldn't hang on much longer. I couldn't raise my head because of the wind, and I pressed my face against the hood. I was about to drop to the ground, and I thought at least my face wouldn't be too disfigured if I died now. Just then the car stopped, because a police car was blocking the intersection. They dragged the driver out, but I was stuck there on the hood, my limbs splayed rigid. Some bystanders helped me off, but I still looked like a lizard.

"You bastard!" I swore at the driver. "You thought you'd throw me off and I'd die? Wait and see how I'll get you back!"

I didn't tell anyone about what had happened, not even Wufu. One shouldn't boast about a good deed. The youthful martyr Lei Feng might have kept a diary, but I wasn't going to utter a word or write anything down. A man with glasses rubbed my arms and legs for me. "You're brave," he said as he helped me to my feet. "What was going through your head when you stepped forward like that?" I said nothing. A city tree must do its best to grow straight and true. I'd come to Xi'an and now I was a true Xi'an man, so I was just doing the right thing for the city. I had no idea he was a reporter. The very next morning, there was an article about me in the paper, alongside a photo. It was a picture of me splayed on the ground, looking like a lizard. I was not pleased. I was even less pleased that it said I was a party member, simply doing my duty as a party member should. Me? A party member? Plus, even though his article was flattering, he also quoted my threats to the driver.

But I'd spoken those words in anger. Written down, they made me sound as uncouth and ignorant as Wufu!

Wufu didn't read the newspapers, so he didn't see the article. In fact, I hadn't seen him for five days straight until now. He complained mightily that I was always gone when they got back from the Dengjiapo dump in the mornings, and by the time I was back, very late at night, he and Eight were sound asleep. He asked what I'd been up to. I told him I'd been busy sightseeing.

"You haven't seen the best yet!"

It was true, I hadn't. "Right, I haven't made it back to the Chain-Bones Bodhisattva Pagoda yet," I told him.

"What are you talking about?" said Wufu, who'd never heard of the Chain-Bones Bodhisattva Pagoda.

"What are you talking about?"

"Turns out that Eight's a cheating bastard, up to all sorts of stuff he never tells us about. He goes straight from the Dengjiapo dump to private clinics where he picks up medical waste and sells it at a place on the outskirts where they reprocess the plastic. IV drip bags go for seventeen cents a pound, needles and IV equipment, two yuan twenty a pound. It's easy money."

Medical waste? Had Wufu got it wrong? That was supposed to be dealt with at the municipal medical-waste-handling center. You couldn't go help yourself to it, and trash depots weren't supposed to buy it either. Wufu just said we were too honest. He'd been tagging along with Eight for nearly a week, and he'd found out that most hospitals didn't send their waste to the center, whatever the rules said, because then they had to pay for it to be disposed of. Instead, most hospitals, especially the private clinics, sold waste directly to trash pickers.

"That wuss Eight's braver than he looks!" said Wufu.

"So you've never seen him getting a bum deal?"

"A bum deal? No! In the last five days, we've made three hundred yuan! I'll take you tomorrow. We'll go on our own!"

22.

It was the first time I'd let Wufu take me anywhere in Xi'an. And I was
up for it. I certainly had no objections to medical waste. I wanted to
make money as much as they did. But what I was mostly interested in
was to see whether Wufu could really do it, and get a good price too. I
was testing him.

We were up early the next morning and left while Eight was still
asleep. We took one cart between us and, when we got to the clinics,
filled two large bags with syringes and IV equipment. Wufu went on
about how powerful my luck was. He and Eight had never picked up so
much stuff at once. The plastic-processing places were in villages to the
southwest of the city. In the fields, the wheat was in full ear. We walked
along a dirt track, and grasshoppers landed on our feet, then flew off
again. Wufu was elated. He started telling me about the village houses,
the high walls around each compound. The iron gates were kept closed,
but you could hear machinery rumbling away, crushing the plastic.
They got most of their materials from recycling depots, as well as from
a few trash pickers like us. After crushing, the tubing and bags went
to make "soft" material, and the syringes went to make "hard" material. The syringes were better quality, crushed or not. The needles were
removed, and the "hard" waste was mixed in with crushed household
plastic, then processed into pellets. From there, it went to factories to
make all sorts of plastic products. Wufu said we could sell what was in

our two bags for a hundred and twenty yuan at least. The "hard" stuff sold for as much as 7,300 yuan a ton. "Dammit," he said, "for that sort of money, you can eat proper meat, instead of just gnawing on bones."

We arrived at the processing plants, and Wufu told me to wait with the cart outside the gate, while he went to ask what price they were offering. He was so desperate to show off to me, but he didn't manage to do a deal. Two places were offering two yuan a pound and another, two yuan ten, but that didn't satisfy Wufu. He wanted to try a village farther down the road.

This was a smaller village. On its eastern edge, outside a mud-walled compound, there was a copse where Wufu made me pull up the cart and wait amongst the trees while he went inside. "Are you mad that I'm not letting you go in?" he asked.

"No, you're smarter than me."

"No, it's not that. It's that you don't look like a trash picker. Last time, they thought we were journalists stirring up trouble."

"Off you go then," I said. And I sat down for a smoke. Was I really someone who alarmed people? I sat mulling this over, sucking hard on my cigarette.

But trouble came anyway, in the shape of a minibus that raced into the village and screeched to a halt. Half a dozen police got out and rushed the gate of the mud-walled compound. This was not good, I knew. My first reaction was to get the hell out of there, taking the cart with me, but I would have to pull the cart past the minibus to do that, and the driver might see that my bags were full of medical waste. I thought for a minute, then ditched the bags in the undergrowth and walked out, pulling an empty cart. *Best to hum something,* I thought, and started a cheery Chinese New Year tune. Suddenly there was a crash. Someone plummeted from the top of the compound wall and lay motionless on the ground. It was Wufu. "Wufu! Wufu!" I called quietly. He got up and stumbled over to me, his head covered in grass and leaves, his face as white as a sheet. "What happened?"

"Police raid." His lips were trembling so much, he could hardly get the words out.

"Quick! Get in the cart! Pretend you're sick."

Thinking back on this incident, it occurred to me that an emergency really shows how intelligent someone is, but you have to keep calm as well. I didn't panic. I got Wufu to lie facedown in the cart, but one leg dangled over the edge because he was a big man. I made him pull his leg in, and we set off. The road was full of potholes, and he kept banging his head against the side of the cart.

"Slow down! Slow down!"

"Shut up!"

As we passed the compound entrance, I didn't look in, and I ignored the minibus, but two people got out of it and stopped me.

"Where are you off to?"

"Taking him to the doctor."

"You're not. You were delivering medical waste, weren't you!"

"Do I look like a trash picker?"

The policemen looked at me. I ran my fingers through my hair, then went to get out my cigarettes to offer them one each. I took out my leather wallet first (so they could see it), then put it back in my pocket and pulled out the packet of cigarettes. The pantomime worked—the police stopped looking at me and looked at Wufu instead.

"And you don't look like a trash picker either?" they said.

"I've got a bellyache! Ai-ya! Ai-ya!" Wufu groaned. He was laying it on way too thick, and the police weren't about to let us off that easily.

"We'll soon find out if you were selling medical waste. Let's see if the people in the plant recognize you!" And they told me to pull the cart inside the compound. That sent Wufu into a panic.

"If I die of a bellyache, you'll be responsible!" he cried.

"You've got far too much energy to have a serious bellyache."

"Well, it stops hurting when I'm angry."

I poked him, and he shut up and lay back down, groaning. Inside the compound, the police asked if I'd been selling waste. Of course, no one recognized me, and they finally let us go.

As we walked along the dirt road out of the village, the minibus roared past us, raising a cloud of dust. Through the dust cloud, I saw the workers from the processing plant sitting inside, handcuffed, their faces pressed as flat as dried persimmons against the bus window as they looked back at us.

"Down you go!" I said. "They've gone. I'm not pulling you any farther." I kicked him out of the cart.

"Oh, mother! That scared the hell out of me!" he said.

Me too. "Why did you fall off the wall?" I asked. Wufu said there was a man inside, pouring water over a homemade plastic-spinning machine that was puffing out steam to cool it down. The arrogant bastard offered two yuan twenty a pound. "Take it or leave it!" Wufu was so angry, he needed to piss, so he went to the urinal. Lucky for him, because when he saw the police charging in, he climbed onto the low urinal wall and climbed from there to the compound wall. He was going to jump but fell off instead.

"Agile, aren't I?" he said.

"Yeah, so agile you've made yourself lame."

Wufu's leg really did hurt him now, and he pulled up his pant leg. He had a big purple bump the size of a fist.

"Well, at least my pants aren't torn," he said. He put his full weight on his leg and straightened it. Then he set off back toward the compound, pulling the cart behind him.

"Where are you going?" I asked.

"To get those two bags." He was a funny one all right. Sometimes he was a lot less brave than Eight; other times, he was so brave, he'd tackle a wolf bare-assed. Now he went straight to the little copse, pulled out the two bags, and brought them back.

In the end, we took the needles and tubes to Scrawny's depot and had a quiet word with him. Would he take them?

"Will it get me into trouble?" he asked warily.

"Just asking," I said.

"Well, if you had the balls to collect them, then I suppose I've got the balls to take them."

"You're not afraid of the police?"

"No net can catch all the fish in the river." And he took the stuff from us. He only gave us one yuan ninety, though, and Wufu was not happy about that. He tried bargaining him up, but Scrawny simply picked up his newspaper and said, "If you think I'm ripping you off, you can go sell them elsewhere."

"Capitalist!" Wufu shouted. "Just wait till there's another Cultural Revolution!"

Scrawny laughed and carried on reading. Suddenly he jerked upright. "Is this you, Happy?" He was looking at the picture of me they'd printed. He showed it to me. "Is this you?" he repeated.

"Yup," I said, and he read it aloud from beginning to end.

"When did that happen?" Wufu asked.

"The day before yesterday."

"You were lucky!" Wufu exclaimed. "Didn't you think about how you were going to die if you let go and fell off the hood?" It was the same question the reporter had asked me.

"Of course I did," I said.

"And?" demanded Wufu.

"Well, I thought people would cry," I said.

"I'd cry!"

"Would you cry because you wouldn't know what to do after I died?"

"I'd know what to do. I'd carry you home on my back!"

What a good bro! I'd never forget he said that. I hugged Wufu. He reeked of sweat. I gripped him by the shoulders and gazed into his eyes for a long time. Then I wiped the boogers from the corner of his eyes and told him, "If I really die, then remember one thing, Wufu—don't go burying me in Freshwind. I want to go to the city crematorium. I'm a Xi'an man while I'm alive, and I'm going to be a Xi'an ghost when I'm dead."

When Scrawny heard this, he craned his neck over the newspaper and asked if I was going to get a city resident's card for my heroic exploit. No, I said.

"And did they give you a reward?"

"No," I said.

His neck retreated inside his collar, and he took out his hip flask. "Hey, Happy Liu, you love this city, but this city doesn't love you back! You want to be cremated, but no one's going to cremate you if you die in the street, or in Fishpond Village, because you won't have a hospital death certificate. Dream on!"

Scrawny always talked like this. He was such a cynic. Wufu and I hated that!

Wufu said fiercely, "If Happy dies, I'm carrying him back home. And if I die, then he's taking me back home. I'm not going to be cremated in the city!" A few months later, I was to remember this conversation with a shiver. Had it been an omen?

The world is full of mysterious happenings, but Scrawny was always making fun of our Freshwind superstitions. The "spirit way," he called it. But what did he know of blue flames that suddenly leap out of the fire, or the glow of a pearl, or the way houseflies turn up instantly even if you crap on the very top of a mountain, or how the owls hoot mournfully every night for a couple of weeks before someone dies in Freshwind?

Wufu was furious. "Scrawny rips us off and jeers at us too! Whatever, let's go eat!" So we had a meal of mutton *paomo* soup and a bottle of *shaojiu* spirits, and we ended up tipsy.

23.

The evening was drawing to a close by the time we got back to Fishpond Village, and in Leftover House's yard, a flock of birds was flying around overhead. Trees are so generous to all comers. The birds settled in the branches of our tree and vanished from view. It was as if the tree itself was twittering and dribbling black-and-white bird droppings. Eight had been back awhile and was heaving a big bundle of plastic bags onto the roof of his cookhouse. They fell off with a thud and landed on a pile of rusty wire netting by the cookhouse door. There was a filthy, sodden quilt on top of the netting, and the flies resting on it all flew up at once. Eight put the bundle of plastic bags back on the roof and laid some mildewed *ganmo* out on the windowsill to dry.

Wufu felt the quilt. "There are spots of blood on it. Did the hospital throw it out?"

"There's still good cotton wadding inside," said Eight. "What's up? You jealous?"

Wufu snorted. "Are you really going to eat moldy *ganmo*?" he asked.

"Not me," said Eight. "But you sneaked two of them the other day. Think I didn't notice?"

"You talk such crap!" said Wufu, and went upstairs.

"You're a bastard, winding Wufu up like that," I said.

Eight laughed and picked up a stick to scratch his back.

"I've got a remedy for itches."

"What's that?"

"Go rub your back against the tree trunk."

Eight was foulmouthed when it came to the government, the rich, cars in the street, and the police, but he never dared swear at me. He just laughed at my teasing and went over to the tree to rub his back, then said, "Don't throw your dirty dishwater off the roof anymore. I don't mind, but she's back."

"Who?" I asked.

Eight jerked his chin at the side door. I heard a woman call out shrilly, "Eight, you son of a bitch!"

Eight hustled me upstairs, shouting back, "Bitch yourself, woman!"

The door banged. She was outside, under the tree. "Did you just go to the shit-house? You left such a big pile of crap, it's blocked the hole. Why can't you flush it away?"

There was only one WC in the building—a squat toilet right beside Eight's room with no door, only a curtain. Anyone wanting to use it had to stomp up to it, to warn whoever was inside. When a squatter saw shoes in the gap at the bottom of the curtain, he'd give a little cough and the other person would go away.

"That wasn't my crap!" said Eight.

The woman had been talking at Eight's door, but when she heard him on the steps, she looked up at us. "So it's dog shit, is it?"

"I was eating melon today. You go and cut it open, see if you can see any melon seeds!" said Eight.

I rapped Eight on the head. "You're disgusting!" I wondered why Eight knew this woman so well.

He whispered to me, "She was in Fishpond long before me. She's an old hand at trash picking, but she went back home for a few months to marry off her son. Her husband's always with her, but they're always fighting. Every spat they have ends in one or the other of them throwing a stool or smashing pots, even stabbing the door frame with a kitchen knife. They fight so bad, I don't understand why they don't divorce, but they fight by day and make up every night. She's fierce all right, but she's lively."

As soon as the woman caught sight of Wufu and me, she clamped her thin lips shut, then ran up the steps after us and booted Eight on the ass. "Flush it away!" she yelled.

Tough-talking he might be, but Eight did as he was told. The woman smiled at me. "Just arrived, have you?" she said.

"That's right. I'm Happy Liu, and this is Wufu. We're your new neighbors. I do hope we're not causing you any bother."

"Hah! The way you talk, I'm betting you don't come from the same place as Eight!"

"That's right, we don't."

"Lucky for me you don't!" And she swore at Eight again. "You and your filthy habits, dirty as a fly!" Then she suddenly smiled. "Isn't it odd how flies don't get sick!"

She wasn't bad-looking; her top half was shapely, though it was hard to see because she wore a baggy jacket. Too bad about the bottom half though. She had big hips and short legs, so she looked as if she'd been put together all wrong. Three times Wufu inquired politely where she was from, but she ignored him and asked me, "Are you on your own? Haven't you brought your missus?"

"I haven't got one."

"It's good to leave someone at home," she said. "The two of us came together, but there was a terrible accident while we were away. We went home for a few months and fixed the damage. Anyway, we thought we wouldn't come back to Xi'an, but in the end we had to. The side room got burned, and the kids need to go to college . . ." She looked down. She had a scar on one eyelid.

"I thought Eight said you'd gone home for your son's wedding."

"Why would I tell him the truth? Don't expect any comfort from him if you've got troubles."

Jia Pingwa

I started to pay attention. This woman wanted someone to talk to, heart to heart, and she wanted that person to be me. She must be pretty smart, to open up to me when she'd only just met me. She must not have had anyone to talk to for a long, long time. Then she actually said, "I have to bottle everything up all day long!"

Turned out that she wanted to talk about her mother. Her mother had been looking after the grandchildren back home. She had a room on one side of their courtyard, while the kids lived in the main part of the house. They'd had dinner, and the kids finished their homework, then shut the door and went to bed. "She didn't sleep a lot, so she sat under the mosquito net, smoking her pipe. The side room was old. Dust kept falling off the wooden ceiling boards, so she kept the mosquito net up year-round. She was a good woman, a ripe old age, but she was still cooking three meals a day for the kids. But she was addicted to that pipe of hers. In our family, women have smoked pipes for generations. I don't know what she saw in it. Anyway, a spark from the pipe fell on the bed quilt and set the mosquito net alight. The kids were sound asleep and wouldn't have known what to do anyway. By the time the smoke woke them up, the fire had enveloped the side room and it couldn't be saved. My poor old mother, when her body was finally brought out, she'd been burned to a cinder. All ten fingers were melted together. When the quilt caught, she'd tried to squeeze the flames out with her hands, but the cotton wadding was on fire. How could she squeeze that out? My poor mother . . ."

Someone shouted up the stairs. "You're gabbing again!" I could see a short man downstairs—must have been the woman's husband—and he sounded annoyed.

"So what if I'm gabbing?" said the woman. "Happy Liu's a poor peasant too, and he doesn't laugh at me! Get a bowl of water and wipe the bed down!" After that, she ignored him and told me they hadn't been back here for months, and that the bed was covered in rat shit.

"Having rats is a good sign. If we didn't have rats, it would mean we were starving!"

Between my efforts to follow what she was saying and making sure to look sympathetic, my head was reeling. I was still sighing over the tragedy of her mother, and she'd switched to rats! Well, if rats were a sign of wealth, then maybe trash was too. The more a city had, the better it was doing.

And trash was what we'd come for. Without it, we wouldn't be here.

"Is that your man?" Wufu asked.

She stared at him. "Do you think he's a lover I've dragged in? What, d'you think we make an odd couple?" Wufu choked and couldn't get any words out. Then he farted loudly. "Anything else you'd like to say?" she asked, then cackled with laughter. Meanwhile, the man was filling a basin from the faucet. "Have you washed that basin?" she shouted down at him. "It's filthy! Are you going to wipe the bed down with that?"

"You're the boss at home," I commented. It was meant as a compliment, but she said, "What do you mean, 'the boss'? My previous old man was the boss. The money didn't touch my hands. I stayed out of it and took things easy." She laughed again, and her eyes sparkled. "I've had two husbands," she said. "The first one was a handsome fellow, like you, but he was also a heartless thief. I gave him two children, and he upped and died on me. Cirrhosis of the liver. I spent sixty thousand yuan trying to get him cured, and he just kicked the bucket. Where was I going to get sixty thousand yuan to repay that debt? I could sell myself over and over but I'd never clear it. This one's from a little gully behind our village. He's not much of a looker, but he's honest, and he does what he's told. He's my rough-around-the-edges guy, not like the fine gentleman I was married to before."

As we stood and talked, the mosquitoes started biting my legs. "Come in and sit down," I said out of politeness. So she came in. She patted the quilt to see how thick it was, took the lid off the wok to see what food we had left over, and undid the bag of flour to sniff at it.

"You've got weevils in the flour," she said. "I've got a fine sieve down-stairs." And she hurried off. She came back with the sieve and four or five large potatoes stuffed into the front of her jacket. "Homegrown," she said. "We dug some up and brought a basket load back with us."

Not half an hour after she'd gone downstairs again, we heard them fighting in their room. There were crashing and smashing noises, then we heard her crying and swearing. Wufu and I came out of our rooms at the same moment. We were about to go down and try to help make peace, when we saw Eight standing in his doorway. He waved us back. Then he came running upstairs and said cheerfully, "They're at it again."

"We ought to stop them."

"The woman acts crazy when others are there. The more you try and calm her down, the madder she gets. Last time I tried, I told them to fight outside. 'The room's too small. Don't smash up the TV,' I said. We'd found it in the trash and fixed it so you could watch one channel. And blow me, she just picked up a stool and smashed it into the TV!"

In the end, we stayed where we were and sat on the steps, listening to the goings-on. There was less of the banging around but more shout-ing and swearing. The woman sounded like she was talking more calmly to him, using rough, vivid village language. It made me feel like I was back in Freshwind; those scolding tones were so familiar, and so warm.

Eight really seemed to be getting off on it. Every time she cussed her husband out, Eight would yell from the steps, "Nice one!"

Wufu chuckled, then laughed silently, and finally got to his feet. "Sleep," he said. The lights grew dim in the distance, stars appeared in the sky, and the bugs in the tree were busy crapping, dripping filth all over our faces and necks like rain.

I knew Wufu was hankering after his missus, but I didn't let on I knew. I only said, "I'm off to bed too." We went to our rooms.

Did it make others happy to have a wife to quarrel with? Listening to another couple fighting and missing being bawled out by my own missus . . . That was a feeling I'd never had. I pulled back the quilt and got into bed. I'm telling you, I thought I'd soon be dead to the world, but sleep wouldn't come. The bed felt lumpy. I turned on the light and smoothed out the bed mat. I found a bit of *ganmo* and chewed on it, looked at the high heels sitting on their shelf, then dusted them. I wasn't sure what I was thinking about, probably nothing. Anyway, I turned the light off again. The moonlight was coming in through the window, but I shut my eyes and saw only dark.

I don't know what time it was, but I was woken by cries coming from somewhere. Were they still arguing downstairs? But these cries were a bit like singing, a bit like panting, sort of vibrato—so strange, they gave me goose bumps. I opened my door to hear better. Wufu had thrown on some clothes and was standing at his door too. "Can you hear it?" he said when he saw me.

"What is it?" I asked.

"She's screaming," he said cryptically.

Wufu's eyes were gleaming like a cat's. I felt foolish. My not having a missus was embarrassing enough in itself. So I had no idea that a woman's cries of pleasure sounded so terrifying, and so seductive at the same time. What I couldn't figure out was, they'd been at each other's throats until after dark, and now, a scant couple of hours later, they were having sex and she was screaming the house down!

24.

We got up at dawn. Another day had begun. Every day was the same, there was no difference between the one before and the one after. Wufu was sitting on the roof, boiling our rice porridge and rolling up his pant leg to look at his cuts and bruises. I leaned against my door, feeling my chin and pulling hairs out with tweezers. Downstairs, the doors to the two rooms opened at the same moment. Eight's saddle patch on his nose looked whiter than ever this morning, and his eyes were puffy. He seemed annoyed and was muttering to himself.

"Going to Dengjiapo today?" Wufu asked.

"Yup."

"Toss your matchbox up here, will you?" said Wufu. Eight went in to get it, then lobbed it up. Wufu tore the striking strip off and pressed it against his wound, then threw the matchbox back down.

"You tore off the striking strip?" said Eight.

"Stuck it to the wound," said Wufu. "It'll make it heal quicker."

"Wound? What wound?" Eight asked. Wufu looked at me and didn't answer. Nor did I.

The woman came out of her room carrying the pisspot. As she passed Eight, she asked, "What did you make for breakfast?"

"Nothing."

"Then give me a minute, and I'll cook you a bowl of porridge."

"Two bowls!" said Eight. "I need two of them after the night I had."

"Didn't you sleep well?" she asked.

"You made such a racket, even a deaf person couldn't have slept!" said Eight.

The woman laughed and laughed. "Why don't you bring your missus here then? Now you see why I don't divorce Mr. Gules, because our sex life's so good."

"Well, keep the noise down," said Eight.

"Why shouldn't I scream if I'm having a good time?" said the woman. That made us all feel despondent.

After that, she screamed every night, and we simply had to put up with it. I got the feeling she was doing it on purpose, to show off. I watched them and wondered how they had the energy to work during the day with all the rumpus that went on at night. But she seemed pleased as punch, always busy at something. She went out to pick trash, then came home to tidy their room, wash their clothes, and rinse the rice. She never stopped talking, laughing, and cursing. He was the exact opposite, keeping his head down and never saying a word. He had his breakfast, then went to the shit-house. He came out of the shit-house and went to pick trash. When it got dark, he came back, had his dinner, then went to the shit-house again. He was a bit of a mystery. The only stuff he did for himself was eating and using the shit-house. The rest was all work. He worked by day and he worked at night.

Wufu said to Eight, "You'd think they'd get fed up, doing it night after night."

"You eat three meals a day—do you get fed up with it? His name's Gules, and it's always 'Mr. Gules this' and 'Mr. Gules that,' but we just call him Goolies, because we figure he's got big balls. Her proper name's Wang Caicai, but she's got such big eyes, we call her Almond, and she's happy with that."

After Goolies and Almond arrived, Wufu and I started to come back from Prosper Street earlier. So, we discovered, did Eight. Almond would shout and swear at Goolies, or she'd pick on us for some minor thing instead. We complained about her nagging and said we'd wouldn't come back till later the next day, but the very next day, we'd be back early again as usual. I couldn't say why. We must have been soft in the head. On one particular day, I'd taken refuge on the steps when I'd gotten back. I couldn't face cooking, and my head felt like lead. Almond was going after Wufu, whose face was as coated with dust as a kiln. "Go stick your head under the faucet!" she said, then when he went, she added, "And watch what you're doing! You haven't got a wolf at your heels! You're splashing water everywhere!"

"Wash it for me!" Wufu said.

"In your dreams!" Almond said. Eight cackled with laughter. Almond ignored him and said to me, "Happy, do you mind if I ask you something?"

I looked up and grunted. I'd almost nodded off, sitting there. "Are you listening to me?" she said. "I want to know who you bought those high-heeled shoes for!"

"For my missus!"

She turned gimlet eyes on me. "You're having me on! Wufu said you weren't married! You've been fooling around with a fox spirit, haven't you? And she gave you the shoes so you wouldn't forget her. Be honest now, am I right?"

"You're blabbering on again," said Goolies. "Scratch my back for me!" And he turned around and presented his back.

She reached her fingers under his jacket, her eyes still on me. Goolies seemed to be really enjoying it. He breathed hard, his cheeks slackened, and he went so limp, I thought he'd slip to the ground. Almond often scratched his back for him in front of us, and it made us itch all over just looking at them. *Do it in your room!* I felt like saying. It put us all in a bad mood. Eight pulled the shit-house curtain down, and Wufu knocked over the basin of vegetable water Almond had put out on the roof to sour in the sun.

"Are you going to stitch my mouth up for me?" said Almond, and turned to me. "Happy, be a nice guy and give me those shoes, please?"

I looked at her, and she blinked. "I'm not nice."

She gave Goolies one more scratch, then pushed him away. "You're so tightfisted! Even if you did give them to me, my feet are too fat to fit in them. I was just sussing you out, and you're as tightfisted as I thought!"

I really didn't feel well, but I forced a laugh and curled up again on my step.

"What's up with you? I'm only teasing. Don't be like that!"

"I'm not right," I said. "I'm stiff all over."

"Are you ill? Come over here," she commanded. "I'll give you a scratch, and that'll relax you." I tried to back away, but she was already behind me, her fingers up my shirt. A woman's hands are so soft! I wriggled in embarrassment, but her fingers raked me gently, and wherever they reached, they tickled, then scratched, and it felt so good that I stopped wriggling. I was worried that my back was grimy and she'd get dirt under her fingernails, but she said only, "Look what a chubby face you've got! How come your body's so thin? Mr. Gules is the fat one!"

Wufu and Eight were jealous at the special treatment I was getting, and they moaned and complained like a pair of ghosts. I never heard the end of it, but, well, everyone's different. From then on, every evening as the clouds in the sky blossomed peony pink, Goolies got his back scratching and so did I. Wufu and Eight tried their best to get on Almond's good side: they swept the yard, sluiced down the shit-house, put up the clothesline when she'd done the laundry, and chopped wood for kindling. Finally, they too got a scratching. Back scratches were addictive, and we started coming home earlier and earlier every day. We'd say hello to Almond, and then, like kindergarten kids waiting for the teacher to hand us pieces of fruit, we'd wait for her to scratch our backs. We lined up, gripped the stair railings, and bent over so she could scratch first one, then the other. When she'd finished with us, she'd slap us on the butt and say, "Off you go!" And we'd get on with our chores, a spring in our step and a smile on our faces. I found a small cooking pot and gave it to her as a present. She showed it to Wufu and Eight.

"If you've got a pot, you need a ladle. I'll bring you one if I find one," said Wufu. He was busy washing a pair of pants, old ones he'd found in the trash.

"Now if you really wanted to show your devotion," said Almond, "you'd give me those pants!"

"But they've got a zip up the front!" Wufu objected.

"All city women wear front-zip trousers," said Almond. And she took them from him. Wufu let her have them, but he grumbled that Eight hadn't given her anything. So Eight got his porcelain God of Wealth, the one with an arm broken off, and gave it to Almond. Actually, it was a figurine of the great General Guan that Eight had found in the garbage one day when a restaurant was being refurbished, and kept beside his bed. Now the figurine went into Almond's room, and she bought incense and prayed to it every morning. She made us do the same. We had to put the incense sticks in their holders with our left hands. She said your right hand was for fighting and for cleaning your ass, so the right hand was dirty.

Pulling the cart around the streets all day left us bone-weary, and we needed more than a back scratch to set us right again. Not that I said that, and Wufu and Eight certainly didn't have the temerity to. Then there were the nights. Almond's screaming made us grind our teeth in fury at Goolies. In Wufu's room, the previous occupant had left a poster of a car with a long-legged girl standing beside it. The girl's legs had three deep slashes in them, so you could see the wall behind. I said nothing. In the public toilets, you often saw drawings of naked women on the walls, sometimes with rude rhymes to go with them. Some appeared on our shit-house wall too, and I was worried Almond might think I'd done them, so one day when I was downstairs, I said, "Who's been scribbling on the shit-house walls?"

There was no answer. Almond came out of her room and said, "You're allowed to do that if you haven't got a woman. But her titties are so big, they look like basketballs!"

"Think you've got big titties, do you?" said Eight from his room. Then I knew that he'd done the drawings. I went to his room, where he was sticking some posters he'd found in the trash around his bed. He was illiterate, so he didn't realize that they were anti-AIDS ads. As far as he was concerned, they had a woman's head on them.

"That's nice, Eight," I said. "Now you can sleep in a woman's lap."

"You can have one if you like," he offered.

"No, thanks, but go clean those drawings off the shit-house walls."

"OK. But you've got to stop Almond screaming."

How could I stop Almond screaming? Her screaming had its good side—I lay in bed and as soon she started up, I got busy with my hand—but there was no way I was going to tell Eight that. I'd been jerking off since I was twenty years old. I didn't know if other men were like me, and I thought if I told them, they'd laugh at me. And now it was just a habit. Every night I lay in bed, waiting for Almond to finish. Trouble was, she was sometimes very late, and I had to wait until midnight before I could do it and fall peacefully asleep.

25.

I was happy in Leftover House, but life as a trash picker was boring, and I was getting lonely. Wufu, Eight, and Goolies hardly uttered a word from morning till night. They were tough, crabby characters who tended to lose patience when they were bargaining for trash and then the sellers wouldn't sell. Nothing made them happier than a street scuffle; they were always in the middle of the shouting and jeering onlookers, and yelling themselves. None of us were into soccer, because we'd never played it in Freshwind, but every couple of weeks in Xi'an there was a match. The soccer field, as it happened, was east of Prosper Street, and heaving crowds of spectators brought traffic to a halt all down the street. The Xi'an team wasn't very good, which enraged their fans, so there were always fights after the match. We didn't go inside because tickets were too pricey. Why would we pay thirty yuan to watch a bunch of men kicking a ball around? On match days, we never made much money, because the streets were so crowded, you couldn't get the cart through, but we liked to pull the carts to the soccer field after the match began and stand outside and listen. Eight went too, and a bunch of other trash pickers. It was as if the soccer field was the city's punching bag. The earsplitting roars—"Fuck! Fuck! Motherfucker!"—made the ground shake. I couldn't understand why they had to vent their rage like that, as if they were full of swamp gas. Why did they have to be so foulmouthed? When tens of thousands of spectators roared in unison,

"Fuck! Fuck! Motherfucker!" Eight used to yell along with them, "Fuck! Fuck! Motherfucker!"

I tried to stop him. "You can't shout here!"

"Why not? Everyone else is yelling, 'Fuck!' Why can't I?"

"They're shouting at the referee and the teams. Who are you shouting at?"

"I'll think of someone," he said.

He was pissing me off, so I grabbed Wufu. "Let's go!"

"As soon as the fans come out, there'll be fights," he said. I very nearly smacked him again. But unlike Eight, Wufu did what I said, and he went with me. Eight hung around waiting. Once there was a big fight and the police turned up. They tried to arrest a man throwing stones at cars. He took off and twisted his ankle, and then got Eight to pull him on his cart. The police caught up with them and arrested the man, then tried to arrest Eight too. Eight protested that he was a trash picker and hadn't been inside at the soccer match. "If you're helping a rioter escape, then you're a rioter too," they told him.

Then they saw his face. They didn't know what vitiligo was. "Dammit, you're sick!" they said. "Is it AIDS?"

"If I'm sick," Eight said, "then you'll catch it too!" So they didn't arrest him, just gave him such a beating that they ripped his pants.

I never wanted anything to do with stupid stuff like that. So on match days, I stopped going out at all. I simply played the flute, and then I talked to my cart since there was no one else to talk to.

My cart understood me.

One day, something happened. I was in a lane at the north end of Prosper Street and a woman was walking in front of me, carrying a plastic bucket. I usually didn't look at women on the street; it was safer that way. It wasn't only that ogling women was a lowlife thing to do. You could get into trouble if she took it the wrong way. But the shoes the woman was wearing were the exact same style of high heels as the ones I'd bought. That was quite a shock! I hadn't seen anyone wearing them until now. Something made me take my courage in both hands and pull ahead of her. I wanted to see her face. Had I seen her before? But just as I went to pass her, one of my cart tires blew out. I saw the woman duck into a nearby hair and beauty salon, the very same salon I'd seen a woman pop her head out of before, and something about the way she held herself and her facial expression made my heart leap. It was like an electric shock. It'd never happened to me before.

Every time I passed the salon after that, I felt like I knew the place, and I couldn't help sneaking a look through the window. A few days later, Wufu and I went in, with the excuse that we needed a haircut, but it was too expensive and we walked out again. The hairdressers were all women, but the woman I liked wasn't there. Was the woman with my high heels the same one I'd seen popping her head out? I wasn't sure, since one of my cart tires had blown out as I'd gone to pass her. It was heavy going, pulling a cart with a punctured tire, and there was no repair place nearby. I was in despair. That was the first time I'd talked to it. "Cart, cart, why did you have to go and blow your tire?" I said. "You have to be strong, so I can pull you. And whatever you do, don't let the inner tube puncture! Do as I say, cart, and I'll wash you well when we get back, and get you nice and clean!" And sure enough, the cart pulled lighter, and just down the street I found a repair place.

The cart understood me. That had happened more than once. Wufu believed me too. The pity was, it couldn't talk back. I wondered who else in Xi'an was as lonely as I was.

The traffic police were really lonely. They stood at intersections, and people streamed past them like ants, but no one gave them the time of day. No wonder they were so grim-faced and cantankerous. I'd observed these traffic police before, and I discovered that as long as you chatted with them when they yelled at you for something, they'd lighten up. One day, I waited with my cart at the intersection and crossed when the light was blinking amber, making sure to walk very slowly. Sure enough, that brought the traffic policeman running. When a traffic policeman crooks his finger and beckons you over, you have to go. Though really, it's just as easy to get one to come to you. He shouted at me to pull over, then told me my trash was improperly loaded and that I should never cross the intersection when the lights were changing. And we started talking.

"Hey, Trash Picker!"

"My name's Happy Liu. Please don't call me 'Trash Picker.'"

"Huh? Want a salute as well?"

"No need for that."

"Do you think you're driving a car?"

"This isn't a main street. There's no rule that says my cart can't pass!"

"Well, aren't you a Mr. Know-It-All!"

"That's because I'm educated."

"Pah! Pull my other leg! A trash picker, educated?"

"If I weren't a trash picker, I could be a traffic policeman!"

"What did you say? Say it again?"

I didn't.

"Say it!"

I chuckled and said nothing.

"Not so talkative now, eh? And what's this?"

"A flute, can't you tell?"

"What's a trash picker doing with a flute? Ridiculous!"

I chuckled again.

"What're you laughing at?"

"I just wanted to shoot the breeze with you . . ."

"And why would I want to talk to you? I'm a busy man!"

"You can still talk when your eyes are busy!"

"Off with you!" He aimed a cheerful kick at my ass. After that, Happy Liu and his flute were regulars at the intersection. I always stopped to chat with the traffic policeman. He even got me to come at certain times to play him a tune.

"This is for you!" I'd say.

One particular day, I turned up with my cart as agreed and the policeman waved at me. I thought he was greeting me, so I waved back and trotted over, but he said, "Get your cart down that back street, quick! There's a roadblock today!" He looked stern again, like he used to, yelling at one driver who grumbled about the roadblock, and pulling the young man's keys out of the ignition.

Xi'an was a city of history and culture, so there were always road-blocks. It didn't matter if it was a foreign dignitary visiting or some bigwig from the central government; on every street they drove from the airport to their luxury hotel, and at every intersection, there was a policeman every ten paces, and a sentry every five. No one could get through, either on foot or by car.

I got myself and my cart down the back street. There were the usual three-wheelers laden with coal, milk, bottled water, and knockoff books and magazines. I told them all, "Roadblock!"

The magazine vendor, who had a flattened nose, said in a nasal voice, "Piss off! Look, there're the garbage cans."

Of course, I'd seen the row of three garbage cans in front of me as soon as I'd reached the back alley. But Flat-Nose was pissing me off. *Think you can look down on a trash picker? Think because you're selling knockoff magazines, you've got education? Pah! Go down the road, off you go, and see if the police will let you pass!* I thought, and went over to the garbage cans. I was a professional, after all, and I couldn't pass a can without taking off the lid and looking inside, in case there was some-thing worth picking out. Sure enough, in the first there were three empty pull-tab cans. You could get five cents a can for them, so that was fifteen cents, and every cent counted. If you went to a store and were a cent short, you'd leave empty-handed. And I'd picked up fifteen cents just like that.

Trash picking was like hawking wares on the sidewalk. If you sold something, however cheaply, as soon as you opened for business in the morning, that meant you'd be lucky for the rest of the day. The same with trash: I figured that the time of day I found my first bit of trash and how much it was worth told me whether the rest of the day's business would be good, and I was always right.

Those three pull-tab cans cheered me up, and I pinged my thumb happily against them.

A girl standing nearby was staring at me, wide-eyed, and suddenly she piped up. "Don't dig around in the trash. It's dirty!"

I smiled at her and made a silly face. "What's your name?" But she ran off.

I rifled through the second bin, but there was only stinky food waste. But, hey, in the third, I found a leather wallet. It was a big brown leather wallet, with a fearsome fish motif on its side. I was really in luck today! I took a good look around me, but no one was there. A sparrow was perched on the branch of a nearby tree, twittering and chirping. It knew my secret now, but I shooed it away. A girl with a waist as slender as a water snake swayed past in a long skirt, flapping her hand fussily under her nose. But at least she hadn't seen what I was holding. Ah well, good looks never brought a girl good luck! Or brains.

Of course, there was still the sparrow. It flew back into the tree, and undoubtedly saw me stow the wallet inside my jacket with lightning speed. Then my cart and I were on our way down the lane. I walked quickly and stared straight ahead, sneaking quick glances to either side. I felt like I'd grown eyes in the back of my head, and even my butt. The sun was shining brightly, and there wasn't a cloud in the sky. The street was crowded with people bustling everywhere. Everyone was so busy—but they were clueless. They hadn't the slightest idea that something momentous had just happened!

Lucky for me that trash pickers were invisible in this city. I stopped by a wall that was painted maroon. There was no one around, only a ball of leaves blown by the wind. I kicked them away, then turned toward the wall and opened the wallet, like a gambler at the betting table taking the lid off the bowl to look at the dice. I wasn't searching for a bundle of notes. All I wanted was the pleasure of owning a quality leather wallet, to go with the pouch I was using right now for my money. There was no money in it, but there were seven cards with magnetic strips on them, a cell phone, a passport, and a motley collection of keys on a key ring.

If it had had three hundred yuan in it, or even five hundred, I would have pocketed it without a qualm and not told a soul. But there were so many things in the wallet, I got scared. Setting off firecrackers was one thing, but handling explosives was quite another! I flung it away from me, as if I'd stuck my hand in a bird's nest and pulled out a snake. It landed at the foot of the wall, and I turned on my heel and left. But I'd only taken a few steps before going back, emptying everything out of the wallet and taking the wallet with me. Another few hundred feet, and it occurred to me that the owner of the wallet must be frantic with worry—its contents were obviously important. I went back again, stuffed everything into the wallet, and tucked it deep inside my jacket. At that moment, I remembered the old saying that good fortune always brings disaster in its wake, and my legs seemed to turn to lead.

26.

I didn't mention any of this to Scrawny when I got to the depot, and I wouldn't sell him the three pull-tab cans either.

Scrawny figured I was stockpiling pull-tabs at Fishpond so I could up the price when I sold them, and he said rudely, "Huh! And everyone always swears blind that Shangzhou husk-eaters are too honest to swipe the shit from the buckets they're carrying!"

Back at Leftover House, I arranged the three cans on the window-sill. I didn't have any incense sticks, but I put my palms together in respect.

"What's all this about?" Wufu asked.

"It's the god of luck!"

"The god of luck?"

"Take a look between my eyebrows . . . Can't you see the light of luck shining there?"

Wufu was really obtuse. He peered at my eyebrows and said there was a pimple between them. It was time I showed him what was what. I got out the wallet and flourished it. He shouted in astonishment. Then I told him the whole story.

He looked disappointed. "A wallet is for money, dammit! Didn't he have any on him?"

All he could think about was money! I showed him the passport. "That's proof that he's been abroad. It's like our ID cards. Only big businessmen use passports! And so many cards! There'll be money on them, for food, for discounts on meals, even for buying goods. Too bad they're of no use to us. Look at the keys, what a collection! Apart from house and car keys, you can tell a lot about someone's status in this city by the other keys they have!"

Wufu started playing with the phone. We couldn't use it because we had no idea how to turn it on. Wufu said that he'd seen old cell phones for sale in the market on Lane Two for three hundred. "If you sell it, Happy, it's as if you picked up three hundred yuan!"

"Think money is all I care about?" I said.

"So you're the emperor's mother, just doing a bit of gleaning for fun?" Wufu retorted.

"Well, some things you can have, and some you can't. Can you have the moon?" I was happy to get small windfalls, every day if possible, but a sudden windfall this big terrified me. I really had no idea what to do. I could throw away the passport, the cards and the keys, keep the wallet and sell the cell phone, but that would be like not rescuing a kid who's fallen into water or seeing someone's house·on fire and not helping put out the flames. I've got standards, after all. So I decided to hand the wallet in at the Fishpond local police station and let them go look for the owner. I had to accept it wasn't meant for me. Then at least I could rest easy.

But Wufu said, "If you hand it in, won't someone think you stole the money from it? Who's going to believe you if you say it had a passport, cell phone, cards, and keys but no money in it when you found it?" He was right. He might have a brain like a sieve most of the time, but today he'd hit the nail on the head. I wondered suddenly if Wufu suspected me of ripping off the wallet or the cash in it. For an instant, I even suspected myself.

"Let's sleep on it," said Wufu. But I couldn't get to sleep. Finally, in the middle of the night, I went over to Gem Han's house on West Lane and knocked on his door. He listened to my story and rifled through the wallet, then looked hard at me. A minute passed, and he said nothing.

Another minute passed in silence. I couldn't bear to look at those pockmarks of his, and I averted my eyes. Suddenly Han began to interrogate me very sternly.

"Did you rip it off?"

"No."

"Did you rob someone?"

"No."

"Really?"

"No, no, no!" I repeated frantically. Han's insinuations were unbearable. Suddenly angry, I wanted to grab the wallet and go. Then Han hooted in laughter. It was a creepy sound, like a screech owl. "We're going to get rich!"

"Get rich?"

Han had turned on the cell phone. There was a bleep, and a message appeared on the screen: *Comrade, you've picked up my wallet. The contents are useless to you, but very important to me. Take the phone. Just give me the SIM card back, and we'll be friends. It's got all my clients' numbers on it. At eight o'clock tomorrow night or the next day, leave the SIM card, the passport, the keys, and the cards in the flower bed behind the third electric pole on Qing Song Road. There'll be an envelope there, with one thousand yuan as a token of my appreciation.*

This was fantastic news. What a good thing I'd come to him. He'd solved everything! I offered him a cigarette and lit it for him.

"Do you think he'll really give us one thousand yuan?"

"You're such a simpleton!"

Me? A simpleton? I knew what he meant though, and I told him straight up, "If we really get one thousand, and divide it in three, that's a hundred left over, and we can have a good pig-out on that!" I knew Han wanted his share, but I was determined to bring Wufu in on it.

"You know what?" said Han. "If the money's really there, he'll be there too, hiding behind a tree, and he'll drag you to the police station and accuse you of theft!"

"Could he really be so devious?"

"What do you think?"

"Then I don't want his money! No one calls me a thief!"

"You know, it'll cost him a pretty penny to replace his passport, and to change all the locks in his house. One thousand yuan's nothing compared to that."

"So what can we do? We're screwed either way!" I said.

"I need to have a hand in it," Han said.

The next evening, Han tried to stop Wufu from coming, but he eventually gave in. I knew what he was thinking: if it came to a fight, Wufu was a good man to have on your side.

I warned Wufu. "Keep your wits about you. Don't simply do whatever Han tells you!"

"I'll just do what you tell me," Wufu said.

We got to Qing Song Road, and sure enough there was the envelope in the flower bed behind the third electric pole. Han tore open the envelope, and there was one thousand yuan. He rubbed each note between his finger and thumb, then went to the lamppost and checked them in the light. "They're real," he said. Then he made me put the wallet down with the passport, keys, cards, and the cell phone inside. Han picked up the cell phone, took out the SIM card, and put it in the wallet. He told us not to say a word. We all looked around carefully, then beat a retreat to the main road. When we got to somewhere quiet, Han opened the envelope and took out five hundred. "That's to split between you two," he said.

We'd agreed to split it three ways. Han was a son of a bitch. But he'd already put the rest away in his fanny pack, so what could I do? Getting that crook Han involved had cost me five hundred yuan. I counted out two hundred and fifty, but Wufu muttered to me, "We've been taken for a ride!" and gave me back ten yuan.

Han wasn't letting us go though. He made us leave our hiding place and scoot, bent double, across the road. We then waited behind a parked car to see who would come for the wallet. After about ten minutes, someone came strolling down the street. We couldn't see his face because he had his back to the streetlight, but he crouched down when he got to the flower bed and swiftly retrieved the wallet. It was a bit like a scene from a movie, and I laughed out loud. I was just about to say we were like spies, when Han leapt out and pounced on the man.

I always knew Han didn't stick to the rules, but this was really out of line. The man had already given us a thousand yuan as a thank-you. Wasn't that enough? The man looked like he was on his own; there were no cronies with him, and he wasn't luring us into a trap. It made us look like scum!

"Gem, Gem!" Wufu and I shouted. Han ignored us. He was gripping the man's arm and saying something to him. A car drove by, and its headlights swept over them. I saw that our man had neatly combed hair and was wearing a checkered shirt with a tie. Then the car was gone and the flower bed was in darkness again. Our man looked familiar. Where had I seen him before? No one I knew was that posh, nor dressed that neatly. So how did I know him? I just felt he was a friend.

"Did you get a good look at him, Wufu?" I asked.

"Yup!"

"Seem familiar?"

"Nope."

Han and the man were still talking. I saw a lot of gesticulating. Then the man went off down the street, and Han came bounding back again.

"What were you talking about?" I asked.

"I said if that stuff was so important, why was he sending us off with only a thousand yuan?"

"Were you blackmailing him for more?" I asked.

"Why mess around with someone as rich as that? I asked him for another five hundred, and I was going to give you two hundred of it, but the stingy son of a bitch only gave me three hundred."

Even if Han had offered it, I wouldn't have accepted. He was despicable! We went our separate ways, and I couldn't sleep all night. We'd started out by earning the man's gratitude, but no doubt he was calling us every name under the sun now.

I pictured his face clearly in my mind, and I said a little prayer that he would forgive Wufu and me. Then I wondered yet again where I'd seen him before.

Hey, wait a minute! I remembered something the monk in Freshwind said . . . Maybe the man had some connection with me in a former life. Was that possible, in such a big city? Suddenly a very bold thought flashed into my mind: Was this the man my kidney had been transplanted into? It was such a strong feeling—it must be him, it must be! I scrambled out of bed, ran next door, and shook Wufu awake. When I told him what I'd been thinking, Wufu put his hand on my forehead. "Are you feeling hot?"

"No," I said.

He patted my face. "Are you sleepwalking?"

"No."

"Then I must be dreaming," Wufu muttered.

I was so annoyed, I grabbed his lips and twisted them. His skin was so slack that I ended up twisting half his face.

"I trust my gut about this!" I said.

"Well, if that's what you believe, that's it then," he said. Wufu always went along with what I said, though when he said that, it made me hesitate. But he told me something that once happened to him. The first time he was introduced to a girl, a friend came with her. The minute he set eyes on the pair, he had a strong feeling that the friend would become his wife. And that was what happened: it didn't work out with his date, and he married the friend. Talking about his missus made him start to miss her. Maybe she was sitting up late, stitching a shoe sole for one of their kids, he said. Well, I suppose even ugly men miss their wives . . . "Such fine, fair skin she had." He sighed. "And her family was better off than mine. It seemed impossible she'd marry me, but she did!"

"Yeah, well, you can stick a flower in a cow pie!"

"That's just what she is, a flower in a cow pie. People are strange, first impressions are right on."

"So do you think my feeling's right?" I said.

"Yup."

I must have gone pale. I couldn't speak, and I felt all choked up. On the one hand, I was happy, at last I'd found my alter ego! And that alter ego was such a fine figure of a man, and wealthy too. But another part of me was annoyed that such an unfortunate incident had led me to him. Han, you swine, turning a pot of rice into vinegar and my alter ego into my enemy!

27.

Days went by, and I kept wanting to go back to Qing Song Road with my cart. But it wasn't part of my patch, and the local trash pickers threatened me. I swore I just wanted to pass through, and if I ever looked as if I was going to collect any trash, they could smash my cart and bash me over the head with a brick. Regardless, I never saw my alter ego. I described him to the Qing Song Road trash pickers in the hopes they might let me know if they saw him.

"What's he to you?" one asked.

"My alter ego."

"You're out of your mind! Get off my patch!"

After that, we had three days of nonstop rain. For practically every business in the city, rain boosted their takings. Not for us. Rain was a disaster. We were stuck indoors, and if we couldn't go out, we couldn't earn. We'd finished our rice and flour, were waiting to sell our newly collected trash so we could buy more, and were angry that we couldn't. We boiled the remaining three handfuls of noodles, but there wasn't even a scraping of salt left in the pot.

"All outgoings, no incomings," grumbled Wufu, "like pissing widows!"

He borrowed a spoonful of salt from Eight. I'd seen Eight gnawing on moldy *ganmo* flatbreads he'd been keeping on the windowsill, but he stopped when Wufu went downstairs, and he started drinking water.

"What are you eating?" Wufu asked.

"Nothing, skipping my meal, just living on water."

"Living on water?"

"That's right. It's what trees do."

I'd been playing my flute upstairs, but Eight's answer was so funny, I had to stop. The odd thing was that whenever I played my flute these days, no one seemed to notice; they just got on with whatever they were doing. It was when I stopped that people felt the music's absence, like fish stranded when the water suddenly drains away.

Almond came out of her room. "Why've you stopped playing?"

"You've got rice for dinner, but our stove's cold. Maybe he doesn't have the heart for it anymore," said Wufu.

"You've got the money to buy classy high heels, but you've got nothing to eat. Who're you saving up for?" Almond filled a big bowl of rice with cabbage and bean curd on top, and brought it upstairs to us.

I wouldn't take it. "If it's a present, I'm not accepting it."

"Did I put rat poison in it or something?"

"I don't want Goolies to hit me."

Goolies shouted up the steps. "I told her to bring it up to you!"

I laughed. "Then it really must have rat poison in it."

"Not so much it'll kill you. Eat up. Then we'll go play mahjong at Fan's," he said.

"Don't you dare!" said Almond. "You lost twenty yuan yesterday. You're not going back there again."

"I'll get Happy to give me advice. I want to win the twenty back."

"Off you go then," said Almond. "Stay out all night if you like. Just one thing: I need sex, and I need it at nine o'clock."

Wufu and Eight cackled with laughter.

"Be a good boy and stay at home, Goolies," I said. "And if you're really bored, then you and I'll play chess. Go buy the chess set, and the one who loses owes drinks."

The house that belonged to old Fan was almost opposite ours. They were pulling down the old building in front and putting up a bigger building, and the alley was full of bricks and sand, but they couldn't work in the rain, so Fan played mahjong with his buddies in the back room. He didn't have a bad life, though he once told Almond, "You and Goolies have it good. You come to the city to earn money, and if you don't get enough, you can just take off and go plant your fields. We can make a living renting out rooms, but what will our kids do, without jobs or land? Our bodies have gotten lazy, life's going to be hard!" He was right too. We were fortunate, I thought smugly. But now here he was building a new apartment building, five stories high, and his monthly income was going to skyrocket! Typical city man, he'd complain whatever his circumstances, just like a pig grunts whether it's skinny or fat. He was making so much money that he'd be able to set up his children and grandchildren with their own businesses, but we'd always be left behind. Even if Fan begged me, there was no way I was going to play mahjong with him.

We ate our food and started a game of chess. You needed a worthy opponent for chess; neither Wufu nor Eight qualified. Turned out that Goolies didn't either. We played a few rounds, and I lost interest and watched as he played against Wufu. Goolies kept taking his moves back, but Wufu was taking the game seriously. They argued, then it got abusive. "Keep an eye on them!" said Eight. "There's going to be a fight." I didn't care. I simply sat there, mulling things over. Sure enough, Wufu grabbed some pieces off the board and flung them into the alley.

"I'm not playing with you, motherfucker!" And he stormed off to bed.

I ignored them. The rain was easing up, but some of the demolition bricks, sodden with rain, were lying in the alley and turning into a lumpy slurry. Passersby, cats, and dogs were slipping and sliding in it, walking with great clods stuck to their shoes or paws. It was quite a sight. I kept my eyes pinned on them, eager to see who would fall over next. Then I saw something even odder: the pile of mud on our side of the alley was covered in green shoots. This was the rubble from the smoke-blackened mud-brick wall Fan had knocked down, and now it was sprouting vivid green shoots of corn two fingers high.

Weird! Three days ago there was nothing on this heap of rubble, and it wasn't even the growing season. There must have been seeds mixed in when the bricks were made, and they germinated with the rainwater. The new shoots couldn't know that they would soon be carted away with the wall debris and all their efforts would be fruitless. They wouldn't even reach six inches in height before they'd be dead.

What a will to live those shoots had, and they were only a lowly form of life! My thoughts naturally drifted from the shoots to us. Wufu was still annoyed and had gone to bed. It was Eight who found the chess pieces in the sludge in the lane. He was angry, swearing at Wufu for leaving the game and at Goolies for changing his mind about his moves. Then he swore at the rain, and at this city where the rich could go off to their karaoke and their ten-pin bowling on a rainy day, and we had nothing the fuck to eat. "The city government couldn't care less! The mayor says he's 'getting down to the grass roots' and 'sounding out popular opinion,' but he never comes here!"

Eight had a bellyful of grumbles. The good thing about corn shoots was that they never grumbled. They were seeds, they simply needed earth and water, and warmth, to put up shoots. Eight didn't hold a candle to them, none of us did.

My head teemed with thoughts: Like, if you had a fishpond with no fish, and no one ever put fry in, you just had to fill it with water for there to be fish within a couple of years. Where did they come from? And like, how did lice get into clothes? We'd learned about Darwin and evolution from our secondary school textbooks, but how did the fish in the pond and the lice in our clothes evolve so quickly? I couldn't figure it out. I wanted to get this stuff clear in my head, but I couldn't. I thought and thought till my head itched, so I stopped thinking. I gave it a good scratch, and a snowstorm of dandruff fell on my shoulders. I shouted to Wufu, because a bird with a red neck and a white tail I'd never seen before had landed in our tree. But Wufu didn't respond.

Almond did. "Everything gets wet in the rain. How come we all get so bad-tempered?" she said.

I just grunted. She had some of the old bricks in her arms and was laying them like stepping-stones in the muddy yard. She laid one brick, took a big step onto it, then laid another. With all that stooping, her straw rain hat had fallen off and her clothes were soaked. They clung to her body and showed off her big ass. She must have had eyes in her butt, because she said, "What are you gawking at? I'm laying these stepping-stones for everyone's benefit. You can help me by bringing some of the bricks down from upstairs."

"What are you doing this for? It's not like we have kids who are going to fall in the mud."

"Because if we don't, this yard'll just turn into a bog. When the weather clears, you make Wufu and Eight bring in some more rubble from outside and pave the whole yard. Come winter, they can rebuild the wall too. We've got the only yard in the alley without a wall."

I bent down and started to pull up the corn shoots.

"What are you doing that for?" Almond asked.

"What are they doing growing here?" I countered.

"They're not doing you any harm. Why can't you let seeds grow? And once we've built the walls up, we'll need a gate, so keep an eye out when you're trash picking."

I chuckled to myself.

"What's so funny?" she demanded.

"You've got it all planned out!"

"You're no different from Mr. Gules. How do you live without planning? Where would I be now if I didn't plan?" And so, as the rain came down, she taught me a lesson. Not how to be bad, the lesson that Han taught me. Almond taught me something different: she showed me how to live. She wasn't an educated woman, and she had no idea she had such a rich philosophy of life. But from then on, as I struggled through life in that city, it was her philosophy that got me through.

She told me that after her first husband died, she lost the will to live, that life had no meaning anymore. But though she got as far as looping a rope over the rafters, she didn't hang herself, and that was because of her old mother and her kids. Once she'd decided to go on living, she made a plan: within a year, she'd find another man to marry, and then the next year she'd clear half her debts. She made up her mind, and she went through with it. She married Goolies and moved him into her house, and they worked their socks off, making and selling bean curd and pulled noodles. They paid off half the debts that way. When two years were up, she made another plan, to clear the rest of the debt and rebuild the house within a year. Though it took two years, she'd done both. She was sold on the benefits of plans by then, and she made another one. Over the next year, she wanted to furnish the house and start saving to put the kids through college in five years' time. Within ten years, she planned to pull down their old house and build a modern apartment in their yard. Twenty years, and she'd open a business in the County Town. In thirty years' time, she'd move the business to Xi'an. She knew she'd be knocking on eighty's door in thirty years, but she kept revising and expanding her plans, even though that took her to one hundred and twenty years old.

Almond's eyes shone as she told me about her plans. "You must never think you're no good!" she said. "You always have more to do! My next-door neighbor, Wang, started out in the County Town with a job at the paper mill, but he lost his job when they went under. He thought he was a goner and, sure enough, three years after he came home, he upped and died. Then there was another guy in our village. He was a hulk of a man, strong enough to kill a tiger, but after he gave his dad a good funeral and built a house for his son and got him married, he told me he had nothing left to do. I knew what was going to happen. What was he going to live for if he had nothing to do? And sure enough, he kicked the bucket a year later."

I looked at Almond. I really liked the way she talked. "I . . . ," I began.

Almond interrupted me. "I know what you're going to say: You've got a pair of high-heeled shoes but no one to wear them, you haven't got a kid or a city residence card, you've got no money, and you haven't got a proper home here. You haven't made your mark yet, but your head's bursting with ideas, isn't it?" What with her gimlet stare and her sharp words, I felt like she'd cut right through my clothes and my skin and laid bare my heart, my liver, and my guts. I was a fine fellow, and Wufu and Eight looked up to me. Lively Shi did too, so why did I suddenly feel as if I'd become as transparent as glass with this woman?

"I . . . I," I began again.

"Am I right, or am I right? What are you thinking?" Almond demanded.

"I'm thinking I want to hug you!" I said. I wanted to take that back as soon as I'd said it. It seemed disrespectful, and my ears turned red.

But Almond said, "OK, but you can only hug my clothes."

She pulled me toward her, a little too suddenly and hard, and I banged my head on her breasts, lost my footing, and fell over. She cackled with laughter. "Mr. Gules, Mr. Gules!" she shouted. "Come and look at Happy Liu! What nerve he's got!"

28.

Wufu was pissed that he hadn't brought any ground-up persimmon and rice-husk mix with him. "Did you used to eat that at home?" he asked Eight.

"No," said Eight. "Our assholes are too delicate. That stuff stops you up."

"That's because you only make it with rice husks and persimmons, so of course you get stopped up," Wufu said. "The way we make it is much better. We mix barley with it."

They got into a squabble about the merits of their local recipes. "Why are you fighting about persimmons and rice husks?" Almond shouted up the steps. "If you're starving, you should feed on imaginary banquets! Why not dream of bread? Is starvation food the best you can do?" Almond had three pig tails and was sitting under the tree, scraping the bristles off in warm water. "Wufu, Wufu," she said, "are you really going hungry?"

"Who says I'm going hungry?" Wufu said. "I've just been to the butcher's to order a pig's head!"

"That's nice," Almond said. "Mind you pull all the hairs out before you cook it."

Wufu and Eight were so annoyed, they took their bowls into Wufu's room and ate there.

"It's all show," Wufu said. "When she's got only rice gruel, she stays in their room and won't come out. She's a trash picker, just like us. How's her life any better than ours?"

"She's got lots of tricks up her sleeve, that woman has," Eight said.

"What tricks?" Wufu asked.

"Didn't you see she's been getting up early these past few days? When we go to the Dengjiapo dump, she and Goolies go to the Ghost Market. The sellers are thieves. The stuff is all stolen—manhole covers, steel from building sites, you name it. She buys it cheap, then sells it to the depot. She's raking it in!"

"So we'll go too," Wufu said.

"They're a bunch of crooks, the lot of them. I don't know about you, but it's not for me," Eight said.

"But we're crooks too!" Wufu said. That was just bravado, of course.

Right after, he told me what Eight had said, and asked if I knew about the Ghost Market. Of course I knew about it. It was scattered along the Horse Passage, the ramp that led to the top of the city wall at East Gate, and was frequented by some very odd characters. The market used to deal in antiques and was held before dawn, so it got called the Ghost Market. Then the antiques business moved to Pagoda Street, but the old market, a place where stolen goods were fenced, kept the name. Once, when I was cycling by, I saw a gang fight—a fat man was being held down, and they were tearing his ear off. There was blood everywhere. It had never occurred to me to buy trash there. But Almond and Goolies had been around a long time and knew what was what. I sighed. No wonder they had pig tails for dinner.

"Can we go?" Wufu asked.

"Well, if there's really trash to pick, and if Almond and Goolies can go, then sure, we can go too."

"When you say that, I feel brave," said Wufu. He rubbed his hands in glee at the prospect.

"Look at you, getting all excited. You look like you're expecting the market street to be paved with gold."

"That's right," said Wufu. "But I'm playing it cool, and I'm not telling Almond, or Eight either."

We were up at the crack of dawn that day. Almond and Goolies hadn't opened their door yet. Inside the shit-house, we could hear a lot of huffing and puffing. Wufu said in a low voice, "Having trouble crapping, Eight?" Eight grunted. "Take your time then," Wufu said. We got on the bicycle, and he pedaled us into town.

At the depot, we retrieved our carts. Then we set off for the East Gate. On the way, Wufu bought four fried *youbing* cakes flavored with scallions. "We need a good breakfast," he said, sharing them equally, and we ate as we walked. He asked how much money I'd brought.

"Two hundred and sixty."

"That won't be enough! What will we do if we find more trash?"

He patted his pocket and told me he'd brought three hundred and ten.

"Leave your pocket alone. You're telling all thieves that you've got money in there."

"Make sure you stick with me when I find stuff, OK?" Wufu said.

I told him firmly that when we got to the Ghost Market, we'd pick up whatever we could. If there was nothing for us there, then we'd just go. "Whatever you do, don't get mixed up with the people in the market! Keep your eyes peeled, and if anything's not right, we take off!" I warned him.

"Got it!" he said.

The street to the north of the Prosper Street intersection was all hair and beauty salons. It made me think of the wild monkeys in the mountains near Freshwind. One monkey would sit down, legs akimbo, to soak up the winter sun, and the next thing you knew, they'd all follow suit. It seemed like it was the same in the city: if the beauty salon at the top of the lane did well, then the whole lane quickly filled with beauty salons. The salons here all had one thing in common: each frosted glass door was half-open and a young woman sat in each doorway, her breasts bulging out from her tight top, one leg, clad in a high-heeled shoe, crossed high over the other and swinging to the rhythm of the music being played in the shop.

Wufu asked, "That salon you were talking about, is it the one at the top of the lane?"

"I'm not sure, there are so many of them," I lied. Of course I was sure. We started down Salon Street, and I found myself tensing up. I stopped eating my *youbing*. My palms were sweaty. Wufu swung his head around and examined every girl in every doorway to see if she was wearing shoes identical to my pair of high heels, but none of them were.

One of them smiled at Wufu. "Shampoo your hair, sir?"

"Shampoo?" asked Wufu.

"It feels good," said the girl.

"Why would I wash my hair when I'm on the street?" said Wufu. The girl bent her head and examined her fingernails. She had flowers painted on them.

I prodded Wufu in the back and continued down the street. When we got to the salon I was looking for, I licked my greasy lips clean, blinked, and pulled myself together. There were three women standing in the doorway, cleaning grime from the top of the door with brushes atop long poles dipped in water. Wufu looked down, and I tweaked his ear.

"I was only looking at their shoes!" he said.

"They're not like mine," I said.

"Did you look?" he asked, and went closer. None of the women had my shoes on. But then something unexpected happened.

A woman with dyed-red hair swiped the door so hard with her brush that she spattered dirty water all over our faces. I wiped my face, but Wufu didn't wipe his and the dirty water trickled down his nose.

"What do you think you're doing?" he said.

Red Hair giggled.

"And why are you laughing?" Wufu said.

"It was just a few drops of water," she said.

"It's dirty water."

"You're a trash picker. Why are you worried about a bit of dirt?"

That made me angry. "Are you saying all trash pickers are dirty?"

"I'm talking about him, not you," Red Hair said.

Now that I'd chimed in too, Wufu raised his voice. "It's not all right to talk about me either!"

As we argued, the salon owner ("boss," the girls called her) came out of the shop. She had very long, stained teeth—real wolf fangs. She told Wufu to wipe his face clean, but he wouldn't. "Are you trying to start a fight?" she said. "Because if you are, I'm calling the police."

"Start a fight? I'm not starting a fight," Wufu said.

"That's because you wouldn't know how to! So you want compensation then?"

"What do you think?" Wufu said.

"Well, I'm not giving you a cent, so you can forget about it," the woman said.

"You mean I just have to put up with it?" Wufu said. "Let me splash her back then!" He reached for the dirty water bucket, but I stopped him.

"Don't you dare!" the woman said. "OK, if you're trash pickers, you can collect some trash. There are two door frames and three window frames upstairs, aluminum alloy. You can have them cheap. Is that good enough?"

"That's fine," Wufu said. But she meant me. She wasn't letting Wufu in. Wufu couldn't believe his ears.

I pulled Wufu to one side and told him we were very lucky to get two door frames and three window frames, that we'd split the money

evenly. I'd fetch them, and he'd go on to the Ghost Market on his own.
All his bravado vanished at that. "On my own?"

"You'll be fine," I reassured him.

He set off with his cart, muttering, "Wolf fangs!"

I ran after him. "Don't forget what I warned you about!"

"Uh-huh," Wufu said, and cursed again. "Wolf fangs!"

It's weird the way things pan out: when we'd first set off for the
Ghost Market, we should have taken another route, but Wufu insisted
on buying the *youbing*, so we ended up going down Salon Street.
Whenever I'd passed before, I'd just glanced in, I'd never stopped, but
today we stopped, because those girls splashed our faces with dirty
water. Then, Wufu should have been the one to get the frames, but the
salon boss picked me instead. Thinking back, I couldn't help but be
amazed how things had turned out so beautifully.

So now I was going into the salon. I'd put my left foot over the
threshold and my right foot was following, when to my alarm, I saw
another Happy Liu coming toward me. Then I realized there was a large
mirror mounted on the opposite wall. By the mirror were three revolving shampooing chairs, with two girls standing behind them. The girls
were nothing special to look at, and they weren't wearing my high heels
either. Maybe I'd got the wrong salon, or maybe she'd left. My heart
sank, and I simply stood there stupidly. "This way," said the owner. I
followed her. Behind the mirror were some stairs. The owner shouted
up the stairs. "Number three! Number three!" I didn't understand why
she was shouting "number three," but then she said to me, "Go on up."
I was surprised that a beauty salon like this had such narrow, steep stairs.
I tried my best to tread softly, but my feet echoed on the boards. There
were around twenty stairs, and you couldn't look up. You had to keep
your eyes trained on them, ten . . . thirteen, fourteen, fifteen, and suddenly I saw a pair of feet in front of me, wearing the exact same style of
high heels as I had at home! I looked up then, to see a woman standing
at the top of the stairs.

The woman smiled at me but said nothing. I stood on the fifteenth step, the toes of her shoes almost touching my forehead because the staircase was so steep. I was scared out of my wits.

When you want something really badly, you imagine every detail, every lovely word that you want to say, ever so calmly, but when the occasion suddenly presents itself, it throws you into a complete panic. I started to sway and almost fell backward.

"Careful," the woman said. "These stairs are steep." She smiled and I smiled back, I don't know why. I stood there, beads of sweat breaking out on my face and head. "Come up," she said. She was about five foot six, long-necked and slender but with broad shoulders, and she was wearing a very revealing yellow top. She had prominent collarbones that seemed to go straight into each shoulder. I shot her a quick glance, then hurriedly looked down. Her pants were black, like her leather shoes.

"Come with me," the woman said. Her voice was low, and she spoke standard Chinese with an accent that softened it, though I couldn't work out where she was from. I followed her. She smelled nice and I breathed in, my nose twitching. It wasn't the usual sharp women's perfume, it was the smell of fresh grass at first light, the kind that lingers on your hands, the smell of a fresh steamed bun when you pull it apart. The corridor upstairs was dark and narrow, lined with doors, each with a curtain hanging in front. The lightbulbs were very dim. We passed three doors before my eyes adjusted and I could see where I was going. I began to relax a bit, and I ran my fingers through my hair and straightened my collar. I felt rather warm, so I wiped the corners of my eyes. Her butt wasn't big, but it stuck out and she walked slightly pigeon-toed. By now, I was absolutely sure that this was the woman I'd seen the first time at the door of the beauty salon, and also the one I'd seen carrying a plastic bucket.

Without looking round at me, she asked politely, "Are you a migrant worker?" How did she know? I wondered, puzzled at how she guessed when I was wearing a suit and leather shoes!

"Yes, I'm a migrant worker," I said.

"Me too." Most pretty women were cold as ice, but she sounded so pleasant, I relaxed completely. I felt quite excited, and my brain started whirring as I tried to speak without my Freshwind accent.

"What's it like working here?" I inquired. "Is business good? Why is the whole street beauty salons?" She answered all my questions, though a bit vaguely.

Emboldened, I said, "May I ask your surname?"

"Meng."

"The same Meng as in Mencius's name?"

"Yes. And it's the same Meng as Lady Meng Jiang who cried the Great Wall down."

She obviously liked the grieving widow better.

We turned a corner and passed another four doors. This salon certainly had a lot of rooms. *Did it double as a hotel?* I wondered. Curious, I lifted one of the curtains as we passed. The door was open, though it was too dark to see inside. I heard a man exclaim, "Hey! Hey!" and a woman's voice, "Horrible man!" I was startled, but Ms. Meng pulled me away and we went to the farthest room. Inside, it was completely empty, except for a bed, and a bathroom in the corner. "There's running water in there. You can take a shower," she said.

"Take a shower?"

"You have to take a shower."

"There's no point," I said. "If I'm moving door and window frames, I'll sweat."

She was taken aback. "So, you're not . . . not a client?"

"Why would your boss let a trash picker in as a client?" I said.

Ms. Meng laughed so hard, her eyes almost disappeared into her sockets, a joyous, slightly silly laugh. She leaned against the bathroom door. "I sure got that wrong!" And she laughed again. I was wondering what it was she'd got wrong, when I heard a groan from next door, and a rhythmic knocking sound from the bed frame. It suddenly dawned on me what kind of a place I'd come to and what she thought I'd come to her room to do.

I felt like such a fool. How could I have been such a fool? I turned on my heel to go, and her laugh stopped abruptly. I ignored her and clattered down the corridor, turned the corner, and bumped my head on the wall. I didn't stop to rub it but simply stomped on. When I got to the top of the stairs, I patted the dust off my suit. There wasn't any dust on it, but I patted it anyway. I wanted to clear my head. Just then, I saw an open door to the left. It led to a balcony where there was a pile of window and door frames. I went out and lifted up one of them. It was covered in dust, and cobwebs stuck to my face.

Ms. Meng appeared behind me, looking embarrassed. "I thought, I . . ."

I didn't say anything because I was busy shifting the frames to the top of the stairs. But the stairs were too narrow for me to get them down.

"Hold them sideways, then they'll go down," she said. She tried to give me a hand, but the door frame jerked forward and one of her shoes tumbled down the stairs. I got it for her. It was identical in style to the pair I had. I gripped it, looked up at her, my nostrils flaring, then I passed the shoe up to her.

She met my gaze. Her eyes shone, but differently from before, a bit like a frightened cat now. In that instant, I felt terribly sorry for her, but what could I say? I'd had so many beautiful illusions about this woman, and she turned out to be a prostitute. What a blow, what a heavy blow! Once I'd moved the frames outside, I settled with the owner, ninety-eight yuan. I gave her a one-hundred-yuan note and waited for my change.

"Are you really waiting for two yuan?" she asked.

"That's what you owe me," I insisted. She dug around in her pocket and brought out a two-yuan note. "Put it in the cart," I said, and turned to go. The note blew away when I reached the top of the lane.

29.

I didn't head for the Ghost Market, or for Scrawny's depot to sell the frames, but simply wandered around with my cart. Down one lane, up another. Someone shouted, "Trash Picker, come pick up this trash!" I ignored him, and he shouted angrily, "If you're not picking up trash, are you out on patrol or something?"

I saw myself plodding along. I heard myself muttering, "Oh, Ms. Meng, I don't care that you're a hooker, but why did you have to bump into me? You must have another pair of shoes. Why, oh why, did you have to wear these high heels today?" As I reached the top of the lane, two kids on Rollerblades suddenly appeared. They hadn't seen me, and there was no way they could stop in time. They ran right into me. I staggered, kept my footing, but the Happy Liu in front of me disappeared. I saw the sign for Prosper Street Lane Two. How had I got all the way back here? I leaned against the street sign, and it crossed my mind that in the old days, when someone was condemned to death, the police made the family pay for the bullet. Was I one of those condemned men? This was cruel, too cruel! A street vendor was selling Xi'an steamed rice cakes, shouting, "Rice cakes! Rice cakes!" A little dog—someone's pet?—trotted by and stopped to look at me.

"Come!" I called it. I wanted to talk to it, but it just came over, cocked its leg, and pissed right in front of me. I felt like swearing at it but swallowed my words. Then I spotted Wufu pulling his cart down the lane. "Wufu! Wufu!"

Wufu saw me but was slow to react. Another look, and he came closer, scowling. "Why are you playing with dogs here? Why didn't you go to the Ghost Market?"

"Shut up, let's go!" I said. Wufu looked at me uncertainly. He followed me, but he hadn't gone twenty paces when he suddenly burst into tears.

This was certainly not a good day for us. Wufu told me about the Ghost Market. Like people said, it sold all sorts of stuff. He'd stopped his cart by a stall when someone offered him a bag of copper piping. Of course he said yes and paid his money, figuring that just that one bag would make him more money than a whole cartload of old newspapers. He pulled his cart away but hadn't got far when a fierce-looking guy ran up behind him shouting, "That copper piping comes from our factory. Where did you get it from? You must have swiped it!"

"I didn't swipe it!" protested Wufu. "I'm not that brave! And even if I was, I wouldn't know where to get it from." He told the guy the truth—that he bought it from someone in the Ghost Market—but the guy wouldn't listen.

He seized Wufu by the collar. "You're dealing in stolen state property, and you're not working alone! How many accomplices have you got? Tell me! Who does the scouting, who steals, who sells, how many times have you done it, how much have you cleared overall, how many times have you raped a woman, and how many did you kill?"

Wufu was struck dumb with terror. Then he fell to his knees and swore blind that he didn't know the person who'd sold him the tubing, he didn't have any cronies, he was on his own. "I didn't mention you!" he told me.

"Well, I had nothing to do with it! What happened then?"

"I told him I was on my own, from Shangzhou, just got here, never been anywhere else in Xi'an apart from my patch on Prosper Street and the Ghost Market. The man whacked me across the face, and I lost a tooth. I bent down to find it, and the man trod on it. He said, 'From Shangzhou, eh? Two-thirds of the criminals operating in this city are Shangzhou migrant workers. The city government has a special unit for beating up criminals from Shangzhou.' Do you think there's really a special unit for beating us up?"

"No, we're not criminals."

"He stamped hard on my tooth and scraped it into the ground! He asked me, 'Want your tooth back? If you go to the police station, you'll be looking for your leg as well!' He twisted my arm, but I didn't lay into him. I felt guilty, because I knew the tubing really had come from a factory. But I didn't give in easily either. When he tried to twist my arm behind my back, my arm didn't bend. I made it as stiff as an iron rod. But then he jabbed me in the armpit, and I'm ticklish so I couldn't stand it, and he bent my arm behind my back. I tried to beg him, but the only thing I could think of to say was what I remembered from movies as a kid: 'I've got a baby at home and an eighty-year-old mother!'"

Wufu said the guy relented then and told him, "Cough up three hundred yuan and I'll turn a blind eye just this once and won't stand up for what's right and proper. I won't put public interests before private interests!"

Wufu had only brought three hundred, and he'd already spent two hundred on the tubing. Luckily he'd stuck half the remaining one hundred in his undershorts, so he took fifty out of his jacket pocket and said, "I've only got this, you can search me!" So the guy did, poking his pants crotch too. "That's not a wallet," said Wufu hurriedly.

"But you could commit a crime with that!" said the man. Wufu watched as the man, his fancy checkered jacket flapping and blowing behind him, walked away with Wufu's fifty yuan and his copper tubing. And then he saw he'd been tricked. Someone popped out from behind a phone booth—it was the very man who'd sold him the copper. When the pair saw him looking at them, they made faces and waved. "Bye!" Then they were off.

Wufu was a sorry sight, his face all creased from crying, one of his blackened teeth missing. "I don't deserve this, Happy!" he wailed. "I've done nothing wrong! Why's this happened to me?"

I was sorry that Wufu had lost two hundred and fifty yuan, but what was two hundred and fifty yuan compared to the catastrophe that had befallen me? Besides, now he'd gotten it off his chest, he felt better, but I had no one to tell my story to. I tried to comfort him. "Stop crying. You're lucky he didn't try to kill you. Have you had lunch?" I dug three yuan out of my pocket so he could get himself a bowl of noodles.

Still sniffing, Wufu said he'd already had a bowl of noodles. "Wipe your tears, and don't tell anyone, all right?" I said. Wufu nodded.

It was blowing hard, and the city streets had turned into wind tunnels, like mountain valleys. Wufu and I set off, pulling our carts side by side without speaking. The wind followed along after us, sometimes blowing the leaves into piles, whipping around our legs, or dropping to nothing, pestering us like a naughty child. Wufu's cart rattled and banged horribly. "You should get another cart, Wufu," I said.

"It was because of that cart that I was screwed over today," said Wufu. "If I'd had a cart with rubber tires, I could have outrun that guy."

"Scrawny's got a three-wheeler he wants to move."

"Scrawny already asked me, but he wants three hundred for it and that's too much. He's not going to rip me off like that!" said Wufu.

"Well, I'll buy it then," I said. "He can rip me off." As soon as the words left my mouth, I felt like I'd said something wrong. "Anyway, I want it, and you can have this one," I hurried on.

"You're giving it to me?" Wufu asked. "I don't have any money to pay you."

"I don't want your money," I said. "And you're due half on these old frames."

Wufu seemed to cheer up considerably at that. "When he groped my pants crotch, why did he say I could commit a crime with that? What did he mean?"

"He meant you could rape a woman with your cock," I said.

"Motherfucker!" Wufu swore, furious. "He can leave my cock out of this. He's a son of a bitch, son of a nun, son of a hooker!"

The mention of hookers plunged me into misery again. I lit up a smoke and took a deep drag. "Have you seen any hookers?" I asked him.

"Nope."

But I couldn't be bothered to tell him my story.

From the doorway of a coffee bar across the way came gales of laughter, from half a dozen young women, all tall with shoulder-length hair and dressed in skinny jeans that made their butts stick out. If you saw one woman standing there like that, you'd just take a look, see if she was pretty, and that would be that. But half a dozen together were like a bundle of firecrackers, and all the passersby stopped in their tracks and gawked.

"What kind of a woman works as a hooker?" Wufu asked.

I looked at the women, and Wufu followed my gaze, then couldn't drag his eyes away. "Keep your eyes to yourself," I said.

Wufu asked, "Are there any hookers there? Point them out to me!"

I found myself blurting out, "There are some in the beauty salon!"

Wufu was taken aback, then looked at me oddly. "In the beauty salon? Did you get a leg over when you were picking up the frames then?"

30.

Two days later, I bought Scrawny's old three-wheeler and let Wufu have my cart. "I've exchanged an air gun for a machine gun!" said Wufu. He did a bunch of repairs on it, then bound the handles with a length of plastic-coated wire he'd picked up. In the seventies and eighties, back in Freshwind, when folks bought bicycles, they wound cable wire around the handlebars. Now here was Wufu, acting like a yokel and doing the same thing. I couldn't let him do that.

"No one notices if you're ugly. But as soon as you try and beautify yourself, you draw attention to your ugly mug!"

So Wufu took off the wire, but he hung a bag over the handles, for his folded paper wallet, his tobacco pouch, a face towel, and some *ganmo* for lunch.

Wufu and I raced his cart against my three-wheeler. Out of three tries, he won twice.

When Wufu was happy, he could act really silly. Like, he'd stick his finger in his butt as he farted, then push his finger under Eight's nose and make him smell it. Or he'd stick scallions up Eight's nostrils when he was asleep. He tried to tell me jokes, but he'd start laughing uncontrollably before he'd even started, and when he finally finished, I couldn't see what was so funny, and neither could Eight and Almond. Or he'd painstakingly tell me a joke and say, "Funny, eh?"

"Sure, it's funny," I said. "But I was the one who told you the joke in the first place."

That'd shut him up for a bit, but then he'd laugh and ask me when I was going to take him to the salon to see hookers. That shut me up. He kept nagging me, and the more I ignored him, the more he was convinced that I'd had a hooker. "I don't mind. I've got a missus, but it's time you got laid."

Was that his way of being sympathetic? I was useless with women. I found one in Freshwind, but she wouldn't have me. I looked for one in town, and all I could find was a hooker. *I'm an object of pity, even to Wufu* . . . And I hawked and spat. The gobbet of phlegm hit the wall like a bullet.

I wouldn't go to the salon again. I made sure to go a roundabout way whenever I went to the depot, and I avoided Salon Street altogether.

But ever since I'd met Ms. Meng in the salon, the vision of her seemed to haunt me, and it was driving me frantic. I couldn't drive her away. In the play *The Romance of the Western Chamber*, the young scholar Zhang Sheng is in mortal danger of pining away for love of Yingying. No matter how hard he tries otherwise, he thinks about her all the time. I used to laugh my head off at this hopeless man whenever I went to the County Town to see the play, but what was I now but another Zhang Sheng? As soon as I got back to my room and set eyes on those high heels up on the shelf, I saw Ms. Meng's face, her lithe movements, the way the tip of her tongue flickered between her teeth when she laughed. I took the shoes down, wrapped them in old newspaper, and stuffed them under the bed, but still, the first thing I thought about when I woke up in the morning was Ms. Meng! What the hell! If all the women in the world died, the only one I would miss was a prostitute! I must be sick in the head.

One morning, I went and sat on the steps for a while. I heard a clattering coming from the next-door yard. Whatever was going on? Did the neighbors have wooden floorboards? It was the same click-clack noise that Ms. Meng's shoes made as she walked along the corridor. When her shoe had fallen down the stairs, I'd seen that she wasn't wearing socks, and I saw her toenails were painted silver gray. I coughed to drive the thought from my head. Down below, Almond was sweeping our yard. There was a lot of swearing: Who'd eaten the daikon she'd left on the edge of the tub? Why was she the only person who ever swept the yard? She swept until she got to Eight's cookhouse. His stove was made of mud bricks, with a wok perched on top. He hadn't washed it after his meal of the day before. He never did until it was time to make the next meal. We all did that. But when she discovered two half-burned ox bones inside Eight's cooker, she started swearing again.

"You've been burning ox bones, Eight! I said the place stank to high heaven last night. It was like someone had croaked! Have you been collecting ox bones instead of firewood?" Then she shouted, "Happy Liu! Happy Liu!"

I didn't answer Almond, so she came upstairs. "Aren't you awake yet?"

"Hi, Almond," I said.

She sniggered and tweaked my chin. "You've been staring into space. Are you hankering after your missus?"

"I haven't got one," I told her again.

"I know that," she said. "A mouth that's never tasted meat doesn't miss it. Then once you've had it, you never stop thinking about it. Do you know Eight hasn't gone home once in a whole year? When he came, his face was purple, but now it's yellow!"

"Purple, yellow, what difference does it make?" I said.

"Well, at the start, he missed his missus so much, his face went purple with holding it in. But now it's gone yellow, and you know why? Every few days, he's at the dance hall in the street behind the Town God Temple. From what I've heard, the customers are all migrant workers or men who've lost their jobs. It costs five yuan to get in, and you get a piece of paper and a bottle of mineral water for that. The place is heaving with dancers, hundreds of them, and then they put the lights out and all sorts of stuff goes on, groping, kissing, cuddling, and sex. The women give the men quick hand jobs, wash it off with the mineral water, slap the paper on, and away they go! When the lights go up, you have to watch you don't slip on the gunk all over the floor, or so I've heard!"

Wufu came running out of his shed, half his face creased from pressing on the bed mat. "Is that right?"

"I was talking to Happy, not to you!" Almond snapped.

"You just think Happy's better-looking."

"Well, he is, so what?"

Wufu swore.

"Why won't you accept it?" said Almond, but Wufu ignored her and shouted for Eight.

Almond slapped her forehead. "Damn, I was calling you because of Eight. How did I get sidetracked? Do something about Eight burning these bones!"

"Maybe he was out of firewood," I said.

"Out of firewood, so he burned bones instead!" Almond was incredulous. "So if you were out of food, you'd eat human flesh?"

"Well, you've told him off. He won't do it again," I said.

"He'd better not!" Then she suddenly added, "What were you saying just now, Happy? Did you say you thought of someone as soon as you opened your eyes? A woman, right? I've had that, you know. When I was crazy in love with my husband, the one that's passed on, I thought of him before I went to sleep, I dreamed about him, and thought about him as soon as I woke up."

"Am I in love?" I said. If this was really love, then had I fallen in love with a hooker? A hooker! I knew perfectly well she was a hooker. Why did I go and fall in love? My breath was coming hard and fast, and my face burned at the thought.

Almond looked at me, eyes narrowed, lips pressed together so her mouth curved like a pea pod. "So you really have fallen in love! Who is it? Who's the fox spirit?" She didn't sound too happy, and I didn't dare look at her. She sighed, and her voice softened. "Well, you can't help being in love, and you can't hide it from me either. But all the little demons and spirits want their pound of flesh from the saintly monk Xuanzang, don't they? Bring her over here, and if she's OK, I'll give you advice. I've got sharp eyes. I can tell a good'un from a bad'un right away!"

"I was only joking!" I protested.

I wanted to stop her chatter, so I started washing the pot and preparing our food. As the fire got going, I thought, *If the fire laughs, then Almond's knocked the nail on the head.* No sooner had the thought flashed through my mind than the fire whooshed and crackled, and Wufu said, "The fire's laughing. We'll have good pickings today!" I shivered, looked into the flames, and said nothing. Next I thought, *If the fire laughs again, it means Ms. Meng isn't really a prostitute. If it doesn't laugh, then she is one.* I waited. The fire didn't laugh. I blew at the flames, and the rice porridge boiled over. I wiped it up, and the fire whooshed and laughed again. A weight fell from my shoulders. Then I began to think back over everything I'd seen and heard at the salon. The people sleeping upstairs must be the shop workers, mustn't they? If people really had been doing it, wouldn't they have shut the door? The next-door bed creaking, that was her giving him a massage, wasn't it? When Ms. Meng told me to wash myself, maybe it was just that I was sweaty. When she started to say, "I thought you were . . . ," she must have meant, *here for a massage.* A massage was nothing. She had looked embarrassed and tried to explain, but a hooker wouldn't do that! How could such a lovely, kind woman be a hooker? Ms. Meng wasn't!

I ate a big breakfast. As Wufu pedaled us to Prosper Street, I blabbed on about all the goings-on in the city. Wufu was impressed that I knew so much.

"You should read the newspapers. You pick up old newspapers all day long. Why don't you read them?" I said.

"Why would a trash picker do that?" said Wufu. "Just the sight of the newsprint gives me a headache. It doesn't matter how many times I read the same word, I keep forgetting it." Suddenly he piped up again. "Almond said Eight's been to the dance hall behind Town God Temple . . . Is that what really happens there?"

"How come you're bringing that up all of a sudden? D'you want to go?"

"Just asking," said Wufu. "You go to the salon, so why shouldn't I ask about the dance hall?"

"Bullshit!" I yelled angrily.

Wufu said nothing more. I was about to suggest going by Salon Street on our way to the depot, but I was too embarrassed now, so we took the usual route. It was getting hotter by the day, and more and more women in the street were in T-shirts and skirts. Spring lasted no time at all in Xi'an.

Wufu and I went our separate ways, and several times I was tempted to go to Salon Street, but I kept finding myself turning back. I had no excuse to go there, and if I saw her, what would I say? Besides, I wasn't wearing my suit today, and I certainly hadn't taken a shower. Between Lane Nine and Lane Ten, where Prosper Street bends, a young couple strolled by, their arms wrapped round each other. The girl's hair was permed and looked like a Pekinese dog. The boy was pale, and he wore a flowery shirt that was a bit girlie for a man. They must have seen me, but they kept on groping each other's butts as they passed. That annoyed me. Did they think they could get away with doing whatever they liked just because I was a trash picker? I looked at the boy again. A proper man was one who was the polar opposite of a woman, but this guy didn't look masculine at all. With his slicked-down hair and powder-smooth skin, he was simply a pretty face, all talk and no action. As for the girl, she didn't hold a candle to Ms. Meng. Her calves were short and the muscles bulged. She wasn't even worthy to pick up Ms. Meng's shoe! I held my back straight and my head high. They were in love, but I was in love too. I, a trash picker, had fallen in love with a city woman. As a humble worshipper, I had dared to fall in love with a bodhisattva!

I was Happy Liu and indeed, how happy I was. So happy but with no one to tell, so I took out my flute and began to play.

31.

This time I was playing for myself, but there were lots of people around. City folk were always drawn to any kind of goings-on, more so than country folk. I liked it when lots of people gathered around to listen. I forgot where I was or what time it was, and I played on and on, and sometimes I'd look someone in the eye and they'd smile back, and then, to my astonishment, I saw a face I knew. It was Ms. Meng!

It really was her. My playing came to an abrupt halt. She had been passing by in a car and stopped to see what was going on. One long leg extended through the open car door, and I saw her flick back the hair that had fallen over her face. She must be a little shortsighted, because she came closer, eyes narrowed. Were lots of pretty women shortsighted, or was that just the proud way they walked, head held high and eyes narrowed? She stood at the back of the crowd, a crane amongst chickens, and when she realized that it was me playing, she exclaimed in surprise and put her hand to her mouth. Our eyes met. If we'd been in a martial arts film, there would have been cymbals clashing and sparks flying.

How I'd suffered, missing her, but now that she was here, it all seemed so easy. I was rather warm and twisted my neck inside my collar. There were cars coming and going behind her; the traffic never stopped in this city, streaming by like an unending river, but Ms. Meng stayed right where she was. The crowds began to heckle me. "Go on! Play! Why have you stopped?" I blew another note and held it for a long time, as if I could draw her to me with it. But someone lowered the car window, and a man stuck his head out. "What are you looking at? It's just a busker!"

Just a busker? I was furious. Who was he? Her boyfriend? Why would she work in the salon if she had a boyfriend with a fancy car like that? How did she get the car to stop in the first place? Was she now going to get back in the car and leave? I took a quick guess at what would happen, and I was right: she headed back toward the car, said something to the man, and the car turned and drove away. As it did so, I suddenly realized that the driver was the man who'd dropped his wallet! I shouted, but not at him. "Ms. Meng!"

She stood at the curb, watching as I pushed my way through the crowds and hurried toward her. She seemed rooted to the spot. When I told Wufu about it afterward, he said I must be making it up. But truth is often stranger than fiction. Yichun and I stood face-to-face at the curb. Imagine the scene: a beautiful, smart young woman and a trash picker standing together, talking as if they were old friends. Passersby thronged around us, gawking as eagerly as if watching a movie. *Go on, get an eyeful, why don't you?* I stuck my flute back in my collar and waved them away. And I was suddenly in a panic. This meeting was so unexpected, I couldn't think of a thing to say. All I could do was smile foolishly. Even to me, my smile seemed fake.

"You've been picking trash?" she asked.

"Yes, I'm a trash picker."

As soon as she spoke, I relaxed, but my words seemed to embarrass her. Why had I said that, as if I was talking to Wufu or Eight? She seemed at a loss for what to say, and began to blush. She reached for my flute, then let her hand drop. "You play so well!" she said.

"Play so well for a trash picker, you mean?"

"You think too much."

"You mean, for a trash picker?"

"I don't look down on trash pickers."

"Really?"

I wished I didn't sound so weird, but I was really excited. The jeans she was wearing made her butt look full and firm, and her legs even longer than normal.

"Really?" I repeated. She looked uncertain and took an involuntary step back. But instead of backing against the parasol sapling, she missed it and landed on the ground with a cry of pain. Her face was covered in sweat, and tears were welling up. Had she twisted her ankle? She was still wearing those high-heeled shoes! I fell to my knees and started to rub her ankle. It was so fiery hot, I hardly dared touch it.

"Take it off, take off my shoe," she said. I took it off and held it as her ankle swelled in front of my eyes.

"This was all my fault," I said, my cockiness all gone.

"No, it's the shoes' fault. The heels are too high," she said.

I helped her up, but she couldn't stand, and as soon as I let go, she sat down again.

She needed to go to the hospital. But if I called her a taxi, and she couldn't put any weight on her foot, how would she get into the hospital and to the reception desk and the treatment room? If I went with her, what would I do with my three-wheeler? There was a saying back in Freshwind: Carelessness makes things go wrong, and a careless dog is a tiger's meal. I'd gotten carried away; it was my cockiness that'd made this happen! "Can you sit on the back of the three-wheeler, and I'll take you to the hospital?" I said. She nodded, breathing hard from the pain.

This was the first time I had taken anyone else on the three-wheeler, and a woman I liked, at that. Surely lots of things were going to happen between Ms. Meng and me, because both times we'd met, it was trash picking that brought us together. I wanted to put my arms around her to help her in, but I hesitated. Would she let me? The cart was messy and dirty, full of old newspapers and plastic cement bags. I couldn't put a pretty woman in there, could I? I pulled out all the trash and piled it against the wall, then spread out my jacket and helped her onto it.

The street was lined with lilac trees clad in dark red foliage. Beneath them, blades of grass, a hand's span high, glinted brightly as the breeze caressed them. There was a single small flower too.

"Are you comfortable?" I asked.

"Yes."

Wearing only my vest, I trod on the pedals and sped off down a side street. It was crowded as usual, and I had to keep ringing the bicycle bell. Bystanders swore as they got out of the way, then fell silent as they saw someone lying in the cart, apparently sick. Then they saw it was a woman, and a pretty one at that. What on earth was she doing, lying in a trash picker's cart? The abuse started up again, and this time it was worse. "What the fuck? Is this his way of getting off with a woman?" Well, yes it was. Heaven had sent me this chance, and I was taking it. With my unparalleled cycling skills, I twisted and turned through the crowded streets, cheerfully diving down one lane, then another, to the accompaniment of shouts and curses.

"Don't tire yourself out," Ms. Meng said from behind me. My back began to itch like crazy, as if someone was tickling me with a barley bristle. I could feel her eyes on my back, my skinny, sunburned back. I turned around and saw that her head was resting painfully against the cart side. I knew it wasn't just the pain that was making her rest her head against the cart side. I realized she was trying to keep her head down, out of sight. I pedaled as hard as I could, thinking, *It was my fault. It was because of me that she twisted her ankle.* But I also thought, *If she hadn't sprained her ankle, I wouldn't be taking her to the hospital.*

I was ashamed at that, and I looked around. "Is it very painful?"

"Do you think I've broken it?" she said.

"No, I don't think so. Careful not to get your hair trapped in the wheels." After two more lanes, I was panting in exhaustion.

"Have a rest," she said. But I wouldn't, I just pedaled harder. She wiped the sweat from my back with her handkerchief. Had she seen the scar on my left side? I almost stopped so I could pull my pants up over the scar. The chain slipped then, after a minute, I put my foot down again. Faster, faster, the beads of sweat flew off my brow.

We got to the hospital, and I helped her into the emergency room, then into the X-ray room. Happily, no bones were broken, it was only a sprain. The doctor gave her painkillers and spent a long time rubbing in safflower cream. She still needed help walking, but it was less painful now.

We left the hospital, and she thanked me, which embarrassed me.

"I still don't know your name."

"Happy Liu."

As everyone else did, she said, "What a great name!"

"Not so great—it didn't bring you happiness, it brought you pain."

"It's because I'm tall, and I've got small feet, and I was wearing high heels. I'm always falling over. I've twisted that ankle twice already." She couldn't get the shoe on again because her ankle was swollen, and she knocked it in frustration against the side of the three-wheeler.

"They're very pretty shoes," I said.

"Men like women in heels, but . . ." She stopped. I didn't know what to say either. She was looking better now, and she took out a little hand mirror to powder her face, lips pursed. She saw me staring at her. "You think I'm vain?"

That started me gabbing again. If I was with a woman who wasn't saying anything, I'd keep quiet too, but the minute she spoke, I couldn't help myself. Words came tumbling out. "I bet you've never ridden on a three-wheeler."

"They're good. I get carsick in cars."

"You're just trying to stop me from feeling bad. That man who was driving you just now . . ."

"He wasn't driving me! I was getting a free ride."

"Quite a guy!"

"He's a businessman."

"The villas off Qing Song Road are full of them."

"That's right, that's where we were coming from."

"Really? Not long ago, he lost his wallet with his passport and keys."

"I think he mentioned it."

"Uh-huh."

"You know each other?"

"Has he had a kidney transplant?"

"I don't know."

"I'm sure he has!"

That was confirmation! That was the man who lost his wallet, and the man who lost his wallet was my alter ego, the man I was looking for. I punched the air in my excitement.

"What's up with you?" she said. I looked at her but didn't answer. *I'm sorry, there's no way I can explain it to you. I couldn't even explain it to the man if I met him.*

I threw another punch, this time at the side of the cart.

"Are you angry?"

"I'm bad-tempered sometimes."

"You are. That day we met, I didn't have time to explain properly before you took off . . ."

I'd avoided talking about the salon, but if she raised the issue, then fine, it was further proof that I'd gotten the story wrong. How could she possibly be a hooker?

I smiled. "I'm really sorry, I mistook you for a hooker."

"But I am a hooker," said Ms. Meng.

I stood rooted to the spot. How could she be? Not her, it was impossible! How could a girl with such honest eyes be a hooker? Would a hooker say it up front, like that? She must be teasing me, like someone good-looking saying they were ugly, like me saying I was a peasant, which was something I'd never believed. I laughed out loud. "What a character you are!"

But she said it again. "No, I really am a hooker."

32.

Yichun really was a hooker. And she explained it to me quite calmly. She told me she didn't try and hide it anymore, but I was the first person she had actually said it to, because I'd acted friendly toward her, and it'd be good for both of us to be honest.

Just then we heard distant drumming from the Drum Tower. The evening sky began to fill with scattered reddish clouds, like rose petals. I didn't look up at the sky, and she sat quite still on the three-wheeler. Shrill sirens came from the end of the street, and the tide of humans and cars suddenly parted like a crack opening in the earth.

"Think about it. What was someone like me doing in a car like that? Well, the man's a regular client, someone I can rely on. He introduces me to other clients, then gives me rides to and from. Don't look at me like that. I need money. That's what we all come here for, but I need lots of it and I need it fast. What would I do otherwise? I can't be a trash picker like you. Every one of the hair and beauty salons on that lane is a brothel, and almost all the women who work there are hookers. Along with washing clients' hair and giving men a shave, they provide services like massage, foot-washing, and sex. The sex is divided into sex on-site and outside visits. In the salon, it's one hundred and fifty yuan. An outside visit is three hundred, or five hundred if you spend the night. I was going to give you a massage that day, but you left without asking me for anything. In two years, you're the only man who's turned me down. I felt so ashamed and pathetic. But it wasn't that I thought you were being noble. Every one of the men I've gone with has more money and status than you. I figured you left because you didn't have enough money to pay, right? I'm not making fun of you. It's just that after you'd gone, I felt sorry for myself, but I felt sorry for you too. Both of us, we're going through hard times, so I thought, maybe I can talk to you—that's why I called after you that day, and that's why I wanted to tell you everything today."

She told me there were hundreds of thousands of sex workers in the city, in dance halls, in saunas and massage parlors, in beauty salons. They all had false IDs, and all gave false addresses, names, and ages. But her last name really was Meng.

"My family name is Meng. My full name is Meng Yichun. I'm from Miyang County. I'm twenty-seven."

She told me it wasn't easy working in the sex trade. Everyone had their own reasons for doing it. "I had a boyfriend from Chengguan in Miyang County. He was called Li Jing. He loved me, but he was violent and a heavy drinker, so we split up. His way of being good to me was to ram a fried pancake down my throat when I'd had enough to eat. I couldn't take that, and I said I was leaving him. He was dead set against that. In fact, he threatened to kill me if I wouldn't marry him. I thought he just said that because he was angry, but every time he got drunk, he'd turn up, shouting and yelling at my home. I went to stay with an aunt for a few months in the neighboring county to get away from him, but he got drunk again and went to my family's home with a knife and said he'd come for his bride. My dad got into a fight with him. Then my big brother came home, grabbed a stick, and knocked him down, but he got the knife out and stabbed my brother in the chest, and killed him. It would have all ended there if he'd killed himself as well, but he went on the run, vanished without a trace. He has to pay for a crime like that. The police spent a month trying to track him down, but they never got him. There were no clues, the trail went cold, and they dropped the case.

"Miyang's a poor county, and the police are underfunded. If the suspects leave the county, and lots do, they can't pursue them, so they simply put the cases aside, but I couldn't let that happen. My mother died young. Then this business made my father ill, and six months later he was dead too. A month after that, someone told me that Li Jing had been spotted in Inner Mongolia. I begged the police to go after him, but they said I had to pay their tickets, board, and lodging. Where would I get money like that? But I was determined the case should be solved! So I came to Xi'an to get a job. I washed dishes in a restaurant, and worked as a housekeeper, but I only made enough to get by. Then I met the owner of the beauty salon, and when she heard my story, she badgered me till I agreed to work for her as a hooker.

"The money's good. Every time I've got ten thousand yuan saved up, I send it to the police back home. They already made one trip to Inner Mongolia and another to Ningxia, but they didn't catch Li Jing. So, I've kept earning money and sending it to them. They've been to the south part of Gansu, to Yunnan, to Wutai County in Shanxi, but they still haven't caught Li Jing. In fact, the trail's gone cold again. It went cold before, and it's gone cold again. But even if Li Jing's fled to the ends of the earth, he's going to pay with his life in the end, and I'll go on earning money. I don't work just in the salon. The businessman you saw has introduced me to his wealthy cronies. They've got plenty of women, but they want someone fresh, and now that they know about me, they pay me several times the going rate."

Meng Yichun told me absolutely everything. It made my belly churn like a washing machine, my guts bouncing around inside. When she'd finished, she smiled again, then pulled herself into a sitting position and started to get out of the three-wheeler.

"I don't think you'll want me to stay now." But I wasn't that kind of person! I insisted she let me pedal her back to the salon. She looked at me, and I looked at her, and I saw her lips were cracked. She'd been talking so much, they were white with spit. I wanted to buy her a bottle of mineral water, but I couldn't find a store nearby. There was a pedestrian bridge across the main road from us, and a small labor market. Before Yichun started speaking, I'd seen clusters of peasants, newly arrived from the countryside, sitting or standing around there. As the evening drew in, some of them signed up for jobs and left, while others drifted off in search of somewhere to stay the night. The only one left now was a girl with a dozen or so apples laid out on a cloth in front of her. I ran across the main road. The girl, an ugly little scrap of a thing, gazed up at me hopelessly.

"Where are your apples from?" I asked her.

"I'm looking for work," she said.

"You've brought apples to look for a job?"

"They're from my family's trees. I brought some with me."

"And you haven't found a job yet?"

"No one wants me."

"Are you selling the apples?"

"Yes, yes, then I can buy a bowl of noodles."

Yet another girl coming to town for work, only she hadn't found a buyer, either for herself or her apples. I only wanted one. I turned them over, one by one, but they were all small, and some were already rotting. I threw down five yuan, took an apple, and ran back across the main road. Yichun held the apple in her hand without eating it. I got on the three-wheeler, and we pedaled slowly off.

At the corner of Salon Street, she got out of the cart. She didn't want me to help her down, and she put her twisted ankle gingerly on the ground a few times. Finally she put her weight on it and said she could walk slowly on her own. I got out fifty yuan. It was all I had.

"What's this for? I never paid for the ride, and you're trying to pay me?"

"I'm not a big businessman. If I was, I'd give you fifty thousand or a hundred thousand to put toward your case."

"You might be a big businessman one day!" Yichun said. Suddenly her eyes filled with tears.

I'd only given Yichun the fifty yuan on impulse, and now that I saw her tears, I didn't know what to do. I patted all four pockets for more money but only found some small change. Her eyes were still on me, growing rounder and darker, and she blinked rapidly. *More tears to come,* I thought, but I didn't dare say anything in case I really set her off crying. At that moment, I was filled with happiness, because when I'd impulsively given her the money, it wasn't me looking down on her as a hooker, but feeling sincerely sorry for a human being even worse off than me. Then as her heavy lids closed and the tears spilled, I felt completely helpless.

I hurriedly pedaled off, like I was running away. I'd reached the end of the lane when Yichun called after me. "Happy! Happy!" Not Happy Liu, just Happy. I paused, and she hobbled after me. I thought she was going to give me the fifty back, or say something. Instead, she planted a kiss on my cheek! This was the last thing I expected, I actually turned my head away, and her big smacking kiss landed on my collar, where it left a lipstick mark.

Yichun *was* a hooker. Only a hooker would be bold enough to kiss me in the street. But that kiss was the best experience I'd ever had.

I thought, *I've never had a woman open her heart to me like this, and I've never been kissed. And now I've been kissed and confided in by the woman I've fallen in love with. I don't care whether Yichun loves me or is thanking me or repaying me, it's really boosted my morale. So Yichun's a hooker, but she was forced into it. She's sacrificed herself to accomplish something truly admirable. And I'm not exactly white as snow myself. I'm willing to buy stolen goods from the Ghost Market. I've gone collecting medical waste, haven't I? Who is white as snow in our world?*

223

Yichun was in no way a bad woman. She was pretty; in fact, she was gorgeous. So was I saying someone that gorgeous couldn't be bad? That's right. A house with nice proportions is built on firm foundations, catches the sun and the breeze, and is pleasant to live in. Only badly put-together buildings are damp, dark, and liable to fall down. Yichun wasn't bad, she was just in a bad place, that was all. Didn't lotus flowers grow from mud?

She and I were alike in a lot of ways. We'd been through hard times, but we were proud too. She saw plenty of fifty-yuan bills in her line of business, but when she'd accepted mine, it showed she accepted me. Now I had a woman I couldn't stop thinking about, and I'd go see her as often as I could. I headed back to Fishpond and tried to pull myself together. A person shouldn't talk about either their sufferings or their joys, but you had to be pretty remarkable to get yourself under control when something so good happened, and not let on about it.

It was evening, and time to get the fire going and put the water on, but Wufu just sat there, whittling away at the heels of an old pair of women's sandals with a kitchen knife. He was so clumsy, he'd never get them level.

"Haven't you made any dinner?" I asked.

"I'm doing these sandals for my missus. They'll be great with flat heels. We've still got *bingzi* cakes. We can soak them in water. They're enough to get by."

I didn't want to just get by on a day like today, and decided we'd have noodles. But when I went to make the dough, there was only half a bowlful of flour in the bag, only enough to boil it and drink it as porridge. On a day when I should have had a nice meal, this was even worse than usual. I decided I'd go for broke: I got out a ten-yuan note, gave it to Wufu, and told him to go to the shop and buy some eggs to poach. "Buy two, Wufu! No, four!"

But when Wufu got back, he was swearing and grumbling about the price of eggs going up. It used to be you could get two for one yuan, and now the shopkeeper charged three yuan for four eggs! He'd bought a small bag of potatoes instead. "Boiled potatoes are nicer than poached eggs!" he insisted.

When you boil potatoes in soup, you don't need to chop them after peeling them. You simply simmer them. Wufu kept taking the lid off the pan and jabbing the potatoes to see if they were done.

"Let them cook slowly. Are you really that hungry?" I said.

"I didn't feel hungry, but as soon as we started cooking, my belly started rumbling."

Wufu took off his jacket. I didn't, because I wanted him to spot the lipstick on my collar. He was so dumb, he never saw a thing. He just said, "Are you breeding maggots in there? Why don't you take your jacket off? You've given me a potato dinner. Let me wash your jacket for you."

"No, no, this jacket isn't going to get washed, never!" I stood facing sideways, so the lipstick mark was toward him, but he still didn't react.

"Let's only have two meals tomorrow. That way we can save a little," he began, then said angrily, "Dammit, other people eat meat, and we can't even afford noodles."

Downstairs, Almond was making mutton dumplings, and even Eight had some spareribs boiling. He kept taking the lid off the pot and tasting, waiting a bit, then tasting again, till eventually Almond got annoyed. "By the time they're done, there won't be any left to taste!"

I told Wufu that just because we didn't have much to eat tonight, that didn't mean we'd always eat badly. As soon as we got some money, we'd go to a decent restaurant and have squid, and sea cucumber, and abalone and shark's fin.

"I can't stand seafood," said Wufu. "I saw someone eating prawns at the night market. I don't know what they taste like. I've never had them."

"What do you want to eat then?"

"Anything but seafood!"

Only pigs eat anything. A phoenix is a phoenix because it's picky about its food. It only eats bamboo fruit and drinks nectar. Mind you, what did that make me? Of course, I knew you should be content with whatever you could get, but if I was trash picking in an apartment building, I'd take a good look at the food pictures on cards stuck inside the elevator and see if I could spot abalone and shark's fin, papaya, and birds' nests. Then as I was eating my bowl of rice or noodles or corn porridge later, I'd imagine how those foods tasted.

Wufu said, "My eyes don't need a feast. I like my porridge noodles the way they are. I can eat any amount of them."

"In Freshwind Township, they cook the noodles in porridge made from cracked corn, but in the County Town, the noodles are cooked in corn flour. Which do you like better?"

"Both."

Huh, whatever he ate he seemed to think was fine. But I liked it the township way, with the noodles made of wheat flour or bean flour or even yam flour, and best of all, when they were made from a fifty-fifty mixture of mung bean flour and wheat flour.

I complained that the porridge noodles we had for lunch the day before yesterday hadn't tasted good.

"It's the pickled vegetables," said Wufu. "They're made with daikon leaves back home, but they use celery here, plus Xi'an scallions are too big and have no bite."

"Remember, the next time you make porridge noodles, boil some soybeans with them, or potatoes, but don't slice them up—chop them into chunks," I told him.

We were having a great time talking about our favorite food.

Almond stood behind us, cackling with laughter. "It's only porridge noodles!" she said. "Make sure all these city folk don't laugh at you!" She was carrying a bowl of dumplings in one hand and a head of garlic in the other.

"Porridge noodles are the best!" Wufu declared.

"Are they as good as dumplings? Which would you choose if you had a bowl of each in front of you?" Almond asked.

"Porridge noodles!" I said.

"Oh, well, then I'll take the bowl of dumplings away," said Almond, and turned to go down the steps.

"Hey! Hey!" Wufu shouted.

I pinched him. "It's only a few dumplings, not enough to stick between your teeth!"

So Wufu said with an effort, "That's right! Porridge noodles are the best!"

Almond got halfway down the steps, then turned and asked, "Happy, what's that red stuff on your collar? . . . Fox demons!" she came back and exclaimed. "It's lipstick! A woman kissed you?" she chortled.

I turned scarlet. I picked up the spoon and stirred the porridge. "Rubbish, who'd want to kiss me? You wouldn't, would you? These potatoes are done."

"That's nice," said Almond. "We've got a thirty-something virgin! You've been hard at work, so you need extra food!" She poured the dumplings from her bowl into mine and took her empty bowl away with her.

When we'd finished, we sat there, patting our bellies contentedly. We figured we'd eaten as well as any mega-rich businessman. I rinsed my mouth with a ladleful of water. Wufu farted thunderously, then strained to see if he could get one more out. I told him to rinse his mouth out, but he just looked at me and whispered, "Are you going back to the salon?"

I grunted.

"Hey, take me too. What do you do there? Let me . . ." He cackled with laughter. "People say there's a big difference between a hooker and a wife. Your missus is like a lump of meat, but a hooker can get up to all sorts of . . . Come here and I'll tell you."

And he pushed his face into mine. I smacked him across the face, but he was smiling so impishly, I couldn't keep up the bravado. I was so happy that I spilled the beans and told Wufu everything that had happened. I guess I wasn't a remarkably self-controlled guy after all. I agreed to take him to meet Yichun.

33.

So I took Wufu to meet Meng Yichun. When he saw the bevy of heavily made-up young women in the beauty salon, Wufu got completely tongue-tied. His face had a sheen of sweat over it, and he kept trying to flatten curls that were sticking up, spitting on his hands and smoothing them down. His hair was very long by now. Dumb people's hair is always stiff as pig bristles and grows like crazy. Yichun offered him a free shampoo and cut. Wufu wanted only a trim, but I made Yichun shave his head completely. She'd just finished when her cell phone rang.

"Are you here? I'll be right out," she said. I looked outside and saw a car parked in the lane. I'd seen it before.

"That's him?" I asked.

"I'm really sorry," Yichun said. "I've got to go."

I had an idea. "Can you introduce me?"

"If you promise you won't let on that I've said anything about him."

I nodded. I told Wufu to stay there and went out to the car with Yichun. I opened the door, and we got in so we wouldn't be seen by passersby. Yichun introduced me as a friend from her home village. The man was wearing sunglasses, and I got the impression that he was annoyed at my being there, but that impression disappeared when he took the glasses off. I learned his name finally: Mr. Mighty. He was about my age but better-looking. I have quite prominent cheekbones, with the skin stretched tight over them, whereas he had full cheeks and fleshy lips and a calm manner, calmer than mine. Was he the recipient of my kidney? Was it there inside him? Was he my alter ego? I smiled at him and he smiled back, a few dimples appearing at the corner of his mouth. He offered me his hand to shake, and I felt our pulses beat in unison. A fantastic thought crossed my mind: I imagined us looking for each other in the spirit world. Or rather, the two kidneys searching for each other. A person was one part yin and one part yang, outer skin and internal organs, or lightbulb and electric current, you might say. Without the current, the bulb wouldn't light up. None of these metaphors were quite right. I couldn't put it into words properly. But we were both happy that we had met.

I could have told him that I'd picked up his lost wallet, but I couldn't very well explain why Gem Han had screwed another three hundred yuan out of him, so I said nothing. Then there was the kidney: I could have told him I'd sold my kidney. I might even have questioned him about how it performed after the transplant, whether there had been any signs of rejection, whether he had to take drugs every day, but I forced myself to keep silent. It would be embarrassing to talk about things like that in front of Yichun. Instead, I clapped him on the shoulder and said, "Good to meet you, Mr. Mighty! I hope you're in fine health and your business is flourishing!"

"Happy Liu, it makes me happy to see you," he responded. "We were obviously meant to meet! That makes us friends, Yichun, right?"

Yichun looked at me. "Yup, we're friends!" I repeated.

"Drop by my office sometime when you're free," Mr. Mighty went on. "I've got something to attend to right now, and I'm sorry to interrupt your conversation, but I have to take Yichun with me. I hope you don't mind."

I felt a pang. Of course I minded. Where was he taking Yichun? What for? I couldn't ask him, so I just stammered that it didn't matter. I pushed open the car door, lost my balance, and fell back onto my seat again. Yichun steadied me, and I slammed the car door shut after getting out.

The car pulled out fast and disappeared into the stream of traffic. The north end of Prosper Street was bustling, with only a narrow slit of sky visible through the forest of apartment buildings. Opposite, a conference was going on at a business center, and hundreds of red banners fluttered from the rooftop, chasing one another like scudding clouds. Amid the earsplitting noise from the gongs and drums and the firecrackers, the cars flowed by in an endless stream, the city's yellow taxis darting in and out of the traffic lanes like crazed rats. I suddenly noticed a stalk of wheat trailing from the undercarriage of one of the cars, and then I spotted another.

Wheat. When the villagers harvested the grain in the summer, they spread it out along the highway so that passing vehicles could crush it as they drove over it. Had these cars come from the countryside? It must be harvesttime. That meant we'd been in town for as long as three months.

I turned back to the beauty salon where Wufu was hunkered down by the doorway. "Why did you let her go? Why did you let her john take her if you're in love with her?" he asked.

I put my hand over his mouth. "Don't talk shit!" Then I turned on my heel and stomped off. I was in love with her, Wufu was quite right, but I couldn't keep her to myself. I couldn't rescue her or stop her from going with clients. If I did, how would she earn the money she needed?

Wufu caught up with me. "Happy! Happy! It was crap what I said. Are you angry with me?"

"When we got here, I told you to treat her with respect, didn't I? Respect! So why are you saying he's her john?"

"I'm sorry, I was disrespectful. But who was that man then?"

I didn't want to tell him that it was Mr. Mighty, the man with my kidney. Anyway, what hurt most was that Mr. Mighty was a john, taking Yichun for sex. I felt suddenly as if I were all skin and bone, my suit

231

flapping on me like a sheet. Wufu obviously felt sorry for me. "Let's go have a drink, bro! It's on me," he said.

I suddenly thought of the Chain-Bones Bodhisattva. That day all seemed a very, very long time ago. But the image suddenly reappeared. *I should take Wufu to see it and read the inscription*, I thought. Only the bodhisattva could console me now. I could tell Wufu why I was so resentful, distressed, and sorry for myself. I turned to Wufu but found myself saying instead, "They've started to cut the wheat."

"Cut the wheat? Already? What date is it today?"

"There were grain stalks stuck to a couple of the cars," I said. Wufu forgot about having a drink and ran over to a shop selling *liangpi* rice noodles to look at their calendar. Hung on the wall, it was a two-page spread with a picture of a curvaceous woman on the left and the calendar on the right. Wufu covered the woman with one hand and counted the days on his fingers. Then he said gloomily, "Harvest day, we're here . . ."

"You've got a missus to do the harvest, haven't you?" I said.

"She's a woman." He was dismissive. "If there's too much rain and if she can't cut the grain in time, the wind will blow it flat and it'll lie there wet and start to sprout . . . Don't you think we should go back?"

"Can't she manage a little bit of land like that? How would she manage if you upped and died?"

"Don't say stuff like that!" Wufu exclaimed, and he spat upward at the heavens, "Pah!" The spittle landed back on his face, and he asked, "Who'll cut your grain?"

"Anyone can cut it," I said, "and if no one wants it, it'll rot where it lies." Actually, I was a little worried about my small patch of land. Freshwind was overpopulated, and land was in short supply. About a third of my patch was a sloping field. I'd grown sweet potatoes on part of the land. The rest was planted with wheat, and before I left, I'd asked my neighbors to keep an eye on it. We agreed that if I didn't come back, they could have the wheat and just give me a measure of grain.

I'd planted Qinchuan number-three wheat variety, applied fertilizer, and irrigated it, so the yield should be at least two hundred pounds of grain. Of course, I was annoyed that the neighbors would get more than half of that for themselves, but it would take days to get home and back, and selling the grain wouldn't even cover the cost of my fares. I'd already worked it out in my head. But Wufu was laboriously doing the math on the ground, using a stick. He did the math several times, muttering to himself, "Not worth it, not worth it . . ." But then he looked up at me. "If we don't go back for the harvest, do you think . . . ?"

"Think what?" I asked.

"Well, Liu Baidou goes back every year to see to his dad's grave. Shouldn't we go at harvesttime?" Liu Baidou was the highest-ranking official Freshwind had ever produced. He was a department head in the County Town government. He'd moved his entire family to a nice courtyard home in the County Town, but every year, he got in his car and went home for the Grave-Sweeping Festival to do his duties. Well, Liu Baidou was Liu Baidou, and we were who we were. If I were him, I'd go home every month, not just for the Grave-Sweeping Festival.

"We're ordinary folk, Wufu. Liu Baidou's a VIP. As soon as someone becomes a VIP, they start saying their village is the most beautiful place in the world, their parents are wonderful, and they go back to revere their ancestors, cuddle the babies, and pass the time of day with all the local characters."

"But we're peasants," objected Wufu. "Not going home at harvesttime, that's . . ."

I cut him off angrily. "We're not peasants anymore! We're city folk. We're trash pickers in the city, so we're city folk!" I always got my way, and Wufu never dared answer back, especially on key matters like this. Besides, I knew Wufu couldn't go back on his own as he had no idea which train to take and where from. Wufu sniffed and said nothing.

I'd been about to take Wufu to Pagoda Street. Changing the subject to the harvest was supposed to make me feel better. But actually it only upset us both. Everything I'd said was meant to convince Wufu, and me too, that we weren't going back, but no sooner had I made up my mind than my head teemed with images of harvesttime in our village. It was as if I could smell the ripened grain, the ladybugs and moths crawling from the sheaves, the sweat on the reapers. I remembered the odors, a mixture of fragrant and sour, wafting through the village streets at dusk. I sighed. It was a sight for sore eyes, the ears of wheat bending in the wind, and it seemed a shame not to pick up even a single grain on the ground. Then there was the stubble, which stabbed your ankles as you toiled in the fields under the starry sky, but not painfully. The blood trickling down your legs like little earthworms was a pretty sight. Then there was the winnowing, wielding a wooden shovel on the threshing floor, getting bristles stuck in the collar of your jacket, and how the more you sweated, the harder they stuck, until you itched all over—and that was a pleasant feeling too. I wanted to say something to cheer Wufu up. "Let's go see some wheat fields!"

His face, which had been creased with misery, suddenly blossomed into a chrysanthemum. There were wheat fields not far from the city center; it was a forty-minute bicycle ride from the highway, so they were within sight. For us, the city of Xi'an was the largest in the world, but it was surrounded by countryside, not like Beijing and Shanghai. Vehicles driving into town brought in mud on their tires, a source of much grumbling by city inhabitants.

Suddenly, we were in a hurry to see the wheat, and we left the three-wheeler and the cart at Scrawny's depot. Scrawny was scornful when he heard we weren't doing a day's trash picking. "You really think prancing off to the countryside on an inspection tour like government officials will make you money?" Huh, he must know everything comes at a price. He was from the countryside too. He didn't get paid for visiting his old mother, did he? Even eating wears your teeth out. Without a decent meal, you have no energy, and not going to see the wheat would make us feel bad—really bad!

When we arrived, we saw the fields stretching endlessly over the flat river plain, a sea of wheat! Wufu suddenly let the bicycle drop, without regard for me. Arms and legs flying, he leapt over the dike into the field, as if jumping into the sea, and was swallowed up. "Wufu! Wufu!" I shouted, hurling myself after him. We had flattened a patch of wheat, but then the breeze picked up and the wheat swept over me like a wave and covered me, then swayed apart and revealed a sky above that was yellow, golden yellow. I stroked off the ears of grain, rubbed them between my fingers, blew the husks off, and eagerly popped them into my mouth. My tongue couldn't separate the grains, so I chewed and chewed and tasted the sweetness of the kernels in my nostrils and mouth.

Wufu was silent for nearly five minutes. Suddenly, like a carp, he took a flying leap out of the wheat and fell back again. "There's nothing like the countryside, bro, is there?" he exclaimed. "We hate it while we're there, but when we're in town, we realize how happy we were in the country!"

I stopped chewing. Wufu's words made me sad. I wished I hadn't brought him to look at the wheat. I couldn't let him say things that like, or he'd never settle in town. "You mean, the city's not as good?"

"Fuck the city! The city doesn't belong to us."

"You earn money from the city. What have you got against it?"

Wufu stared at me dumbly. "I'm not comfortable in it."

"Well, give it time. The city gives you money and it's our city, so you'd better start loving it."

"I love my missus, and I feel sorry for her," said Wufu, and he started to cry. He was in his forties, but he cried so easily.

"You're embarrassing, Wufu, useless! You should be ashamed of yourself!"

"But what kind of a life we are living! Whenever I think about it, I feel like crying."

"Fine, cry all you like. There's no one around, so have a good cry."
At that, Wufu really did burst into a flood of tears. He was saying something, but the words were so garbled, you couldn't make heads or tails of it. He howled and he bawled, and I got up and left him, and went for a walk along the riverbank. I came to a slope where the wheat had already been cut, tied into thick sheaves, and stood upright in shocks. I strolled amongst them, noticing how some of the sheaves seemed to whisper amongst themselves, or looked hopefully around them, or turned their backs on one another, sulking. I turned around to find that Wufu had followed me, his face still streaked with tears.

Why had he stopped crying?

"You were bawling as if your dad died," I said.

"Were you in the township when my dad died? He got liver cancer. It was a long, painful death, and when he finally snuffed the candle, he went out with a smile."

"If he died smiling, why can't you smile?" I asked. I was fed up with his mumbling and turned to walk up the slope. There were a few stalks of common sow thistle with brightly colored flowers, and I snapped one off. The stem bled white sap, which immediately turned black. Wufu picked all the thistles and stuffed them in his pocket. "That'll do for the pot," he said, then added, "Bro, when I die, who'll cry over me? Will you?"

"No, I won't!" I exclaimed. Wufu stared at me in shock. "I won't!" I repeated.

"You won't cry, eh? Fine, don't then." He was annoyed. Then he gave another wail, which ended up sounding like a groan, or a harsh laugh.

34.

We left the wheat fields and headed back to Fishpond. We stayed up late that night. Now that we'd satisfied our nostalgic longings, we urgently needed to make up for what we'd lost on the trash picking. That was the only way to stop ourselves from moping. We wandered through the village night market, in the hopes of finding some trash or getting work loading or unloading stuff. As Wufu put it, "Even if we have to rip it off, we've got to get ten yuan today." But no one wanted goods shifted at night, and no one was buying anything heavy they wanted carried home. There were plenty of empty beer bottles, but mostly the drink sellers collected those. Our haul was only a few dozen plastic mineral water bottles. We were just passing a hotpot restaurant when Wufu said, "There's Gem Han." I went to stand on the other side of the road. Sure enough, there he was. I could see him through the restaurant window with a hotpot, a big plate of lamb kebabs, and a cluster of bottles of beer, which he was consuming all on his own. I wanted to go in to see him.

"If we go in when he's eating, he'll make us eat, and then we'll have to pay for it," objected Wufu. I said that was OK. "Then you go in, and I'll wander around outside," he said, and he disappeared. I went in, and Gem Han made me share his meal. He told me that my nephew, Goodson Liu, had been to see him.

"Goodson's come to town?" I was surprised. The young man must have had another fight with his dad.

"Hasn't he been to see you?" Gem Han was also surprised. "I gave him your address."

"Does he want to pick trash as well?" I asked.

"No, he doesn't. But I have a friend who has a coal store, and he's going to sell coal for him. That kid's like me. He's going to do well in town."

"That kid" was a brute and had been at odds with his dad from the day he was born. The pair of them fought about his going to school every single day. My big brother told me that it wasn't that his son couldn't learn, it was that he just refused to. He was a kid with ambitions, and they didn't include studying—he was a real troublemaker. I said a kid like that would go far. A placid kid might be no trouble, but he wasn't going anywhere. It was the troublemakers who made waves. "Right," said my brother, "he takes after you." So now Goodson had come to town, no doubt intent on following in my footsteps, but he still hadn't come to see me even though he knew quite well where I was. He was disrespecting me, going to see Gem Han first and avoiding his uncle!

I was annoyed with Han too. I'd regarded him as a nobody in Freshwind, but here he was in Xi'an, the self-appointed agent for anyone coming to town, like God Almighty! Damn him, he was still a nobody! We finished eating, and he shouted for the bill. But he didn't take out any money, so finally I took the hint and said, "I'll settle up," though I thought to myself, *You had your dinner. I don't see why I should pay your bill.* I made a big show of stopping him paying while fishing around for money I didn't have. "I'll settle up," I repeated. Finally, he capitulated, pulling out a hundred-yuan note and giving it to the owner.

"Now why did I let you do that?" I said.

"And you're loaded, are you?" He made a point of opening his wallet to put away his change, pulling out a stash of money between finger and thumb before tucking the fifty-yuan note in with the other bills. As Gem Han was going through this performance for my benefit, I heard a ruckus coming from the other end of the night market. Customers looked up, wondering what was going on. Just then, two police officers escorted a man out of the lane, to a police three-wheeler van parked at the main intersection. The man had his arms twisted behind his back, and the police were struggling to undo the rope that held his pants up. They finally succeeded, and his pants dropped to his ankles.

"My pants, my pants!" the man cried. "You should be ashamed of yourself!" one of the officers shouted at him. They bound his hands and were pushing him into the van when the man twisted his head and shouted back at the street, "Decheng still owes me three yuan fifty!" He must have been yelling at his missus, but the cluster of gawking onlookers couldn't identify her. The police tried to stuff his head inside, but he refused to bend his neck and they couldn't get him in, until someone jabbed him in the armpit and in he went, though his butt still stuck out. The onlookers jeered, but the police didn't crack a smile, and the van squealed away.

News travels fast. It was a trash picker who'd been caught snipping forty feet of electric cable from a freestanding advertising billboard. Luckily, no one knew who I was, but the owner knew Gem Han and asked him, "Mr. Trash King, is that one of yours?"

"No, no one who lives in that lane has anything to do with me." What a disgraceful thing to say.

Then the owner said, "Trash pickers, they're all thieves, the lot of them!"

Gem Han spluttered, then said, "Are you quite sure that one was a trash picker?" He seemed in a hurry to get out of the restaurant. So Han the Tyrant was a pussycat when it came to dealing with the locals!

"Do you think the food and drink sellers in the night market are all paying their taxes like they should?" I piped up.

I said that mainly to annoy the restaurant owner, but he came back with, "Very good point! And what do you do?"

"He's one of my guys," said Gem Han.

"You're quick on the uptake," Gem said to me as we went out the door. "These people think they can pull one over on us because they're locals and we're outsiders, and they're always trying to rip us off!"

"Does everyone know you?" I asked.

"Of course they do!"

I suppressed a smile and turned it into a cough.

As we walked down the lane, he said, "How have your takings been lately?"

"So-so," I said.

"I can't stand lying," he said. "Come with me to Lane Three and see what the others say."

When we got to Lane Three, there were a few trash pickers milling around. They greeted Gem Han politely. "Have you had your dinner yet, Boss?"

"Why wouldn't I have eaten yet?" said Gem Han. Then he turned to one trash picker. "You haven't been to see me all month!"

"I've got the money ready. I'll see you tomorrow," said the man. Then Gem Han said to a bald man, "I'll fix it for someone else to share your patch, hmm?"

"If anyone else comes, I'll starve! Not that it's my place to say anything, of course," said Baldy hurriedly. Then he pulled Gem Han aside and tried to sneak something to him. But Gem Han said, "Don't be so sneaky! When you pay your dues, it should be open and above board. Give it to him, he'll collect it." Baldy passed one hundred yuan to me. We walked through three more yards, Gem Han and I, and three more trash pickers handed over a hundred yuan each. Gem Han made them give the money to me. Outside the yard, I handed over the four hundred yuan to Gem Han. I knew what he was getting at. "We haven't been to see you either," I said.

"Well, now you know," he said. I saw Gem Han to the lane where he lived and went back to Leftover House. Wufu was still up, sitting on the bed and counting his money. He always handed over the big notes to me to look after, but he kept some change in a cloth bag, covered with a plastic bag and stuffed into the crack in the corner. His small change consisted of one- and two-yuan notes and a heap of copper coins. Just when he'd finished adding them up, the light went out. He hurriedly pulled the bedcover over the pile and stood guard at the door, convinced that someone had seen him counting his money and was going to sneak in to rob him while the lights were off. To be doubly sure, he shouted down the steps, "Goolies! Goolies!" There was an answering shout.

"Eight! Eight!"

"What?" came from Eight's room.

Satisfied, Wufu shouted, "Why has the electricity gone out?" As he spoke, the light came on again. He quickly checked that there was no one on the steps, went back into his shed, and counted again. This time one coin was missing.

He dived under the bed to search. His butt stuck up in the air, and his pants crotch split, so his ugly goolies hung out. I came in right then and kicked him. "What the hell are you doing?"

He backed out and shook out the quilt. A one-yuan coin fell out and skittered across the floor. Wufu hurriedly grabbed it. "Fuck you! Think you can get away from me again?"

"How did you get back so early? Did you see the police arrest a trash picker?" I asked. It seemed he hadn't. I explained about the theft of the electric cable.

"I don't know why the police don't arrest all the Fishpond trash pickers, and Gem Han as well, and just leave us two," said Wufu.

"If it was just you, you wouldn't earn any money."

"What do you mean? I took in at least twenty yuan this evening."

I was astonished. "How did you do that?"

241

"Didn't you have to pay twenty yuan toward Gem Han's dinner? At least twenty yuan? Well, I didn't, so it's like I'd earned twenty yuan!"

I'd had enough of talking to him, so I went to bed. Then I immediately got up again, turned the light back on, and looked at the lipstick stain on my collar. Took the high-heeled shoes out from under the bed, unwrapped them, and put them back on the shelf. From that day on, I got into the habit of saying Yichun's name to those shoes every night before bed. I imagined her in my room, lying in my bed, and my hand crept between my legs.

What a scumbag I was being to Yichun. I knew I shouldn't, but I couldn't help it. The evening I saw Gem Han to his home, he asked me how my sex life was. I said I didn't have one. I told him that when I couldn't hold out any longer, I jerked off, but I was sure that wasn't good for my health, so I'd try and hold out, until it got too much for me again. Gem Han said if I really didn't want to fork out on a dance hall, I should use a twig to scoop the wax out of my ears and that would take my mind off it. I did that, and told Wufu to do it too, but just as soon as I looked at those high-heeled shoes, I was lost again. Yichun was a caterpillar who'd wriggled her way into my heart.

35.

It was getting hotter by the day, too hot to wear a jacket. I left my shirt buttons undone. If Wufu only moved a muscle, he was covered in sweat. He went bare-chested and rolled his pants up to his knees. I covered up with a red T-shirt I'd bought because I had no biceps to speak of, and you could count my ribs when I breathed. One evening when we got back from Prosper Street, we passed a restaurant with bits of wood piled up outside, left over from a reno job. We bundled some up to use for fuel, and then Wufu found an old digital watch amongst the stuff. He fiddled and fiddled with it but couldn't make it work, so he gave it to me. "You'll look grand in that," he said. "With your T-shirt and that watch, no city man will dare tell you it's not working."

I put the watch on. And seeing as I was so grand, I wasn't going to walk along pushing a bike with a bundle of firewood on the back either. "If a city man's walking along with a country boy, you don't ask the city man to push the bike."

"Fine, fine," Wufu said, and took the bike.

When we got to the turnoff for Fishpond Village, we saw someone going into the phone bar, where the public phones were. From behind, it looked like Eight, but how was that possible? He wouldn't be smartly dressed in a fully-lined tracksuit top, would he? We gave it no more thought and headed for Leftover House.

Almond was in the yard, washing a plastic garbage can lid in the sink. The garbage can had some soured vegetable water fermenting in it, with a layer of white bubbles floating on top. She'd just skimmed off a layer of scum. "Oh, you're back," she said. "It's hotter than hell today. Do you want some?" Wufu drank a ladleful. I unloaded some of the firewood for her and left some at Eight's door too. "It's very sour," she said. "Help yourself to a scoop, if you want to put some in your noodles."

"OK," I said. "Is Eight back?"

"He came back a long time ago. He was cursing and swearing that there weren't enough people to harvest the grain back home on his patch. He might have gone to call his missus."

Wufu looked really worried, but I glared at him and he said, "I'm not calling. If my missus's tired out, I can't help that. She should act like I'm dead and gone!"

"Well, you haven't gone home because you're earning money here," said Almond. "If you've got a heart, send her some money tomorrow." She immediately added, "Eight doesn't send money home. He buys himself fancy clothes instead. Not that any fancy clothes are going to look good on him!"

Wufu and I exchanged looks. So it was Eight we'd seen in the doorway of the phone bar. "Where would he get the money to buy clothes like that? Do you think he stole it?" said Wufu.

I told him he should keep his trap shut, and Almond agreed. "There's a crime crackdown right now, and they're after people like us. Don't ever say that he might have stolen it."

"He's such a show-off, he spent ages prancing around in front of me, and I bet he'll do the same to you when he's back," she added sourly.

"He can prance all he likes, but no one should mention his new clothes."

The words were hardly out of my mouth when Eight turned up, his face set in such a grim expression that I was scared. "What's up?" I asked.

"That fucking Cripple Qian!" Cripple Qian? Who was Cripple Qian? "I called the village post office, and Cripple Qian refused point-blank to get my missus for me. It's only a *li* away, but he couldn't be bothered! He just wants her to give me an earful!"

"Your wife's too busy with the harvest to give you an earful!"

"She sure wasn't too busy! My ears were burning today!"

"But is she still your wife?" muttered Almond.

This last comment was said very quietly, and Eight didn't hear. He washed his face, then puttered around the yard. He made sure we could see him cursing and swearing that the streets were so dusty, what the hell was the city mayor doing about it, sitting in his office all day? All this time, he was patting the dust off his jacket, but we pretended not to notice. Wufu was having trouble not laughing, and I made a face at him. Wufu hunkered down and stopped looking at Eight.

Eight looked crestfallen. He asked Almond for some of her soured vegetable water, but she said no. "What do you mean, you're thirsty? Why are you wearing a great thick jacket like that? It looks like something you'd wear to your own funeral!"

"I got it, so why shouldn't I wear it?" Eight glared at her.

"No need to explode! What's put you in such a temper?" said Almond.

"The weather, it's so hot!"

We all jeered and tried to peel his jacket off him. Wufu sneaked his chance to wipe snot on it. After dinner, our rooms were full of mosquitoes, so we kept the lights off. We lit sogon grass to fumigate the rooms, and we sat in the yard, chatting. Not about anything in particular, just this and that. Like, why did city folk all have mosquito nets, so all the mosquitoes flocked to us? Then we chatted about the deli at the entrance to Fishpond Village where they sold a beef dish called "General Zhang Fei beef," which was very good. Eight kept trying to talk about his clothes, but we refused to take the bait and instead kept talking about the beef dish and discussed how the beef dish got its name. Wufu said it was because the general was a tough guy and the meat was tough too, and was it buffalo beef? Almond looked down her nose at Wufu and said scornfully that the beef was cooked till it was very dark in color and that was why it was named after the general. Wufu slapped at the mosquitoes on his face and managed to kill one. "A damned female!" he said.

"Are you dissing me?" Almond said.

"Not you!" said Eight. "That was a stripy mosquito. City folk are particular about the way they dress, and that goes for city mosquitoes too!"

Almond changed the subject again and decreed that no one was to wash their clothes in the yard at night.

I laughed. "If you keep trying to stop him talking about clothes, he'll burst! Where did you get your new jacket, Eight?"

"It'll be you that bursts, not me," said Eight huffily. Then he told us about his jacket, and it put a serious damper on the conversation: this morning he had spotted someone about to jump from the roof of an eight-story building. There were some gawkers clustered underneath. It wasn't unusual to see jumpers in the city, but they didn't really want to kill themselves. They were mostly migrant workers, protesting unpaid wages and hoping that the threat of committing suicide would shame their boss into paying up, though Eight thought that never actually worked. But then the bystanders started jeering at the man on the rooftop. "Jump! Go on, jump!" They even started throwing stones at him. Eight protested. "Don't make him jump!" but no one paid attention. He tried to get someone with a cell phone to call the police, but still no one paid attention. The shouts and jeers got louder—"Jump! Jump! Jump!"—until the noise was unbearable. The man they were goading turned toward Eight and bowed, hands clasped together in the old-fashioned way, but as Eight was about return the bow and shout at him to come down quick, the man turned back toward the jeering crowd, bent low, and then jumped. His jacket was torn from his body by the force of the fall and landed in some flowering shrubs at the foot of the building. As the man lay on the concrete, his skull smashed, the bystanders all took off, but Eight stayed. He covered the corpse with a sheet of cardboard from his cart. Then he addressed the body. "You're such a fool. They told you to die and you died!" The police turned up and took the body away, but they left the jacket behind.

"You took his jacket?" exclaimed Wufu.

"Well, the police didn't."

"You didn't point it out to them?" said Wufu.

"He bowed to me before he died, and I figured that meant he wanted to give me his jacket. Otherwise, why would the wind have torn it off him and dropped it in the shrubs?"

I'd read an article in an old magazine about a bandit who, when he'd killed someone, used a stone to smash their teeth so he could extract the gold fillings. That might have been Eight if he'd been born in more lawless times.

"It's a good jacket, worth hundreds of yuan!" said Eight. We all spat skyward and made Eight move away from us. The spirit of a man who had died a violent death still clung to his jacket, we told him. "You're just jealous. The ghost will be looking for his boss," said Eight. We fell silent. There weren't even birds chirping in our tree, but the bugs were still pissing on us from its branches. A mournful cry came from somewhere.

"An owl?" said Wufu.

"You don't get owls in town," said Almond.

My head was still full of the jumper. How could all those bystanders goad him into jumping like that? But he was a migrant worker, and to city folk, it was like watching a performing monkey. I didn't feel like talking about it anymore, so I changed the subject. "Who knows how many migrant workers there are in Xi'an?"

"Around half a million?" Almond suggested.

"More like a million, I'd guess," said Goolies.

"That's a million people not getting the harvest in!" Wufu exclaimed.

I hurriedly changed the subject again. "Xi'an's developed so quickly, some old city folk don't recognize its streets anymore. And all the heavy construction work is done by migrant workers, every bit of it!"

"We give it everything we've got," said Eight, "and the fucking city folk still don't respect us!"

"Well, you didn't respect the migrant worker either," I said. "They egged him on to jump, and then you took his jacket!" I cursed myself for returning to the suicide again and got up to see how the fumigation was going in my room. The mosquitoes were gone, but the smoke was so thick, I had a coughing fit. I took a bowl of water back to the others.

Wufu had a swallow and said, "If I was the country's leader, I wouldn't bring a million migrant workers to town. I'd let the townsfolk do their own work—or starve!"

"If you hadn't come to town, you'd pretty soon have starved to death yourself," retorted Almond. That sobering thought shut us all up. We slapped our legs and faces—the mosquitoes seemed to be biting everywhere.

"Have you seen the newspapers over the last few days?" I asked. No one had. "You collect old newspapers all day and you never read them!" I said. "There's a plan to erect a statue to migrant workers in the park. And there's been a discussion about who it should be modeled on."

"On Wufu and Eight," said Almond.

"Not me. Happy's better-looking," said Wufu.

"But if it's modeled on Happy, it won't look like a migrant worker!" Almond objected. "And Wufu's all paunch and no brain."

Wufu erupted. "If I'm ugly, then you be the model!"

"Well, I'm not much to look at, and I'm loud-mouthed, and I'm a bit short, but at least I have a figure!" And she drew herself up to her full height, making her breasts stick out high and proud. Wufu harrumphed and went upstairs to fix the fan in his room.

Wufu had picked up an old box fan on his rounds, and when he plugged it in, the blades actually turned. So he cleaned off the grease and used it. It didn't cool him down much because it only puffed out the odd gust of wind, and feebly at that, but now he nailed up a shelf over the bed for the fan so at least he could feel the wind on his head. Wufu's head was brick-hard, and he still rested his head on a brick instead of a cotton-padded pillow, so he certainly wasn't worried about having a draft on his head. We were still talking downstairs, and the noise seemed to be bothering him, so he clattered and banged on the shelf like he was playing percussion at the opera. I went up to have a word with him about it.

And that was when it happened. Afterward, I asked Wufu how he'd known to fix his fan at that precise moment. Had he had a premonition that something was going to happen?

"Premonition?" he said. "Sure, I did! Anyone who gets on my bad side has it coming to him!"

He was obviously just shooting his mouth off, and I warned him, "Don't say stuff like that. However rude we four families are about one another, if something happens, we've got to look out for one another."

Then we heard a car horn in the lane outside and a beam of light shone on the tree, its shadow growing first tall, then small, on Wufu's wall. "Looks like a ghost, that shadow," I said.

"Then it's one Eight brought back with him," said Wufu. The words were hardly out of his mouth before the sound of running and a shriek came from downstairs.

Then two people came thundering upstairs and pushed Wufu's door open. "Which one of you's Gules?" they asked. They were in regular clothes, not uniforms, and they looked aggressive. Wufu's door had been ajar anyway, and when they gave it a kick, it bounced back, so they kicked it again. One of them brought out a hardbound notebook and brandished it. "Police!" he shouted. I couldn't see the notebook properly, and I thought they were burglars.

I stepped back until I was against the window. There was a small hammer on the sill. "We're trash pickers. We have no money, comrades!" I said.

"Which one of you's Gules?" they asked again. One guy, towering over the rest of us, undid his jacket and used the front to wipe the sweat from his face. That was clearly designed to intimidate us: we could see the handcuffs hanging from his waistband. Wufu was trembling.

"Mr. Gules? Not us," I said. "Wufu, get out the cigarettes. Offer them to these officer comrades."

Then the fan fell off the shelf with a crash. The men paid no attention, just pushed open the door to let out the cigarette smoke that was making them cough. The door sprang back and slammed shut again.

"It doesn't mean to. It just doesn't shut properly," Wufu said. He took out the cigarettes. One had come apart and he smoothed it shut with his lips, then offered the cigarettes to the policemen.

They ignored him. "What are your names? Show us your IDs," they demanded. We always had them on us in case we had to produce them in a hurry.

"My name is Happy Liu, and he's Wufu," I said. "There's no Happy Liu here," the man with the cuffs said, looking over our IDs.

"Oh, er, Hawa was my given name, but I changed it to Happy after I came to the city."

"No name changes allowed!" he barked. I said nothing. Why couldn't I change my own name? The officer looked at Wufu, then back at his ID card. Wufu hurriedly said that the photo wasn't good because it had been taken when he was sick. But the officer only seemed interested in Goolies. Where did he live? I hesitated. Wufu said we hadn't come with Goolies. He lived in one of the rooms downstairs. We heard a shrill screaming from Almond. She sounded like a stuck pig.

"Shut your mouth!" someone shouted. There were no more screams, but we could hear sobs. Our two officers clattered off downstairs. There was a lot of noise—stern shouts, weeping, the sound of smashing pots, a bang—and then silence fell. After a while, we heard talking, someone slapping the table, something being kicked and bouncing across the yard. Eight came running up the steps, ashen-faced. "There's been a crime committed!" He sounded as if he meant murder.

Had Goolies killed someone? We didn't dare go down. We didn't know what to think. After half an hour, the men departed, but they didn't take Goolies and Almond with them. When the three of us went downstairs, we found Almond slumped on the floor of her room, shaking all over. But Goolies, surprisingly, was his usual self. "It was nothing, nothing," he said. "The police just wanted me to identify a picture and answer a few questions, that's all."

"You really didn't kill anyone?" Wufu asked.

"Would I be capable of doing a thing like that? Get up, Almond." But she couldn't stand. She'd pissed herself, and her pants and the ground were all wet. Goolies said that a man from his village, a trash picker in another district, had been killed. The perp was a local. The murdered man had been in Xi'an for ten years and had saved 120,000 yuan over that time. The perp was a drinking buddy of his. One day the victim went to withdraw money from the account at a cash machine and the perp followed him, sneaked a look at his pin number, killed his friend, and took off with all his money. The police had found an address book in the victim's room with Goolies's address in it, and so they had come to ask about the victim.

Goolies smiled. "They showed me a picture of the dead man, but how could I recognize it? The head was all swollen up, one eye ball was hanging out. Turns out, eye balls are attached to a really long thread. Then there was the tongue. The tongue . . ."

By that time, our hair was standing on end, and we stopped him. That he and Almond were both OK was all that mattered.

36.

It was a dismal evening. First there was Eight telling us about the suicide. Then it was Goolies talking about the murder. We were all scared out of our wits, but finally everyone calmed down. Almond, of course, swore at Goolies, for knowing a murderer and leaving his address with the victim. "Now that the police have been here once, they might keep coming back if they don't solve the case! Are you trying to frighten me to death? And suppose the murderer comes by here, the police can get you for harboring a criminal! You'll end up in prison or get shot for that! Do you have a death wish?" Her face was wet with tears and snot.

As for Goolies, he hadn't killed anyone, or harbored a criminal, and he wasn't afraid of the police, but he was afraid of this woman, and of her weeping and wailing. "I can't stand this. Let's pack up and go back home to the countryside."

That made Almond even more abusive. "And what are we going to feed ourselves on there? Wind and farts?"

"You get the blame whether you go or stay, Goolies. Some missus you got yourself!" Eight added.

Almond rounded on him then. It was all Eight's fault for taking a dead man's jacket and bringing disaster on them all. "If the police show up again, I'll tell them you've taken a dead man's clothes."

Eight was furious. "If you dare tell the police that, I'll make sure they know what you've been up to in the Ghost Market."

Almond looked at Wufu and me. I looked back, and she went pale. Then she went for Eight, trying to clamp her hand over his mouth, but he stuck his foot out and tripped her. Goolies reached toward the chopping board but didn't touch the knife that lay there. Instead, he picked up a matchbox: "I'm going to bash your head in!"

Things were getting out of control. Wufu was rooted to the spot, so it was up to me to pull things back from the brink. "Stop it!" I shouted in my most commanding voice. It worked. They stopped. I didn't try to adjudicate. After all, how could I? I simply said, "In a family, things sometimes get messy, and we've just got to live with it." And I laid down two rules, which we kept until the day we left Fishpond and went our separate ways.

Rule one: no airing dirty laundry in public. We should keep our stuff to ourselves. If Wufu ever said that Eight had taken the dead man's jacket, then everyone would accuse Wufu of taking it. If Eight said Almond was a fence for the thieves in the Ghost Market, then everyone would say it was Eight who was the fence. Rule two: no one was allowed to bring strangers back to Leftover House, or tell anyone our address. Anyone who disobeyed these two rules would be kicked out by the others.

Eight still looked annoyed, but Goolies put his arm around him. "Her bark's worse than her bite, you know. Leave her alone," he said.

"Men don't fight with women. I am leaving her alone, but you said you wanted to bash my head in!"

"Oh, that was all for her benefit," said Goolies. "Come on, bro, stay up and play a game of chess with me tonight!" Almond looked outraged, but Goolies hustled Eight out of the door and into Eight's room. He was back before long. "I didn't mean it. It was just to get him into bed." He smiled at Almond. She didn't smile back, so he went to the shit-house to get their chamber pot.

I felt sorry for Goolies. Almond was a capable woman, out picking trash, then coming home to cook, but it was always rice, her favorite, no vegetables, just rice mixed with a little soy sauce. Goolies liked noodles, but he never got any.

That evening, when Goolies returned with the chamber pot, I didn't go back to my room. The fight was over, I could see that, but we still had a problem to resolve: What was to stop the perp turning up here and then the police coming after him? I suggested they make themselves scarce for a while. I gave them my nephew's address, they could go there. Almond could see the sense in that, but she wanted me to keep an eye on their place, and make sure no one touched the bundle of plastic tubing, or even a stick of the firewood stored on the steps.

It was midnight before I got to bed. I dreamed of Yichun. How strange! You'd think that after the scary evening we'd had, I'd have been dreaming of the murder and the police. The whole affair must have reminded me of Yichun's big brother and made me think about what I could do to console her, because what I actually dreamed was that Yichun and I were cozying up like a pair of lovebirds. That was strange too.

In my dream, we were sitting in a coffee bar. I ordered two teas, and the waitress told me each tea cost twenty yuan. What a rip-off! Was the tea made of gold leaf? I ordered it anyway; it was their best. Then Yichun said she wanted coffee. I couldn't see the attraction of coffee, it was as bitter as Chinese herbal medicine. The odd thing was that the coffee bar was full of young women, each with a coffee cup in front of her, flipping through fashion magazines full of handsome guys and beautiful women, cars, and furniture. Well, Yichun was young and beautiful, so she needed her coffee. I sneaked a glance at her. I knew you shouldn't stare at a woman's face. That was how lowlifes behaved, she'd be turned off. I met her eyes but hurriedly looked away as if a noise outside the window had caught my attention. I pretended the chair wasn't in the right place and shifted it a bit, and caught sight of her feet. She was wearing sandals, and her toes were like the plump white shoots of potatoes sprouting in a cellar. A feeling I couldn't put into words made me blush to the tips of my ears.

"You're embarrassed!" she said. "You're sweet when you're embarrassed." That made me very happy. What a lovely woman she was. I gazed at her, and she quietly looked back at me. "Can't you see in my face that fate's dealt me a rotten hand?" she said.

That was nonsense. She was beautiful. I tried to guess how many hairs she had on her head, and where she got that rounded nose and clear skin without a single pimple. If I reached out and touched it, it would be like touching a pane of glass.

"You shouldn't get too close to people when you talk to them," I said. "You're exquisite, but you don't want people staring at you."

She pouted. "Don't be a pain!" I liked that. All the same, when an ugly person makes a face, it's funny, but when someone good-looking does so, it's a bit scary.

"You really shouldn't make faces," I told her.

"Can't you see in my face that fate's dealt me a rotten hand?" she repeated.

"There's nothing wrong with your face. If you've had bad luck in life, it's because you're too beautiful. And why does being too beautiful bring bad luck? Well, it's like with flowers. A gorgeous blossom attracts bees and butterflies, and passersby pull the stalk toward them and sniff—they can't help themselves. And eventually someone plucks the flower."

"I was born unlucky," she said, "and it rubbed off on my brother."

I could think of nothing comforting to say to that, so I just sat silently, sharing her gloom. She went on. "I'll be old by the time I've avenged my brother."

I so wanted to say, *Oh, Yichun, I love you . . . I'll marry you when you're old.* But I didn't have the nerve. If she was disabled and unable to look after herself, then she might let me marry her. Even if we didn't marry, if only she'd let me dedicate my whole life to looking after her. I imagined going trash picking during the day and coming home in the evening. *Yichun, I'm back!* I'd say to her. I'd buy her clothes, I'd bring her *youbing* to eat, and we'd sit in our room, slapping the mosquitoes and chatting about whether we should repaint the walls and whether we should put a sofa under the window. It would be an upholstered sofa, comfy to sit on. Oh yes, we'd buy a washing machine so she wouldn't have to wash the clothes by hand. I'd put in a row of hooks over the window for strips of bacon and dried bean curd to cure. Where would the crock for vegetable pickles go? Should we have some chickens as well? And a puppy, a Pekinese, to keep her company while I was out trash picking. We'd have a black one. Most people preferred white Pekinese, but I thought black ones were nicer. Yup, a black one. We'd fight sometimes, of course, that was normal, that was what made a family. But I'd never make her cry. If the spat got too bad, I'd hold my tongue and coax her into a good mood, or play my flute for her.

My dream went on all night. A thought surfaced: *This is a dream, only a dream.* But I was in it so deep, I couldn't wake up. Eventually, I had an urgent need to piss, but I still didn't want to wake, so I kept my eyes shut and pissed out the back window, then climbed back into bed. Too bad the dream didn't return. Eventually I fell asleep again and dreamed about coming back from Prosper Street to find the high-heeled shoes missing from their shelf. *Shoes, shoes, where are you?* I cried. Then I looked down and realized I wasn't wearing any shoes either. I ran barefoot through every street and lane in the city. It was only when Wufu knocked at my door that I woke with a start. I was covered in sweat, and the sun was already quite high in the sky, shining brightly through my window.

Wufu told me he'd slept badly too. He'd woken early but hadn't gone to the Dengjiapo dump again. It kept going through his head that the trash picker had been murdered because he had money, and maybe he should send all his savings home to his missus as soon as he could. "Is this your way of showing your appreciation for her hard work?" I asked, and got his savings out for him. He had fifteen hundred yuan. He wrapped a thousand in paper and put it in a black cloth bag, and wrapped another layer of wastepaper around the outside.

"Ready?" I said.

He added a pair of stinky old shoes to the package. "Ready!"

I had saved fifteen hundred, and I took out four hundred and stuffed it in my pocket.

"Are you going to send money too?" Wufu asked in surprise.

"No," I said. "I'm feeling a bit anxious and having some money reassures me."

"Really?" Wufu sounded skeptical.

"Really what?" I asked.

Wufu leered at me. "You're going to . . ." He stopped speaking.

"Spit it out!"

I knew what he was trying to say, but I sounded so fierce, he fell silent. He put on some cloth shoes. They had a hole in them, so his toes stuck out.

I got dressed, putting on my suit and leather shoes, of course, and plucking the whiskers from my chin. I armed myself with an old magazine too.

As we left, Wufu was still grumbling about how difficult it was to make any money.

"You sound like an old woman! Look at the magazine I'm carrying . . . Doesn't it make me look educated?" I said.

"Just like a teacher!" he agreed.

We took a taxi to the post office. Wufu protested a taxi was too expensive, but I told him it was the only safe way and he gave in. I put him in the back, and I sat beside the driver with the cloth bag in my lap, so Wufu couldn't get the money out to pay. The driver looked at the cloth bag but said nothing. After a while, he wound down his window. "Something stinks," he said. I knew the odor came from Wufu's smelly old shoes. *Hah! If you knew how much money there was under those shoes, you wouldn't say they stank!* I thought. I began to read my magazine. It made me look quite cultured.

We got out of the taxi, and I paid the driver. He checked each bill to make sure it was genuine, so conscientiously that I flared up. "Look at me! Do I look fake?" I made a point of getting a receipt from him, though I had no use for it. I took the receipt, got out of the taxi—and forgot the bag.

Out on the street, I told Wufu, "Mark my words, when people disrespect you, you have to stand up to them!"

"Where's the bag?" Wufu asked.

"The bag! I left it in the taxi!" It had driven away. We started running madly after it. I couldn't run as fast as Wufu because I had leather shoes on. He kicked his cloth ones off and streaked away like a leopard. Maybe the driver heard our shouts, or maybe he saw us in the rearview mirror, because he slowed down, didn't stop, and simply flung the dirty old bag out the window.

He flung it with such disgust that one shoe fell out and rolled down the street. Wufu opened the bag and checked that the money was still there. Then his face cracked a goofy grin.

After that shock, I felt very guilty and kept my hand firmly on the bag. We sent the money and went to the depot to pick up the cart and the three-wheeler. When we got to Prosper Street, I said, "Is my hair a mess, Wufu?"

"It's fine."

"Look at the back!"

"It's fine," he repeated. Then he smirked.

"What's so funny?" I demanded.

"I know you're on the lookout for someone."

"Who?"

"I'm not saying." Then he told me, "Mind that money you've got on you." He went off to his patch, pulling his cart.

Wufu may have been simpleminded, but he'd guessed my intentions. And he was right. I was on my way to Salon Street, because I wanted to give Yichun some money.

37.

Goolies said it was losing at mahjong that reminded him to send his missus some money. But giving Yichun some money was something I'd been planning for a while. I wanted to give her money because of what she'd told me about her life. Once I had that idea fixed in my head, I couldn't let it go. But I had no idea how to get it to her, or how much.

Most of the front doors in Salon Street were still shut but there were plenty of people around, mostly clustered around the snack stalls. Xi'an wasn't short of snack stalls, everyone in China knew that, and they were at their busiest early in the morning and late at night. Normally I couldn't pass those rice cakes, oil tea broth, and soft bean curd stalls and the wonderful smells that wafted from them without my mouth watering.

But today I ignored them. My ears burned and my heart pounded as I headed straight to the door of Yichun's salon. It was still closed, and I felt somehow relieved. How could I be glad not to see Yichun? But for an instant I was. In Wufu and Eight's eyes, I was an arrow shot from the toughest of bows. Once I made up my mind, I never veered off course. They had no idea that *that* deep in my heart, there were certain things I couldn't cope with. I was as hopeless as they were. I was just more self-possessed, better at concealing it.

What was I doing here though, if not meeting Yichun? I knocked hard. There was no sound inside. I peered through a crack in the door, then saw a notice hanging on it, stating that they opened for business at ten o'clock. I pushed the three-wheeler to one side and stood there, looking at the railings of the building opposite. *If a bird settles on the railings, that means Yichun's going to start work.* But no bird came. Someone passed me, and I asked the time. He looked at his watch without stopping and said it was ten o'clock. Ten o'clock and still no one to be seen? The owner of the watch had a bit of leek from his breakfast pancake stuck in his teeth. I scraped the gap between my teeth with my fingernail and rubbed my eyes. I heard a cheeping, and there was a bird perched on the railings. I was just looking at it when Yichun turned up on the back of a motorcycle. She gave me a friendly wave. The motorcycle stopped, and she fluttered from it like a butterfly.

"Hey! You haven't paid!" the biker shouted.

"How much?" She turned back and exclaimed, "I really did forget!"

"It didn't look like it, the way you jumped off so quickly!"

"How much?" she repeated.

"Five yuan."

"But this trip's always three yuan."

"I went the long way around."

"You did it on purpose, so you could charge me an extra two yuan."

And she put down three yuan and ran over to me. The biker was about to come after her, but I shook my fist at him. "Where d'you think you're going?" He stopped and spat toward the lane. I spat too, and it landed farther than his. "You're a bad man!" I said.

Yichun giggled. "If you hadn't been here, I would've had to pay an extra two yuan."

"Next time someone tries to pull one over on you, come to me!"

"Actually, I'm the one who ripped him off."

I wasn't too happy when Yichun said that, but I didn't say anything. She hadn't had any breakfast, and I would have liked to share some soft bean curd with her, but she was in a hurry to open up and clean the salon. So I went to buy her some snacks. I'd reached the snack shop at the head of the lane, but before I could choose anything, Yichun was right there behind me.

"I'll pay!" she said, and dug around in her pocket.

But I slapped a hundred yuan down. "A pound of the soft cakes!" How could I let her pay? This was my opportunity to show her how I felt. We argued.

The cake man weighed out the cakes and wrapped them up. "That'll be five."

"I've given you the money," I said.

"Who did you give it to?"

"I put it on the counter, a hundred-yuan bill." But the money was gone. Another man was leaning on the counter, super skinny, with a tuft of dyed red hair, whistling. Where was that money? "I put that money down right here. Don't tell me I haven't paid," I said.

"Well, I haven't got it!" said the cake seller. I looked at Red Hair. He was leaning on the counter, his eyes fixed on the God of Wealth sitting high up on his shelf, still whistling. I gave him a furious stare and stopped arguing with the cake seller, then simply got out five yuan and paid for the cakes.

None of the other workers were there yet when we got back to the salon.

"Did you really put the money on the counter?" Yichun asked.

"Absolutely. That bastard with the red hair must have taken it," I said.

Yichun was all for going after him, but I stopped her. "He's never going to admit it, so I'll never get it back. Hell, it was only a hundred yuan!"

"You're not upset about it?"

I was, but I hadn't wanted to make a fuss in front of Yichun, and Red Hair must have guessed that when he palmed it. I told Yichun to eat up while I swept the floor. She fed the cake into her mouth in little bits so as not to spoil her lipstick. It looks very refined when a pretty woman eats this way. She told me to help myself, but I didn't, so she picked up a piece and went to put it into my mouth for me. I shook my head, and the cake landed under my nose. I stuck out my tongue to lick it up, and it tasted like the best cake in the world.

You could see she was enjoying it too, sitting on her chair and swinging her long legs. She was leaning slightly backward, her face brimming over with pleasure.

"You're out early today," she said.

"I'm usually earlier than this."

"There's nothing on your three-wheeler."

"I came straight to see you."

"Is anything up?"

"Yes."

"What?"

"I came to give you four hundred yuan, but one hundred got stolen, so it's only three hundred now."

Yichun wet her fingertips and collected the crumbs that had fallen on her knee. Then she stood up and went to pour me some hot water. Her back to me, she said, "Why would I take money from you? I don't want your money!"

I put down the broom and stuffed the money into her purse between a makeup case and some tissues. Then I zipped it up again. I grabbed a paper cup and took it over to her. "Here!" I held it out for the water. The cup was made of soft paper, and the hot water nearly spilled. I could hear her breathing. She'd stopped chewing and was quietly watching me. Then she went over to her bag, unzipped it, took the money out, and put it on the table that the broom was propped against.

"I don't make much money, but don't turn down the little I can afford," I said without turning around. She was still watching me. I went back to the table, picked up the money, and put it back into her bag. "If you were doing OK, then maybe I would ask you for money, but it's you who needs it."

Yichun was eating her cake again, chewing and chewing, and chewing . . . Suddenly she got up and shut the door, then took off her jacket.

"Come with me. I can't take your money for nothing," she said softly.

My head was in a whirl. Never in a million years did I imagine Yichun would do this! I couldn't deny that I wanted her like crazy, but I wasn't giving her the money for that. The thought had never entered my head. *Oh, Yichun, did you really think I'd take advantage of you? That I was just a john?* The reason I didn't respect the rich guys who were so generous to Yichun was precisely because they only did it so they could spend their lust on her body. They were johns, just more kindhearted than the usual.

"No, no, I'm not your john . . . ," I protested. She looked crest-fallen, and I wished I hadn't been so abrupt. What did I mean, I wasn't her john? That Yichun was nothing but a hooker? I was reminding myself she was a hooker, and reminding her too. *Happy Liu, you stupid idiot!* I tried to correct myself. "No, no, I didn't mean . . ."

But Yichun said quietly, "I know you're not a john, but I'm a hooker and I can only thank you with my body." I opened the salon door and fled.

When I first thought of giving her money, I didn't imagine it would be easy to get her to accept it, but I figured I'd work on her until she did. I even imagined leaving it on the floor and taking off. Since Yichun didn't come after me now, I stopped in the street. Mission accomplished, I was elated at my success. The trouble was that we'd ended up talking about her being a hooker. I'd done everything I could to avoid it, but I'd gone and done it, and I should have been ashamed of myself. Whatever my motives—sympathy or a desire to help her—had it done her any good? As soon as that thought popped into my head, I tried to banish it. It was true, I did sympathize with her, and I did want to help her, but more important was the fact that I liked her; I loved her. I'd made my money, cent by cent, as a trash picker, and her accepting it drew us closer together. Even though money wasn't the same as emotion, still, once you loved someone, you wanted to spend money on her in any way you could. Money was a tightrope that I was edging along toward Yichun.

But . . . but . . . why was Yichun so ready to take her clothes off for me? "Hooker" wasn't something you should say out loud, but Yichun did just that.

I suddenly felt uneasy, in a way I never had before. I wanted to cry, but I couldn't. I wanted to rage at someone, but who? I was like a cat on hot bricks. I trod hard on the pedals and cycled over to Prosper Street and onto Lane Ten. I kept my head down and ignored the shouts of "Trash picker! Trash picker!" At the north end of the lane, whom should I see but the bastard with red hair, sitting on a concrete bench and eating a fried dough stick. There were three more on a piece of paper in front of him.

"Someone's shouting for you! Are you deaf? Are you a trash picker?" he asked. I got off the three-wheeler and went over to him. "I've got spare parts here. You interested?" He undid his jacket. He had a wire fastened round his waist and, hanging from it, some scaffolding clamps from a building site. "For anyone else, four yuan each. You can have two for five yuan. Want them?"

"Sure," I said. Then I spat on the dough sticks lying on his newspaper. "Let me have a couple. I haven't had breakfast," I said. Red Hair wiped his greasy hand on his pants and pulled himself to his full height, fists at the ready. I grabbed him by his collar. "Get my money out! Now!"

"I didn't take your money," he said.

"Get it out! Get it out!"

Red Hair took seventy yuan out of his pocket. "I bought the dough sticks and a pack of smokes. This is all that's left."

I released him, and he dropped to the ground with a thud. I turned to go, but I was worried he might try and jump me, so I said, "I've been doing this job since you were just a gleam in your daddy's eye!"

And I made a point of walking away very slowly, keeping a close eye to either side for his shadow. But he wasn't following me. Now that I'd let off steam and felt much better, I pedaled to the little park and sat down to eat my fermented bean curd.

Quite calm now, I went over what'd happened in the salon and wished I hadn't run away. *Happy Liu, how did you want Yichun to behave? Maybe she was just trying to be nice to you. Anyway, she did nothing wrong. What did you expect from her?*

I was worried that my running away might have annoyed or upset her.

I almost went back to the salon to see her, then decided not to. It was only three hundred yuan after all, and going back would be making too big a deal out of it. I wasn't the kind of man to make a fuss. She needed money, so I'd given her some of my earnings. It was no big deal! There was nothing more to be said. Now that I regarded Yichun as my girl, I was right not to worry.

38.

From then on, I redoubled my efforts to collect trash, working until dark. Every time I saved three hundred yuan, I went to the salon and gave it to Yichun. Of course, she tried to refuse it, but she took it in the end. The second time I went, she wasn't there, and I left the money with the owner to give to her.

"Who are you, anyway?" the woman asked me.

She obviously thought I was one of Yichun's clients, because she asked me how many times I'd been with her and why she hadn't gotten her cut from Yichun. The bitch! I hurriedly explained that I wasn't a john. Trash picking might be a lowly job, but this was honest money. I was from Yichun's hometown, I'd borrowed from Yichun, because someone was ill in my family, and now I was paying the loan back. I was kicking myself for saying this, for taking the coward's way out, but that was what I said, what I had to say.

The third time, I waited for her on her way to work. I gave her the three hundred, and she refused it. She tried to give me back the money I'd left with her boss the last time too. I put the money on the sidewalk in front of her, turned on my heel, and left. I thought she'd pick it up once I'd gone, but she turned on her heel and left too. When I'd gone a short way, I looked around. She'd vanished. I had to go back to pick the money up. Then I discovered that on the outside of the roll of bills, she had written my name, very small, eight times! My heart thumped.

When had she written my name, and why? I sniffed the bills, thinking that there was nothing in the whole wide world that carried as many stories as money. Every bank bill had so much to tell, but surely this one, the one with her writing, had the most beautiful story of all. I kept it, and put the rest in a paper bag and deposited it where she would see it when she left work that night. Then I waited out of sight. She picked it up and looked all around but didn't see me. Finally, she took the money with her.

That was a good way of doing it. The next time, I left the next three hundred yuan in a paper bag on the sidewalk for her to pick up. She seemed doubtful, peered around, and finally spotted a three-wheeler under a tree a long way down the street. "Happy Liu!" she shouted.

Ha-ha-ha . . . I'd been found out. I walked over to her, a goofy grin on my face. Ha-ha-ha.

She smiled back. Then, as I got nearer, she stopped smiling and said sternly, "This is a lot of money, Happy Liu! You're working in the city for your mom and dad and wife and kids, and you're spending money like it grows on trees!"

I told her in all honesty that I had no parents, or wife, or kids. "I want to give you money—I want to."

"Just a few hundred yuan?"

"I'm not a big businessman."

"Well, at least we've got that straight!"

"But I've got to help you."

"You can't help me out. In fact, I won't let you. I know what you're doing—you're laughing at me."

"No, I'm not," I protested. I was desperate to express my feelings, but I just couldn't get them out, at least not clearly. My cheeks were bulging with the effort, and I started to stammer.

Yichun stood there and burst into tears. "You're a trash picker. How much money can you earn? And why would I want your money? What are you trying to do, Happy Liu? Can't you see, this is the way I am, and you can't change that!"

I finally managed to get a few words out. "When I give the money to you, I feel better. That's all I'm trying to do, to feel calmer."

"You're so dumb!" she said. That felt like when she told me off for being a pain, and made me really happy. All I could do was grin, and she sighed. Then she grinned too. After that, whenever I gave her money, she took it without objecting. Though she asked me every time how much I'd kept for myself.

"I don't earn big money, but I have something coming in every day, enough to keep me in food and drink," I said. She took one bill out and tried to give it back to me, but I just slapped it back into her hand. "Don't worry about me!"

Wufu used to tell me that once he earned all his money, he was going to get drunk, then go home and fling it all down in front of his wife and say, "Here's the fucking money!" I'd laughed at him for being crude, but now I realized he wasn't being crude; he was showing how unbelievably proud of himself he was. Nowadays, I would sit in the three-wheeler with Yichun, and tell her the day's news, and anything interesting I'd picked up. She would listen quietly, her expressions changing with my mood. She was adorable, her eyes were so gentle. I was elated. "I'll sing you a song," I said. It was an old folk song from Freshwind:

> "Thirty *li* of mountain slopes, forty streams
> of water, I'm off to see my girl every second
> day, and now I've gone bow-legged with
> running!"

"You're very funny," she said, and she unwrapped some chewing gum and popped it into my mouth. But I don't like peppermint, so I chewed it twice, then spat it out.

Now that I had a woman, there was so much more to life in the city. In the dead of the night, as I lay on my bed thinking about how superior Yichun was to all the other women I'd met here, I'd let my thoughts run wild about what we'd do next time I saw her, but every time we met, I made myself sober up. We'd talk and talk, and never run out of things to say. We talked about the countryside, about our hometowns, about Xi'an. We always agreed, and we often found ourselves saying the same thing at the same moment, and she'd get so excited, she'd pummel me on the back with her fists. One afternoon, I went with her to the post office to send five thousand yuan to the county police in charge of her brother's case. On the way back, we bumped into a hawker from southern Shaanxi who was carrying a bag of walnuts, and I bought a dozen for her. I sat Yichun on a park bench while I hunkered down to crack the walnuts with a stone. Her face was the same color as the flowers nearby, and I went into a sort of trance as I bashed away. One must have had a mind of its own because, after I struck it, it spun toward her and landed under her legs. As I bent down to retrieve it, my face almost brushed hers. She blushed scarlet, and I could see her hair trembling. It was the first time I had seen her so shy. Did she imagine that I'd aimed the walnut at her on purpose and was going to kiss her? I hurriedly picked up the walnut and went back to bashing it. *I can't take advantage of you just because I'm trying to help you, Yichun,* I thought. I struck the walnut again and succeeded only in hitting my hand.

I sighed. It was all because the first time I gave her money, I'd backed off. The thing was, I didn't want the money to give me any advantage over her. It was as if I was looking at her through an old-fashioned paper window, and I couldn't bring myself to poke a hole in it!

What kind of person was I, anyway? Proud of my high-and-mighty stance, and at the same time an idiot who couldn't pluck up the courage to kiss Yichun. I always bit my nails when I was out of sorts. It was a bad habit of mine. I gave the walnut kernel to Yichun now and sat there chewing my nails. She must have heard the crunching sound, because she laughed.

"What are you laughing at?"

"What's up with you?"

"Nothing! Nothing at all!"

"So if it's nothing, why are you biting your nails?"

I stopped hurriedly.

"It's a sign of immaturity," said Yichun. That reduced me to a state of utter embarrassment. It was true. With Yichun, I was totally immature.

"Am I really immature?" I said.

"Yup."

I mumbled some nonsense.

"See? Just a few words from me and you get like that. Isn't that immaturity?"

As she stuffed a walnut into my mouth, she asked when I would take her to where I lived. To Fishpond Village? I suddenly felt astonished and deliriously happy and overwhelmed with gratitude, all at the same time. But I was secretly dismayed too. I didn't mind breaking our rule not to bring strangers to Leftover House, not at all. I was simply worried that she would be turned off by where I lived, and that it would turn her off me.

Go for it, Happy! I told myself. If she was going to be turned off by where I lived, so be it. What trash picker ever had a decent place to live? And maybe she wasn't like that. She must be well aware that clean things could grow out of muck and filth.

As we walked, I kicked away a bit of broken brick on the road. I pointed to a large puddle of sewage. "Mind the water." There were some planks of wood lying higgledy-piggledy in the lane. I kicked them away too. They had nails in them and I scratched my foot, but I didn't say anything.

When we got to Leftover House, I shouted for Eight. I didn't want him leering when he saw me arrive with a woman. I was delighted when I realized he wasn't there. And a long-tailed bird sat on a branch of our tree, chirping away. Today was a good day!

"Would you like to use the WC?" I said, pointing in the direction of the shit-house. I wished she would, because then I could quickly tidy up my room, or at least fold the quilt neatly and put the lid on the unwashed pan. But she didn't.

We went upstairs.

"My room's a mess. Don't laugh."

Yichun, sweating from the walk, sat down on the edge of the bed and kicked off her high heels. She looked around curiously. "It's very neat and tidy." I had no hot water or fruit, and I couldn't find anything to offer her. "Why aren't you sitting down?" she said. "You must be tired."

I finally found some crispy bottom-scrapings left over from last night's meal, sitting on the windowsill. "Have you ever had bottom-scrapings? Try it! It's tasty," I urged her.

Yichun took it and nibbled. "We eat scrapings like this at home," she said. That was good. I stood in front of her, watching her eat.

"Nice?"

"Yup. You have some too."

"No, you have it all."

She nibbled again and gave me the rest to eat. It was exactly the same as when she'd given me some cake at the salon. But this time, the blood rushed to my head, and I was suddenly in such a panic that my mouth didn't close over the scrapings and they fell to the floor, and the cat pounced. It was the cat from the yard next door. It had never been in my room before, but it must have followed us in, ready to scoot off with the scrapings. "Get out!" I aimed a kick at it and tried to retrieve the food, but Yichun stopped me. She pursed her lips, pushing half the scrapings she had in her mouth into mine. In a daze, I went to take the scrapings from between her lips, but as I did so, the pieces fell to the floor and my lips met hers instead. Inside her parted lips, her tongue was slippery as a fish. I held it between my lips.

Somehow we must have pulled each other's clothes off, but that was all a blur. Suddenly I became aware that the quilt was on the floor, and there was Yichun's smooth body outstretched on the bamboo matting on the bed planks. My first thought was: How did that happen? Most nights I'd lie there, wondering when this moment would come, and I'd get ramrod stiff. But now she was in my arms, and I was kissing her over and over, but I just couldn't get it up. The more frantic I got, the more hopeless it was, until I was covered in sweat.

"Are you still a virgin?" Yichun asked.

"This has never happened to me, it really hasn't!"

Yichun sat up and began to stroke me gently. The cat was still crouched in the corner, its beady eyes gleaming at us, and I threw a packet of cigarettes that I found by the pillow at it. Yichun put her arms around me and laid me down, but my you-know-what was still so dead to the world, it seemed like it would never wake up.

"This isn't me! I can get it up normally, so why not today?"

"You're too anxious, and the bed's hard," said Yichun. She leaned over me and began to wipe my sweaty face. I could see that her back was crisscrossed with marks from the bed mat.

"Is the bed uncomfortable?" I asked.

"A little," she said. I felt bad. This wasn't the right kind of room or bed for this. *I'm so sorry, Yichun.* I kissed her again, all over her body without raising my head.

"Whose are those high heels?" she suddenly asked.

She was looking up at the shoes on the shelf. "They belong to you," I said.

"Nice try! But I don't believe it. Why would you have my shoes?" So then I told her the whole story. Yichun's eyes misted over, and she held me tight. "Thank you!" she said, planting a kiss on my forehead. I got the shoes down.

"If it's written in the stars that we should meet, then these shoes will be just your size!" I slipped them on her feet. Good God, they fit her perfectly!

I told her to take them with her, but she said she'd leave them here, so whenever I looked at them, I could think of her. I wasn't having that. I took her old shoes and put them up on the shelf. They would really give me something to remember her by. And when she went home with her new shoes on, then she could think of me.

39.

Finally, I was a man with a sex life! After she'd gone, I found one of her long hairs. I carefully folded it in a piece of paper and put it under the pillow.

As luck would have it, just as she was clipping down the lane in her new heels, whom should she bump into but Eight. He stared after her, then came racing up the steps to find me.

Meanwhile, I was in my room, seeing stars. Yes, really, my room was full of twinkling stars. When I got close to them, they disappeared, but as soon as I went over to the door, they reappeared, twinkling away, tiny bright dots of light, especially around the bed. Very strange. I finally figured out that they were from Yichun's sparkly makeup. I knelt down and picked up a dozen or so of the sparkles between my finger and thumb. Then I turned around—there were another dozen or so behind me—and there was Eight, licking his fingers. He had been eating a fried cake when he'd spotted Yichun, and the syrup had gotten all over his fingers.

"Got yourself a hooker, did you?" He leered at me. I stared at him. There was still one sparkle on the bed, and I sat down on it. "I've never seen a hooker as pretty as that," he said. "You only get them in big hotels. How did you get her to come here?" I threw the pillow in his face, but before it hit him, the cat pounced on his foot and drew blood. That got rid of him. When he'd gone, I saw the piece of paper with her hair inside, where the pillow had been. Luckily Eight hadn't spotted it. I went to pick up the pillow and heard Eight on his way downstairs. He didn't sound at all annoyed. "Fancy people eat fancy food, and you certainly got yourself a fancy woman!" Was I a john? Maybe I was. I mean, Yichun was a hooker, there was no doubt about that. Whatever her reasons, she was in the sex trade. If I wasn't giving her bits of money, would she have come with me? I thought I was a cut above Mr. Mighty and his cronies, but hadn't I had sex with Yichun too? Sex of a sort, anyway, even though it hadn't quite worked out.

I suddenly understood how Mighty and his cronies felt. All the same, I couldn't help feeling a bit smug. She did business with them, but she came to me even though I hardly gave her anything. She couldn't have come for that little bit of money. In other words, when she came with me, she didn't come as a hooker, and I certainly wasn't her john.

I sat on the bed to rest. The bed was too hard. I needed a new one. I wasn't in the mood for trash picking that afternoon, so I simply sat there and looked out the window at the porcelain-blue sky. Xi'an skies were usually murky and gray, but today it was so clear, you could see the Zhongnan Mountains in the far distance. I got out my flute and piped a tune. Strangely enough, as soon as I began to play, I got a hard-on. When I'd needed it, it couldn't be bothered to stir itself, but now that there was no call for it, it was crowing. Dammit! I suddenly thought of the Chain-Bones Bodhisattva. Maybe Yichun was a living reincarnation of the Chain-Bones Bodhisattva. I'd found my very own Chain-Bones Bodhisattva! I yelled for Eight.

Eight was sitting in his doorway, picking over his trash, his face and hands blackened with dirt. "Do you know Pagoda Street?" I shouted in excitement.

"Yup, there's a pagoda there, but I've never been in."

"Want to go?"

"I'll come if you want to go," said Eight. So I took him. He wanted to take his cart, but I wouldn't let him. I forked out for a taxi instead. We walked past all the little shops selling curios and reached the Chain-Bones Bodhisattva. The bearded man wasn't there anymore. I bought a ballpoint pen and a notebook, and squatted down to copy the inscription. Eight grumbled that the pagoda was nothing special. "I know you paid for the taxi, but you owe me a meal now," he said.

"How come?"

"Because you got lucky today." I stared at him, then continued to copy the inscription. I was thinking of pasting the paper above my shelf.

"I bet this was your first time. After my first time, I had to make a load of mud bricks. Usually you need an hour's rest after making mud bricks, but I kept going for half the night and never felt tired."

"I was nice enough to take you on an outing to the pagoda, and all you do is talk hogwash!" I said angrily.

That shut him up. He watched me copy the inscription, then asked, "What's that mean?" I read it to him, but he couldn't make heads or tails of it. So I explained this was the pagoda of the Chain-Bones Bodhisattva, she was buried under here. I told him the story of the Chain-Bones Bodhisattva, burbling on and on about her. Eight tried to look as if he was listening, but his gaze wandered. He spotted five empty beer bottles not far off and quickly retrieved them. Then he came back. "Go on," he said.

"Go to hell!" I said. Why had I ever bothered to bring him? He was worse than Wufu.

"These bottles would earn enough to buy a meat bun," he protested. He could see I was angry.

"All you know how to do is pick trash and stuff your face! I brought you here, so I'll buy you a bun to eat. Let's go!" I put my pen and notebook away and went back to the curios market. On the other side, there was a stall selling meat buns.

Eight caught up with me. "I don't want a bun. I'm going to Hibiscus Garden. I want to see if the scenery's prettier there."

I couldn't stay angry with Eight anymore, and I smiled. When the din from the night market at Fishpond disturbed my sleep, I made myself think of it as a nice noise. Now I turned my anger at Eight into amusement. "Fine, let's go to Hibiscus Garden. Anywhere else while we're out?"

"Is it true they spent a billion on those gardens?"

"That's what the ads say."

"Our country must be rich!"

"Well, Xi'an is booming. They're building a new finance center on South Avenue."

Eight started on a tirade. "I just can't get my head around it. The city spends a billion on a park, millions on a concert in a stadium, and even more on this or that exhibition. But if they've got money to burn, why do they only spend it on the city? The villages get poorer and poorer, and we don't have a cent to rub together!" He was working himself up into a rage, cursing and swearing. I turned to look at myself in the window of an antiques shop and adjusted my jacket and pants. Looking back at me in the glass was another me, laughing at Eight just like I was.

"Why are you so grouchy, Eight? Are you sick?"

"Nope."

"Come look in the window," I said.

He came over. "What are you looking at?"

"Look at yourself."

"I don't like looking at my vitiligo."

"Smile," I said.

He smiled.

"Our life in the city, it's like this shop window. If you're angry, it's angry too. If you smile, it smiles with you!"

Eight fell silent.

When we got to the entrance to Hibiscus Garden, in the square outside, I told Eight, "I'm coming in with you." I'd already made up my mind I wanted to go in this time. I wanted to go to the best viewing place in the gardens and write, "Happy was here." But just as I was telling Eight that he mustn't breathe a word about this to Wufu, who should turn up but Lively Shi. Strange that I kept bumping into Lively. Birds of a feather, maybe. But no, we were completely different. Maybe it was divine providence, fixing it so I could learn from him and become a real city man.

Lively was standing on the steps at the entrance to Hibiscus Garden. He looked as fat and grimy as ever. He had a large placard in his hand with "Ticket cheat!" written on it. Everyone going in and out of the gardens had to pass by him. He stood there, his big head bowed, shining with sweat.

"Lively! What are you doing?" I called to him.

I heard someone say, "This dirty fat man wanted to get in without a ticket. There're always gatecrashers outside Hibiscus Garden. When they're caught, they're made to stand here as punishment."

Suddenly I was furious. I went over, grabbed the placard out of his hand, and tore it into pieces. "What are you doing standing here, making an idiot of yourself? Isn't it bad enough you don't have any money or a ticket? Why make a spectacle of yourself? Go on, scram!"

Lively looked at me, then he looked at the ticket collectors nearby. He didn't move. "Scram, I said!" I shouted at him. I gave him a kick in the ass, and he went, dragging his feet reluctantly and staring back at the ticket collectors.

The ticket collectors were watching but didn't interfere. Lively finally picked up speed and disappeared.

I stomped off too, my hands clasped behind my back. I wasn't just acting as if I was a government official. I really felt like one. "Achoo!" I sneezed.

Eight ran and caught up with me. "Happy, Happy! You let Lively go! Why didn't you get into trouble?"

"It's my air of authority." I was a trash picker; I would never have had that air of authority if I hadn't been with Yichun, the most beautiful girl in the city!

40.

As I said, I'd set myself certain targets for city life, and my next step was to buy a bed. I figured that, even if I couldn't buy a bed frame, at least I could get a springy mattress to go on top of the bed boards. I went window-shopping and checked out the prices: a mattress cost at least five hundred yuan. But the mattress wouldn't stop me from giving Yichun her regular three hundred yuan, come what may. So I had to think of a way to earn extra money. But where was I going to do that? There was only one place: the Dengjiapo dump. I used to hate it when Wufu and Eight went scavenging there in the mornings, but now I went along with them.

I was astonished at the hordes of people at the dump. They chased after the dump trucks like a pack of dogs, and some of them even got buried as the garbage was tipped out. But they simply jumped up again, wiped their faces, and rummaged madly through the trash with their rakes and hooks. Dust flew everywhere, and the air was filled with plastic bags—red, white, blue, and black—and the shouts of the pickers. Shacks made of branches and cornstalks surrounded the dump, full of women and children and dogs. The women and children ran in and out, tying and bundling together the various cement bags, bits of broken plastic, empty paint cans, and wire and scrap metal their husbands or fathers brought them. Then they sat down on top of their bundles and ate their *ganmo*. A fierce scuffle broke out for some reason, and we could hear crying. There was a chase, which ended in the man being chased throwing down a big laundry bag. I stood there in bewilderment. I had no idea what to do. I felt that I shouldn't have come, and that Wufu and Eight shouldn't have come either. Wufu shouted. He was shouting at me. I saw that he and Eight had taken possession of a pile of trash, and I ran over to him. Wufu was bent over, pawing through it. His face was filthy, and the sweat left runnels in the dirt so he looked like a villain from Qinqiang opera. He had his butt stuck in the air, and the crotch of his pants had split again, exposing his goolies for all to see. But it all seemed quite normal here. Whenever he found anything, he tossed it over to me and I sorted it out. The cardboard boxes were sodden, and the wire came encrusted with bits of cement. The plastic shoes, old shopping bags, and aluminum pots and bowls stank to high heaven, and then a casserole missing its handles came flying my way, and the rancid chicken intestines inside it landed all over my head.

"Hey! Hey! Who's going to buy this old pot?" I shouted. Wufu threw a pair of shoes over. I swore angrily and threw them into a nearby ditch.

"Those are my shoes!" Wufu protested. He'd taken them off because the slurry was getting inside and making his feet slip around in them. He didn't want to ruin them. I had to retrieve them from the ditch. Eight wasn't doing any collecting. He stood nearby, armed with a stick to keep marauders at bay. A lot of people were watching us from a distance. A dog barked furiously and tried to get near us, but Eight brandished his stick and rushed it. As the dog backed away, it fell over, and then the people cleared off too.

We finally sifted through the trash without further incident, and we collected pretty decent stuff. But by now we looked more like dung beetles than humans.

Every time we got back from Dengjiapo, Wufu and Eight ate a couple of *ganmo* stuffed with pickles and chilies, then set off for Prosper Street with their carts. But I had to wash myself first. I did this in the shit-house. I hung a pot with a hole in the bottom from the beam overhead and stood underneath. The water trickling out made a good shower. The only trouble was the water soon ran out, and I had to keep yelling at Wufu to come refill the pot. Wufu and Eight just jeered at my showers.

"Go ahead! See if you can wash off your peasant skin!"

We'd never agree on the importance of being clean. Let me give you a few examples: I always changed my clothes when I went to Prosper Street; Wufu and Eight didn't. I plucked the whiskers from my chin; they didn't. I stopped to look at the fashions and the mannequins in shop windows I passed; they said, "Those aren't real people!" I commented on the style of this building, or the windows in that building, and I was eager to know if it was a foreign head of state visiting or some official from Beijing when we hit a roadblock. They just said, "Leave it alone, Happy! What the hell's it got to do with trash pickers like us?" They picked holes in everything I said, and when the three of us were together, I had the impression that Wufu was drawing away from me and much preferred cracking jokes with Eight instead. I felt sorry for them. They were so poor that their minds were poor too. But there was always one whale in a shoal of fish, and one phoenix in a flock of birds, so I couldn't get angry.

I felt sorry for them, but I'd never abandon them. It was like when Yichun and I were walking together, how my ugly face made her look even more beautiful by contrast and her beauty boosted my confidence. Well, it was the same with me and Wufu and Eight.

Eight had one thing going for him: he kept his lips sealed. He never breathed a word to Wufu about me bringing Yichun back to Leftover House. Wufu was not exactly quick on the uptake anyway. When he realized I was taking two bits of fermented bean curd with me when I left in the morning, instead of one, or that I was playing the flute more than before, or that whenever I had a spare moment, I stood in front of the mirror plucking my whiskers, or cleaned under my fingernails with a piece of split bamboo, he just asked, "How have your takings been?"

"Fine!" I'd say.

"Mine haven't been bad either," he'd say, "but it's a pity no one's given me any more clothes."

"Have the sweatshirt I picked up. It's just got a big number 'five' printed on the back. Maybe someone wore it for a sports match, then threw it out. Want it?"

Wufu rushed into my room for it and finally saw I had an old pair of high-heeled shoes on my shelf instead of the new ones. He thought that Almond must have sneaked in and swapped them out before she left. When I spilled the beans, he was open-mouthed with astonishment. Now that I'd started to tell him about Yichun and me, I couldn't contain my excitement. I laid it on thick as I told him how beautiful she'd looked that day, but Wufu wasn't impressed. All he said was, "Aren't they all the same when they strip down?" He didn't believe she was at all good-looking, but he was happy that I wasn't a virgin anymore—nothing would convince him that we hadn't gone all the way.

When I said we hadn't, he asked, "What happened next?"

"She left."

"Did you give her any money?"

"Yup."

"You didn't finish the job, and you still gave her money?"

"You think the money was for that?"

"Don't give her any next time!"

"Why not?"

"Because when it comes down to it, she's a hooker. When my missus gave me my first child, she had a difficult birth. But with the second, it was as easy as taking a crap. Your Ms. Meng's a hooker. It doesn't mean anything to her to do it with you. And you keep giving her money, money that you've scraped together, cent by cent, with the trash you've picked!"

"You don't understand anything! I'm telling you—and I'm serious—don't talk about her that way. She gave that up long ago. I don't want to hear you calling her a hooker!"

"But she is a hooker!" he insisted.

I got so angry, I ignored him. In fact, I ignored him for two days and two nights. I knew he was cooking rice, and making it good and thick, every time he came back to Leftover House. I saw the fresh ginger he'd brought for me and left on the chopping board because I had a cold, but I still refused to have anything to do with him. I read aloud from an old newspaper to Eight. Eight wasn't interested, and I had to force him to sit and listen, but whenever Wufu came within earshot, I shut up. I got hold of an orchid plant and divided it into two. I left half in a bowl on my windowsill; then I stood outside my door and shouted down to Eight, "I've got a potted orchid for you!"

"I'll take the pot and leave the orchid," he shouted back. I heard Wufu crying in his room.

When he cried, I felt I'd gone too far. I made dinner that night. I cooked pulled noodles, and I went to the store at the top of the lane to buy two eggs to poach with them. When it was done, I filled a bowl for me, then filled another bowl and left it on the chopping board. Wufu came out and carried the bowl into his room. When he was halfway through the bowl, he discovered the egg. "You bought eggs?"

"If you don't want it, put it back in the pot." He laughed then and swallowed his poached egg whole, in one gulp, nearly choking on it.

After that, I didn't talk about Yichun anymore, and he would find an excuse to make himself scarce if we were going to pass by Salon Street. There were quite a few evenings when we went home to Fishpond separately, and I knew he was giving me a chance to see Yichun on my own. After a while, I realized that most of the time when I got back, Wufu wasn't there, or Eight either. Once, old Fan said to me, "Why haven't you gone with them, Happy?"

"Gone where?"

"To the dance hall in the street behind the Town God Temple. Didn't Wufu tell you?" I was going to ask more, but Fan's missus was coming across the street toward us, so he shut up. The next day, I looked as I passed Town God Temple. There was the dance hall. So Wufu and Eight had gone behind my back and were hanging out there. They must have been jealous that I had Yichun. What a pair of lowlifes! But I sympathized with them and never let on that I knew.

Still, I kept a careful eye out for any changes in them. They were as lively and garrulous as always, only Wufu was getting bossier with Eight, and I couldn't figure out why.

One evening, I was upstairs cooking, and the two of them were playing chess under the tree. They'd agreed that withdrawing a move wasn't allowed, and that for every game lost, the loser had to cough up one yuan. So they were playing for real, neither letting up and both shouting and yelling. After Wufu lost a game, he got really wound up. Eight had taken his shoes off, so Wufu shouted at him that his smelly feet were putting him, Wufu, off his game. Eight put his shoes back on and said the loser was allowed to throw a temper tantrum. Wufu insisted on another game, with the loser paying two yuan, and he promptly lost again. Eight took the money and got up to go.

"Oh no, you don't!" said Wufu. "Another game, and the loser pays four yuan!"

They played on, until Wufu said he was thirsty and told Eight to get him a bowl of water. While Eight was gone, Wufu moved his horse and finally won the game. But Eight wasn't paying him four yuan. He said he'd pay one. They started to argue. Eight coughed up another one yuan, and then Wufu jumped on him and tried to snatch the money away. Wufu was bigger, but Eight was stronger, and Wufu only succeeded in hitting Eight across the face, which made him furious. He tore up the one-yuan note and flung the bits in Wufu's face.

I saw it all from the rooftop, and egged them on. "Keep going! Why are you stopping?" But Eight stomped off to his room, swearing.

Wufu picked up the torn-up bill and came upstairs. "That idiot still thinks he can win!" And his face cracked a broad smile.

"What are you smiling at?"

"If he hadn't left, I'd have beaten him up."

"Do you have to pick on him?" I filled a bowl with noodles for Wufu to take downstairs.

"You want me to take him a bowl of noodles?"

I bellowed at him, and he went off with the noodles, extracting one between finger and thumb and slurping it up on his way. When he got to Eight's room, he put the bowl down by the door. "Hey, listen up, you haven't paid your debts, but we're still feeding you!" And he picked out another noodle and slurped it up.

The next evening, they settled down to another game of chess. This time, they didn't play for money, but whoever lost had to buy the booze. I reasoned that any kind of betting sours friendships, but that drinking brings friends closer, so I didn't try to stop them. Anyway, Eight lost and had to buy the booze. "I bought it, so I need my share," he said, and proceeded to get very drunk. He didn't behave like Wufu who got maudlin and sniveled about his missus. Eight cursed and swore, and then fixed us with a glassy stare, behaved like a dumb idiot, went into his room, and collapsed on the floor. He slept there all night, and that was where I found him, sprawled on the floor and just opening his eyes, when I went to the shit-house in the morning. "I thought I was still drinking in Wufu's room," he mumbled.

"You wouldn't know if you were dead."

"You're right. When you die, it's no different from being drunk. You'd probably think you were still drinking." He staggered to his feet and shouted, "Wufu! Why didn't you help me into bed when I got drunk? You left my door open and let the mosquitoes in, and they bit me all night!"

41.

About ten days later, there was another downpour. Wufu got up that morning and pointed furiously at the sky. "We can't go trash picking. That's another day wasted!"

"Just sit and think about things," I advised him.

"What things? I'm going to take a piss and then go back to sleep. Don't call me for breakfast."

I found a bottle of liquor, still half-full. As I drank, pleasant daydreams came to me about Yichun.

Wufu came back from the shit-house. "You shouldn't drink on an empty stomach. Have some snacks with it!" he said. *Memories are the best snacks,* I thought. But Wufu interrupted my train of thought. "Happy, you need to go sort out Eight," he said in a low voice.

"What's up with him?"

"His room's empty."

"He's not in his room?"

"He hasn't been in his room for a few nights." That was unexpected. I stared at Wufu. He looked as embarrassed as a girl, red to the gills and avoiding my eyes. I suspected he was ashamed. This was serious. He admitted that he and Eight had been going to the dance hall behind the Town God Temple for a hand job at ten yuan a go. He kept saying that old Fan had put Eight up to it, and that he, Wufu, had been away from home for so long, he couldn't resist and had let himself be tempted too.

He finished his story and looked at me. I knew what that look meant: *You've got Meng Yichun, but we have to scrape the bottom of the barrel.*

I didn't take the bait. I just said calmly, "Forget all that, Wufu. What's happened to Eight?"

As he explained, I got very worried. It went something like this: Eight had hooked up with a woman in her forties with such big buckteeth, she couldn't close her lips over them. He'd boasted to her that he was a factory worker. She didn't believe him and said no factory worker would have skin as dark as his. Eight said he worked on boilers, had done so for twenty years or more. The perks were really good: you got issued a pair of gloves, a towel and soap, and a bag of rice every ten days. The woman was impressed and took him home. She lived in a 1970s air-raid shelter, inside the north city wall. Eight went once; then he went again, and this time he took Wufu with him. The shelter was divided into countless tiny rooms, with partitions made from branches and cornstalks. The woman's room was the farthest in, and nice and cool, though the light wasn't good, nor was the air. It smelled like rotten pickled cabbage. She'd had lily-white skin in the dance hall, but out in the open air, her face looked sallow and dark, her teeth stuck out more than ever, and they were stained yellow.

"What's wrong with yellow teeth? Didn't you say all women were the same when they stripped down?" I asked.

"How d'you always remember what I say? I'm not talking about whether she's a good woman or not. It's the other people in the air-raid shelter—they're a rough bunch. Eight's been going there a lot, and I'm worried he's gotten himself into trouble!"

I kept drinking. Things didn't look good.

"He didn't come back last night, and he's still not back . . ."

I didn't offer a drink to Wufu.

He was still looking at me, as if I were a judge pronouncing a sentence. When I'd finished the bottle, I said, "Go make some food." Wufu wasn't happy, but he went anyway. He boiled some porridge, muttering to himself as it sputtered and bubbled. I couldn't make out what he was saying, and I didn't care. When the porridge was cooked, he said, "You eat. I'm going to sleep."

"You've got to eat too! When we've eaten, you'd better take me to the shelter."

So Wufu took me by bike to the north wall. The rain pattered down, and he got lost three times before he finally found the shelter entrance and we squeezed in. It was a long tunnel, lined with partitioned-off cubicles, like he'd said, and we kept stumbling over old paint tins and empty beer bottles. Cracking sounds echoed around us. Anyway, we tracked down the sallow-skinned woman. Eight wasn't there, and the woman was brewing up herbal medicine from a packet labeled "For Hepatitis B." A man was sitting on the mat. His shoes were covered in mud, and he was frantically scratching his legs. His eyes shone green as he looked at us. "Who are they?" he demanded. "I bet if I'm not here, you're like a bitch in heat!" The woman quivered, even though he wasn't looking at her.

"No, no, I don't know them," she protested. I sensed danger. This man seemed to have the woman completely under his thumb, and he looked like an escaped prisoner, or maybe he'd served his sentence and now couldn't get a job.

"We're searching for someone from back home," I explained. "Have you seen a man called Stone Huang? A stocky fellow, bald as a coot."

"Get out!" the man roared. Wufu tried to act tough, maybe thinking I'd be right by his side. But I'd never confront a tough guy openly. Wufu was about to get us into big trouble.

"That's no way to talk to us!" Wufu said belligerently. "Who are you to tell us to get out?"

The man lumbered to his feet. "Who am I? Come here, and I'll tell you who I am!" I tried to stop Wufu, but before I could get hold of him, he went closer and the man seized his jacket collar. Wufu was tall, but he looked like a sheaf of corn in the man's grip.

"I took an ax to someone, the police caught me, and I got away. This woman's mine to use whenever I want, and if I don't choose to, no one else had better think they can get their hands on her. Understood?" And he jabbed Wufu in the mouth.

I had to intervene at that point, even though there was no way I could knock him down, so I jumped on him. But he was like an Amur leopard. Before I could get close, he'd knocked me flying. My suit jacket got hitched on a wooden stake. He kicked me again, and a great rent tore in my jacket. He'd ruined my suit! Fired up with fury, I went for him, using a low trick I'd seen women in Freshwind use on their men: I headbutted him and at the same time grabbed his testicles as hard as I could. "Ai-ya!" he screeched, and collapsed on the floor.

The punch in the mouth had spun Wufu around. Now he was searching for a stone but couldn't find one. There was a wooden stake across the door of one of the cubicles, with a rope tied to it, attached to the door frame of another cubicle. Wufu went to grab the stake, and tugged and tugged but couldn't move it. "Hit me if you dare!" I shouted at the man on the floor and, jumping to my feet, I ran over to Wufu. But instead of helping him, I ran away, pulling him with me.

When we'd gotten a good distance, we looked back. The man wasn't coming after us. Wufu was still annoyed and still looking for a stone.

"Why are you still trying to fight him?" I asked. "Didn't you hear? He's a prisoner on the run."

Wufu rubbed his mouth. A trickle of blood ran down. "Why did you drag me away? The two of us could have dealt with him," he complained.

"We were getting in too deep. There's no point in us getting killed. We've got to learn to look after ourselves."

"What a lousy day," grumbled Wufu.

I was sore about my suit, but I said, "Change what you can change, adapt to what you can't change, put up with what you can't adapt to, and let go of what you can't put up with."

"Who said that?" he asked.

"It was in the papers."

"If anyone finds out about this, we'd really lose face . . ."

"If we don't tell, who's going to know?"

"We know."

"Forget it!" I said. It was over and done with. We took the old Horse Passage along the foot of the city walls. It was still raining and chilly.

Wufu asked, "So, have we given up on Eight?"

"No, we can't do that! Eight won't realize that fiend's at the woman's place. He's so dumb that if he goes there again, he'll get himself killed."

But the rain was coming down in sheets, and Eight was nowhere to be seen. Xi'an wasn't Freshwind. It was a place where dangers lurked around every corner. Even so, Wufu and I decided to hang around the city wall to wait for Eight to appear. Just as we got to the end of the Horse Passage, Eight came staggering toward us. He was pulling his cart, a sheep's intestines hanging from the handlebars. As soon as he spotted us, he pressed his straw hat down on his head and dived into an alley.

I shouted after him, "You think you're invisible under your hat?"

Eight's mouth gaped, and he stuttered, "How . . . how? What are you two doing here?"

"No, what are you doing here, Eight?"

"I . . . I bought a sheep's intestines. Not easy to get a hold of . . . I went out really early for it . . . We can have hotpot, right?"

"Is that so?"

"Of course!"

"But we thought you were off to the air-raid shelter?"

Eight's sallow face turned as yellow as the paper offerings in a temple. He knew Wufu must have spilled the beans. "You gab like a woman!" he said furiously to Wufu. He pulled out a smoke and offered it to Wufu; then, just as he was about to take it, Eight passed it to me instead. "Listen, Happy, that woman . . . We're all away from home . . ."

"Did you know she's sick?" I asked. "What if you've caught something from her? D'you want to die?"

"Don't exaggerate, Happy! She's a good woman. She really looks after a man. She's not sick, she just caught a cold. That's why she was making herbal medicine. Whatever Wufu told you, it's just sour grapes."

"Sour grapes, huh? Fine, go ahead, but there's a man there, ready to chop your legs off!" Wufu retorted.

"You've been to her place? And there's someone else there? Don't mess around with me, Wufu!"

"I'm not motherfucking messing with you!" Wufu said.

Eight looked dismayed. "Was the man her husband?"

"Don't know."

"Her lover?"

"Don't know."

"He must be her lover! I saw some size-ten flip-flops there once. Dammit, why shouldn't I go? You've been!"

"Go ahead! Go get yourself killed, if that's what you want!" And Wufu told Eight what had happened in the air-raid shelter. Eight slumped down onto his haunches.

We headed back to Fishpond Village. Eight washed the sheep's intestines, stewed them, and asked Wufu and me to join him. I turned up a bit late, and they'd already gotten started. The intestines were tough, as if they hadn't been cooked long enough. Wufu chewed and chewed. Eight told him, "Just swallow it." Wufu took a large bit out of his mouth, looked at it, then put it back and swallowed it in one gulp. I suddenly remembered something. "Eight, how have you been feeling these last few days?"

"Fine. I've been sleeping a lot though."

"Do you feel sick?" I asked.

"I do when I get up in the morning, but I don't bring anything up."

I stood and went upstairs, pulling Wufu with me.

"What's up?" Wufu asked.

"Eight might have hep B," I told him. "Don't eat anything he cooks, or use his dish or bowl."

"What's hep B? Is it really that bad?" Wufu asked.

"It's a disease of the rich. You can't work, you need to rest a lot, and eat good food."

"But Eight's so poor!" Wufu was puzzled. He tried to puke up the food he'd eaten but couldn't, so he just swilled his mouth out with boiled water.

We couldn't afford to be sick here. We especially couldn't afford a disease of the rich. And poor old Eight had caught it. I felt really sorry for him—I couldn't tell him what he had, or tell him to go and get treated. From then on, the more we tried to avoid eating his food, the more enthusiastic and generous Eight became. Every time he had something good for dinner, he brought us a bowl. Of course, we thanked him, but as soon as he'd gone, we tipped it out. Wufu was very jittery. He kept saying he hadn't had sex with the woman, just groped her breasts once, but he had eaten Eight's food, so could he have caught hep B?

"Does meat, like red-cooked pork, sound good to eat?" I asked.

"Are you buying some?"

"Every time you hear the word 'meat,' you get a gleam in your eyes, so that's all right!"

Wufu grabbed my arm. "What do you mean, 'so that's all right'?"

Obviously I couldn't explain exactly what hep B was, but I knew about it from Freshwind, where it was called "drum disease." My father died of it. It made you not want to eat meat, especially fatty meat. Just the mention of it made you puke.

Wufu cheered up. "I can't have this disease. My family's too poor and my kids are only young. If I caught hep B, they'd all be finished, wouldn't they? And God wouldn't let that happen. Anyway, some meat really does sound good to me. Just last night, I dreamed I was eating a big piece of meat."

To prove he didn't have hep B, and to celebrate it, Wufu bought three pounds of meat. He had no sugar to caramelize it, so the meat never colored and instead stayed milky white. I took only half a bowl, but Wufu filled his bowl and squatted down at the top of the stairs with it. He wolfed down a great hunk of meat, then picked out another great chunk with his chopsticks and stuffed it into his mouth. Oil dribbled down his chin. "Good, eh, Happy?" Before I could answer, he answered himself. "Fucking good!"

Thank heavens for that.

I just said, "Chew your food, otherwise you'll choke to death!"

"At least I'll die eating!"

We talked and ate, and Eight, who had been sitting under the tree in the yard, looked up and dropped heavy hints. "That smells good, whatever you're cooking . . ." He caught sight of Wufu's oil-smeared mouth, and felt sure we'd call him up to share the food. But the call never came, so he got annoyed and went into his room, humming a Qinqiang opera tune. Then he came out and called up, "Wufu, the clouds this evening look like tiles. Does that mean it'll be even hotter tomorrow?"

"Yup." Wufu had chosen to sit on the steps to have his meal. That way he could tempt Eight upstairs, and if Eight saw the meat and was sick, that was incontrovertible proof that he had hep B.

"Have you had your dinner?" Wufu asked.

"Nope."

"I've made red-cooked pork. Want some?"

"Yup!" Eight was practically drooling.

Alarmed, Wufu shot an anxious glance at me and whispered, "He says he wants some."

I was astonished too. "Then give him some. Give him all the meat in the pot, Wufu."

And Wufu said to him, "You really want some? Bring a bowl then."

"Why didn't you bring a basin?" Wufu grumbled when Eight fetched a big bowl. He served him five slices of meat and firmly put the saucepan lid back on.

Was it possible that Eight didn't have hep B after all? I watched as he ate one slice after another. When the last slice dropped to the ground, he rinsed it and put it in his mouth. Well, that was good if he didn't have hep B. When you spat a gob of phlegm into the garbage can, the can didn't complain it was dirty, and the flies didn't worry either.

42.

When it was clear that neither Wufu nor Eight was sick, the pair started to hang out together again. Every evening, after dinner in Fishpond, they wandered around the night market. I warned them to stay away from the dance hall, and Wufu swore solemnly that he would. He said he'd keep an eye on Eight and stop him from going too.

"You never want to hang out with me these days," I complained.

"Eight's an ass without a halter. He needs me with him to rein him in," said Wufu. I smiled. Wufu had learned to order people around too. He smiled back. He'd lost a front tooth just a couple of days before, so it was a gap-toothed smile.

One evening I went to the depot to trade in my pickings, and Scrawny asked, "What's up with Wufu? Is he sick?"

"Like hell!" I said. But I was puzzled because Wufu had gone to Prosper Street with me in the morning. I hung around the depot waiting, but he never showed up. I suspected Eight had inveigled him into going somewhere else. Fuming, I went home to give him shit. As soon as I got to our yard, I saw Wufu and Eight sitting under the tree, having a drink.

"We were waiting for you. We've left you half a bottle," said Wufu. I grabbed the bottle and flung it on the ground.

Wufu looked dumbstruck. "What . . . ?"

"Earned some extra cash, did you?" I said.

"Yup," Wufu said.

"So you thought you'd just bail out, did you?" I said, my fury mounting.

"No, we didn't!" Wufu cried.

Eight had rushed over to retrieve the broken bottle and drink the dregs. I wasn't shouting at him. After all, I hadn't brought him to the city, so I wasn't responsible for him.

"Well, if you didn't bugger off, what happened to your trash?" I asked Wufu.

"That's not the only way to earn money," he protested.

"Well, if it didn't come from trash, you must have earned it from a ghost."

"I did," he agreed.

He held out a fifty-yuan bill. I refused to look at it. He put it on Eight's windowsill. "It's real, not ghost money!" he said. A sudden gust of wind took the bill, and it floated skyward.

"Ai-ya!" Eight shouted, and made a grab for it. It stuck on the shit-house wall, and he retrieved it. "This is real money, Happy. We got fifty each."

"Fifty yuan? What did you do to earn fifty yuan?" I asked even more furiously. For Eight and Wufu to get that much money, they must have stolen it. But how did they get away with it without me there? I stared at Wufu. I felt oddly like a snake with a rat, immobilizing it with my beady eyes and drawing it inexorably toward me.

Wufu hemmed and hawed. "Come on, spit it out!" I said. I was the boss around here, and I wasn't going to let him off the hook. Eight pulled Wufu to one side and gave him a daikon. They'd had two daikons to eat with their drinks.

"Go ahead, tell him," Eight said. "If you don't, it looks like we stole it, and then there'll be trouble! If you don't tell him, I will!" So Eight did. He said that in the morning, he'd gone to Lane Two in search of Wufu. He wanted them to look for the woman who lived in the air-raid shelter. He'd dreamed about her several nights running. (Eight looked embarrassed at this and sneaked a glance at me.)

"Tell him the truth," said Wufu. "Did I agree or not?"

"He refused," said Eight. I snorted. "It's true," said Eight. "Even when I offered to buy him a meal, he still refused. Just then, a woman called us over. She said someone had died in an apartment at the top of a high-rise, right when there was a power outage. She offered us a hundred yuan if we'd carry the stiff downstairs. 'Was it illness or a murder?' I asked. She said it was suicide. 'Oh, it must have been a woman then,' I said. 'They've got no moral fiber. They only have to get into a fight, and they're threatening to do themselves in.' She said it was a man. 'A man, killing himself?' I said. 'A government official,' she said. Would we carry him down? We didn't want to do it. Government officials ride in cars when they're alive, so why should we carry him on our backs now that he was dead? I mean, the spirit doesn't leave the body for three days after death, so it would be bad luck. Still, it was hard to turn down a hundred yuan. Wufu asked if we were going to do it. 'Yup,' I said, 'where else could we earn a hundred yuan?' We went upstairs. He was a fat man. He'd hung himself from the stair banister in his apartment, and his tongue stuck right out. The neighbors were saying he was the head of his department. The city government was running a massive investigation into corruption, and there had been thirteen arrests. He'd been called in for an interview. He came home and did himself in.

"I figure he did it because he'd been accepting bribes, don't you think, Happy?" Eight went on. "Maybe he knew he'd had it, but he thought the trail would go cold if he died, and they'd have to drop the case, so by dying, he could protect other officials, and in turn they'd look after his family for him. What do you think?"

"That's smart of you. How do you know stuff like that?" I said.

"Something like that happened in our county—that's how I know," said Eight. "So, I got the corpse on my back, and Wufu stood behind me, keeping it steady. What a weight! I nearly fell flat on my face. I can carry someone weighing a hundred and fifty pounds, no sweat, but I don't know why a dead body feels so heavy. The worst was his tongue, like a snake on the back of my neck. I said, 'Tie the tongue in,' and Wufu tied a towel around it, but it came loose. So someone produced a sheet and wrapped the corpse in that, and I heaved it on my back again."

"Anything else?" I asked. I didn't want to hear any more about the tongue.

"I got it downstairs," said Eight. Wufu had stopped eating his daikon. "It didn't feel right, to be carrying a corpse. We asked the family for a bottle of spirits to splash on the body, to chase the evil spirits away. And here's the bottle."

I sighed. I knew I'd done them wrong, but I had to keep looking stern, or it wouldn't be good for my reputation. I took off my T-shirt and went upstairs.

"I owe you a drink," I said.

Wufu and Eight visibly relaxed. "Fuck it!" Eight said. "A few more greedy officials should die!"

Wufu loosened up too. "Why do you owe us a drink?" he said. "You cuss at us because you love us! You always have our best interests at heart. Laugh, Happy. When you laugh, me and Eight feel easy."

I snorted. Right away, Wufu ordered Eight, "Get those things out, and give them to Happy!" Eight pulled something out of his pocket—a pair of black square-framed sunglasses. The city was full of people wearing them; it was part of power-dressing. We used to make fun of them, because from a distance it looked like crows had pecked their eyes out.

"Where did you get these from?" I asked.

"I really didn't want to carry the corpse," Eight said. "It had such a long tongue, so they gave me some dark glasses that were sitting by the bed. But even with the sunglasses on, I could still see the tongue."

"Obviously. They're not glasses if you can't see through them. They must have belonged to the dead man. He probably had a black trench coat too. Black trench coat and black sunglasses—I've seen plenty of rich men dressed like that!" I spat on the glasses.

"What's up? You think they're bad luck?" Wufu asked.

"Yup," I said. "But you sprinkled them with the liquor, didn't you?"

And that was how I came to own a pair of sunglasses. Though the official was greedy, he died with nothing. He couldn't even keep his sunglasses; they'd come to me! I went to my room, shut the door, and put them on. They fit me just right. Then I put on my suit. And my leather shoes. A new me appeared in the triangle of the broken mirror on the windowsill. No one would have believed I'd come from Freshwind. Most city folk, on the other hand, if you dressed them up in peasant outfits, would be the ugliest men and women in the village, even uglier than Wufu and Eight. It was impossible to see myself full-length in the mirror, so I tried something new: I put the mirror on the shelf and stood on the bed. There I was finally, all of me, reflected in the mirror. Very impressive! *Who are you?* I asked myself. *Happy Liu!*

There was a knock on the door. It was Wufu. I hurriedly took off the glasses and put them away. I wanted to give Wufu and Eight something in return. Maybe I should give Wufu the gold plastic boat on my windowsill. You saw boats like that in lots of shops; they were there to wish the business "smooth waters." And when I'd found one in the trash, I'd taken a liking to it. Wufu could have that. But what could I give Eight?

Wufu came in with some water for the orchid. "You're getting very fond of the orchid!" I said.

"I know they grow all over our mountain slopes, but having one here in the city, well, that makes it precious," he said.

"Here, take the orchid," I said. "I'll give the 'smooth waters' boat to Eight."

But Wufu said, "I don't want anything. And don't give Eight the boat either."

"Isn't it good enough?" I asked.

"You keep it; then you'll have 'smooth waters.'" Wufu smiled flatteringly. I grunted, and he said, "If you have 'smooth waters,' then so do we."

43.

Now that I had my shades, of course I wanted to go out, and of course I wanted to see Yichun. But in the afternoon, the wind picked up. That was the only thing wrong with Xi'an: it was very windy. The wind sounded like wolves howling or ghosts wailing outside the window, or a mob going at it with clubs and hammers and bricks. It kept me awake this evening. Wufu came out a few times, first to tell me to make sure my window was shut, or that it would bang and break the glass, and then to tie down the piles of sorted trash in the corner of the rooftop and weight them with a brick, and then again to shout down to Eight, "Why don't you take that stuff off the roof of your cookhouse, in case it blows away in the wind?" But Eight was sleeping like the dead, and no amount of yelling was going to wake him.

I came out. "You've been yelling so long, just take the stuff down yourself!"

"You think I'd help out young Junior there?" retorted Wufu. But he went up anyway. There were three sacks of brown paper up there, plus a bundle of plastic bags, and he picked up the bundle to throw it down, missed his footing, and fell with a loud crash.

"Wufu! Wufu!" I yelled. I was scared stiff when he didn't answer. I ran and switched on my room light so it would shine out and I could see what was going on. Then I ran down the steps. Wufu, stark naked, was sitting on the bundle, peering at his crotch. "Are you OK?" I asked.

Jia Pingwa

"I banged my balls, but it's nothing. I landed on the bundle."

"Why haven't you got any clothes on?"

"I don't wear anything at night." Then he yelled, "Eight! Eight! If I've damaged my balls, you'll have me to answer to!" But Eight still didn't wake up.

By daybreak, the wind had dropped a bit, but then it started to rain, and the wind blowing the dust around turned the sky a murky gray. Of course, rain was a good thing, but now it was raining mud. Wufu stood bare-chested on the rooftop for a while and got brown spots all over him. He looked like a sika deer. There was no trash picking to be done on a day like this, and Wufu grumbled, "Who'd have thought we'd have to take the day off, right after earning fifty yuan!" He asked me what I was going to do.

"What can I do?" I said. I thought nostalgically of the big ox shed back in the village. The commune once kept thirty head of oxen there, but when the land was contracted out to individual families, the shed was left empty. After that, in bad weather, it was used as a social club. It was a shame there was no space as big as that in Xi'an for migrant workers to gather when it was raining. That way, I could have met more folks from back home. We'd have talked and laughed and got our complaints off our chest, and brought snacks to share. The city never considered our needs. There was nothing for us to do except have a drink.

But Wufu decided it was extravagant to be boozing again, after yesterday. He didn't want to fork out himself, and he didn't have the face to ask me to go, so he shouted to Eight, but Eight objected. "Why is it always me who has to go?"

"OK, OK, I'll go," said Wufu. "Better have a drink while I can get it. After all, tomorrow my trap might be sewn shut!" He started down the steps, then stopped. "But it's not good to drink if you're in a bad mood. Let's drink the pickling liquor instead, and we can play drinking games." I smiled, but he really did come back up, ladled out a big

304

bowlful of liquid from the pickled-cabbage pot, and shouted down to Eight, "Bring us your dried bean curd, Eight!"

Eight had bought a bag of dried bean curd out of his fifty yuan, but he was in his room and not answering. "I nearly busted my balls last night, bringing down your stuff! Can't you spare a bit of dried bean curd?" Wufu thumped down the steps. Eight was peering out through the crack in his back window. "What are you looking at?" Wufu asked. Eight waved him over. Wufu went in and looked too. A window faced them in the neighboring yard, and the curtains weren't drawn. They could see a man and woman going at it on the bed, getting into all sorts of different positions. Wufu and Eight stood glued to the spot. It went on and on, and finally they got tired of watching and came upstairs with the bean curd.

I didn't drink the pickling liquor, but Wufu and Eight did, egging each other on with shouts of "Drink! Drink! Drink yourself drunk!"

Then Eight asked, "Can you eat you-know-whats too?"

"What you-know-whats?" I asked.

"That radish."

"Of course, you can eat radishes." They roared with laughter until tears ran down their cheeks.

Finally, Wufu said, "We shouldn't tease Happy." And he told me everything they'd seen through the window. "It's too bad—I've been married all these years, and I had no idea you could do it so many ways. Country folk and city folk really are as different as night and day." He sighed. There was a sudden crash, the door blew open, and the plastic piping from the rooftop landed under the tree.

"What a wind! Does that mean a sandstorm's coming?" I wondered aloud.

"You don't get a sandstorm after rain," said Wufu.

Eight looked out and swore violently. "Motherfucker!" His outburst startled us, but I didn't bother telling him not to swear like that, and the three of us simply sat listening as something in the lane was hurled to the ground with a great clatter.

Finally, Wufu poured out the pickling liquor. "That's enough. If I drink any more, I'll have a pickled belly. Why don't we wander around the village? There are plenty of stores, and we might be able to collect some stuff that's blown down."

"Because some of Gem Han's people have the contract for Fishpond Village," said Eight. "I used to pick trash on the streets around the entrance to the village, and Gem Han once warned me that he might slap a fine on us if we go up there again."

"We won't take the carts, just a sack. Why would we bump into Gem Han?" Wufu persisted. Of course, I didn't go, only watched them set off with their sack, then went and fixed my bicycle.

Once I had the bike fixed, my plan was to go into town and see Yichun. Whenever the weather was wet and gloomy, sort of "yin," I always found myself thinking of Yichun, I don't know why. Maybe because when heaven and earth seemed to mingle, women and men had the urge to mingle their yin and yang as well. I was embarrassed to go out while Eight and Wufu were around, but now they'd gone. Buddha have mercy on me, I actually called out her name, "Meng Yichun!"

The storm had emptied the streets, and I pedaled along on the bicycle, leaning hard into the wind. If the wind and rain got any fiercer, I'd be blown off and plastered against the old city wall. And if the wind dropped without warning, I would have fallen in the mud for sure. I felt like I was doing acrobatics. I wondered if Yichun would be touched, when she saw I'd come out in this terrible weather to see her. I imagined her scolding me, calling me a fool, an idiot, for risking life and limb like that, and then relenting and rubbing my rain-drenched hair dry with a towel. When a woman who loved you was annoyed, she'd pummel you on the chest with her fists, or rather, what passed for fists, more like cotton balls, really. *Careful, Yichun,* I'd say. *Don't break my sunglasses.* And I'd bring them out of my pocket, not like I was showing off but quite casually. And Yichun would give a cry of surprise. *Oh, what gorgeous sunglasses!* Then she'd put them on me and admire me from this way and that. And so I daydreamed on . . . I even dreamed that I'd love it if the heavens opened up and rained down flying stones and broken tiles on me as I arrived at the salon door. Then when Yichun saw me, she'd say, "Ah!" and faint with excitement. But when I finally got there and pushed open the hair and beauty salon door, she wasn't there. Why hadn't she come to work? Had she gone somewhere else? No one in the salon knew. They just told me she hadn't been there for two days. I asked where she lived, but none of them were willing to tell me. I decided to call her, but the salon didn't have a phone, so I scurried off to a general store and borrowed their phone. She answered, her voice hoarse and a bit muffled.

"Hello! Hello!" I shouted down the line. "It's me, Happy Liu!" I could hardly make out what she was saying. "What's up? Are you crying? Eh? What?" I asked.

"No, no, I'm not," she said, but she sounded all choked up.

I was frantic to know where she was, but she wouldn't tell me. I coaxed her and questioned her, and got annoyed with her, and the store owner stared. He removed a vase of flowers from beside the telephone because I was waving my hands around and he thought I might break it. Eventually I extracted her address and asked him for a pen so I could write it on my palm, jabbing the fleshy part with the point of the pen. Then I put the phone down, grabbed the bike, and set off at a run. I swung myself onto the saddle—and, dammit, the chain came off.

Down two streets, onto a narrow lane . . . I must have looked like a drowned rat. I parked the bike downstairs, ran up thirteen flights of stairs, and pushed open her door. It was a cubbyhole of a room, with a tiny TV, a wardrobe, and a cot for a bed. Meng Yichun was sitting on it, wiping away her tears.

She told me the county police had been in touch: there were new clues to follow, and so she'd sent them another ten thousand yuan.

The police officers had gone off on a trip to Swatow, and to Mount Potala in Zhejiang, but it was all a waste of effort. They called her when they got back to Xi'an, and she went to see them. They'd asked her for more money, to cover their hotel expenses and meals, and they also demanded money for the train tickets from Xi'an back to Miyang County. "Where am I going to get more money? Do they think money grows on trees?" Yichun wept. "Are they chasing a criminal or going on vacation? They were staying at four-star hotels. Why couldn't they have stayed in cheaper places? They wanted money for cigarettes and tea, and they wanted to go to Hibiscus Garden while they were here. Where can I get that money from?"

On the bed, she had laid out seven bills with Chairman Mao's head printed on them, seven hundred yuan altogether. She lit a cigarette and took a fierce drag on it. Then she puffed out smoke from each nostril, and the bank notes turned into frosted leaves in the morning mist.

"Yichun, Yichun," I said.

She didn't look at me, simply stared at the bank bills. Then she reached out with the tip of her cigarette, and a small singed hole appeared in one of the bills. "Oh, Chairman Mao, Chairman Mao, why don't you look after me?" The tears pattered down. I put my arm around her, and she slumped on my shoulder and sobbed. It felt like her whole weight was resting on me. I tried to stand up, because I was sopping wet, but I couldn't. I sat there on the bed, wetting a large patch of the bedding. I didn't know what to do. I wanted to cuddle her, but I didn't know if she'd think that was OK, so I just sat there motionless, letting her cry. My gaze alighted on the only picture on the wall, the photograph of a man who must have been her brother, if the high-bridged nose was anything to go by. I addressed the photo silently. *If you're a ghost, why don't you go after your killer? You could demand a life for a life, and he'll be so frightened, he'd cave in straightaway. Huh? Why not?*

But I actually said, "That's outrageous! Let me go find them. Which hotel are they in?"

"There's no point in going. Mighty went to see them." So Mighty had turned up, or more likely, she'd asked for his help. Did she always turn to him in a crisis? She trusted him, that much was obvious.

"Mighty went to see them?" I repeated. Yichun was still sobbing into my neck, wetting it with a mixture of tears and snot. "Don't cry, Yichun," I begged her. "We'll think of something. There's always a way." I rooted in my pocket, pulled out three hundred yuan, and pushed it into her handbag. Normally, when I gave her money, I had to do a lot of talking. Now I said nothing, and the bills curled up in a tight roll as if they were embarrassed to be seen. Though Yichun did see, she too said nothing. As before, she took the roll of money and counted it out, bill by bill. Most were one-yuan bills. One had a corner folded over, so she flattened it carefully and carried on counting. At the end, she counted out twenty yuan and gave them back to me. "You need to eat."

"I've hardly given you anything!" I protested. "Why are you giving me some back?" But she stuffed the money into my jacket pocket and buttoned it. She sat back on the bed, and I sat opposite her. She was wearing the high-heeled shoes I'd given her, but the sight didn't titillate me the way it used to. Did Mighty go see them? I couldn't get the question out of my head. Yichun didn't yet feel about me the way she felt about Mighty, and it was true, I didn't measure up to him, especially at this critical moment. In silence, we gathered together the bills spread out on the bed. A small alarm clock by her pillow ticked away, each tick a hammer blow to my heart.

We heard footsteps. Someone was coming upstairs. Mighty? Meng Yichun looked up, then asked me to get the door. I opened it, but there was no one, only the sound of a door shutting one floor down. Another resident coming home. I sat back down on the bed.

Meng Yichun was twisting her hair around her fingers. Her hand seemed soft as cotton fluff. I felt as if it would get smaller if I gripped it. But I didn't. I simply patted it and said, "OK, I'll be off now."

Then she said, "The weather's terrible today. Did you go trash picking?"

"Nope."

"Then you came specially to see me? The moment I had a problem, you were there for me."

"But I'm useless," I said.

I went to the door. Outside where I'd left my shoes, there was a bag of garbage. I picked it up, intending to take it down for her, but she called, "Come here!"

I put the bag down and went over to her.

"If you're not busy, don't rush off," she said. She took her ring off her finger. It was a very pretty one. Then she put it on again.

"You got something for me to do?" I asked.

"I bought this ring for three thousand yuan five years ago. I'd like you to ask around and see if anyone'll buy it. I'll take two thousand for it . . . No, forget it. Where are you going to find a buyer? But can you sell the TV for me? Even if it makes only a little money . . ."

"But then you won't have one to watch," I said.

"Well, you don't have one, do you? I can always buy a bigger one later."

I picked the TV up, but then I was worried about the sunglasses. "Put your hand in my inside pocket." She put her hand in and pulled out the plastic bag with fermented bean curd, then a handful of ten-cent bills, then the sunglasses. She didn't seem surprised by the sunglasses. She put her hand back in, but I said, "There's nothing more." She looked at me and said quietly, "There's your heart."

I saw tears hanging from her eyelashes, and instantly it took me back to Freshwind and the village pond, and the rushes covered in dewdrops, and my reflection when I looked into the pond.

I leaned toward her and kissed her.

"Be careful going down the stairs," she said.

I carried the TV down carefully. I had to carry it a long way before I managed to sell it off to an electrical repair shop. I had a nasty fight with the store owner before I managed to screw twenty yuan out of him to add to Yichun's savings. I had to put up with him abusing me, calling me a dirty rogue.

"Fine, I'm a rogue, but give me the twenty yuan," I said.

44.

I went to give the money from the TV to Yichun, then headed back to
Fishpond. Wufu and Eight were there, wet and muddy. They looked as
if they were about to say something until they saw my stony expression.
I went into my room and went to sleep.

It was hunger that woke me. It was the middle of the night. I
crawled out of bed, got a daikon from the chopping board, and chewed
it up. I got out all my savings and counted the money out on the bed. It
came to only a thousand yuan. I stuffed four hundred in my pocket, and
wrapped up and hid the remaining six hundred again. I got back into
bed, but then got up again and took another hundred from my savings.
You're so stingy! I berated myself. We should each get half. I would give
that five hundred to Yichun tomorrow. Then I was assailed by doubts
again. What possible use could five hundred yuan be in cracking her
brother's case? It was a drop in the bucket. *Mighty, why don't you give
her eighty or a hundred thousand? The same goes for her other rich clients.
They could pay all the costs of catching her brother's killer in one fell swoop,
couldn't they? I just don't have the money! Money,* I sighed. *Beats me how
I'm supposed to get it.*

I went back to bed. I'm telling you, I expected to dream about
money. In fact, as I was dozing off, I imagined I took a big stash of
money over to Yichun's. If I found Mighty and his entrepreneur cronies
with her, so much the better. I wouldn't give them a hard time. In fact

I wouldn't say anything at all. I'd simply put all the bills down on the bed, bundle after bundle, so much of it that the pile would come up to my nose.

But when I finally fell asleep, I dreamed that I was running down the main road again, barefoot, and up thirteen flights of stairs to Yichun's.

"You here?"

"Yup."

"I was just about to call you, and here you are!"

And she told me she wanted somewhere else to live because this room was costing her too much. Would I help her find somewhere cheaper?

"Come live with me."

"With you? What do you mean?"

For a moment, I was tongue-tied. Then I took my courage in both hands. "Yichun, I want us to live together. Maybe I'm jumping the gun, but that's what I want, for us to live together."

She looked at me but shook her head.

"Is it because Leftover House isn't good enough for you?"

She shook her head again.

"Yichun, I love you, I really love you. Let's live together."

"I know you love me, but it's impossible."

"Why? Aren't I good enough for you?"

"I'm not right for you. It's not that you're not good enough. It's that you can't support me, and you'll never put up with what I do."

I almost choked with emotion. "Don't go back to the beauty salon. With your looks and brains, can't you find another job? Or we could go trash picking together."

"What other job is going to earn me enough money? And without money, the police will never crack the case." She sighed. "There's no going back for me."

"Then I'll put up with it. I'll put up with anything you do."

She shook her head again.

"Are you in love with Mighty? You go to him for everything. Do you want to marry him?"

"I depend on him. I was in love with him once, but he wouldn't marry a woman who did this."

She stood there, looking at me, and I looked at her, but she suddenly disappeared, and all that was left was a pair of high-heeled shoes on the floor.

When I woke up, I wasn't sure whether this had been a dream or had really happened. I had such a bellyache, it felt like a cat was clawing inside me. OK, so it had been a dream, but why had Yichun and I talked about so many things, and why had I heard every word she said clear as a bell in my head? My dream was telling me something, something I couldn't bear to hear. Dammit, it was a dream, a dream! What actually happened was always the opposite of what happened in a dream. I waved it away and crawled out of bed. I slapped my cheeks hard to try and clear my thoughts.

Wufu was up earlier than me and had breakfast ready—a pot of pumpkin and potatoes. "The weather's much better," he greeted me. I grunted.

"Something up?" he asked.

"I'm fine."

"But you looked so grim last night, it scared me." He served me a bowl of pumpkin and potato, wiped a pair of chopsticks on his sleeve, and made a face.

"You've just dirtied the clean chopsticks! What's up?" I asked.

"My arm hurts."

I rolled up his sleeve. His arm was all purple.

"Eh?" I exclaimed.

"I didn't dare tell you. I thought you'd yell at me."

"You got into a fight?" I said angrily. "How many times have I told you not to go picking fights? You shouldn't even watch other people fight. You're too dumb, that's why! You get all fired up and hurt yourself when what's happening is none of your business!"

"I learned my lesson last time I cheered on someone else's fighting," Wufu protested. "But I did this yesterday. I went to the lanes at the village entrance with my sack, and I got fleeced. I was so angry with myself, I banged my arm on the wall."

I gave him a look.

"There are a lot of bad people in Fishpond nowadays," he said. "They target us trash pickers. Eight said so too. He got screwed over twice. Two guys blocked his way and demanded fifty yuan. Eight said he didn't have it, so one of them said, 'Thirty yuan'll do it.' Eight said he didn't have thirty yuan either. They picked up a broken brick and said, 'Want to stay around here?' Eight emptied his pockets. He had only ten yuan, so they called him a stingy bastard, took the ten, and bought some beer with it. They still wouldn't let Eight go. They wanted to give him the empty beer bottle."

I asked, "Why are you talking about Eight? You haven't told me what happened to you."

"I'm coming to that. So I was walking along, carrying the sack, when suddenly a motorcycle stopped right by me. There was a man riding it, with a woman sitting behind, and two sacks loaded on the front. 'You taking aluminum?' the man asked me. 'Yup,' I said. 'How much per pound?' he asked. 'Eighteen yuan,' I said. 'This is good aluminum ingot, best of its kind,' the man said, and got off, unloaded one of the bags, and opened it so I could see there really were aluminum ingots inside. I weighed it, ten pounds—at eighteen a pound, that was a hundred and eighty yuan. I got my money out to pay him. It was in small bills in different pockets and in my shoes. I counted it three times and handed it over."

"And then?" I asked.

"I've been fleeced before, so I'd made sure to look at their faces first, and I only bought their aluminum because they didn't look like rough types. I was going to sell it to the depot for twenty-two yuan a pound, and that would have been a nice profit. I even felt sorry that you weren't with me. But right after they left and I went to pick up the sack, it felt heavy. *Odd,* I thought, *maybe I under-weighed it.* I found somewhere quiet, opened the sack—and the aluminum had turned into stones. The motherfuckers switched out the aluminum when I was counting out the money," he wailed. "I'm useless, aren't I?"

"You are," I said.

"If you don't stake a dog down, it'll run off and take your rope with it! Why do things like this always happen to me?"

"Because you're always trying to make a quick buck."

Wufu looked despondent. Suddenly he said, "Eat up! I was going to make rice gruel this morning. Then I thought, no more slop, let's have something a little more solid! Eat up, Happy!" I had two bowls, Wufu had three. Then he put his bowl down and made a strange gargling sound.

"You shouldn't eat so much when you're angry. It'll make you sick!" I said.

"I'm not angry, but it's over a hundred yuan—it's like I didn't go out trash picking for two whole weeks . . . Almond said they hadn't been out picking for a month."

We hadn't had any news about Almond for a long time. "Have you seen her?"

"They came back yesterday."

"Are they OK?" I asked.

"They look all right, only they've both gotten thinner. Almond's lost so much weight, you can't see her tits anymore. I asked them what they'd been eating, if they haven't been out trash picking. Almond said they'd been sleeping during the day and working nights unloading concrete on the northern edge of town."

It was a throwaway remark from Wufu, and that was how I took it. But then, just as we were leaving, there was Almond shouting up the steps at me. "Do you want some *jiaotuan* corn pudding? I just got some fresh cornmeal. It's good and springy!"

"You're back!" I said.

"Yesterday. You never dropped by to see if we were dead or alive. You're heartless, you are. Out of sight, out of mind!"

I laughed. "How could I know? I get home and go straight to sleep. If we'd known, we would have sent a reception committee to the top of the lane!"

Almond really had gotten thin, and she'd cut her long hair short.

Eight came out carrying a bowl and tapping the side with chopsticks. "I've made some rice porridge, Almond. Want some?"

"If you want some *jiaotuan*, bring a bowl here. I don't want your porridge—you never wash your pan clean."

Eight tipped his porridge back into the pan and brought over the bowl for Almond to fill up. He was trying to talk with his mouth full of pudding. "The night . . . night . . . before . . ."

"Swallow your food, then talk," Almond said.

"I just burned my mouth!" said Eight, swallowing. "The night before last, I had a dream about you. I dreamed you'd come back."

Goolies came out of their room. "You were dreaming about my missus?"

"I dreamed it was raining so hard, Leftover House collapsed, and I put Almond on my back and carried her out and ran and ran all night."

"Careful not to run yourself into the ground," said Almond.

Almond was her old lively self, but I had no time for banter, nor was I in the mood. I was in a hurry to get to Prosper Street.

45.

Pickings were not good that day either. It was past noon, and I'd only gotten a bundle of old newspapers and a broken aluminum washtub. There was a furniture store across the street, and I saw mattresses being carried out. It reminded me of my plan, I should go take a look. Even if I couldn't buy one right now, at least I could see what they had. I went inside. The mattresses were just what I wanted. They bounced you around when you sat on them. Yichun would never scrape her back on one of these. The store was doing a brisk trade in beds and mattresses, and as soon as a client made a purchase, a porter was ready to transport it. The porters were charging a lot, so I offered my services to a customer. But I hadn't even settled on a price before three porters hustled into the shop. "Where the hell did you come from, donkey head? If you think you can scrounge from our manger, you're looking for a fight!"

"Fine, fine, I won't interfere." Then I added, "But let me tell you, if you ever have the nerve to pick trash, I'll trash you!" And I went back to my three-wheeler on the other side of the street.

It was a scorching day, and I felt drained. The streets were jam-packed as usual, and countless shoes—big and small, flat-heeled, high-heeled—passed before my eyes, none of them stopping for an instant. I remembered my dream. Why didn't I ever have any shoes on in my dream? And why did Yichun disappear so suddenly, leaving only her shoes behind? I looked up, wishing someone would talk to me, but not a single passerby noticed me. The road surface radiated heat, and I felt like I was being roasted, first my face melting, then my innards, then my arms and legs.

"Happy Liu! Happy Liu!" The old boy who collected parking charges outside the tea shop was waving at me. "Have some water, Happy!" Well, if he was going to call me Happy, I'd better pin a smile on my face.

"A penny for your thoughts," he said. "I've been watching you staring into space over there. How have takings been lately?"

"Fine," I said. That was bullshit. What earthly use was it giving Yichun three hundred here, four hundred there? How long would it take for her to win justice? I needed to get going, and fast. I pedaled away. Two more lanes and I'd collected only a heap of rusty wire mesh. I cycled on, panting hard, my legs as heavy as lead. *What's up with you? If you don't keep moving, you'll never earn any money!* I admonished myself. I was puffing and blowing so much that the smallest slope, or rather the smallest stone, brought me to a halt. But I had to keep going.

By the time I got to Lane Seven, I'd at least collected a couple of bent window screens. I was just loading them onto the three-wheeler when Wufu came toward me, pulling his cart. He hadn't had any better luck than me, his cart was only half-full, and none of it would make him much money. We exchanged smiles and stood there in silence. I offered him a smoke.

"Why's there not a breath of wind?" I complained, though we'd hated the last storm that ended only a day ago.

"Bring on a cyclone! Bring on a sandstorm!" said Wufu.

We looked up at the sky. It was covered with turbulent clouds, but there was no wind. At a nearby construction site, six skyscrapers were going up, each with dozens of stories already built. There was a roar of machinery, workers swarming like monkeys over the scaffolding. We always stopped for a while whenever we passed this spot, because workers often pilfered bits and pieces and were happy to offload them on us. But not today.

"Let's wait a little longer," said Wufu. We parked the cart and the three-wheeler under a tree where the workers could see them. An enormous cement mixer started up with a deafening noise, and a line of pushcarts waited underneath. The cement mixer spurted a slurry of cement into each cart, and a laborer pushed it away. They were bare-chested and burned black from the sun, scurrying around on stick-thin legs, like a bunch of ants. One of the laborers lost control of his cart as he passed by our tree and yelled, "It's running away with me!" He hung on, but it careened toward us, the handle flinging the laborer to the ground. Wufu and I shouted in alarm, and Wufu tried to stop the cart.

"Wufu! Wufu!" I called after him. He had stopped the cart, with its load of wet cement intact, but he had fallen on the ground. He crawled to his feet and so did the young laborer. Both were OK, apart from scraped hands.

"What way is that to push a cart? Eh?" I rebuked the boy.

"Keep your voice down! If the foreman hears, he'll dock my wages!" He sounded pissed off, but all the same, he reached inside his jacket, pulled out a large metal nut, and dropped it into my three-wheeler. "That'll do, right? Now, give me a smoke!" He had a cheeky smile, standing there in the sunshine.

"Do they want any more laborers here?" I asked.

"You want to push a cart?" he asked.

"How much do you get in a day?"

"Ten yuan."

"And if we just came at odd times, how much would we get?"

"You get your board and lodging. No one comes and goes as they please." After I gave him his cigarette, he said, "Come after dark tomorrow, and I'll sell you three steel tubes."

When he'd gone, Wufu said, "Are we going to come here looking for odd jobs?"

"Well, if we worked on the carts in our spare time, it would be OK, but not if we were stuck here all day. We'd earn more by trash picking."

"But you can take stuff from the construction site and sell it," objected Wufu.

"And how many steel tubes can you rip off?"

At the depot, Scrawny sat at the stone table at the gate, sipping from his flask as usual. He jeered at us because we had so little to sell. "You know Nine Wang?" he said, and took another sip, wrinkling his nose till it looked like a purple head of garlic.

"Who's Nine Wang?" Wufu asked.

"He's from Shangzhou, like you," said Scrawny. "He's been six years in Xi'an, and he's picked enough trash in that time to buy himself a house on the north side of town. Never seen anyone so dumb as you two!"

"We couldn't pick enough even if we ran ourselves into the ground!" said Wufu. Then he turned to me. "Why are people so different? We both spend our time trash picking, but Scrawny sits here boozing."

"Remember this," said Scrawny. "In this world, there are people who ride in sedan chairs, and people who carry the sedan chairs." I was so annoyed, I ignored him. What a pain in the ass! When Scrawny weighed Wufu's bundle of newspapers, there was a bit of rope hanging down. Wufu quietly put his foot on it, adding three pounds to the weight. I coughed, and Wufu gave me a meaningful glance. I said nothing. Scrawny went to pay Wufu fourteen yuan.

"Give me fifteen," Wufu said, "and I'll give you change." He took the fifteen, then said, "I haven't got one yuan. Do you really want it?" Scrawny insisted, Wufu said he was stingy, and in the end I forked out the one yuan.

After we'd left the depot, Wufu told me off for giving Scrawny the one yuan.

"It's not worth falling out with him for that."

"Here." He took out a one-yuan coin.

"I don't want it."

Wufu was playing with the coin. He tossed it up in the air, caught it again, and covered it with his hand. "Heads, we'll be lucky tomorrow. What do you guess, heads or tails, Happy?"

"Heads it is!"

Wufu was excited. He held the coin between finger and thumb, then put it in his mouth and bit down on it.

"It's not a silver dollar!" I said, and walked on.

Wufu was silent for a while, until he suddenly cried, "Happy! Happy!"

I turned to look at him. He had gone pale.

"What's up?"

"I've swallowed it!"

How could he have swallowed a coin as big as that? We were both worried. I tried to get him to throw it up, but he couldn't. I got him to stick his finger down his throat. That worked, and he puked up his dinner. Finally, there was nothing left to come up. But the coin was heavy and was still in his belly. What could we do? He might die from it. What if it got into his intestines and got stuck, what then? We'd better get straight home so he could drink oil. I remembered that back in Freshwind, a kid who swallowed a thimble was given rapeseed oil to drink, and she crapped it out.

Eight had a bottle of cooking oil, and Almond brought Wufu half a bowlful as well. Wufu swallowed Eight's oil, and followed it with Almond's half bowl.

"What a moocher!" said Almond. "With that much oil inside you, you'll be shitting so much, you won't get to pull your pants up in between!" Sure enough, Wufu was soon off to the shit-house, where he crapped in Almond's pisspot. He had a second crap, and a third. Still no coin. Wufu was still in there, crying, with us sitting outside and chewing our fingernails. It was like waiting outside the delivery room, said Almond. Finally, with a ping, the coin fell into the pisspot, and Wufu came out, covered in sweat, with a one-yuan coin in his hand. We all breathed a sigh of relief.

"So you're our goose that lays the golden egg! We'd better look after you, Wufu," I jeered.

"You're lucky. If it hadn't come out, you'd be a stiff by morning . . . You know people used to swallow gold to commit suicide in the old days. And gold and steel, same difference," said Almond.

"At least if you'd died, you'd have died eating money. No shame in that!" Eight said.

We had a good laugh, but we wouldn't let Wufu sit with us, because he still stank. Wufu was exhausted and went upstairs to look for something to eat. Almond started to regale us with tall stories of how they had spent their time away.

"How did my nephew Goodson treat you?" I asked.

"He was polite, but he didn't find us anywhere to live at the coal yard. We found a shed nearby and holed up there." I felt bad for them, and it must have shown on my face because Almond said, "Why are you looking like that? Goodson doesn't run the company! But that kid's learned a thing or two. You can do a lot better delivering coal than trash picking."

"How much better?" I asked.

Almond was a tad vague on the specifics, but in the end she said, "Well, he wears a suit, and he's always going out for kebabs or beer. He's a young man about town, compared to you!"

"A thief who lives beyond his means," I said. Then I asked what she and Goolies had been living on.

"We got by," said Almond. "Did nothing during the day, unloaded cement at night."

That was the second time I'd heard about unloading concrete, and I started to get interested. I told Eight to go get a fan for Almond, so that while she fanned the mosquitoes away, she could tell us about the unloading job. But Almond took the fan and rapped Eight on the head with it. "Did you touch that cardboard on the steps while I was gone?"

"Nope."

"Really?"

"Well, I only took three pieces. I'll pay you back."

Almond turned to me. "You wanted to know about unloading concrete?"

"Sure, if I can earn more money that way."

"Huh, what's up with you? Haven't you got enough money?"

"Who ever has enough money?" Eight said.

"Talking out of your ass again!" Almond said.

46.

We decided we'd all go unload concrete. Want to know what that means? Well, here's how Almond described it: "You've all seen the labor markets, right? They're outside the city walls and under pedestrian bridges. Country folk are always there, hammers, brushes, shovels, hooks, saws, and brickies' trowels at the ready, all antsy for a job. The company bosses or the labor contractors do the hiring. They inspect you all over, ask your age, look at your ID card, measure your height, estimate your strength. Then they pat you on the behind as if you were a mule or a horse, and say, 'You, I'll take you!' Some people get picked as soon as they arrive. Those are the lucky ones. Then there are some who can't get a job for a couple of weeks. They stand there, chewing on stale *ganmo*, or they lay out a few jujubes, cauliflowers, or apples they've brought on the ground and try and make a few cents. The fruit and the seller, they're both on sale. Often the fruit has started to rot, but the seller just sits by the side of the road, head bowed. Country folk flock to the city to earn money doing jobs that city folk don't want to do anymore, the dirty, heavy work, like demolition, excavation, road building, dredging the city moat, carrying sand and bricks, plastering walls, washing pots in restaurants, caring for the sick . . . City folk don't want to do stuff like that, so when companies—state-owned or private—buy cement or coal from Tongchuan, they need country folk to unload it. Tongchuan is a big center for coal and cement, and dozens and dozens of trucks bring it into Xi'an every day. Or rather, night, because the municipality doesn't allow trucks into town by day. Coal is brought to the west side of the city, and cement to the north side, and out-of-work country folk fight over the trucks. If you can get on one, you ride them to the depots where the goods are unloaded. You get twenty yuan for unloading a truckload of cement and thirty yuan for a load of coal. More and more country folk are turning up, but there are only so many loads, and every evening there are pitched battles near the west and north beltways. The amount of shouting, yelling, arguing, and fighting is horrendous."

Almond and Goolies had been unloading cement on the north side of the city, having heard about it through a friend. They knew that area, so we decided to go with them.

After we were through picking trash that evening, we made ourselves some good, thick rice porridge and downed it. Bellies full, the five of us set off toward the beltway. Almond made Goolies, Wufu, and Eight sit beside the beltway and told them to stay put. Then she had me go with her a few hundred feet up the approach road where we stood and waited. We were all in our oldest, dirtiest clothes, with bags or plastic sheeting over our shoulders, but Almond looked neat and fresh, and even powdered her face with the aid of a small mirror she held under a streetlamp.

"Do I look pretty?"

"Yup."

"Got to act young."

Whenever a vehicle came by, its headlights glaring, she could tell whether it was a cement truck. She gave me a shove into the shadows while she jumped into the center of the road, arms and legs flung wide. When a truck came to a halt, she shouted, "Driver! Driver!"

"This is unloading work, not a job for a nice girl like you."

"There'll always be someone to unload for you. How about I keep you company?"

"And what else'll you do for me?"

326

"You watch your mouth, mister!" And she opened the cab door and jumped up. "I'll sit on your hood, shall I?"

"My hood, eh? You do that!"

"The hood of the cab! The cab!" She gestured to me, and I scrambled onto the back of the truck.

When we got to the beltway, there was a rush of people, but I shouted, "We've already got unloaders!"

When they still tried to scramble aboard, Almond shouted in her fiercest voice, "Wufu! Eight! Pull 'em off! Aren't there any rules left in this world? We're unloading this truck!" Goolies, Wufu, and Eight grabbed the climbers' legs and hauled them down, while I pried off the hands that appeared over the truck's sides. As soon as they were gone, Goolies, Wufu, and Eight got on board, and the truck ground into gear and moved off.

The people left by the roadside cursed and swore. "That fucking woman's harder than a man, and that goes for her you-know-what too!"

"What you-know-what? She's got no you-know-what!" Shouts of laughter.

When we got to the depot, we unloaded the cement bag by bag. It was utterly exhausting work. It was OK if the customer got you to unload them where they were needed, but often you had to carry them into a building, and that was terrible. Almond didn't carry any bags herself. She kept the driver company in the truck cab while Goolies and I offloaded the bags, and Wufu and Eight carried them inside. They were like beasts of burden, standing there, heads lowered, while we loaded them up, and then trotting quickly away. Eight was stronger than Wufu. Wufu could carry two bags, Eight carried three.

"Are you OK?" I asked Wufu.

"Sure, just hungry."

The bags were sewn closed, but as soon as you moved them, cement dust flew everywhere, and you were soon covered in it. If you tied a towel over your nose and mouth, then you couldn't breathe, so you wadded up the towels in your mouth instead. The worst was when it got in your eyes. Then if you wiped them with the back of your hand, you got even more dust in them, and it was really painful. Poor Wufu and Eight were soon drenched in sweat, and the dust turned to cement.

"I can't see—my eyes are clogged up!" Eight cried. His hands were too coated to clear them, and so were ours, so Almond got out of the cab and came to wipe them with her sleeve. Then she looked under his eyelids, and said, "They're fine now," and got back into the cab.

We four didn't look human by the time we'd finished unloading a truck; you couldn't tell who was who. Almond took the wages and handed them out to each of us. "Goolies . . ."

"Here!" Wufu and Eight said together, and we all laughed.

"You're not bushed, are you? Still got energy?" she said.

"Now that I've got money, I've got energy!" Wufu said.

"Good," she said. "Then you can go do one more load." And we took the truck back to the beltway.

At twenty yuan a truckload, that made four yuan each. We couldn't do more than four trucks a night, at most, and some nights we only got one. We got home at midnight, fell into bed, and were dead to the world.

The next morning, we'd be back trash picking as usual. The five of us soon got quite a name for ourselves on the beltway because we snagged the most work, and that was all due to Almond. I jokingly started to call her "respected elder sister-in-law," and Eight and Wufu followed suit.

"What's so elderly about me? An old ox still needs sweetgrass!" Almond grumbled.

"'Respected little sister-in-law' then. You should have a bigger share of the money."

But Almond said, "It's true that those who earn don't labor and those who labor don't earn. But I don't want your money. It's enough for me that you wanted your little sister-in-law to have it. It's the thought that counts."

"You'd better be careful, little sister-in-law," I warned her. "Those drivers have been away from home for years. They might take advantage of you."

"If Mr. Gules isn't worried, then you shouldn't be. Do you take me for a fool? The day before yesterday, the driver with the mustache put his hand on my thigh, but I pinched him, and he didn't dare try again. He's so bald, his face goes right over the top of his head. And he thinks he can get it on with me?"

"You were being nice to that young man last night," I said.

She gave me a quick wink, and whispered, "Not another word from you! Mr. Gules already went after me about it. The guy isn't married, and he groped my tits. He'd never seen tits before, so why shouldn't he? It's no big deal. And it's nice to know I'm not too old to attract a young man!"

She gave me such a fiery look that I had to bend down to tie my shoelaces. That made her cackle with laughter. "I'm no spring chicken, and I don't have firm young breasts anymore, but aren't I doing it to get you work?"

By the time ten days had gone by, we were finding the unloading really hard. The old-timers disappeared, but many more came to fill their places. Rumors spread like wildfire in the labor markets that this was the place to earn money. It was like a gold rush, with people streaming in. Come evening, it was mayhem on the beltway, with trucks and people everywhere. And now they were coming in groups, each group with a woman in it. There were scuffles and fights over every truck, and sometimes blood was spilled. One evening, we'd already taken possession of a truck when we were thrown off by another posse. In the tussle, victory went to the strongest and the nimblest. Wufu pulled several off, but he couldn't scramble on himself, though he kept trying. Someone below had hold of his legs. He was kicking hard; then his shoes came off and vanished in the darkness. After that, he jumped down and faced up to them. "Looking for a fight, are you?" He took a punch in the gut and yelled up to me, "A brick, Happy! A brick, hurry up, Happy!" By this time, the other group was in possession of the truck.

"He's taken a beating, and he still says he's happy?" they jeered, brandishing sticks at us. That time we definitely came off worse.

Almond was furious. When the truck had gone, she rounded on Wufu. "You're such a loser! Where did your strength go? He threw your shoes away, but you couldn't use your hands? You dumb pig!" she yelled as she searched for his shoes in the darkness.

"I stopped him fighting," I said. "Goolies's too short-assed, and I can't fight, so if he did get into a fight, he and Eight would be dead."

"You can't fight?" Almond said.

"Only with words, not physically," I said.

"So in a war, you'd be a deserter?" she said, but she laughed. "What soldiers I've got! Look for his shoes, all of you!" It was after midnight before we found them. Almond was furious again. "I thought they were shoes worth looking for! These have holes in the toes, and it's your fault we haven't earned any money and lost sleep!"

Then just as she chucked Wufu his shoes, she stepped in a hole and twisted her ankle. That meant she couldn't come with us, and we found it even more difficult to get unloading jobs. It got worse: one evening we found that a whole crowd of people had been staking out their patches all day, armed with stout sticks to keep us away from the beltway. I walked up and tried to reason with them. Heaven belongs to everyone and so does the earth, and we were all looking for work, I argued. Their response was, "We've only got one pancake, and it's small. If you take a bite, that's one less bite for us, isn't it?"

I tried again. "It's first come, first served, you know. We're old-timers, and you've only just turned up. You can't push us out by force of numbers. That's dominating the market."

They came back with, "'First come, first served?' If the city belongs to everyone, why doesn't the city give you work?"

I tried again. "C'mon, we're all country folk, poor laborers. Let's talk this through." I got an uppercut for that and stumbled backward. I didn't fall over, just leaned against a lamppost.

"Who the hell do you think you are? Our teacher?"

"I'm Happy Liu!"

"Well, there's nothing for you to be happy about here!"

I tried a different tactic. "I assume you're hungry."

"Yes, we are! So what are you offering us?"

I laughed loudly and withdrew. Xi'an city folk didn't see us, but they didn't treat us too badly either. The ones who really had it tough were this type, who came from the countryside to get laboring jobs. I went back to the others. "Let's go. At least we have our trash-picking work. This lot are dirt-poor, and brutal too!"

47.

And that was what happened. We'd been pleased as punch to earn an
extra five hundred yuan each, but then that door slammed shut. Worse,
we'd gotten used to going out at night to unload trucks, and we were all
keyed up to do it. Now we were at loose ends, deflated like punctured
soccer balls. Goolies and Almond shut their door and went to bed early,
I sat on my bed, chewing things over, wiping the shoes on the shelf
clean, and thinking of Yichun. The mosquitoes whined around me. I
chased them away, and they came right back, biting me all down my
back until it burned like fire. I put the shoes down and went to the wall,
slapping them one by one, till their blood was smeared all over the palm
of my hand. It stank. Was it their blood that stank or mine? I sat back
down and carried on wiping the shoes clean and thinking of Yichun. At
least I had her to think about. Lonely old Wufu and Eight were chatting on the rooftop, swapping stories about the dance hall and straining
their ears for goings-on in Almond and Goolies's room below—and
probably wondering why they hadn't started yet. They stayed awake,
waiting, and carrying on with their tales of the dance hall, annoyed that
they could remember one or two hookers' faces but had no idea what
their names were.

  I went back over everything Yichun and I had talked about from
the day we'd first met. I remembered all her movements, how her hair
swayed as she turned around, how her little ears and her cheeks flushed

slightly when she looked up, how her waist moved as she skipped up the stairs, how she turned her toes a little bit inward when she leaned against the door, the shape of her butt when she bent down to pick something up . . . Ai-ya! The images unfolded in front of my eyes like a movie, until my heart overflowed with sweetness. I don't know when I finally fell asleep, because I saw the same images in my dreams.

I got up the next morning and made breakfast. Wufu's room door was still shut. I called him, then called again, and he finally emerged. He looked at Goolies standing below, holding his breakfast bowl. "You're such a pain, you two!"

"What have I done to annoy you?" Goolies asked.

"If you want to get your rocks off, why can't you do it earlier? How are we supposed to sleep if you're going at it so late at night?"

I pulled Wufu into his room. "You're so embarrassing. Let's get going."

"I want to give you the whole five hundred I earned. Stash it away for me."

"You should keep some with you, to buy trash."

"I've got a hundred and twelve—that's plenty. If I carry any more around with me, it's tempting fate. I might lose it, or I might end up in the dance hall."

I kept my five hundred on me because I was planning to give it to Yichun. "What day is it today, Wufu?" I asked.

He didn't know, but Almond said, "The seventeenth."

"A good day!" I said.

"The eighteenth is a good day. What's special about the seventeenth?" Almond said. But I was proven right. This time when I gave the money to Yichun, it all went smoothly, and I got properly introduced to Mighty as well. I had mixed feelings about this. I wanted to get to know him, even become his friend, but our relationship with Yichun got in the way. Of course, I couldn't be sure that he had that kind of relationship with her, but I didn't want to ask in case the answer upset me. I did ask her if Mighty had asked about me, and she said he hadn't. So I figured that, well, we were both good people, and we could each help Yichun in our own way. Wufu had mentioned Mighty to me once. He'd asked which one of us had gotten to Yichun first. I twisted his lips and jerked them. He was insulting Yichun, and insulting Mighty and me too.

This time when I met Mighty, I was even more firmly convinced that Yichun was my bodhisattva. When I gave her money, I wasn't helping her; she was guiding me, and drawing Mighty and me together.

Yichun and Mighty were standing talking at the top of Salon Street. Yichun saw me first and waved cheerfully. "Come here, quick!" Then Mighty saw me and composed himself. He nodded politely and as he did so, put his right hand on his stomach, smiled, and bowed slightly.

Of course, I was equally courteous in my response. "Mr. Mighty, how do you do?"

"Are you Happy Liu?"

"I am."

"I'm very pleased to see you again," he said. But then he began to say good-bye. That surprised me. Did he not want to hang around with me? Did he not want to be seen with Yichun?

Yichun said, "Are you going?"

"I'm sorry, I've got something going on. Happy, you're Yichun's countryman. Stay and chat."

But Yichun wasn't having that. "No one's going," she said firmly. "It's been hard enough to get you two together, and I have things I want to say to you both." And she took us to a teahouse across the street, saying, "It's on me!"

In the teahouse, Yichun told me all about Mighty's business. And she told him all about how I picked trash and how I gave her the money I saved.

"Really? Really?" Mighty was very surprised.

"Aren't I just following your example?" I said.

"My example?" He pointed to himself.

"Yichun told me that you've been helping her."

"Yes, well, that's so she can pull enough money together to get justice."

"Of all the people I've met in Xi'an, you two have been the best to me," Yichun said. "Now you should give each other a hug."

And so we did. Mighty's hands clapped me on the back, and my sunglasses, in my jacket pocket, dug into my chest. I didn't dare get them out though. I gave him a hearty embrace in exchange, but I was worried that he'd smell the fermented bean curd I'd been eating, so I turned my head to one side. I could feel his heart beating. And his kidney was beating in time with my one remaining kidney. Or rather, both my kidneys were beating. The bowl of orchids on the table quivered.

Yichun stood there, quietly observing us, a foxy gleam in her eyes. Then she lightly clapped her hands. *Thank you, Yichun. Without you, how would I ever have met Mighty?* It would have been a miracle for my two kidneys to have met otherwise, in this vast sea of a city. And there I was, hugging a man of his means and social status. Too bad Wufu wasn't here to see it, and Eight and Almond and Goolies, and Gem Han and my nephew Goodson. Everyone from Freshwind should have seen it.

Happy Liu, oh, Happy Liu! I said to myself. *You always thought you deserved to be a city man. And you can certainly act the part, bossing people around and strutting along, chest puffed out. Sometimes you even think yourself better than rich entrepreneurs like Mighty. But one hug from him, and you have to face the fact that you're really a countryman, come to pick trash in the city.*

I gave him a little push and we separated. I patted the dust off myself and dusted off Mighty too.

You're putting yourself down again; no need for that, Happy. Mighty's looking at you warmly, he's reaching out his hand and grasping yours, pulling you to a chair. If you refuse him or take too long, you're lowering yourself to the same level as Wufu and Eight. Lift your head up, look Mighty in the eyes. You're brothers in the city!

"Which streets are your patch? Is there plenty of trash to collect? What are your daily takings? It must be hard work!" He seemed genuinely concerned.

"Yes, it's hard work, but meat pasties don't fall from the sky. What job isn't hard work?"

What a fine suit he had on. I said I'd met a few company bosses, in real estate, pharmaceuticals, foreign trade, and investments, and although they had cars and secretaries, and frequented fancy hotels and restaurants, when I collected trash from outside their homes, I saw how exhausted they all were when they came home, and I'd heard their families complain about the pressure they were under. I wondered what kind of watch Mighty wore. I noticed he had a bracelet of prayer beads on his right wrist. Was he a Buddhist? *Your hair's thinning too, Mr. Mighty, and you have dark circles around your eyes. You can't be much older than me. Your face is less sunburned, but you have more wrinkles than I do, and then there's the kidney . . .*

"My patch is the ten lanes along Prosper Street. I take in between ten and twenty yuan a day, not bad," I said. I wondered if I should tell him about the wallet, if I should mention the kidney. Maybe best not to . . .

Mighty smiled and nodded. "You have a funny way of talking," he said. That embarrassed me. OK, so I was funny, but Mighty was quite calm. "Do you smoke?" he asked.

"I'll have one," I said. As I got up to take it, I put my hand to my back. Why was it aching, again? But I wouldn't tell him. It was enough that I knew why.

Now Yichun was talking. She was puffing me up to Mighty, saying I was so intelligent, capable, kindhearted, reliable, and then there were my looks: I was fine-featured and definitely had class. If I wasn't on a three-wheeler, no one would know I was a trash picker from the countryside. There was more to me than met the eye. I was a crouching tiger, a hidden dragon, not some earth-bound creepy-crawly. The way she went on, I got a little embarrassed. When someone said nice things about you, it was like when a drunk was talking to you: you couldn't echo what the drunk was saying, but you couldn't contradict him; you just had to listen. Finally, she got to the point. "Mr. Mighty, Happy Liu's work is so hard, and trash picking never makes a lot of money. Couldn't you give him a job in your company?"

Mighty laughed out loud. "Meng Yichun's taking me to task!"

"That's right," she said. "In fact, I'm begging you."

I waved dismissively, but Mighty was already firing questions at me. "Have you ever been a salesman?"

"No."

"Worked in finance?"

"No."

"Do you have any skills?"

"Only as a laborer."

Mighty looked pensive. "Could you watch the gate at the company offices? It's not heavy work. You just have to be there twenty-four/seven. Could you handle that? I can fire our gateman and offer you six hundred a month. How about it?"

Meng Yichun was delighted and tugged at my shoulder. "Of course you can handle it. It's only six hundred yuan, but if you do a good job, Mr. Mighty will be sure to give you a pay raise."

I said, "Thank you, but . . ."

"What are you saying?" said Yichun.

"I'm saying, I came with Wufu, and he's never been away from home before. He relies on me for everything. I'd worry about him trash picking on his own." I looked Mighty in the eye.

He said, "We can't split the job between two people."

"Then can you find something for Wufu to do?" I asked. Mighty didn't like that. Yichun was glaring at me too. *I'm sorry, Yichun, I can't do what you want me to do.* It was the first time I'd put Wufu before her, but a friend was more important than a lover. I explained to Mighty, "Let me fix Wufu up. As soon as I can find him something suitable, I'll come work for you.

"I'm truly sorry, you'll think me ridiculous," I went on, "but Wufu and I came to Xi'an together, and I'm responsible for him." Mighty was still smiling and said he admired my loyalty. Then he said his good-byes. When he'd gone, Yichun scolded me.

"You can't force someone to give me a job," I said.

"But his company's huge. It's nothing for him to find a job for one or two people."

"I don't think he wants me there."

"But he said he did, and he was smiling."

"That's because he always smiles. He knows I'm with Wufu, but he only offered work to me. And he knows I couldn't hold a job like that. And it's only six hundred a month. Does he know you told me about you and him?"

"What do you mean?"

"What does he not want me to know? Why's he acting so friendly and decent to me?"

"You think too much!" She poked me on the forehead. I stood there and let her, like a good boy. Then I got out the five hundred yuan and gave it to her. She took it and poked me again. "Suspicious, that's what you are!"

Well, if I was, so be it. "Have your police officers left?" I asked.

"I borrowed a thousand yuan off my boss so they could go home."

We didn't talk any more. She just took a hundred-yuan bill from the five hundred and gave it back to me, and I stuck it back in her pocket.

48.

I never took Mighty up on his job offer because Wufu really did need me. I've already said we must have had some karmic connection from our former lives, because he was glued to me like cooked daikon between your teeth, and I couldn't get rid of him. Wufu heard about the job offer, and he promised with tears in his eyes that he'd look after himself, go out and pick trash by day, come back to Fishpond to sleep, never go anywhere else, never answer back if anyone cussed him, never lift a finger if someone hit him, and if he missed me, he could always find me at Mighty's company offices. But the more he talked, the more I felt I couldn't leave him. I told him I wouldn't go anywhere without him. And he got down on his hands and knees and kowtowed to me.

"Get up, Wufu! Get up! Are your legs made of jelly? Why are you kowtowing for a little thing like that? Go buy a bottle! Let's have a drink!"

He came back with an armful of beer bottles, on which he'd spent almost all of his takings from the last few days. He shouted to Eight, Almond, and Goolies to come to his room and told them it was his birthday. "Drink with me! C'mon, let's get drunk!"

We did that, and then Wufu went to the shit-house. He was gone a long, long time. I thought he'd fallen in, so I went to look for him. He was sitting on the shit-house floor, unable to get up, but still clutching a bottle. "Happy! My bro! I'll never be able to pay you back. I'll just drink, drink till I'm drunk . . ."

"You're already drunk," I said.

"No, I want more!" He raised the bottle to his mouth and glugged more down. "Happy, I'm not a woman. If I were, I'd let you screw me, but I'm not, and the only way I can pay you back is to make myself ill with drink, to drink till my stomach bleeds!" I grabbed the bottle from him, hefted him onto my back, and carried him out of the shit-house.

When I turned Mighty down, Yichun had been disappointed, but she let it go. Every few days, I'd drop by the salon at lunchtime to see her, and sometimes she'd be there and sometimes she wouldn't. If she wasn't, I'd get a stone and make a mark on the wall opposite the salon door. That was our arrangement, and she'd know I'd been there. If she was there, she'd pop out with a mug of tea and make me drink it. There was always a dab of lipstick around the rim and I'd say, "That's where I'm drinking from." She'd smile.

I always asked her, "Any headway?" When I first started visiting, she'd grumble about the lack of progress, but later she refused to answer, just snapped impatiently at me. She looked pale. I didn't blame her, and I stayed passionate about going to see her. The trouble was that every time I left her, I felt as if someone had stuffed a handful of weeds into my heart. *When would the murder ever be cleared up?* I wondered bitterly. I had no idea how much more money she could earn, and how much more Mighty and his entrepreneur cronies would give her. And what use was the pittance I gave her? That was the worst thing. When I started giving her money, I'd felt as proud as an errant knight of old, but as time went on, and a resolution to the crime seemed as distant a prospect as ever, I lost that sense of pride. I dreaded seeing a fleeting anxiety cross her face when I handed over my money, hidden under her customary smiles and affectionate words.

"They'll wrap it up soon," I said.

"How have I harmed so many people?" she said. I'd been thinking I'd go to her hometown, chase down the police, and work with them to crack the case, but how could I? I even thought of holding a collection box in the street, but when I told her that, she began to cry. She told me that Mighty had talked of publicizing her plight in the newspapers too. The trouble was that as soon as it was known that she was in the sex trade, what would that do to her reputation, even if the case was wrapped up? The funds simply had to be raised in secret. But how long would that take? I thought of telling Eight and Wufu and Almond and Goolies about it all, but even though Yichun was a bodhisattva to me, they would never believe that a hooker could be a bodhisattva. I racked my brains for a few days, until my head started to ache. I decided to take my friends to Pagoda Street. Then once they heard the Chain-Bones Bodhisattva's story, they were filled with pity for Yichun's predicament.

"What's her name?" Almond asked.

"Meng Yichun."

"Is that the woman you told me you think about as soon as you wake up?"

"That's her."

"Why don't you bring her to meet us?"

"I'm embarrassed," I said.

"I thought I had a hard life," Almond said. "Imagine there being another tragic beauty! What are you going to do?"

"Beg you to help me think of something."

"That's what I figured," Almond said. And she talked it over with Wufu and Eight, and they came to an agreement. Every day each of them would put aside two yuan for Yichun. It hadn't been my intention to ask them for money, but Almond had the clout and the ability to do this, and if they all took up a collection, even though two yuan a day wasn't much, it showed their support for Yichun and me. After that, every evening like clockwork, Almond took around an empty rice jar and got everyone to put in their two yuan. I put in mine just like the others. Almond and Goolies needed to put in only two yuan since they were one household, but after a moment of hesitation, Goolies put in two yuan for himself too.

These were my trash-picker friends, and I was so grateful to them! Normally, no one would give you a cent. If you were a cent short when you went to a shop for a needle, or a restaurant for a bowl of plain noodles, you'd go away empty-handed.

But five days later, when I went to give the fifty yuan we'd collected to Yichun, she flew into a rage. "Who told you to go telling them my affairs? Do I want all of Xi'an to know I'm a hooker? 'Cuz that's what I am! I don't need your friends' sympathy! If I never get justice for my dead brother, then so be it! Go away. I don't want to see you again! Take the money back! Every cent of it!"

She was incoherent with rage. A storm of tears followed. I felt injured. I really wanted to explain that my friends weren't enjoying a joke at her expense, but Yichun just threw the money back at me, pushed me out the door, and slammed it shut.

Why was she being like this? I'd never seen this side of her, so hysterical, so pig-headed. Maybe this was how she'd gotten to this point, splitting up with her boyfriend and then, when he murdered her brother, starting work in the sex trade.

Or maybe Yichun had never respected me at all.

If she'd accepted that I was her man, then surely she wouldn't have flown off the handle like that. I remembered my dream. Maybe she'd only regarded me as a friend, and maybe it was because she really needed to get it all off her chest that she'd told me about her life, and she'd kept in contact with me because we understood each other and shared a common language. But as soon as something happened that seemed to harm her interests, she'd shrink away, like a touch-me-not flower. She'd retreat into herself, shutting herself off from the outside world.

You can be very hurtful, Yichun. But maybe she didn't care. Maybe she was incapable of having feelings for anyone. I left her apartment building. The trees on the street were dropping their leaves. I didn't stop to play my flute, or shout for trash. I just pedaled along until I got to Lane Ten and then stopped and sat on the ground, too listless to move. At the intersection with Prosper Street, there was a hundred-year-old walnut tree, which had dropped its catkins so it looked like the ground was covered in caterpillars. If the walnuts were dropping their catkins, it meant summer was nearly over and the weather should start cooling down. How had I landed in this mess? Why did city life make me feel like I was a piece of iron being forged in a furnace one minute, then dropped into water the next? I stared at the catkins. They really had turned into caterpillars, wriggling toward me.

"Hey! Happy Liu!" A guy in glasses was calling me. He was from one of the residential compounds up ahead, and he told me to take the three-wheeler to Building Five, as he had old books to sell me. People with glasses are usually educated, and educated types aren't given to chatting with ordinary folk, so I didn't ask him any more questions, just waited until he'd gone, rubbed my face to wake myself up, then pedaled after him.

I waited a long time outside Building Five, but he didn't come down. When he eventually appeared, he was not carrying any books. He told me he'd left the key inside the apartment, and the door had shut on him. Could I crawl through the window from the outside? I followed him up to the fourth floor, but I was too scared to crawl along a very narrow window ledge and push open the window. The man was hopping from one foot to the other in his anxiety, so finally I said, "I'll break open the door for you. Do you have your ID card?"

He didn't have his on him. I got mine out; I always carried it on me because the police were always stopping people with three-wheelers to check their IDs.

"You're going to open the door with your ID card?" he asked.

I told him I'd heard my nephew say that you could slip it down the side of the door by the lock, shake the door, and wiggle the card, and the door would open, but I'd never tried it. And I succeeded in opening the door. That cheered us both up, and he sold me an armful of books.

I had just gotten downstairs when an old lady turned up with a bag of rice on the back of her bicycle. I recognized the lady—a woman I liked who always had a smile for me.

"Bought some rice, have you?" I asked.

"That's right."

"Do you have someone to carry it upstairs for you?"

"I'll wait for my grandson to come back."

I went ahead and carried it up to her apartment on the seventh floor. When we got there, she asked, "Where are you from?"

"Shangzhou prefecture."

"I've been there. The land's very poor."

"It's all right."

She got out two yuan to give me, but I wouldn't take it. How could I take her money simply for carrying her bag of rice? But she said, "If you don't take it, I'll be indebted to you. You must take it." I didn't like that she didn't want to owe me a debt of gratitude; it was like she was rejecting my kind gesture. Anyway, two yuan was too much for carrying a bag of rice to the seventh floor, and I wouldn't have agreed to do it if she'd told me she wanted to give me that much for it!

I went downstairs. The man whose door I'd opened was there, talking to someone.

"Did you lock yourself out of your apartment, Professor?"

"I did indeed."

"How did you get it open?"

"The trash picker opened it for me. He slipped his ID card between the door and the frame and pushed it through, and the lock opened!"

"The trash picker can open doors? But he's always in and out of our courtyard. We must put a stop to that!"

"He's very honest," protested the professor.

But his friend said, "Using an ID card to open the door, how honest is that?"

Suddenly, I lost my temper. "You'd all better watch your doors in case I break in and burgle your apartments!"

The pair of them were very embarrassed. They looked at each other, then disappeared into the passageway. I headed toward the exit, swearing I'd never come in here again.

Then the old lady came trotting after me, still trying to press two yuan on me. "Hey, take it! Do you want me to feel guilty every time I see you?"

I kept going without turning around.

I retrieved my three-wheeler and pedaled back onto the main street. Back in Freshwind, there were only a dozen lanes, any of which would take you to the center. When you saw the hen with the tufted crest, you knew who it belonged to. And looking at the sow, her tail stuck out because she was about to crap, you knew where her house was too. And that old man carrying a grandchild on his shoulders, you knew perfectly well whether the grandchild was his daughter's or his son's, and whether the in-laws were Pock-Face and his missus, or Baldy. I caught myself thinking all this . . . for what? No one had tied a rope round my neck and dragged me to Xi'an. Now I was here, I should talk like a Xi'an man! I was thinking of parking the three-wheeler by the flower bed and stopping for a smoke, but there was a cop there, so I pedaled on till I found a low wall to leave it by, and sat down to stare into space.

Meng Yichun. For some reason, as soon as I sat down, I thought of her. I remembered one story she told me: a passerby saw a woman being mugged, her handbag taken, and he set off down the street in pursuit. The mugger knifed his pursuer and left him unconscious. Another passerby carried the injured man to a hospital, but he died, whereupon his family accused the Good Samaritan of having killed him. It was hard to do a good deed nowadays. I opened the professor's door for him—did that mean that everyone in the courtyard was now going to install burglar-proof doors? The old lady had been right: she owed me nothing if she paid me two yuan. Our feelings toward each other bound us together in Freshwind, but only law or money bought trust in Xi'an.

You think Yichun has no feelings for you, that she has no feelings for anyone, but why does she see you so often? Just because she wants your money? It's not like there's much of that! You're narrow-minded, oversensitive; that's what you are! I berated myself. *Why do you give her money? Why does that fill you with pride every time? Is it just because she's in trouble, and that makes you feel like you're a hero instead of a trash picker?* I remembered another dream I'd had in which I was talking to a tree, telling it I hoped the police would keep investigating forever, that the murder would never be cleared up. What did that mean? That I wanted her always to be the weak one? Weaker than me? So that I could control her? *Shame on you!* I thought.

It dawned on me why Yichun had been so angry that I told Wufu and Eight, as well as Almond and Goolies, about her. I should have kept her business to myself. I decided to go see her again. I scolded myself for being oversensitive, suspicious, weak. The next time I gave her money, I wouldn't make any demands of her, no matter how she acted toward me. Until the case was over, then we'd see.

49.

And if I wanted the case to be cracked soon, I had to earn more money. I thought of what Almond had said about Goodson and decided that Wufu and I would go see that nephew of mine.

It was true that he was doing much better than I was. When he went out every day to deliver coal, he didn't take a cart or a three-wheeler. Instead, he had a three-wheeled motorcycle. The coal yard was run by someone from Shanxi, the pile of coal was like a mountain, and there was a row of six machines pressing coal briquettes. Customers got their briquettes pressed on the spot, and then Goodson delivered them. If no customers came, he loaded up his motorcycle and called his wares in the street. He'd made quite a name for himself, and he had a business card: "King of Briquettes," he called himself.

The King of Briquettes was not exactly friendly, but he didn't ignore us either. He took us to his room and went out to buy a dish of pickled vegetables with fish, and a basket of steamed *ganmo*. He lived in a shed of about sixty-five square feet that backed onto the compound wall and was roofed with a plastic sheet, with the top edge attached to the wall. He had a bed, a coal stove, and a bit of rope strung across the corner from which hung a suit and also a tie.

Wufu and I were hoping to get work selling coal too, but the King of Briquettes wasn't having that. He warned us not to go looking for the boss either, because the boss did what he said. And that was because he,

Goodson, controlled supplies to all the local state-run organizations and private customers. The kid clearly had no sense of family loyalty, but he did let us have some coal, and when we were finished trash picking in the evenings, we could sell it in the New East Street night market. That was his patch too.

Goodson had been a poor student when he was back home and didn't shine at all, but once he'd arrived in Xi'an, he quickly learned how to turn his hand to anything and make a profit. He took us to the New East Street night market, where most of the stalls sold beef or mutton *paomo* soup. On the way, he asked us, "Do you know how the Qin defeated the other six dukedoms and took control of all China?"

"You think you know because you went to junior secondary school? I went to senior secondary!" I said.

"OK then, tell me!" he insisted.

"Because they had Yingzheng as their ruler."

"It's obvious you don't know; let me explain. The people of Qin liked their *paomo* soup, so they took their beef and mutton and flatbread with them to the battlefield. Speed is of the essence in war, and it didn't take them long to cook and eat their soup. But the folk from the six dukedoms had to sit down and rinse their rice, pick over their vegetables, and prepare all these different dishes, and while they were at it, the Qin soldiers killed them in their camp. It was the food that defeated the six dukedoms!"

"Oh."

Goodson strutted along, full of bravado, then took out a pack of cigarettes and offered one each to Wufu and me. He had one clamped between his lips, and he could shift it from one side of his mouth to the other without using his hands. It turned me off from lighting my cigarette. The New East Street night market was on an impressive scale. There were some shops, but most of the market consisted of vendors with roadside stands, each with a lightbulb hanging over the front and a washbasin full of water. The vendors stood there, shouting their wares, white hats on and a towel slung over one shoulder. Our King of Briquettes was lecturing us again: China had eight major cuisines, but Xi'an wasn't one of them. Why not? Because Xi'an was the capital of thirteen dynasties, and whenever the emperor was in residence, the other regions of China competed to bring him their dishes, so that Xi'an became one great banquet table, with every kind of delicacy laid out on it, and gradually its own culinary traditions died out. But formal cuisine aside, its tradition of street snacks flourished and could all be found here in the night market: *paomo* mutton soup, sliced tripe, dried persimmons, *hulatang* peppery beef soup, pork steamed with rice flour, marinated bean noodles, noodles with spicy meat sauce, big-knife noodles, spittle noodles, noodles in soup, *liangpi* noodles, steamed rice cakes, *mashi* cat's ear noodles, oil-tea broth, steamed meat dumplings, and *youta* steamed rolls.

Wufu was impressed. "How come you know so much?"

"Don't encourage him!" I said. "He'll drive us crazy with his bragging if you do."

So we stopped responding, and he stopped talking. But I have to admit, that kid certainly knew his way around, and the vendors all seemed to know him. "Briquette King, aren't you selling any briquettes today?" they called out.

"These two will be selling them for me, so take care of them."

"Hiring laborers, are you?"

The stands all needed coal but only in small quantities; mostly they bought just enough for that day because they didn't want to have to lug it home and back the next day. When we were at loose ends, Wufu kept his eyes peeled for trash lying around, like empty bottles and lunch boxes, but the vendors would only give him the boxes, not the bottles, and they made him clean the tables too. But Wufu was very polite to them and collected a lot of boxes.

The work and the long hours took their toll, and after a few days, we were exhausted. We'd get back to Fishpond every night at one or two in the morning, and we were so tired by then, we could hardly stay upright. Wufu kept falling asleep as he pulled his cart along. We couldn't have that, so he got me to lead him along, him holding one end of a stick and me the other end. He actually walked along asleep, sometimes even snoring. There was hardly anyone in the street at that time of night, but the traffic whizzed by fast and furious. Every time a car came by, I'd stop, and he'd wake up and ask, "Are we there yet?"

"How can you sleep and walk?"

"I was dreaming just now, I was eating . . ." Then he shut his eyes and went back to sleep. He had an ugly mug when he was asleep. I felt like I was pulling a walking corpse.

The Briquette King could see we were very tired and let us sleep in his shed instead of going back to Fishpond. But Wufu snored as thunderously as a bellows. Sometimes he stopped altogether, then started again with a great snort. That scared me, because I thought he'd choked. It was getting on my nerves, and the Briquette King couldn't sleep either. He tried stuffing cotton balls in his ears, then throwing things at Wufu. Every time he scored a hit, it stopped the snores for a little while, but then they started up again. By morning, Wufu was covered in stinky shoes and socks and pillows and all our clothes. So the Briquette King refused to have Wufu stay in the shed, and Wufu went back to Fishpond every night, while I stayed over. We arranged to meet at the trash depot every morning, and Goodson would give me a lift to Prosper Street on his coal rounds.

One evening, I was on my way to the night market with the coal, and as I passed a hotel, someone from the hotel hailed me and asked for a load. She said the cashier had gone home, so I should come back for the money the next day. This was the first time I'd sold a complete load, so I headed back early, bought a fish, and stewed it once I was back at the shed. I wanted to show the Briquette King how good a cook I was. He turned up with a dog.

"I've had a good day, good takings," he said.

"My day's been even better—I sold a whole load of coal."

"What a braggart!"

"Well, I wouldn't buy you a fish otherwise, would I?"

He took a woman's purse out of his inside pocket. "For you, since you bought me the fish."

Handbag snatching was a common occurrence, and I looked at him doubtfully. The way he behaved, I wouldn't have put it past him. "Where did you get that from?"

"I found it."

"You didn't steal it, did you?"

"You can't keep your mouth shut, can you?"

My face got stern. It was my duty as an uncle to instruct him on how to behave. "Look at me," I said.

He looked at me.

"Did you steal it?"

"No, I found it!"

He was even more stubborn than Wufu.

"You stole it!"

"If I stole it, don't you think I'd keep the contents and sling the purse?" He dipped the ladle into the pot, cut the fish in half—and gave half to the dog tied up at the door.

"Why are you feeding the dog when we haven't had our dinner yet?"

"So what if I feed the dog?" He glared at me and picked the other half of the fish out of the pot. I went to stop him, but he pushed me hard, and the pot tipped over onto the floor. He grabbed the purse and made as if to throw it over the compound wall. I grabbed it back, and he bellowed furiously at me. I smiled. If he was angry, that proved he was innocent. If he hadn't lost his temper, I would have marched right out of there. I had no intention of spending the night with a purse snatcher.

"Generations of the Liu family have never produced a thief or a bandit. Now, did you find the bag or not?" I lectured him.

"If you weren't my uncle, I'd clobber you," he said.

"Don't go thinking you're better than your uncle. You're still wet behind the ears when it comes to city life. I'm telling you, if someone else steals a purse, and empties it and throws the purse away, don't pick it up. There's so much bag snatching nowadays, they'll think you're a thief! What was in it?"

"What was in it? Tissues and a makeup mirror."

I turned it inside out, and that was all there was. But then a necklace, wrapped in a bit of paper, fell out too.

My nephew grabbed it from me. "I can get a few hundred yuan for that trinket."

"Goodson," I said, "I found that. The least you can do is give me half the money you make on it."

He threw fifty yuan at me and glared contemptuously. What a way to treat his uncle! I went out and bought another fish and made dinner again. This time we filled our bellies and then went to bed. I tossed and turned, unable to sleep. The Briquette King was adding up his money under the quilt. How much did he have? All I could hear was rustling as he counted out the bills.

"If you want to count it, come out from under there. I farted in the bed," I said.

He ignored me.

"How much can you earn in a day?" I asked.

"Go to sleep, why don't you?"

It got later and later, but the dog kept barking; it was driving me up the wall. The Briquette King got up and brought the dog in. It walked all over the bedding and settled on my pillow, until I slapped it angrily away. Then it moved over to my nephew's side, and I finally dropped off.

From then on, the dog became the Briquette King's pet, and he bought it food every day. I'd get back late at night to a cold stove and an empty pot, and find the dog's bowl full of fish and pork spareribs.

Of course, I couldn't let it go. "What have we come to Xi'an to do? To earn money and save money. You'll have plenty of places to spend your money in the future."

He made a face at me. Honestly, I didn't want to be there at all, but I needed to earn more money, so I had to put up with him.

The worst of it was I'd been back to the hotel three times to collect on the load of coal I'd sold to them. They told me I needed to speak to the person who'd bought it from me. But all I could remember was that she was around fifty, with gray hair. They went and asked her. Yes, it was true she'd made the order but they didn't have the money now, I should come back in a few days. But when I went back, the doorman wouldn't let me in. I stood in the doorway, getting angry, until the lobby manager called security. "Get him out of here!" And I was thrown out.

"Do you want me to try?" the Briquette King asked.

"Are you going to beat them up? There's a whole bunch of bouncers. You can't take them all on."

"I won't beat them up. I'll beat myself up. I'll just slash my forehead." He already had two white lines running down his forehead, perfectly healed scars.

"Have you slashed yourself before?" I asked.

"Once, when the SCOUT patrol confiscated my bike and fined me five hundred yuan, I was frantic, so I slashed my forehead. They gave me the bike back and didn't ask for the fine either. One officer even said, 'This is one tough guy. Why not give him a job as an auxiliary?' But I didn't take it."

After that, I really couldn't ask him to collect the debt for me. When I was thrown out one more time by the hotel security, I decided to tell my nephew that I had the coal money.

But he didn't come back that night. What had happened to him? I wasn't worried that he'd lost his way or got beaten up, not like Wufu, but he might have had an accident on his motorcycle or got into a fight.

At two o'clock in the morning, I went to the coal yard to ask why he hadn't come back.

"Did you look to see if his motorcycle was here?" the gateman asked. I went to the parking lot, and the red three-wheeler motorcycle was there. "Are his suit and tie there?" I went back to the shed. They were nowhere to be seen. "Then there's no need to worry," said the gateman. "Other people get beaten up; your nephew doesn't."

What did that mean? I went back to the shed to wait. Still no sign of him. I went to bed. The mosquitoes were biting hard that night, every last one from the yard seemed to be in our shed. I couldn't sleep, so I started to think of Yichun. Was she being kept awake by the insects too? Was she lying there, counting her money over and over? Did that make her think of me? Did she wonder why she hadn't seen me for so long? Or was the thought of me fleeting, like water spilled on a glass table, vanished as soon as you wiped it up with your finger?

How I wished that Yichun's mosquitoes would come bite me.

50.

The next morning, he still wasn't back. I got to the depot earlier than Wufu. When he turned up, his clothes were so dirty, you couldn't tell what color they used to be. "If you slept a bit less, you could spend more time washing your clothes. Aren't they uncomfortable?" I said to him.

"Nope."

"You may not be uncomfortable, but other people feel uncomfortable just looking at you!"

"Picking trash all day and delivering coal by night, how do you expect me to stay clean?"

"The maggots in the shit-house manage to stay white! I was going to take you to see Meng Yichun, but not now."

Wufu wasn't angry. He simply said, "No wonder your clothes are so clean." Then he fished inside his jacket and took out three hundred and fifty yuan. "Almond passed the hat and told me to give this to you."

I'd been gone all this time, and Almond was still passing the hat. I felt a lump in my throat.

Good luck starts bright and early, and I'd woken up in a good mood. Maybe today I'd be lucky. Sure enough, as soon as I got to Lane Ten, I picked up a bag full of pull-tab cans, something that had never happened to me before, and then on Lane Eight, I bought some old window frames and security grills left over from a renovation job. When I got to the luxury hotel, I bumped into the old guys staring up at the building and stretching their neck muscles as they clustered around the newspaper board. Each of them had a bundle of old newspapers for me. My three-wheeler was piled high, and all I needed now was for someone I knew to see me. But the old guy who sold parking tickets wasn't hunkered down outside the teahouse, the security guard at the hotel wasn't there, and the door of the liquor shop was still shut. I didn't see anyone I knew. I pedaled slowly away, in no hurry to get back to the depot, wandered down Lane Nine and turned onto Lane Ten.

At the turnoff for Lane Ten, there was an old man with a mynah bird in a cage. He turned to look at me, then turned back and puttered on. Damned fool! But the bird in the cage called out to me, "Happy Liu!"

The old man took his bird for a walk every day. Sometimes the man hailed me with a friendly greeting, "Hello, Happy Liu!" Other times, he ignored me. But the mynah bird knew me and always greeted me without fail.

"How are you?" I addressed it.

"How are you?" the bird repeated.

"Sing a song!" I said.

"Play your flute!" it responded.

The bird knew my mood better than the old man. I got out my flute and started to play a folk tune,

> "East slope, west slope, sing mountain songs
> on every slope . . ."

But the old man took no notice, just carried on walking. He was in a sour mood today. *Fine, be sour. I'll just carry on playing,* I thought. I started the tune again, from the beginning:

> "East slope, west slope, sing mountain songs

on every slope, sing till the hills are filled with
the sound of singing, oh, blessed life . . ."

I played and played, and then I stopped because I saw Yichun
waving at me from the opposite side of the road. Oh, so she could still
wave at me! If she'd met me in the street and had still been angry and
ignored me, I would have been heartbroken, but she hadn't. She seemed
as vivacious as ever. I took my courage in both hands and pedaled across
the road, making a dozen or so cars slam on their brakes.

We stood by a garbage can. She looked at my load and said,
"Haven't you done well today!" But standing in front of her, I didn't
know which way to look. Meeting like this was all too sudden. I'd rolled
my pant legs up because I was riding the three-wheeler, and one side
was longer than the other. I was worried I smelled sweaty too, so I stood
with the garbage can between us, though Yichun didn't seem to notice.
Her cheeks cherry red, she said, "I thought you were angry with me. I
thought I wouldn't see you again!"

"You were scary that day," I said.

"Was I? Well, sometimes women have days when they're in a good
mood, and then they have their off days. I'm sorry I was off with you."

"No, it was my fault," I said.

"So you didn't come because you were scared of me?"

"I thought you wouldn't see me." That sort of slipped out. I sounded
petulant. If I'd heard someone else speaking in that tone, it would have
set my teeth on edge. It wasn't my style at all. I flushed scarlet.

"You're embarrassed again!" Yichun reached out as if she were going
to jab me on the forehead, but then simply patted the dust off my
clothes. That put me at ease better than anything. The trouble was that
I didn't understand women. Sometimes they were so very nice, but if
they got angry with you, they could be really bitchy. But now I had to
act like a man, so I held my head high and said how much cooler the

weather was today and how I'd lucked out, and then said, "Your clothes are pretty today!"

"My clothes are pretty? Or I'm pretty?"

"You."

"Then look at me properly."

"No, I don't want to. Those people over there by the shop are looking. What will people think of you, being with a trash picker like me? You go, and I'll dump this at the depot. Then I'll drop by the salon."

"No!" This time, she sounded petulant.

So we walked side by side to the depot. The streets were packed. Any more people and there'd have been a human traffic jam. A smart, pretty woman walking along chatting and laughing with a grime-covered trash picker drew some odd looks from passersby.

"Have you put on weight since I last saw you?" I asked.

"You're so tactless! Nowadays, you're supposed to tell a girl she's slim!"

"But you *are* plumper! And it suits you!" I protested.

"Really? Maybe that's because something good happened."

"Is the case cleared up?"

She shook her head and told me that she'd saved another five thousand yuan and sent it off to the police. But what was making her happy was that Mighty had finally agreed that Wufu and I could work for his company. Not at the gate either. Plus, she had collected a big bag of old clothes from Mighty and his cronies, all fine quality, just a little out of fashion.

"Thank you so much!" I said.

"You know what they say, 'Birds of a feather flock together.' Does that make me a trash picker too?"

"I'm taking you out to dinner!"

At the depot, Scrawny kept sneaking looks at Yichun. I aimed a kick at his butt.

"Who's that?"

"A friend."

"If you've got a friend like that, your name's not Happy Liu."

"It's *because* I've got a friend like that that my name's Happy Liu."

"Right, so even a Shangzhou husk-eater can get himself a looker from the city for a girlfriend, can he?"

We had a sumptuous meal in a small Sichuan restaurant, two veggie and two meat dishes, and an egg-and-tomato soup. My treat, of course. Afterward, we went to the salon, and sure enough, she got out a big bag for me. It contained suits, shirts, and underpants—and shoes, all of them leather.

"Go upstairs and try them on."

When I said I didn't want to go upstairs, I saw a trace of embarrassment cross her face. But she didn't object, just took me to the teahouse we'd been to before and got a room there. We went in and shut the door, and she took out each garment, one by one, and made me try them all on. Finally, she selected one of the shirts and a suit for me, and added a tie. Then she pushed me in front of the mirror. "Who would have thought it? You look so dapper! A real company boss!" The tie felt like it was strangling me. I pulled it off and was about to take off the suit, when she came up behind me and put her arms around me.

I tried to turn around, but she said, "It's only the clothes I've got my arms around, so don't go getting any ideas!" I put my arms around her anyway.

"My auntie's in town," she said.

I had no idea what she meant. "Who?" I had my hand down there, and when I pulled it away, there was blood on my fingers.

"You men, you're gross!" she said.

This wasn't how I'd wanted it to be, but when she teased me like that, I forgot all the rules I'd laid down for myself.

"It's dirty," she said.

"Not to me," I said.

"It'll give you sores."

"I don't care."

"Well, you may not, but I do," she said. So I behaved myself. But to comfort me, she said she'd come do it with me at Fishpond as soon as she could. "But not on that bed mat," she said. I told her I'd definitely buy a mattress. The waitress knocked at the door, with hot water for the pot, so we stopped messing around and sat properly on our chairs.

"How did you persuade Mighty to agree to take Wufu and me on?"

"You don't need to know exactly how, but he agreed."

"He might have agreed, but I don't want to see him every day."

"Why not?"

But Yichun was bright enough to know exactly what I meant. She was quiet for a while, then said, "If you go work for him, it won't be nearly as hard as trash picking."

I leaned over and gripped her hands. "Yichun! Yichun!"

But she said, "That's enough of that. Today's a good day. Let's talk about something else, OK?"

But we didn't know what else to talk about. I felt in my pocket for a cigarette, and there was the three hundred and fifty yuan Wufu had given me.

"I'll have a smoke," said Yichun.

I passed her the money with the packet of cigarettes. Then I passed her the lighter, together with a roll of bills I had on me; I hadn't counted it, but I knew it was about two hundred.

She tried to refuse it. "Why are you still giving me money? I've just sent them five thousand."

"Will it be enough?" I asked. I stuffed the money into her pocket. "This isn't much. If you don't want it, you can throw it away."

"You're splashing it around today! Have you been earning more?"

I didn't dare tell her about Almond passing the hat, so I simply said I'd been selling briquettes.

"Is selling briquettes better than trash picking?" she asked.

"Not really." And I told her all about my nephew, Goodson the Briquette King, and about the coal yard and about the hotel stiffing me on the coal I'd sold them. Her eyes grew wide, and she got straight on the phone to Mighty. Mighty said he knew the hotel manager, and he'd contact them. They wouldn't dare not pay me after that. "You can collect your money tomorrow," she said, putting the phone down. "Just say Mighty sent you."

I nodded, though I wasn't sure I believed in Mighty's almighty powers.

I went to the coal yard dressed in my new suit. The Briquette King still wasn't around. The man at the gate told me he'd come back during the night, taken a nap, then gone out on deliveries. He'd pushed a stick through the door ring-pull to lock it up, as usual. The dog was tied to the bed leg and had pissed on the sheet, which was scrunched up on the floor. I dragged the dog out and tied it to a tree outside, then started to mix dough and make *mashi* cat's ear noodles. We always used to just roll the dough on a board, but today I was in a good mood, and I washed my straw hat and used the broad brim to roll out the noodles. The noodles came out nice and curly, with the straw pattern on them. Just as I was finishing, the Briquette King came back.

"And what mischief were you up to last night?" I said sententiously.

"Can't you be a bit more polite? I was out drinking!"

"For the whole night? And you took the purse and the necklace with you?"

"None of your business!" He went outside, then suddenly came back and asked, "Where's the dog?"

"Isn't it tied up under the tree?"

"Where?" he said. I went out. Sure enough, the dog was gone. He started shouting all over the coal yard, "Lily! Lily!" He'd actually called the dog "Lily"! But Lily didn't come.

He ran back in again. "Who told you to tie up the dog outside? Eh? What did that dog ever do to you?"

"If it's gone, it's gone. Why are you yelling at me? Isn't your uncle worth more than a dog?"

He jumped to his feet and smashed his cell phone on the ground. I wasn't going to put up with this sort of behavior. He was really driving me nuts, and I wasn't taking that from anyone, let alone from my nephew! I was leaving. He yelled after me, "Take off my suit!"

"Look in your room," I said. "Is this my suit or your suit?"

I thought the Briquette King might come running after me to admit he'd been wrong, but when I looked around, he wasn't there. So I left.

51.

Back at Fishpond, I divvied up the remaining clothes amongst Wufu, Eight, and Goolies. That made us four men unique in Fishpond, the only trash pickers wearing designer-label suits.

"The suits," the locals called us after that. Some of them even wondered if we were really trash pickers. What kind of a trash picker would wear a suit like that? People from the street committee came around to question us, and took our carts and three-wheelers in. They thought we were only pretending to be trash pickers. There were far too many people making complaints against the local authorities nowadays, and maybe that was what we were up to. We finally convinced them we weren't. We got our carts back, but there was still whispering that we'd swiped the suits.

The other three stopped wearing suits. Hey, they were born to be at the bottom of the heap, and that was where they'd stay. No number of smart suits could change that, and there was nothing I could do about it.

I still wore my designer gear, and when I went to the local market for some Sichuan spicy rice noodles and saw Gem Han approaching, I marched straight up to him, and he actually stepped to one side to let me by. When he realized it was me, he grabbed my arm. "Is it really you?"

"Yes!"

"Why are you dressed like that?"

"They're only clothes."

"Listen to you! You're more of a city man now than I am."

"I've been to see you a few times, but you weren't there."

"Coming to thank me, were you?"

"Of course, but I have something to tell you too."

I told him that we'd kept to the rules and hadn't done anything that would give him a bad name. We had worked really hard and were earning enough to get by. The trouble was that our patch on Prosper Street was a bit small, so could he give us a few more streets?

I was pleased that I was so fluent, and calm and relaxed. But suddenly I realized I'd gotten it wrong, that cheeky grins were no way to address Gem Han. He was the boss, the King of Trash. Sure enough, he squinted at me, said, "OK," and strode away.

I should've at least invited him for a meal of Sichuan spicy rice noodles. I went back and told Wufu about my encounter with Gem Han. Wufu responded, "I don't think he'll go hungry!" Still, I felt uneasy.

Things that've gone wrong keep coming back to haunt you. Like how a pot with a crack will always leak. It turned out I had offended Gem Han. Not only did he not give us more streets, but two more trash pickers appeared on Prosper Street. They were scruffy, wretched-looking individuals, obviously newly arrived from the countryside. We should have been kind to them, but you can't cut a daikon at both ends, and we acted tough and told them to piss off. But they insisted that Gem Han had sent them. They didn't dare try to beat us up, but they didn't go either. This was too bad, and Wufu blamed me for it. I asked Eight and Almond and Goolies what we should do. Eight started cursing and swearing, cursing officials who went on about being public servants and serving the people, but who were actually out to take whatever they could get for themselves. I told him to cut the crap. Gem Han wasn't an official!

Then Eight said, "We'll drive them out by force. We'll use weapons. I'll do it for you!"

"Don't go making more trouble for Happy," said Almond.

As she saw it, if the newcomers hadn't been sent by Gem Han, they would have gone by now. If they refused to go, it must be because they had Gem Han's support, and in that case, we couldn't drive them out. We needed to talk to Gem Han.

Wufu kept at me to go, nagging me like an old woman.

"Why should I?" I said. "If you can't find a butcher, do you just eat the pork with its hair still on it?" Instead of going to see Gem Han, I played my flute.

"So you're not going?"

"No, why?"

"You crapped, now wipe yourself!"

Then he rephrased it. "Because you're the boss."

I carried on playing my flute. Secretly, I'd planned a way out: once we figured there was no future in trash picking, we could just pick up and go work for Mighty. I hadn't mentioned this to Wufu, or to Eight and Almond and Goolies, because I felt that Mighty would prefer to keep his distance from me, and I felt the same. I certainly didn't want to make trouble between Yichun and him. Besides, it would be a pity to give up trash picking, and even more of a pity to part from our friends. But Gem Han had turned his back on us, so we'd have to tackle Mighty and his company.

Poor Wufu, he had no idea what I was cooking up. He didn't eat any dinner, just shambled off to bed and slept through to the next day. He got up, puffy-faced and with a blood blister at the corner of his mouth. We went back to Prosper Street and were greeted by exclamations of surprise from the residents. There were so many trash pickers around all of a sudden! Wufu asked if they'd seen two other trash pickers, one with a long face like a gourd, the other with a thick neck. "Yes!"

they said. Wufu huffed and puffed with rage and picked up a brick to put in his cart.

"Don't do anything stupid!" I said.

"If we don't fight, what are we going to eat—wind and farts?"

"Fight if you want, but I'm not getting involved."

"You don't need to," he said. "If I win, I'll buy you a drink, real *baijiu*, and if I lose, you can buy me a Band-Aid." He was so dumb! I went into a furniture store, leaving my three-wheeler outside. It was the fifth time I'd been in. The owner had a kind face, and we bargained over a mattress. Finally, just as I'd gotten him down from five hundred to four hundred, Wufu came in.

"Come look at this mattress," I said to him.

His hands were grimy, so he didn't dare touch it, but he admired it. "What a nice bed! City folk are so lucky. I bet they dream in color on a mattress like this!"

"Lend me fifty yuan. I've only got three hundred and fifty."

"Who are you buying this for?"

"For myself. I'll let you sit on it when I get it home."

Wufu's jaw dropped, and he waved his hand in front of my face.

"What are you doing?" I asked.

"Are you crazy? We're trash pickers. Why would we sleep on a mattress like this?"

That made the owner turn to Wufu. "You trash pickers aren't just messing with me, are you?"

"No one's messing with you," said Wufu, pulling himself up to his full height.

"Then you're making trouble!"

I pulled Wufu to one side. "Don't say anything else! I need fifty yuan. Will you give it to me or not?"

"No!" said Wufu.

I was really losing face in front of the shopkeeper, and I raised my hand to give Wufu a slap, but he got in first. He charged at me like a bull and bundled me out of the shop.

I was furious, but I didn't want to lose any more face, so I smiled. "Fine, I won't buy it then. Did you find the other two?"

"No, they must have been fucking scared and keeping out of sight, but their carts were by the road, so I let the tires out."

Now I'd have to protect Wufu again . . . I'd said I didn't want to get involved in a fight, but this silly mutt had let their tires out, and if they came after him, I couldn't just let him be beaten up. I looked around, but there was no sign of them. "Come on, quick!" I said, and we ran off, Wufu going even faster than me.

We didn't collect much trash. Wufu was as restless as a sow in heat and kept muttering to himself. I leaned against the lamppost and to calm him down, said, "Maybe the heavens will rain meat buns!" Wufu duly looked up at the sky, which was streaked with cirrus clouds like a newly furrowed field. Then a pebble fell from the lamppost, startling us, but it was only a sparrow, tiny as a wine cup, which flew away.

"Don't worry, Wufu," I told him. "Things will get better, believe me."

"OK," he said.

But it worried me that we'd been waiting for days for Yichun to come tell us when we should go see Mighty. I'd imagined that once I'd bought the mattress, she'd come to Fishpond one morning or evening, and make herself comfortable on it. Did some mysterious cause and effect exist between her nonappearance and my failure to buy the mattress? Another day passed, and she still didn't come. I was frantic. I finally went to the salon to find out where she was—and was greeted by news of a catastrophe.

It was the thirteenth, and it certainly was an unlucky day. The sky was overcast and the air felt colder. Summer would soon be over.

Before I set off, I reminded Wufu to put his jacket on, and I moved the orchid from its place on the windowsill to the floor, to keep drafts off it. Orchids were easy to grow in the summer, but their leaves would wither the moment it got cold. Wufu had been telling me to toss it, but I didn't want to. I'd spoken to it just this morning: *Now, make sure to look lively until I've bought the mattress so that Yichun can see you!* As I spoke, there was a crash, and the shelf fell down. One of Yichun's shoes hit the floor; the other fell on the orchid, getting wet and overturning the orchid bowl. It was a bad omen for sure! But I was too dim-witted to appreciate it at the time.

The news was that Yichun had been arrested. She'd been in the Rehabilitation Center for five days. I stood by the wall outside the salon, our wall, where I'd left a mark for her each time I'd come to see her. There were more than twenty marks there, but Yichun was gone. I knew there were always risks in her line of work, but Xi'an was such a big city and there were countless sex workers. When a bird crapped overhead, what was the chance of the shit landing on you? The fat assistant at the salon, the one Yichun got along with the best, told me that the salons on this street had always been safe, because two of the officers at the Prosper Street police station had relatives who ran salons here, and all the owners knew the local police and kept them well supplied with gifts. What had happened was that a senior anti-vice official from Beijing had arrived to do a cleanup of Xi'an, and the city police had clamped down on dance halls, bathhouses, and beauty and hair salons. The raids had been carried out by special squads, without informing the local police. Yichun was unlucky and got caught in the firing line. The day it happened, half a dozen police swooped in, terrifying the downstairs staff, who were told to line up against the wall and not move. The salon owner tried to get to the desk, on the pretext of finding some cigarettes, so she could press the panic button and warn those upstairs to hide, but they wouldn't let her. Three officers rushed upstairs and brought down Yichun and her client. She hadn't resisted or cried out, and when the owner tried to cover her head with a towel as she was taken out to the police van, she pulled it off. She didn't want her hair mussed. She even turned to look at her reflection in the glass.

"They took twenty-eight couples from up and down this street," said Fatty. "They took Yichun and her client, and later they came back for the boss."

"The boss had it coming to her!" I said.

"But they let her go!"

"How come?"

"When the anti-vice official went back to Beijing, the boss pulled strings and got herself out."

I went to see her. She wasn't plastered with her usual makeup, and her face looked unpleasantly coarse and flabby. "Where's Meng Yichun?" I demanded.

"In the Rehabilitation Center, where else?" she shot back, nasty as always. I'd have to be more conciliatory. I begged her to pull strings to get Yichun out too, but she said she'd already put in a word. The answer was that Yichun could go free upon payment of a five-thousand-yuan fine. "Do you have the money?" she asked. How could I possibly lay my hands on that amount of money? I'd never so much as sniffed at five thousand in my entire life.

"But Meng Yichun's your best employee. She's the one who lays the golden eggs. You must get her out!" I protested.

"You get her out—she's from your hometown."

"I haven't got the money."

"Nor have I." She sat there, dragging on her cigarette and puffing smoke in my face. I felt like punching her, but I controlled myself, and just kept begging her to help, sweet-talking her, saying things like how Yichun would pay her the money back without fail; like how Yichun and I would be forever in her debt, we'd be her beasts of burden in the next life; like how I'd go to the salon every day from now on and wash sheets, light the stove, clean the toilet, and I'd call her "Auntie." I just got, "If you gave me five thousand, I'd call you 'Grandpa'!" And she grabbed the mop and started pushing it across the floor. I took the hint and left, wiping the tears from my eyes.

52.

Leftover House was my lair, and like an exhausted, wounded animal, I headed back there to lick my wounds.

I felt all choked up. I had to sleep, to make everything go away. But I couldn't. I'd been finding it very difficult to get to sleep on this bed, because after Yichun's visit, every time I lay down, I got a hard-on. Now it was driving me wild, and I had to jerk myself off. I'm telling you, I was numb with tiredness, and so confused, I felt more dead than alive. Then I heard a sound. It was that cat. It had sneaked in and was crouched at the foot of the bed, looking at me. It had been there when Yichun and I were in bed together. What was it doing here now? I suddenly felt terribly ashamed. Why was I still horny, when things were this bad? I pulled the quilt over my head.

Poor Yichun. I imagined her being dragged down the steep stairs by her hair, intimidated, humiliated. *Had she been interrogated?* I wondered. I'd heard about that, how they shone a bright light on you, didn't let you eat or drink, didn't let you sleep for nights on end. They threatened you, swore at you, sometimes tied you up and beat you. You were pretty? They wouldn't let you wash your face, or comb your hair. Then they dragged you in front of a mirror to make you look at how ugly you'd become. Or they asked you the same question, over and over again, and made you confess over and over the details of what you did with your johns, so they could get their kicks by virtually gang-raping you. I couldn't bear to go on thinking like this. Maybe Yichun was shut in a cell on her own, with no window or light, and had to sit on a freezing-cold concrete floor. What was she thinking about? Was she thinking about me? She'd know I must have heard the news by now. Was she hoping desperately I'd get her out? But I didn't have five thousand yuan! All I could do was wait until Wufu and the others got back, tell them everything that had happened, and talk about raising the money.

The first to arrive were Almond and Goolies. They were burning ghost money by the water tub downstairs, and the light from the flames flickered on the windows of my room. I opened my door.

Almond said, "You're back early, Happy?"

"What are you doing?"

"I dreamed of my mom last night. She was telling me the house was no good. I knew that meant she wanted me to rebuild our house, to stop people in the village from laughing at us. So at lunchtime today, I sent money back home, and on my way back from the post office, I bought some ghost money to burn for my mom."

Then she asked, "Happy, if the ash flies upward, does that mean that my mom got the money?"

"That's what they say."

"Amazing she can find it in a city this big!" Almond laughed. "Anyway, why are you back so early? Is something up?"

I couldn't start talking about us raising money now, so I just said, "Nothing's up, nothing at all."

Almond knocked her head on the ground before the pile of ashes. Then she ran up the steps, pulling 184 yuan out of her pocket. As she gave it to me, she turned to look at Goolies, who was still kowtowing to the ashes, and said quietly, "This is what Wufu and Eight and I got together for Meng, Meng . . . What's her name?"

"Meng Yichun."

"This money's for her. I had to twist it out of Eight. He was grumbling about why we were still collecting money, even though he said he would when we first made the agreement. That man's so unreliable!"

My hand shook as I took the money. "How's Yichun doing?" Almond asked. "When are you going to bring her to see us? Happy, what's up? You look terrible!"

"I'm fine."

"Screw that! Let me give you a back scratch!" she said. She wasn't going to take no for an answer. She pushed me against the railing, and her fingers snaked inside my jacket.

I didn't know when Eight would get back, and I wasn't counting on him anyway. But as soon as Wufu entered the yard at dusk, I asked him to come up to my room, and I told him what had happened to Yichun. Wufu hunkered down on the floor without a word.

"Say something," I said.

"You haven't got any money. I haven't got any money. Eight certainly hasn't got any. Have you talked to Almond about it?"

"She's got even less to spare. Besides, she just sent money back home."

"So what can we do?" Wufu said.

"I have no idea," I said.

"Well, if you don't know, I sure as hell don't," Wufu said. "But if you can't spring her from jail, then at least you should go and see her."

"She's in a rehabilitation center; that's what I've heard," I said.

"Where's that?"

"I don't know."

"Didn't you tell me there wasn't a lane or a street in this city that you couldn't find?" Wufu said. I didn't answer him.

"Can't we find enough money in the trash? You found Mighty's wallet that one time. Tomorrow we'll go through all the garbage bins in the street, and if Meng Yichun's meant to get out, maybe we'll find some."

I always figured Wufu wasn't going to come up with any decent ideas, and sure enough, talking to him was a waste of time. Finally, I said, "Go get me a ladleful of Almond's vegetable water."

"You can't drink cold stuff after the start of autumn," objected Wufu.

"My belly's on fire."

He got a bowl and took it downstairs. But something he'd said reminded me of Mighty. Why didn't I go see him? Of course! I should go see Mighty. Mighty could help her. The salon owner never mentioned him; he must still be in the dark about Yichun.

I'd go see Mighty. And I'd take Wufu along with me!

We didn't have his cell phone number, so the next morning I found out where his offices were on Shangyi Street and we went there. Just when things had looked really bleak, here was light at the end of the tunnel, and I cheered up. I was grateful to Wufu. Wufu was a toe rag, but even a toe rag could come in useful, to block a drafty window for instance. So on our way to Mighty's offices, I told Wufu about Mighty's offer to give us work with his company, and pointed out that this had all been mediated through Meng Yichun.

"Meng Yichun's a good woman," Wufu commented. Then he added, "Pretty, and so good too."

"She's certainly good. Not many women are so pretty and so good as well."

"Buddhists say that when someone's pretty, their 'inner eye' is blind."

"Bullshit." Then I remembered my analogy. "If someone's attractive, it's because all their proportions are right. It's like a house. If it's well built, then it's well ventilated and airy, and then the sun shines in, and of course it's sturdy too. A house that's just thrown together any old way is none of those things."

"So I won't last long then."

"Don't be so gloomy!"

Wufu laughed. Then he scooted across the street and rifled through a garbage can till his hands were all dirty, but he found nothing.

Four toughs stood at the entrance to Mighty's offices. Wufu pulled me aside. "That's the police. Do you think they've come to pick up Mighty as well?"

"Take a good look . . . security guards or police?"

"Well, even if they're guards, they look more like police than the police do!" He sounded defensive.

We went inside, but Mighty wasn't there. Someone called his cell phone and told us he was at a restaurant. Mighty asked them to pass the phone to me. "Hey, Happy Liu! Come on over; I'll treat you both to lunch!"

Mighty was a good man. Merciful Buddha! Wufu chortled when I told him. "When a big boss invites you for a meal, what do you think we'll eat?"

I issued stern reminders. "Whatever it is, don't guzzle your food. Chew it slowly and don't slurp. Don't talk too much, and when there's something you've never eaten before, watch how other people are eating it, and don't stare, just casually glance around."

There were four or five other people at the table with Mighty. Fellow businessmen, he told us, and then he introduced us as trash pickers who were about to start work with him. Mighty's friends didn't appear to be looking down on us; in fact, you could tell he mixed with really decent people. For their part, they couldn't say enough good things about Mighty: what a wonderful fellow he was to have friends like Wufu and me, and to invite us to a meal, and what a pity the media weren't in attendance to give it a little publicity. Then one of them told a joke: A government official was in the mountains assessing the public mood at the grassroots, and distributing donations to the poor. One old peasant was given a bed quilt, and the official asked how he passed the day. "The old peasant didn't understand his accent, so he thought he'd said 'pissed,' not 'passed.' He said, 'Just one piss a day, not a whole-day piss!'" There was loud laughter. Wufu didn't understand but laughed along with them anyway. I didn't.

Mighty called the waitress over. "Bring us some more dishes, and some steamed minced pork in lotus leaves!" Wufu looked at me, but I said nothing. The dishes began to arrive, but apart from a large plate of steamed pork in lotus leaves, there were no more meat dishes, just carbs and greens like buckwheat noodles and oat noodles, pease porridge, spicy stewed bean curd, fried eggplant, stewed daikon, steamed mountain yam, stir-fried bamboo shoots, bracken flour skins, dried pea pods, scallions and wood ear mushrooms, and walnuts, dates, and toon shoots. The table was covered with endless little dishes. There was every kind and shape of noodle, as well as millet porridge, and bowls stacked three tiers high, with gruels of green beans, wheat berries, and black rice.

"The Empress Dowager Cixi had sixty dishes at every meal, so it's sixty dishes for you as well. Dig in!"

Three times, Mighty personally helped us to the steamed pork, and finally put the dish in front of us so we could help ourselves. He and his friends didn't eat much. They spent most of the time telling dirty stories, each one cruder than the last, and they burst out laughing after each one. It didn't look as if he knew about Yichun, but I couldn't ask him. In fact, I couldn't get a word in edgewise at all. I didn't eat much, just sat up straight, then worried that my mind was drifting, so I pinched my leg hard. If anyone looked at me, I made sure to smile politely at them. Because I was sitting like that, my lower back started to ache, and I rubbed it with my hand. Then I put my hand back on the table and waited, trying my best to maintain a dignified calm. Wufu finished the steamed pork and sat there too, but he looked uncomfortable and kept squirming in his chair. I kicked him, and he sat up straight and put his hands on the table. Ai-ya! His fingernails were so long, and encrusted with dirt! I kicked him again, and he whispered, "What's up?"

"Listen to what they're saying."

"I don't understand their accents."

"Your hands!"

He looked at his hands. They were covered in oil, and he licked them. I jumped to my feet.

"Don't stand on ceremony, Happy. Do you need the restroom?" said Mighty.

"No," I said, "the WC."

"The WC *is* the restroom," said Mighty. "Waitress, take him to the restroom."

I was expecting Wufu to say something embarrassing, but not me. My face flamed scarlet. I'd only asked to go so I could get Wufu to wash his hands, but Wufu just sat there without moving. "Are you going to the restroom, Wufu?" I said.

"Yes, I need a piss," he said.

In the restroom, I made Wufu wash his hands. "We call the WC a shit-house, and here's another name for it—restroom," I said.

"I thought we were going to have delicacies like squid and sea cucumber, but we never . . . ," said Wufu.

I told him to zip his mouth.

Back at the table, Mighty and his friends were inquiring about one another's bodily functions. Good heavens, they had high blood pressure, high cholesterol, and diabetes, and they were talking about whose had gone up and whose had gone down, and who'd scored all of the Three Highs, as they called them. "It all comes from eating," Mighty pronounced. "In the past, we were short on food. Now there's no end of good things to eat, and we eat ourselves sick."

"How can you eat yourself sick?" Wufu muttered under his breath.
"Don't butt in," I told him.

"Our goldfish kept dying," one of the men said, "and we finally found out that they'd died of overeating, not starvation, because the housekeeper kept feeding them."

Another said, "Maybe our children won't have these diseases when they're adults. They live on KFC and McDonald's, so by the time they're grown, they'll be used to eating good stuff."

"Ai-ya!" sighed another. "In the old days, we worried about not having enough to eat. Nowadays, we worry about what's best to eat. Mr. Mighty, you've been in very good health since you got your new liver, haven't you?"

"Not bad at all," Mighty said.

I had realized by then that Mighty and his cronies were sticking to their carbs because they were overweight and had health problems. But what really shocked me was that last comment, that Mighty had a new liver, not a new kidney! So he hadn't had a kidney transplant? He didn't have my kidney?

"How about some chicken soup? Chicken soup, waitress!" Mighty ordered.

"Make it a local, free-range chicken!" one of them said.

"You're so fussy! Your girls have to be foreign and your chicken has to be local!" another said.

I said to Wufu in an undertone, "Did you hear that man say Mighty had a new liver?"

"That's what I heard," Wufu said.

"Did you really hear him say that?"

"Yes."

Suddenly my ears were burning, and my eyes clogged up like they were full of eye boogers. The lights on the ceiling merged into a blur of white, and when the waitress came, it looked like there were two of her. Mighty hadn't had a kidney transplant? How was that possible? The whole reason why I was convinced I was a city man was that my kidney had been transplanted into Mighty, and now it turned out that wasn't true! Oh, Mighty, Mighty! When I met him, I thought it was karma, but it was nothing of the kind. We owed no karmic debt to each other at all!

How could something like this have happened? I didn't hear what they were saying anymore. I was simply looking at Mighty in a daze. Suddenly he'd become a stranger to me, and an ugly one at that. They all carried on chatting to one another and urging food and drink on us, but I wasn't paying any attention. I felt cold, and my legs were trembling under the table. Mighty was talking to me. "Happy, why are you not eating? Eat up!" I picked up my chopsticks and helped myself to a piece of bean curd.

It was tasteless. How could bean curd be so tasteless? I was worried Wufu would make fun of me because I'd rambled on about Mighty having my kidney, but he had gone back to his chicken soup, which he was enjoying so much that his forehead was beaded with moisture. I went to the restroom again, washed my face, and sat down on the toilet seat. I heard Mighty ask Wufu, "Good soup?"

"Very good!" Wufu said.

"Eat up the meat too. Where's Happy?"

"He's gone to the toilet," Wufu said.

"Again! Has he got a kidney problem?" I was worried Wufu might let on that I'd had a kidney removed, but luckily he didn't, because he had his mouth full of chicken and couldn't talk. I flushed the WC, to give the impression that I'd had a crap.

Well, if Mighty hadn't received my kidney, so be it! So what if he hadn't? I could hardly blame him for that; it wasn't his fault. At least my kidney was somewhere in the city.

There was a small window in the restroom, and I opened it to get a breath of fresh air to calm me down. But as soon as I opened the window, an icy draft blew in. The weather had changed. I shut it again and went to stand in front of the mirror, waiting until my face looked better, then walked out. On the table, the dishes had been cleared and replaced with dishes of watermelon, but the flesh was pale instead of red, as if the color had been bled out. I swallowed a piece, seeds and all.

53.

The meal ended, and Mighty's friends left.

"Mr. Mighty," I said, "there's something I need to tell you."

Mighty smiled in that cultured way of his. "Didn't Ms. Meng fill you in? In another week, you can start. Construction's begun on the perimeter wall at Fengyukou."

"What's Fengyukou? Didn't you say we were going to work for your company?" Wufu asked.

Fengyukou was a valley in the Qinling Mountains, forty *li* south of the city. Goolies had told us they were building a lot of holiday villas there, with hot springs, a golf course, and a safari park. The villagers there were pretty smart; they'd gotten rich just by selling free-range hens' eggs. Almond had said she'd take us to have a look, and if we couldn't make enough from trash picking, we could always go raise free-range chickens! But with Almond, she said something one evening; then she'd forgotten it by the next morning. In any case, we didn't go.

"It *is* my company," said Mighty. "We've just bought a big plot of land in the mountains, about five thousand acres, and we're building a villa development. Our land encircles five mountain peaks, and your job is to stick red flags on each of the peaks every morning, and take them down every evening . . ."

"Like hoisting the national flag in Tian'anmen Square every morning?" Wufu said.

"It's not the national flag; it's the company flag," Mighty said.

"Just sticking the flags up?" Wufu said.

"Just sticking the flags up!"

Mighty had the wrong end of the stick completely. And I was angry at Wufu for blabbing on like this.

"Wipe your mouth, Wufu," I said. He wiped it, and I whispered to him, "What did we come here for? Where is your sense of priorities?"

"Oh! Oh!" he muttered, and went downstairs.

I said to Mighty, "Did you know that Meng Yichun's been arrested?"

I'd be telling a lie if I said that Mighty went pale, slumped down on the sofa, and wept as if his heart would break. Instead, he got up and shut the door, sat down again, helped himself to a toothpick, and picked his teeth. Avoiding my eyes, he said, "Yes, I knew that."

He knew! He knew, and he still took his cronies out to lunch, laughed and joked with them, and acted as cool as a cucumber to me!

"You knew?"

"The salon boss phoned me. Ai-ya! Our good little Ms. Meng, how did she get mixed up in all that?"

What did he mean? He was acting as if he had no idea what Yichun did for a living! "You mean you didn't know that . . . what she did in the salon?"

"I didn't know until her boss called me."

"So you and she . . ."

"What are you talking about?" Mighty flatly denied there was any "you and she." If only . . . How I wished there really had been nothing between them. But I couldn't believe that Yichun had told me lies. And several times I'd seen him collecting her and bringing her back with my own eyes, and my eyes hadn't told me lies either. If Yichun wasn't in trouble, I'd have been delighted to hear Mighty deny it all, but today I was shocked and furious.

It was probably because, being a big company boss, he was embarrassed to admit to anyone that he went with prostitutes. Well, I wouldn't rub his nose in it. I sighed. "Anyway, Mr. Mighty, we have to help Meng Yichun."

"Of course," he agreed. "Have you been to see her? You should, you know. I'll buy some cigarettes. Ms. Meng likes a smoke. You can give them to her from me."

"Five thousand yuan will get her out—that's what her boss said. That's all we need!"

"Don't listen to anything that madam says. It's all lies. Once someone's inside, no amount of money will get them out."

"Yes, it can. The old woman's out. Can't you try? All she needs is five thousand, and she'll be free!"

"You don't understand, Happy. We have to be principled."

Was this Mighty talking? Mighty? Yichun had regarded Mighty as her closest friend, and when everything was calm and peaceful and when he was full of lust, that was how he acted, but as soon as things went wrong, he was only concerned about his own interests, and he became a completely different person. He was willing to hire two people just to go stick flags on mountaintops every day, but he wouldn't cough up five thousand yuan to help Yichun! He was tight as a duck's ass! Principled, my foot!

"Mr. Mighty, Mr. Mighty!" I tried again. Just then, a young woman, perhaps his secretary, pushed open the door and came in, carrying a glass of water and three pills. She stood between Mighty and me and urged him to take his pills. He popped them into his mouth and washed them down with the water, then said to me, "Let me see what I can do, Happy. Go home and sell your three-wheeler, and come back in a week. I'll give you a slip to take to Personnel . . ."

I left Mighty to his medicine and went downstairs. There was a glass partition where the stairs curved. I thought it was an open door and walked right into it, and it cracked. The waiter came running, and I said, "I'll pay for it. How much is it?"

But he said, "No, it was our fault. I'm sorry, sir." He supported me with one hand and looked to see if my head was bleeding. I retched and vomited bile.

Wufu was waiting for me downstairs. It was blowing a gale outside, and his face was covered in dust. He saw me with my hand over my mouth. "What's up?"

"Mighty won't pay to get Meng Yichun out," I said.

"I told you, rich folk aren't like us. You went on about how that Mighty was good, but how fucking good is that? He forked out for a new liver to give him a few more years of life. That's how careful with money he is, the motherfucker!"

"You sound exactly like Eight."

"What's wrong with swearing? Just because I've eaten his food, is that what you're saying? OK, I'll vomit too!" He stuck his finger down his throat and puked everything up. "Right," he said. "Now I don't owe him anything."

It was still blowing hard, in fact harder than ever, and the sky had turned a lurid yellow. I said nothing, nor did Wufu. We just hurried along.

Maybe it was fate. After all, daikon seeds grew into daikons, and cabbage seeds grew into cabbages. Yichun had gotten into crime for the sake of another crime. I wasn't Mighty, I would only ever be Happy Liu. I gave a couple snorts of laughter as I walked.

"What are you laughing at?" Wufu asked.

"We're lucky! We didn't sell our carts and go work for Mighty, and we're not going to!" By the time we'd walked down one more street, the sky had gone a frightening black and the wind was ferocious. "Is it evening?" I asked.

"We've only just had lunch!" said Wufu.

Mighty had made me so angry, it had addled my brain. "Well, if it's not nighttime, then a storm's coming," I said. I never expected a sandstorm like this though.

Back in Freshwind, we had three sandstorms a year, but I thought that the high buildings and the greenbelt around the city would keep them out of Xi'an, or at least make them less violent. But I was wrong. By the time Wufu and I got to South Avenue, we could no longer see the sun, and the air was filled with sand. Distant buildings were invisible now, and the whole city seemed to be fading from sight. The streets were a melee of cars and pedestrians scurrying for cover, and half an hour later, they were deserted. Even the traffic police disappeared. All around us, we could hear the wind howling like a pack of wolves, wailing like a banshee. Leaves from the trees, scrap paper, and bits of plastic sheeting bowled drunkenly along the streets.

"Good, that's good, Wufu. The heavens are angry!" I said.

Wufu paid no attention. He was busy running after the garbage, collecting whatever he could grab and swearing when it got away from him, the words torn from his mouth before he'd finished saying them.

I stood in a shop doorway. It was closed, but I pressed my back against it and squinted upward. In the primal chaos of the sky, I thought I saw Yichun. *I'm sorry,* I silently told her. *I'm so sorry. I can't buy you out, no one can. You'll just have to buckle down and do your "rehabilitation."*

Maybe it was better this way. She could get her brother's case out of her head. She wouldn't need to go with those men and wrong herself. At least this was a way out for her.

If that's what heaven decrees as your punishment, then you'll just have to put up with it. It's only three months, I said to her.

And when you get out, then you'll learn who your true friends are. Mighty with the new liver will never be my rival again.

I truly have a woman now, and that woman really has a man, and his name's Happy Liu! I muttered to myself, looking up into the sky. Suddenly, a flowerpot crashed to the ground from the third floor above. I realized my face was wet with tears.

The pot lay in fragments not more than a foot in front of me, but I didn't feel any fear. I bent down and picked a flower out of the debris. It was a rose.

There was another crash, a pane of glass this time. Wufu came running back, his arms full of trash. "Come away from the building!" he yelled at me. I didn't move. He put his booty down and pulled me away. "Has the wind gotten your brains? Do you want to get yourself crushed?" The stuff he'd collected blew away.

At least my head was clear now, clear enough to tell Wufu off for making a big fuss. I wasn't so easy to kill. I'd only just gotten settled in the city, and I still had plenty of stuff to do. I wouldn't die even if the whole building crashed down! Wufu didn't bother to chase after his garbage. "Let it blow! Harder! Till the whole city turns to trash!" he said.

"We've got to run, get back home as fast as we can, Wufu. I'll race you!" I said. We raced each other, our clothes billowing behind us like balloons, until the wind tore the buttons off and our jackets flew open, and it was as if we'd grown wings. I was still holding the rose, but the petals had all gone, except for the last one, which I put in my mouth and swallowed. Wufu ran and ran, but the wind was blowing him off course, and he veered toward a lamppost. "Watch out for the lamppost!" I shouted, but he couldn't stop himself and crashed into it.

54.

The sandstorm blew on into the evening. Back at Leftover House, I gathered up all the suits from Mighty, including the one I'd been wearing and the ones I'd given to Wufu, Eight, and Goolies, and handed them over to Gem Han.

This was how I explained it to Wufu: Gem Han was the first person we went to see when we arrived in Xi'an. Now we were going to see him again, and that meant a new beginning. "Has it ever occurred to you that by the time you've gathered a goodly amount of wisdom and knowledge, you're old and death is staring you in the face? Don't you wish your child could start from where you are now, instead of starting from the beginning? Well, mark my words: the Happy you see in front of you isn't the same Happy who arrived in Xi'an. We're starting again on the basis of the wealth of city experience that we've accumulated."

I rapped smartly on Gem Han's door.

"Who is it?"

"Happy Liu!" I answered. Wufu wiped his nose. He'd had a runny nose ever since we got back from lunch. He wiped the snot on the door frame and added, "And Wufu!"

Han invited us in. He was working on a bottle of red wine, attacking the cork with a knife. Finally, he got a pair of chopsticks and forced the cork down into the bottle. "Who gives a bottle of wine as a gift without giving a corkscrew too?" he grumbled. He looked over the pile of suits we'd brought with us and examined the labels. Then he tried them on and asked where we'd gotten them.

I told him we hadn't stolen them or found them in the trash, and that they hadn't been worn by anyone who was sick or dying. "Believe me, I've got my principles. Don't you remember that when you had to leave the village quickly because they wanted to beat you up, they were searching every lane, and I gave you a *ganmo* to eat and got you away?" The reminder was deliberate. I didn't want Han acting stuck up, or trying to rip us off.

It must have worked. Han waved his hand. "Was I really such a no-good turtle in the Freshwind pond? What a joke!"

It was time for me to butter him up a little. "Exactly. And now look at you!" I said. "You're the South Side's King of Trash!"

"Is that all you think I am?"

"No! Not at all! You have to shore up your influence in the trash-picking world and create the Shangzhou Gang!"

"Fine, fine, Happy," he said. "I can tell you're a man of vision."

"We're just tadpoles swimming with a big fish," said Wufu.

Han handed out cigarettes. "You'll lose your tails with all that swimming!"

"A tadpole without a tail is a toad, isn't it?" said Wufu.

"That's what I am," said Han. "A tailless tadpole-turned-toad. Chairman Mao was a toad, a big toad at that!"

"Nonsense!" I said.

"I'm not as educated as you, but I can recite his poem about a toad by heart," said Han.

> "Sitting in the pond like a crouching tiger
> Nourishing the spirit in the shade of the willow
> Come tomorrow, springtime begins
> No creature dares make a sound."

"That's a good poem!" I said.

"Of course it's good," Han said. "Tadpoles become toads." I held the mirror so he could see himself in the suit. He had a fair-sized paunch, and the suit was a bit tight on him.

"Just like a toad!" Wufu said. We all laughed.

I explained to Han that the suits belonged to a businessman I knew. He had too many to wear, so he gave a few to us, but they were too classy for us to wear. "We'd ruin them, but they're just right for you."

"When you come to the big city," Han told us, "it's smart to get to know people who are rolling in money, the more the merrier. Anyone who hates wealth and hates the wealthy won't last long here."

I nodded sagely. Then I said, "There's something we need to report to you. Two trash pickers arrived on Prosper Street, and they had the nerve to say you'd sent them, using your name to intimidate people, so we had to break their legs for them!"

"You broke their legs?" Han exclaimed.

"Well, we were about to," Wufu said.

"Don't even think of it! I did send them."

I put on an appalled expression. "You sent them? Impossible!"

"They came and asked me for work. I didn't want them to starve, and there are so many offices on Prosper Street, and wealthy residential blocks, rich pickings, so I sent them over to scrape together enough to eat for now, and I'll transfer them somewhere else later."

"That's just wrong," I said. "Prosper Street is a small patch, and two extra trash pickers . . . They're taking the food out of our mouths!"

"I've only had three bowls of rice gruel all day today, no proper meal," Wufu put in.

"And we're your country folk," I added. "The house nearest the water should get the moonlight first."

"OK, let me be clear," said Han. "Do you know who introduced those two men to me?"

"The city's mayor?" I guessed.

"Now you're being sarcastic. Why would the mayor come looking for me? And I wouldn't go looking for him either. I'll only ever be in trash," said Han, "but I've got ambitions beyond being the South Side King of Trash. I've teamed up with the South Side's biggest scrap merchant, and we're going to swallow the small trash depots and set up a company. So when this guy introduced those two to me, well, you can imagine, I had to find them a job, didn't I? If you'll put up with it for the moment, when we've set up the company, then you two can take over a subdepot."

"Gem, now you're talking!" said Wufu.

I'd only ever thought I'd be trash picking for three or four years, and then I planned on becoming the second Gem Han. And here he was dreaming up new schemes! *Gem Han, you're such a sly one. You make me green with envy!* If he really set up a big company and put us in charge of a subdepot, then Wufu could bring his wife and kids to live with him, and I could get Yichun to move in. I definitely wouldn't allow her to work in the beauty salon anymore. That john of hers, Mighty, could go screw himself!

But Yichun was at the Rehabilitation Center. I had to stop thinking about her; it was bringing me down. "Gem," I said, "you've dreamed up a big pancake for us, but we're hungry now. Can you lend me some money, and I'll pay you back in three months, with interest?"

"You want to borrow money? How come everyone from back home wants to borrow money from me? Just the other day, Zhang the Plug asked me for a loan. He wanted to buy a cobbler's machine and open a shoe-repair stall. My principle is never to lend money. So I gave it to him. I gave him one hundred and fifty yuan! I told him I didn't want it back! What do you want the money for?"

"Nothing, nothing," I lied. "A relative's in the hospital in Xi'an, and I was thinking of asking you to lend me five thousand, but now I can see you need your money to invest in the company, so forget it . . ."

"But I still have to help you!" said Han. "How about if I help you both earn a ton of money?"

I gave a little laugh, but Wufu said, "We can't even earn a bit of money, so how are we going to earn a ton?"

"It isn't everyone who can earn big money," Han said. "If I sent those other two, they couldn't tell east from west or south from north. They'd be no good. But if you want, I'll get Mr. Lu to talk to you. He's due here today."

I looked at Wufu, who said, "Shall we?"

"So long as I can earn five thousand as quickly as possible," I said.

"OK, I'll go with you, wherever it is," Wufu said. Han pressed some numbers on his cell phone, and shortly afterward, a man turned up. This was Lu, a company president, Han told us. Lu was carrying a greaseproof paper bag containing a large chunk of braised beef to go with the drinks he and Han were about to have. I wondered how a man who bared his teeth like that could be a company president. Wufu didn't believe it either, and disappeared, saying he needed to take a piss.

I had some trouble understanding Lu's accent. According to Han, Lu was from Qishan County. Qishan folk had the northerners' steadiness and the southerners' ability to think on their feet. His company was on a roll. He'd acquired a site in Xianyang, where they needed a trench dug for a pipeline, and they'd pay fifteen yuan a yard, board and lodging thrown in. If we wanted to go, a truck would depart from Fishpond Village the day after tomorrow, and we could hitch a ride. With that settled, Lu bellowed to Han to get out the bottle. They offered me a drink, but I said no, and I went to take a piss.

Wufu was sitting on the WC, a beaming smile on his face.

"What are you smiling about?"

"I'm not smiling. I'm straining!" Wufu had a face permanently creased with worry, like a pig, but when he was taking a crap, his face wrinkled in a smile.

"Well, you can smile for real," I said. So he did, but it didn't improve his appearance.

"Is it settled?" he asked.

"Yup, we're digging a trench, fifteen yuan a yard."

"Five yuan?"

"Fifteen," Han said again.

"But we can dig three or even five yards a day!" Wufu was so excited, he jumped up to jab me with his fist, and his pants fell down to his ankles.

"Finish your crap," I said. I waited outside, wondering if this good news hadn't come a little too quickly. Was it too good to be true? Before long, Wufu came out.

"Had your crap?" I asked.

"No, I couldn't. I've had a touch of constipation the last couple of days . . . Do you think he's going to cheat us, with a face like that?" He went back to Han's door and peered through the crack. "The man's got a chunky gold bracelet on his fucking wrist, so it might be the real deal!" He was so happy, he leapt into the air and landed with a thud. Our luck had finally turned.

All the same, I said, "Calm down, Wufu. Don't look too excited, or Lu will start to wonder if he's being too generous, and he might go back on his offer."

We never signed a contract. I wasn't used to having contracts back then; I never even thought of it. It was just a laboring job, and not even long-term. But after we'd said good-bye to the pair, who were still drinking and eating their beef, I made a point of saying to Han, "When this is finished, we'll be back to pick trash."

"Of course, of course!" said Han.

Xianyang wasn't far from Xi'an, but we'd never been. I decided to get Eight, Almond, and Goolies to go along too. If we had our friends with us, we wouldn't be lonely. Besides, it's less tiring when men and women work together.

But Wufu was dead set against it. "How many ways can you slice a daikon? If you do less digging, I'll do more. It's just digging, not like trash picking, where you have to get along with people. And I'll dig six yards a day!" he boasted.

I had every confidence in Wufu, and besides, there was a bit of me that selfishly wanted to keep the deal to ourselves, so I decided we wouldn't tell the others. "If you dig six yards a day, it'll be a gold mine!"

Wufu was doing the math. "Six yards a day at fifteen yuan a yard, six fives are thirty, carry three, six times one is six, plus three. Good God, that's ninety yuan! How many yards would the trench be? Maybe thirty? Or fifty? The longer the better! Ten thousand yards!" He stopped trying to do the math and said, "We have to keep quiet about this."

"Why?"

"Don't tell a soul. Don't take the lid off the steamer till the buns are cooked. If you let a draft in, they won't cook through."

Did I need him to tell me that? Back at Leftover House, Wufu got his clothes together, then sat down on the flat roof and fixed his shoes. The heel had come off one of them, and he nailed it on again, his lips pressed firmly together, his face red with concentration. Eight was under the tree, sorting his latest trash, wire, and screws into one pile, Coca-Cola and mineral water bottles into another, plus wastepaper, and an aluminum window frame, which had to be pulled apart. He broke it up by smashing it with a stone. Clang, clang, clang.

"Eight, do you know what the four worst sounds are?" said Wufu.

"What?"

"A pig being slaughtered, a pot being scraped, a donkey braying, and a shovel hitting stone."

"So you can do doggerel, can you?" said Eight.

"Just cut it out! You're deafening me!" said Wufu.

"This is aluminum."

"Even if it was an aluminum ingot, how much would you get for it?"

"Now who's talking? Got some steel tubes, have you?"

"You're scared of me!" Wufu retorted, but said nothing more. When he'd broken up the frame, Eight chose a piece of brown paper from the wastepaper pile and folded it into a wallet. "Watch how I fold it, Wufu," he said.

"Why are you folding it up so small?" Wufu asked.

"It's not small. How much money do we trash pickers earn, anyway?"

"We might earn big money one day," Wufu said.

"There's no 'one day' for a trash picker," Eight said.

"One day you might earn ninety. That's nine hundred in ten days. Three nines make twenty-seven. That's two thousand seven hundred a month!" Wufu persisted. I looked at him. He was really letting his mouth run away with him. I coughed, and he finally shut up and nailed on his heel with a piece of iron piping. Then he started again. "Eight, you . . ." He hit his finger with the piping and stuck it in his mouth. At least that shut him up.

"Happy Liu! Happy Liu!" someone was shouting. I craned my neck and looked below, where old Fan, dressed in a bright red sweater, stood holding a bunch of garlic chives. He came into the yard and up the stairs. What did he want? He normally squatted in his doorway, completely ignoring us, a tea mug in his hands. He clearly thought he was too good for the likes of us.

Wufu stretched his leg across the stair, blocking Fan's way. "Put your leg down, Wufu," Fan said.

"That time I was pushing my cart into the lane and you were sitting there, you never pulled your leg back," Wufu said.

"And how would I remember a thing like that?" Fan said.

"You may not remember, but I do!" Wufu said.

"Ai-ya, Wufu! What's made you so cocky all of a sudden?"

I butted in at that point. "Wufu, Wufu, a blind dog doesn't sit in the middle of the road." I was really going after Fan as well.

Fan put his arm around me and said he wanted to talk to me, then dragged me into my room. He asked to borrow money from me, said his missus was a dragon. She held the purse strings, and she'd gone off to her family, so could I lend him two hundred yuan? I gave him the two hundred. He swore me to secrecy and went back downstairs. On the way, he ruffled Wufu's hair, and Wufu flung his hand off.

I jumped up in excitement and began to play my flute, the tune with the words that went,

> "We came from the grasslands to Tian'anmen
> Square, we hold the golden goblet high and
> sing a song of praise . . ."

"What was that all about?" Wufu asked.

"Know what Fan came for? He came to borrow money from me!"

"Borrow money from you?"

"Borrow money from me!"

"And did you lend it to him?"

"I did."

"You couldn't borrow from Gem Han, but you go lending him money?"

"Why not? Even if I had only five hundred left, I'd lend him two hundred! Think about it, what does it mean, him borrowing money from me?"

"What does it mean?"

"It means that in his eyes, I'm rich!" Wufu looked at me suspiciously. I rapped my flute against his forehead.

Wufu's hair had grown again, coarse and curly. Thick people always had thick hair.

55.

For our midday meal, Wufu and I mixed our remaining flour, then crushed leaves from the Sichuan pepper tree at the village entrance to flavor the dough, and put *laobing* to bake on the side of the wok. Then we cooked all the rice we had left, and we bought some bean curd to make a spicy stew. We gave Eight a bowl of rice and bean curd, and the same to Almond.

"Is it your birthday, Happy?" she asked.

"Does it have to be a birthday for us to have a decent meal?" I said.

"You'll never guess, we're going to . . . ," Wufu began, but I pinched his butt.

"We've eaten your food often. Now it's time for us to give something back!" I said.

That Wufu, he'd been telling me to stay cool and calm, but he couldn't stop himself from letting the cat out of the bag. But we'd decided not to let anyone come with us, so why tell them and make them jealous? Even the best of friends would be pissed if they had watery gruel and we had thick porridge.

The next morning, Wufu wanted me to send all his money back home. After all, we were about to earn big money. I agreed and went to the post office to do it for him, though I did suggest he only send half. But he didn't want to, just told me to send it all. It wasn't much, only six hundred. He started to do the math on his fingers and worked out he'd sent home a grand total of twenty-eight hundred. "I've eaten the same as you and drunk the same as you, and I've saved nearly three thousand, but you've got nothing to show for it," he said.

"Well, that's quite something," I said.

"And that makes me a good man, doesn't it, a man who treats his missus and kids fairly, right, Happy?"

"You want me to deliver your funeral eulogy, eh?" I said.

As soon as the words were out of my mouth, I realized it was a bad joke. But Wufu said only, "You go right ahead and deliver that eulogy. Once I've earned big money, no one in Freshwind will dare call me a useless son of a bitch ever again!" That made me yell at him again for being shortsighted and lacking ambition. I'd often said he should make long-term plans and not be satisfied with things as they were. How was I to know that Wufu's words were an omen and that a catastrophe was waiting for us right around the corner?

Even the most intelligent person slips up now and then. And I really screwed up that day. No sooner had I sent off the money than I rushed from the post office to the beauty salon at the northern end of Prosper Street. I always used to do this whenever I sent Wufu's money home; it had become a habit. It was only when I'd gotten to the door of the salon that I remembered Yichun wasn't there. I stood despondently by the opposite wall and made a scratch on it. "Will you tell Meng Yichun to find me if she comes back?" I said to the salon boss.

"She won't come back, will she?" she said.

"Of course she will, maybe in three months, maybe tomorrow!"

I spoke so fiercely that the woman said, "Where will she find you?"

Where indeed? I was headed to Xianyang, and I had no phone. I didn't know what to say. I simply turned and ran down the lane. "Psycho!" I heard her shouting after me.

I ran and ran; then my footsteps slowed, and I suddenly felt a bump on my shoulder. Instinctively, I ducked and kept jogging, until it felt like someone was trying to trip me with a stick. I looked, and there was Lively Shi.

This was a huge city, but somehow I was always bumping into Lively. Was he haunting me? He was in his beggar's disguise today, limping and propped on a bamboo cane. He was holding out his pot. "I don't have any money to give you!" I said.

"You're going to earn five thousand yuan, and you don't have any to spare?" he said.

"And where am I going to get five thousand?"

"You've been mumbling that you're going to earn five thousand, so you must have some money!"

"Is that what I've been saying?"

"You have."

I stared at him, then after a minute, kicked his leg. He straightened up.

"Why don't you do some work? Anything's better than begging. You have to pretend to be a cripple if you're going to beg, but if you keep doing that, your leg will never straighten again." There was a wedding party ahead of us, a dozen or so garlanded cars parked outside a house, and a crowd thronging around the bride as she left the building. Firecrackers exploded.

Lively said, "I'm not pretending to be a cripple." And he threw the stick away. "You've brought me good luck. Here's a wedding. Wait here. I'm going to beg from the wedding guests. I'll bring you a red envelope too." He went over to the wedding sedan, turned, and repeated, "Wait for me!" He sat down in front of the wedding sedan. I couldn't hear what he was saying, but I could see him humbly cupping his hands and talking, and someone gave him a red envelope containing cash. He carried on talking and cupping his hands, and got another red envelope. He took it with a chuckle and moved out of the way, saluting the bride with clasped hands. The procession of cars moved off, and he ran over to me, insisting I take one envelope. I refused. "You've got to take it," he said, and tore open the envelope. Inside were two yuan.

"You did all that bowing and scraping, just for two yuan?" I said. "Why don't you come to Xianyang? Wufu and I have a job digging trenches."

"It's hard work digging trenches," said Lively. "Give me a smoke."

"It's fifteen yuan a yard. You still don't want to come?"

I gave him a cigarette, and he stuck it between his lips. "Why would I want to do hard labor?"

I snatched the cigarette away. "Then go beg for your food!" And I turned and left, thinking, *Where on earth do people like that come from? If you beg because you're destitute, then I'll help you, but if you're just too lazy to work, then you deserve to starve in the street!* But I'd only walked a couple dozen feet when Lively came running up behind me and said he wanted to go with us. Did he really mean it?

"I haven't told anyone else about this," I said. "I'm only telling you to save you!" Lively nodded earnestly, and I took his begging pot and flung it away. Then I thought he might pick it up again, so I ground the fragments under my foot.

"Walk ahead, and straighten up!" He walked straight, but after a while, his leg gave way beneath him. "Straighten your leg!" I insisted. I took him back to Leftover House, and Wufu was very annoyed. He thought that Eight was better than Lively, but in the end I brought him around. "Eight makes a living in the city. Do you want Lively to be a beggar for the rest of his life?"

"Are you the government?"

In fact, I had another reason for wanting Lively with us, apart from saving him. He was a lot more interesting than Wufu and Eight. There are some people who are good for you, who really help you out, but they aren't interesting and you don't want to be around them. Then there are people who are the bane of your existence, but they're interesting and you enjoy being with them.

We headed for Gem Han's place that afternoon and, sure enough, there was a big truck parked and waiting, loaded with coal. Mr. Lu hadn't shown up; there was only the driver. He told us we'd have to sit behind him, so I climbed into the backseat. "Get out of there!" the driver said.

"Isn't this the right truck?" I asked.

"Get in the back of the truck."

"You want us to sit on the coal?"

"You prefer a throne?" the driver said. He had a woman with him, and she sat in the front passenger seat.

Dammit, there was only that one woman. The backseats stayed empty, and he wouldn't let us sit in them. That driver was not a nice man. We got into the bed of the truck. "I'm sitting here with Wufu. Why are you sitting here too?" Lively said.

"Because I get carsick in the cab," I said.

"So do I," Lively said. There was a tarp covering the coal, and we sat on it. Wufu muttered curses at the driver for putting his girlfriend first. He must have eaten a big lunch because he kept farting. Every time Wufu swore at the driver, he squeezed out a fart.

Finally I said, "C'mon, Wufu, if the three of us sat in the back, it would cramp their style, us gawking at them, wouldn't it? And we wouldn't feel comfortable about the situation either."

"She's up to no good, that's for sure!" said Wufu. "Did you see her, Happy? Is she good-looking?"

"She's got thick ankles, and she shouldn't be wearing a skirt."

Lively made himself a nest in the coal and lay down. "I'm not interested in women," he said. The truck drove out of Fishpond Village and through the streets of Xi'an, heading for Xianyang. Normally, as trash pickers, we got to see the buildings and storefronts on either side of us, but the truck took us along one overpass after another, so we got a completely different view of the city. Freshwind has a chain of mountains outside the town, as I said, but here in the city, there's a chain of buildings. City folk call us mountain people, but they're mountain people themselves. Wufu was exclaiming, "Look, look, isn't that the

Great Wild Goose Pagoda? Look, you can see it from here! And, look! That must be the tallest building in town, the fifty-five-story one! I've heard about it, but I've never seen it. It really is tall!"

"You're pathetic, Wufu," said Lively.

"Me? Pathetic?"

"Yup!"

"Huh! A beggar, calling me pathetic? Let me ask you this then: Do you know the South Side King of Trash, Gem Han? Do you know Mr. Mighty the businessman?"

"Nope. But I know the mayor and the chief of police."

"Be careful what you brag about! How do you know the mayor and the chief of police?" said Wufu.

"I've seen the chief of police in the homeless hostel. He brought the mayor over to ask me some questions, and I gave the mayor my formal complaint letter." Lively was getting the better of Wufu, and he knew it.

"Eight, Eight!" he shouted, like he always did when he wanted Eight to stand up for him. He'd forgotten Eight wasn't there.

"Who's Eight?" Lively asked, but Wufu ignored him.

I laughed, then asked Lively, "Did you really file an official complaint with the mayor?"

"I pursued it for eight years. I'm an old-timer."

"What was it about?"

"I've forgotten."

"Forgotten?"

"What was the point in remembering after I became a Xi'an man?" He fell silent and closed his eyes. So I didn't ask any more. Whatever his story, the fact remained that he was a beggar now. The truck had passed through the suburbs and onto the West Side highway where we picked up speed. The wind was bitterly cold, and it lashed us across the face. We were fine, since we were all wearing sweaters, but what was annoying was that the wind got under the tarpaulin and made it balloon up, threatening to blow us off at any moment. We lay on it to keep it down, and huddled at the front end of the truck. Wufu took one corner and Lively another, but it kept flapping up again, so they came to an agreement: Wufu wrapped himself in one corner and clung on like grim death to the side of the truck, pushing his feet against the side, but his feet kept slipping, so Lively pushed his feet against Wufu's. "Press as hard as you can against my feet!" he said. I crawled between them and grabbed their arms, and we kept the tarpaulin down.

At one point, we went over a bridge, and Lively bounced up in the air and fell heavily back down again.

"Sit up," I said. "You're getting jolted lying down. It's dangerous."

"I can't sit or squat. It hurts my hemorrhoids," Lively said.

"You've sure got a lot of problems!" Wufu said, and tied a piece of rope around Lively. Then he lay back down, one hand gripping the edge of the truck and the rope wound around the other.

The wind grew stronger and the shaking more violent. The jolts raised a storm of coal dust, which turned us all black. Only our eyes and our teeth stayed white. Even Wufu's yellow teeth looked bright when he opened his mouth. "Happy, didn't you say the boss was sending a truck to pick us up?" Lively complained. "Is this it?"

"You've got a truck to ride in. What's wrong with that? How would you get there otherwise? You're getting a free ride!"

"I'm not angry at the boss, just the driver. Hey, you! You're going so fast, is this a shortcut to the crematorium?" Wufu said.

"Don't say stuff like that. You'll be the death of the driver, and then we'll all be dead," Lively said. So Wufu bad-mouthed the driver's girlfriend instead.

If anyone was going to swear, it should have been me. I was covered in coal dust from head to toe. I could wash it off my head, but my suit would never be the same. I took the jacket off, but then I was cold, so I put it back on. "No more swearing now. Let's talk about something else," I said. "Tell us about begging, Lively. How do you do it?"

Lively perked up. "Want to know the Art of Begging? I'll tell you, if you give me a smoke."

"You can't smoke in this wind! And what does the Art of Begging mean?"

"That's what we traveling beggars call it. It's like you could call trash picking the 'Art of Picking.'"

"It's just begging," Wufu said. "Why do you give it a fancy name, like you're so educated?"

"Think you know everything? Do you know how many professions there are in the Art of Begging? Do you know the difference between the Nice and the Nasty beggars? And what 'party begging' means? It's not just begging for a meal—we have higher ambitions than that. We want to get blessings, we want to be infected with happiness, whether it's at a wedding, a longevity party, a baby's first-month party, or a dinner for the teacher when the kid gets into university."

According to Lively, a beggar could use culture, or force. A cultured beggar played and sang; the rough ones tricked people or took what they wanted by force. The Nice beggars included the Friendlies, who kowtowed and held out their hands in supplication; the Weasels, who knocked and weaseled their way into houses; the Bodhisattvas, who took their missus and their kids with them, to look more pitiful; and the Pretenders, who spun hard-luck stories or pretended to be cripples. The Nice ones didn't like the Nasties, who created a ruckus so they could pick people's pockets on the sly. And some of the Nasties were bag snatchers, and broke into people's houses.

When Lively finished talking, he asked Wufu, "So, who has more professional knowledge, you or me?"

"There's no such thing as a good beggar," Wufu said.

"Are you telling me you've never snatched anything?" Lively said. Wufu opened his mouth to protest, but he got a mouthful of coal dust and shut up. What trash picker had never stolen anything? You can't walk a long road without picking up a bit of mud. Best not to go there.

"Talk about something different," I said.

"Did you know there was a National Coal Conference in Xi'an last year?" Lively offered. There was nothing beggars didn't know.

"Tell us more," I said.

Lively sneered at us, then said, "It lasted a week, and there were well over a hundred thousand participants from all over China. The hookers did a roaring trade, and ten days later, their piss was still black with coal dust."

As soon as he mentioned hookers, I thought of Yichun. I wanted him to stop talking, but Wufu was listening. "Yes, I heard, but it's all a load of crap. The mine owners don't dig coal themselves, so why would the hookers piss coal dust?"

Lively looked down his nose at Wufu. "No sense of humor, and no education either," he said.

But Wufu wasn't giving up. "Are you talking about me?" he demanded.

"Yes, you!"

Wufu dropped the rope he was holding, and Lively slipped off the mound of coal he was lying on. Wufu followed with a kick, Lively crawled up, then fell again, and finally gripped Wufu's leg, and they both tumbled off the coal heap.

56.

When we got to Xianyang, we washed our faces in the restroom at the company offices, then went up to the third floor to see the company president, Mr. Lu. He was totally different from the first time we'd met. We smiled at him, but he didn't smile back. He just said to one of his minions, "Take them out! Get them on-site!"

That made me quite angry. Apart from anything else, I appeared foolish in front of Wufu and Lively. They both looked at me. "Let's go," I said.

Once outside, Wufu said, "If I'd known he was so stuck-up, I wouldn't have bothered washing my face!"

"What's up with Mr. Lu?" I asked the woman. "He recruited us, so why did he kick us out?"

"He didn't kick you out! He said, 'Take them to eat,' not 'Take them out'!"

"Well, I heard quite clearly 'Take them out,'" I protested.

"Mr. Lu's from Qishan County," she said. "He wants me to give you a meal before you go to the site."

So that was it! "We misunderstood!" I said to Wufu and Lively.

"The Qishan accent is impossible to understand," Lively grumbled. The woman explained then that Mr. Lu had had a lot of problems after he arrived in Xianyang. People mocked him for his accent, but he'd made the business huge, to the point where he could require everyone in the company to learn Qishan pronunciation. That cheered up Wufu and Lively, and they started joking about all the things they were going to have: abalone and shark's fin, red-cooked pork, and the like, until the woman told us we were having a nice meal of pulled noodles.

"What are the features of the Qishan pronunciation?" I inquired.

"Different tones, plus words like 'chi' sound like 'chu,' and 'ru' sounds like 'ri,'" said the woman.

"Chi"—"eat," and "chu"—"out." "Ru"—"in"... and "ri"—"fuck."

We did eat a meal of pulled noodles—then, and for breakfast, lunch, and dinner every day after that, because that was what the company gave us. A giant grain depot was being built, and four or five cylindrical silos already towered over our site. Where the foundations were being laid, a cluster of tall rigs had been erected and rammers were pummeling the ground. The trench we were digging was behind a row of new buildings, currently unoccupied. Across the trench and some wasteland, you came to a village. On the east side of this was a derelict building where we were to live. Every morning we walked through the village to get to the site, and every evening we went back through the village to our abandoned building. It was a village of farmers, but they knew that as soon as the grain depot was completed, their village would become part of the city, just like Fishpond had. Consequently, they were busy building new houses as fast as they could, so they'd get more government compensation when the houses were demolished. The lane through the village was a jumble of small eateries, but company rules said we had to stick to pulled noodles. The good thing was you got a big bowlful, and they were well seasoned, the way we liked them.

On the first day, Lively wanted some noodle water to wash them down. "Bring me a bowl of noodle water, nice and hot, good for the digestion," he yelled. I told him we had to get going, but he said, "Hurry the plow, but let the food take it nice and easy. I need my noodle water!"

Wufu and I didn't wait for him. We wanted to go to the derelict building to get some rest. It must have been a government office originally, but almost all the windows and doors had been ripped out. We claimed an empty corner room on the second floor, with the only remaining door. It had no lock, so we wedged a stout stick across it from the inside. We felt completely safe; after all, what did we have to lose? We each had a bedroll. Wufu's and my bedding was pretty decent, but Lively's was so encrusted with filth that you could hardly see its peony pattern anymore. He had no pillow; he rested his greasy head on his shoes or a brick.

The day after we arrived, we were dozing after lunch with the door unbarred, when we were woken by the creaking of the door. Some kid came in, took a look at us, then turned to go. The door creaked again. "Wet the hinges with some water from the bowl, then they won't creak," I told him. I knew he was a thief, but we had nothing to steal, and I felt like a joke.

The lad looked at me. "Whatever, joker!" Then he kicked over the bowl of water as he went out the door. The water snaked its way to my bedding and soaked my shoes. We went back to sleep.

Lively couldn't sleep though. He stripped off his clothes and still couldn't sleep. "Go bar the door, Wufu," he said. "If a woman comes in, she shouldn't see me like this."

Three women did come into the building; we'd bumped into two of them when we'd moved in. They were coming out of a room on the other side of the building and scurried away as soon as they saw us. We thought that was odd, so we went to look in the room and discovered they'd gone in to pee. Then Lively told us he'd seen a woman on the first floor taking a crap—some rooms were being used as a public WC by passersby and villagers who were in a bind. That really pissed us off—what kind of accommodation had Lu fixed us with? A few times, we took it up with the foreman. We still had to live there, but we did get three mattresses stuffed with rice straw, which helped keep us warm at night. I used a lump of coal to scratch a notice on the wall by the entrance: "Pissing and shitting strictly forbidden. Offenders will be punished." It had no effect at all. Later, I added a new notice: "Beware, haunted house." That put a stop to it.

By the time we'd done five days of trench digging, we knew we'd been had. The first three days, everything went smoothly and we dug twenty yards between us. That was three hundred yuan, a hundred each. We'd never even approached daily takings like this before. I was, of course, busy working out how long we'd have to work before I had the five thousand yuan I needed to get Yichun released. I'd also made an agreement with Wufu that as soon as we had five thousand yuan between us, I'd take it and go back to Xi'an alone, get Yichun out, then carry on here until I'd earned enough to repay him.

"But that'll leave me and Lively alone together!" Wufu objected. "I can't handle him!"

"It'll only be for a couple of days."

"Then bring me some nice spiced stewed beef. I couldn't take my eyes off that piece Mr. Lu was eating."

Obviously, we weren't going to tell Lively about Yichun, but he overheard some of our conversation. "Are you going on about money again? Where's the money?" he demanded.

Wufu pulled me to one side. "You can take the money back to Xi'an when we've got five thousand, but where will we keep it until then? We don't have a box or cupboard to keep it in, and the door has no lock. I don't trust Lively."

"Then keep it in the pocket of your undershorts."

"I sleep naked. I guess I'll have to wear something now," Wufu said.

Though Wufu didn't trust Lively, Lively was very nice to him and kept saying that he was going to buy him booze. He said he planned to spend everything he earned on drink, except for ten yuan a day. He said he never kept more than ten on him at a time.

But Lu didn't pay us by the day. There was no money stashed away in Wufu's undershorts, and Lively didn't have ten yuan on him either, so he had to keep begging smokes from me.

On the fourth day, we hit stone in the trench. After a whole morning's work, we'd only dug a couple of feet. The villagers told us that there'd been two sets of laborers on the building site already. They'd worked their butts off for a few days and then given up and gone.

Meat pasties don't fall from the sky, I thought, so I went looking for Lu. I was careful to affect my best Qishan accent and tried to make two things clear. One: We wanted better wages and conditions. Currently, we weren't even earning as much as we had by trash picking in Xi'an. We ate pulled noodles for breakfast, lunch, and dinner, and we were sick of them. Every time we burped, we got a sour taste of soybean paste in our mouths. Then there was the accommodation: it was getting colder in the derelict building, so we couldn't sleep. Two: if he wasn't willing to give us better rates and conditions, then he should pay us what we were owed, and we'd go. Lu's little eyes grew exceptionally wide, and he muttered a lot of stuff in a very quiet voice. From what I could make out, he was saying that there were hundreds of curio sellers in the Pagoda Street antiques market, and a score of them left every year, and a score of new sellers came in.

"What are you talking about?" I asked.

He mumbled again, something like, Why weren't we satisfied? How much did we earn as trash pickers, anyway? What was wrong with a little stone? What did we expect when we were digging a trench? Bean curd?

"We're not afraid of hard work, but this is too hard!" I told him. He said we should look at it this way: it was a free world, just as joining or leaving the party was a free choice. He couldn't force us to stay, but if we left, he wasn't paying us for the work we'd already done. I talked tough with Lu, and he talked soft with me, soft like cotton balls, cotton balls with needles stuck in them. It was true, you should never lay your cards on the table with the boss, unless you had the upper hand. Otherwise you were inviting humiliation. My attempt to negotiate was a complete failure. What was I going to report to Lively and Wufu? I hunkered down on the floor in front of his desk and was silent.

"So that's my line," he said. "Go think about it." I got to my feet and caught my head on the corner of his desk. Two drops of blood spilled on the floor. Lu didn't want me to wipe it up. I quietly palmed a miniature pagoda perched on a decorative rock under his desk, and I left.

I'd seen it when I was crouched on the floor, and it startled me. The Chain-Bones Bodhisattva! It wasn't actually her, of course, but the pagoda looked just like the Chain-Bones Bodhisattva Pagoda. I couldn't leave bleeding and empty-handed; I had to take the pagoda with me. Besides, the pagoda was a timely reminder that if I didn't keep digging, I'd be back in Xi'an with nowhere to pick trash, and how would I earn the five thousand yuan then? I went back to the derelict building, where Lively was complaining that Wufu had seen a woman coming in to pee and had done nothing to stop her. Wufu protested that if she wasn't scared of ghosts, how was he supposed to stop her from peeing?

"You just wanted to see her butt, I'll bet," Lively said.

"It was like white marble," Wufu said.

I swore at them, then told them about my head and what had happened with Lu. I didn't tell them the whole truth. I simply said, "Mr. Lu hasn't agreed to give us a pay raise, but he hasn't refused point-blank either. He wants us to carry on with the job, and when we've finished, if we hit more stone, then he'll up our pay, depending on how difficult the work is. There's nothing to be done about the board and lodging."

"I can't stand any more pulled noodles," Lively said.

"You've tasted so many different cuisines, you've gotten greedy, huh? What's wrong with pulled noodles?" Wufu said. "What I want to know is, if we hit more stone after this, did he say how much he'll up our pay by?"

"Not precisely."

"In other words, he didn't."

"What do you mean? If we hit more stone after this, he won't dare not to up our pay. I broke the skin on my head bumping it. Next time I'll bang it so hard, I'll look like a skinned sheep!"

As soon as I mentioned blood, Wufu took my head in both hands and peered at it. Then he pulled a lump of cotton wadding out of his bedroll, burned it to ashes, and rubbed the ash on the wound.

"It's nothing," I said. "Lu gave me a pagoda as I was leaving." I'd brought it back to the construction site and placed it on a small square stone. Now that I had this pagoda, I felt Yichun was keeping her eye on me. We carried on digging. After another day's work, we'd rubbed the pads of our fingers raw, and even though we hadn't slacked off, we'd done only three yards between the three of us.

Toward evening, the foreman came to check our work and said we weren't digging deep enough; we had to go back over it. We worked until nightfall. By the time we got back to the derelict building, I was limp with exhaustion. My back ached all over. When I was standing, I couldn't sit down, and when I was sitting, I couldn't stand up again. I was nowhere near as fit and strong as Lively and Wufu.

"I'll scratch your back for you," Wufu offered.

"It doesn't itch. Everything feels tight. Thump it for me instead."

He started to hit me, but he couldn't get the rhythm, or the right place either.

"Down a bit, down, left a bit—don't you know your left from your right?" I said. I was bent forward and Wufu was banging on my back, but his palms were cupped, not flat, the idiot! I told him just to use the sole of his shoe.

He was afraid of hitting me too hard, and even though I kept saying, "A bit harder, a bit harder," he still didn't dare use real pressure.

"Get Lively to come do it instead!" I said.

That infuriated Wufu, and he muttered as he hit me. Bang, bang, bang! My spine tingled, and I felt as if my bones were shuddering loose and my exhaustion was being pushed out from my joints. He beat faster and faster, harder and harder, as if venting his anger on me.

I groaned. The slapping and banging evened out.

57.

We dug for two more days. There were fewer stones, but we hit a layer of granite. Great chunks of it too, and you couldn't get any leverage with a pick; the only impression we'd make was a small white pit in the rock. So we had to use a sledgehammer and drill rod to break up the surface, then work away at the cracks with the pick again, till we could pry the stone out. Whenever it was Lively's turn with the sledgehammer, he always missed the drill rod and complained that the hammer was bruising his hand, so I took the drill while he used the pick on the cracks I made. It was pretty cold by now, and there was an icy wind. Wufu's hand started to bleed—the skin between his thumb and forefinger had split. He said to the foreman, "Can you give me some lard?"

"What for?" asked the foreman.

"To rub in the crack. Then I'll heat it over a flame and it'll heal," said Wufu. This was a folk remedy from Freshwind to treat cracks in your hands or feet from the winter wind.

But the foreman said, "Where am I going to get lard from around here? Just use a Band-Aid on it. I'll get you one from the village pharmacy."

Lively insisted he'd go instead.

"Forget it, keep working!" I told him.

"I thought you were taking me to heaven, but you're taking me down to hell! If I carry on like this, I'll be digging my own grave before long."

Lively went and didn't come back at noon, nor that afternoon. He clearly felt that no work gave him the freedom that begging did. He was a born scrounger; I knew that now. I was worried that his departure would affect Wufu's morale, but Wufu only said, "He's not interested in becoming decent!"

But that night, Lively staggered back and told us he'd begged twenty yuan, spent ten in a restaurant on roast pork and beer, and still cleared ten yuan! "And all without breaking a sweat!" as he put it.

"What a loser!" said Wufu.

"I'd rather be a loser than look like you," said Lively. "Your face has shrunk so much, it's no bigger than the palm of my hand!" Wufu felt his face. "Have I gotten so much thinner?" he asked me.

"Don't listen to his bullshit," I said, and told Lively, "I brought you to Xianyang to make an honest man of you, and you've started begging again! If you carry on like that for the rest of your life, you'll die in the street, and no one'll bury you."

"So what, let my corpse stink," Lively said.

I flared up. "Get the hell out of here and don't come back tonight!" I don't normally lose my temper, but when I do, I explode like a powder keg. Lively said timidly that he wouldn't go out again. He came over and tried to pummel me on the back. I told him to piss off, but he insisted and grabbed my leg, so I fell on my face. He got on my back and started to slap it. He was better than Wufu at hitting the right spot. Then he said, "Do you belong to the party, Happy?" I didn't answer. "If you do, then I want to be in it too!"

But the next day when we were about to leave for work, Lively said he needed to piss, and he took off again. Out early, gone the whole day and back late, he kept doing it. I was thoroughly disillusioned with him by then, and I missed Eight. Eight was foulmouthed, but he was a reliable worker. I thought of getting him to join us, but he had no phone, so there was no way of contacting him. Wufu didn't care: Lively had worked a few days, and we simply wouldn't pay him for the other days.

"If you were the boss, you'd be like Lu!" I said.

"If I were up to beating Lively Shi, I'd beat him to a . . . ," said Wufu, then stopped. Lively was back. He could see we'd been bad-mouthing him, and lay down on his bed without saying a word. Then he took off his undershorts and tossed them in the air, and they landed in the pot we used for boiling water. We were about to yell at him, till we saw he was lying there stark naked, with a condom on his penis. That really shocked us. We jumped on him and began to pummel him. Was he simply showing off? He confessed then—he hadn't done anything bad, but he'd been begging in the red-light district, because you could get good money there, and he was afraid that if he had the money, he'd want to spend it on sex, and he might get the clap and what would he do then? So he bought a condom. We pinned him down and pulled the condom off him and made him blow it up into a balloon. Then we stamped on it and burst it.

It was midnight by the time we went to bed. Wufu and Lively snored thunderously, but I couldn't sleep for thinking of Yichun. I took the little pagoda out of my pocket and put it on the windowsill, where I could almost see it in the gloom. I must have gone to sleep, because at some point I woke up again and was startled to see Yichun standing at the window. "Yichun!" I cried, but when my eyes focused, I realized I was looking at the shadow of the plane tree in the moonlight. The shadow was waving wildly in the wind. Wufu and Lively were still sound asleep. I buried my head in my quilt and wept.

Always before when I'd shed tears for Yichun, I'd done so silently. This time, I howled. I was sure it was because of this little pagoda that I woke up thinking of her, and maybe she woke up thinking of me. Each of us in the chilly darkness of our separate rooms, unable to meet, but still missing each other. Still, now that I had the pagoda, surely that meant that Yichun and I would meet again, just as soon as we earned that five thousand yuan.

I got up at the crack of dawn and stood looking at the plane tree. Its leaves were fading to a bluish green. I began to play my flute, and two birds, with red heads and white tails, flew over and into the tree. They disappeared from sight, but I could still hear them chirping.

The flute woke Wufu and Lively, and they got up too. "Why are your eyes all red?" Wufu asked.

"They're fine!"

"Last night I dreamed of Meng Yichun," said Wufu.

"Don't mention her name!"

"Why not?"

Oh, Wufu, you want me to talk about her, but I didn't know how. I want to let her go, but I can't do that either . . . "Breakfast!" I said. "Then work. We need to hurry."

At the site, I placed the pagoda on the square piece of stone, and we began to work as hard as we could. At midday, we took a rest. I got out my flute and played a tune to the pagoda, and Wufu took a quick trip to the village store to buy a back frame.

It was the kind of wooden frame you strapped to your back, used to deliver coal to apartment blocks. Wufu was certainly getting better at using his brain—he wanted to load the back frame with the rocks we dug up so he could carry them out of the trench. But when he came back from the village, all out of breath, he also had a big bundle of discarded plastic tubing in his arms. "Happy, there are no trash pickers in the village," he said. "We can go picking in the evenings after dinner."

I was annoyed. "Dogs never get out of the habit of eating shit, do they? You've come here to dig ditches. Let's focus on that!"

Wufu said nothing, just jumped into the trench with his frame. I was in a bad mood, that was the problem. I shouldn't have lost my temper with him. After a while, I said, "Take a rest, Wufu."

"I'm not tired." He loaded himself up with a large rock, puffing and panting as he struggled out of the trench. He smiled at me.

"Save your breath, don't smile," I said.

"I was thinking about my missus," he said.

"Why are you thinking about your missus? It's still broad daylight! And be careful not to lose your footing."

Wufu heaved himself and the rock out of the trench. It thudded to the ground, and he kicked it. He told me that one springtime, he and his missus had gone deep into the mountains to barter rice for corn with the mountain folk because they were short of grain. For a pound of rice, they could get a pound and a half of corn. It was her birthday while they were away, but she couldn't have longevity noodles or poached eggs in the mountains, so instead, he hoisted her onto his back and carried her up the slope and down again. "And my wife's a fat woman, so carrying this stone reminded me of her."

I was touched at his story but didn't say anything. *When Yichun gets out, I'll buy a mattress for sure. I'll load it on my three-wheeler and get her to sit on top. Then I'll pedal her from North Avenue to South Avenue and from East Avenue to West Avenue,* I thought.

From another construction site farther away, a dozen rig-mounted rollers were pounding away, making the earth tremble and echoing my promise.

Why were foundations laid like this here? Back in Freshwind, houses were built using stones for foundations, while in Xi'an, they drove piles in using rammers that looked like grain rollers. I'd never seen such huge iron rollers, pounding downward from their rigs. Wufu took a break, and I poured him some water. Then a man came over from the other site.

"What does he want?" said Wufu.

"Maybe he's thirsty. Do you want some of our water?" I asked.

The man was standing on the edge of the trench. "Are you trash pickers?"

Wufu and I looked at each other in dismay. "What do you mean? Can't you see we're digging a trench?"

"My name's Bull," said the man, tossing us a couple of cigarettes. I didn't move, but Wufu caught them midair.

"So how come I heard you're trash pickers?" Comrade Bull said.

"Are you doing the foundations?" I asked.

"Of course we are!"

"Why are you doing it that way?"

"It's new technology," said Comrade Bull. "Do you want to come see it? You mean you really don't pick trash? I could have sworn you were trash pickers!"

"What do you mean?" I asked again. "Because we're poor and ugly, that makes you think we're trash pickers since trash picking's the roughest job there is?" I was furious. Wufu had stopped drinking and picked up the drill rod, ready for a fight.

Comrade Bull laughed. "I didn't mean anything at all. I've been a sanitation worker in my time. I just thought if you were trash pickers, we were in the same line of business."

"Happy, he's into waste. Aren't trash pickers a cut above them?" Wufu had opened his big mouth again.

But Comrade Bull took a flying leap across the trench and cried enthusiastically, "I knew we could be friends!" And so we were. Whenever he had a free moment, he'd come over for a chat, and he got us to watch him work on the foundations. He really had been a sanitation worker, and there were three more like him in their gang, as well as a former trash picker. They'd formed their own company, called Responsible Groundworks, Inc., and that got Wufu and me excited. Waste and trash collectors could set up their own companies! Bull told us their company chairman was a highly trained engineer who had invented and patented various technologies useful in groundworks, sanitation, and machinery, and their construction teams used this new technology. Laying the foundations for this huge grain silo was a challenge: it was on a slope of heavily weathered diabase, and because the depth and hardness of the bedrock varied, they couldn't use piles or dynamic compactors, only DDC (whatever that was) would do. When we packed up that day, I told Wufu, "It's a new dawn!"

"But it's getting dark. What do you mean, it's a new dawn?"

"You never got beyond junior secondary school, so you don't know that you can have two dawns on a day with a solar eclipse."

Wufu swore.

I couldn't be bothered to give him a tutorial on astronomy. "Just work hard, Wufu," I said. "Gem Han's a trash picker who set up a company, and these sanitation workers are working on a DDC project. Who's to say, maybe one day we'll be transformed into dragons too!"

"We'll run our own trash depot! Scrawny has a three-room house and his own yard—we'll have a four-room one!"

"Are we only aiming at a subdepot?" I asked.

Wufu looked stunned. "Yes, there really are no limits to what we can do if we think big! I'm going to kiss you!" He threw himself at me, but I held him off, so he blew me a kiss.

I made as if to catch it, then flung it away. "It stinks!" Silly man, aping the manners of city folk!

The two of us burst out laughing.

58.

Comrade Bull certainly cheered us up, and our good spirits lasted for several days. The weather got colder but brighter too, and the leaves on the trees turned red and yellow, clothing our derelict building and the building site in brilliant colors. Why were the trees putting on such a gorgeous show? I felt it was especially for Wufu and me.

Another good thing: the day after the gingko tree in the village turned golden, Mr. Lu gave us a large plastic bottle of booze. We were eating our pulled noodles in a village eatery. Wufu went out to the WC in the backyard and came back to say the yard was full of discarded metal drums that we could buy. He was bringing trash to the derelict building every day, and he planned to take it to the Xianyang depot to sell. I'd told him I didn't like him trash picking here, but he went ahead and collected it anyway. He haggled with the eatery owner. He was going to get it cheap, but we had very little money left, and even if we didn't set any aside for a rainy day, we couldn't afford to buy all this trash, I told him. Wufu started complaining that we'd done all this work and Lu hadn't paid us what he owed us. He didn't have some devious plan to cheat us out of our wages, did he? Wufu's words made me anxious. After all, I'd gotten Wufu into this. If that really was Lu's plan, we had to do something about it.

"Don't worry," I told him. "I'll go see Lu this afternoon."

In our three weeks on-site, Mr. Lu had been by a few times. Every time he turned up, we twisted our tongues around his Qishan dialect and asked him politely for our wages. The first time, we each got five yuan, the second time it was thirty, and the third time, he gave us another sixty each. That afternoon, I went to see him again, and this time I wasn't messing around. I told him we wanted our fares to get us back to Xi'an and three weeks' worth of pay. If he wouldn't pay us the fifteen yuan per yard, we'd make do with twenty yuan a day, which was what we earned as trash pickers. I made it sound like a threat, but we didn't have a lot of other options. Lu said, in his soft, blurry accent, that there was no way he wanted to cheat us of our wages, and we'd get it all when the trench-digging project was completed. Then he took something out of a cupboard—it was a plastic bottle containing more than a third of a gallon of *baijiu*.

He carried on, mangling his words so much that I could hardly understand him. "However poor you are, the kid's got to be educated. However broke I am, I've got to pay the hooker, so I'm certainly not going to cheat you of your wages, am I? Just finish the work. That will be good for me, and even better for you. Fifteen yuan a yard is much better money than twenty yuan a day, and you don't have any quarrel with money, do you? Have this *baijiu*—take it and drink it."

I calmed down then and went off, carrying the bottle of *baijiu*.

It was a still, moonlit night, and birds twittered in the branches of the plane tree. Wufu and I sat drinking in our derelict building.

"He's not a bad guy, that Lu, is he?" said Wufu.

"It's not a question of whether he's a good or a bad guy. Our luck's turned, and everything's going our way."

"Then let's drink!"

"Yup! You drink as much as you like!" We hadn't had *baijiu* for ages, and three cups each went down really nicely. We were flying high. We'd soon drunk half, and Lively still wasn't back.

"How come the beggar's not back?" I said.

"As long as he isn't dead, he'll be back. That's the kind of man you brought with us! Drink! Let's finish it before he turns up!" We started with some finger-guessing games and forfeits. Wufu's fingers were really clumsy, and he kept getting the numbers wrong, so I beat him every time. "I'll never beat you. Let's play Tiger Sticks."

But he was still losing more than he won, and he got so drunk, his eyes were like two slits, and he could hardly open them. Then we heard footsteps outside.

Wufu quickly stuffed the bottle under the quilt and said, "The beggar's back!" But the footsteps never came upstairs, and soon they stomped away into the distance. "The fucker's not coming back. He's gone and died somewhere." We got the booze out again and downed another cup each. "Do you think the beggar's really gone and died?" Wufu asked.

"He's been sleeping rough for years!" I said. "Why would he die now? He's got nine lives, all beggars have!"

"Happy, do beggars always die far from home?"

"They just die on the job . . ."

Wufu suddenly looked worried. When he got worried, it made him look exactly like a pig.

"What an ugly face!" I said. But then he started to cry.

"You're hammered."

"No, I'm not . . . Am I going to end up dead on the job? What'll happen if I don't make it home?"

"Lively doesn't care about things like that."

"Lively hasn't got a missus and kids. I have, and I care."

That annoyed me—after all, I didn't have a wife and kids either. "Nothing you can do about that if you're dead," I said.

"Yes, there is. You've got to look after me!"

"You mean I look after you when you're alive, and I've got to carry on after you're dead?"

"I've got to be buried back home in Freshwind. That's where my spirit belongs, nowhere else," Wufu insisted.

"You're just hammered."

"I'm not!"

Wufu downed another cup and said, "You brought me here, you get me home. Otherwise, how will my spirit get home? You've got to take care of it!"

"OK, OK. If you die, I'll get you home, all right?"

Wufu gave a great shout of laughter. He kept laughing and laughing like a maniac.

"You're completely wasted," I said, but Wufu's guffaws got me laughing too.

"Have some more!"

"Drink! Drink!" And we clinked cups again.

"Hey! There's two of you!" Wufu tried to point at me, only he was waving his finger somewhere past my ear.

And I could see all these Wufus floating around the room. It was just like when the Monkey King cloned monkeys out of his hairs, all with exactly the same noses, eyes, and mouths. Then Eight and Almond and Lively were there too. "You're Wufu, and Eight and Almond and Lively too!"

"I'm you! Eight and Almond and Lively are all you!"

"All me! All Happy Liu!"

And we kept on like this, cracking up with laughter. All of a sudden, Wufu—all the Wufus—slumped down in a heap, and Eight and Almond and Lively too. "Stop playing around!" I shouted. Then I went down like puddle of sludge.

The wind picked up and blew out the newspaper pasted over the windows, and it made the door creak and groan on its hinges, but we lay there, blissfully unaware. Suddenly, something heavy hit me on the back. I thought it was Yichun, standing by the mattress and kicking me with her high-heeled shoe. "You shouldn't be sleeping on the floor on a cold day like this."

There was another kick on my ass. I didn't mind the pain, but there was dirt on her shoe and I wiped it off. "How did you get here, Yichun? I never told you I was coming to Xianyang. I was trying to earn a pile of money to get you out and to give the police to crack that case of yours. How did you find me?"

Yichun's face turned coarse and broad, and with a start, I realized it was the site foreman.

"You're not Yichun?"

"How long are you going to sleep?"

"Hey, what time is it?"

"Nearly lunchtime and you haven't started work. If you want to sleep, go home and sleep!"

I crawled to my feet. We must have been in a drunken stupor since last night. Wufu was fast asleep on his back, fully dressed, in one corner of the room. He was covered in dirt, his mouth was wide-open, and he looked ferocious.

I shoved him, and he muttered without opening his eyes, "Eight, there's another one over there . . ."

The foreman gave him a kick and shouted at him to get up.

Afterward, when we were outside, Wufu told me he'd been dreaming of money. He and Eight were pulling their carts when they saw the police chasing a thief. The thief suddenly threw a handful of cash at passersby. The bills floated down on them like snowflakes, and everyone scrambled for their share. The police couldn't get through the crowd. Wufu, like an idiot, held a bill up to the light to see if it was a fake, and when he went to get more, there were none left. "Chairman Mao, where are you?" he shouted. Just then, he saw a bill floating over the pavement barrier like a butterfly. He yelled to Eight to get it, and the pair of them tried jumping over the barrier, but the crotch of his trousers got caught and banged his goolies so hard that the pain made him sit down on the fence.

At the first kick from the foreman, Wufu opened his eyes and said, "My money, where's my money?"

This time, the foreman kicked Wufu so hard that his shoe came off. He hopped across the room to retrieve it, yelling angrily, "Quit dreaming about money! If you don't get working on that trench, the only money you'll get will be ghost money!"

That pissed me off. "Who do you think you're talking to? We've come to work—we're not your slaves!" I'd seen slave owners beating up their slaves in films. I kicked his shoe farther away. He was a cowardly little squirt when it came to it, our bent-nosed foreman, and he shut up.

"Come on, Wufu," I said. "Do up your buttons and let's get to work."

"What about the other one?" the foreman asked.

"He stopped working here a while ago."

"Stopped working here? He's not getting any money then!"

"He doesn't like money!" It had just occurred to me that Lively Shi hadn't been back all night. Wufu put on all the clothes he'd brought with him, and then pulled some filthy cotton waste out of Lively's ragged old quilt and stuffed it in his shoes to keep his feet warm. We picked up the pick, shovel, drill rod, and sledgehammer and started down the stairs, purposely waiting for the foreman to leave first. We were on the front steps of the building when Wufu's left leg gave way and he collapsed against the wall.

"Still asleep?" I joked.

"My leg, what's up with my leg!"

"Isn't it stuck to your body?" I pulled him up, but as soon as I let go, he sat down again with a thump.

"This isn't my leg. I can't make it work."

"It's just pins and needles from being asleep. I'll rub it for you." I rubbed his leg, but there was no reaction. His face had gone a waxy yellow, and sweat was pouring off it.

"Talk nicely to your leg," I told him. This was what I always did when I was in bed or resting and had nothing better to do. I was used to talking nicely to the various parts of my body, like my eyes, nose, throat, arms and legs, and all my innards. I spent my life doing hard physical labor on a half-empty stomach, and my body parts still worked well for me, so I made a point of thanking and encouraging them. I had only one kidney left, and it now had to do the work of two. It kept me nice and healthy, and that was why I was always polite to my kidney.

I leaned against the plane tree. Its leaves had colored up since yesterday. The reds were bloodred and vermilion; the yellows were copper and saffron yellow. There were dark greens and light greens, and sea blue and indigo blue. The sun shone brilliantly, and a leaf spiraled gently down to the ground. "Talk nicely to your leg, and it'll be all right."

Wufu sat on the ground and said, "Please move, leg. Please don't scare me. I'm a dead man if you don't start moving!"

"Hah! Wufu, where did you get such a way with words?" I teased him.

Wufu carried on talking nicely to his leg. Then he made a huge effort and tried to lift it. He got it only two inches off the ground, and the effort made beads of sweat stand out on his head. I was at his side now. Something was wrong.

"Is it really not working?" I asked.

"Happy, I'm really scared. My head aches," he said. Then he slumped back onto the ground, and I knew it was serious.

59.

I shouted for the foreman, but he'd disappeared off to some far-off pit on the site to do a crap. I thought of carrying Wufu to the hospital on my back, but I didn't know where the hospital was, so I put him down and ran into the village. At the nearest store, I called for an ambulance, then ran back to the derelict building. Wufu was sprawled on the ground, his face the color of the dirt.

The foreman finally turned up when I returned from the village, and he came with us to the hospital. Wufu could hardly keep his head up in the ambulance. I held him. "Wufu, hang on. It'll be all right once you get to the hospital." Wufu's pupils suddenly rolled out of sight. That scared the hell out me. I shouted his name, and they reappeared.

He looked at me and asked, "Why am I going to the hospital? How can I . . . ?"

"Don't worry about that. I don't know what's wrong with you, but we have to get you there quickly."

"I'm a goner, aren't I?" His pupils rolled into the corners of his eyes and disappeared again. I shouted, "Wufu! Wufu!" but he didn't answer this time. Tears oozed from the corners of his eyes, thick as beads of sweat, and flowed slowly down his cheeks.

He wasn't the only one crying. I cried too. What on earth was wrong with this big strong man? Wufu, who could eat and drink us all under the table, who could work harder than anyone. There hadn't been any warning that he was going to get so sick. It couldn't have been because the foreman kicked him. Was it the booze? But he'd sobered up by the time he got up. *God, don't let anything be wrong with Wufu!*

"Please drive faster," I said to the ambulance driver. I was sure he'd be all right once we got to the hospital. That was always what happened to me. Whenever I got sick and went to the hospital, I always spent so long waiting in line that I never actually saw a doctor. My head or my stomach always stopped hurting by the time it was my turn. Illnesses don't like doctors.

But when we arrived, the doctor diagnosed a cerebral hemorrhage. "Whose patient is this?" she asked.

"Mine," I said.

"I have to issue a fatal illness note," she said. I was so shocked, I thought my legs were going to give way. As she was writing the note, I did something I'd never done before. I knelt down in front of her and begged her to operate. She was a young doctor. She looked at me and said she'd consult a colleague.

"Clean him up!" she said. Wufu had crapped and pissed himself on the way in the ambulance, and the crotch of his pants was full of it. He stank to high heaven. I wiped him clean and soaked a towel to wash him.

An older doctor came in, examined him, and said, "He has brain herniation."

I had no idea what brain herniation was, but I said, "Wufu can't die! Anyone else, but not him!"

The senior doctor said, "There's not much point in operating, but we can give him maintenance therapy. Hurry up and settle the fees, and get him admitted."

Rich people could afford maintenance therapy, but we had no money. The fees turned out to be thirty yuan per hour, and in addition to other treatments and drugs, that totaled sixty yuan an hour. The admission deposit was twenty thousand yuan. Where were we going to get that kind of money? *Wufu, you never were any good at making money. How could you get so sick?*

The foreman was pressing me. "Does Wufu have high blood pressure? Is there a history of heart disease in his family?"

I knew he was trying to wriggle out of any responsibility. I said, "You've got to go tell the boss. This is a matter of life and death! He's got to do something about it!" I didn't talk about whether it was his responsibility. I just needed to keep him on Wufu's side.

The foreman gave me a packet of smokes and patted Wufu on the head. "Imagine scaring us like that!" he said, and went off again to ask the boss what to do. He came back with eight hundred yuan, then made me count it out bill by bill and sign a receipt for it. Then he said he was going to the restroom, and vanished.

Luckily, Lively Shi stayed with me. It was pure luck that he had returned to the construction site when he did—he'd been away for three days and had decided to go straight back to Xi'an. However, he was walking down an alley toward the bus station when he heard someone shout, "Stop that thief! Stop that thief!" Someone was cycling toward him, with someone else running after the bike. "I'm a clever guy," he said. "I crouched down by a tree at the end of the lane, and when the cyclist passed me, I grabbed a bundle of cotton rags and threw it at the wheel. It caught in the spokes, the bicycle fell over, and the briefcase hanging from the handlebars flew off. The cyclist scrambled after it, but I put my foot on it. He said, 'You're in luck!' And he jumped on his bike and took off. I said, 'I don't want your luck!' I spat, and my foot didn't budge. I kept my foot on the case till the runner caught up with me. You wouldn't believe the amount of money stuffed into that briefcase! The man thanked me, peeled off two hundred-yuan bills, and gave them to me. But I said that was stingy. He had all that money, and he was only giving me two hundred. What did he take me for, a beggar? The man apologized, said he didn't mean to treat me like a beggar, and gave me another hundred. I told him I was a beggar, but right now I was a hero doing a good deed!

The man asked me, 'Are you really a beggar?' And I swear that's the first time ever someone's been surprised at my being a beggar! He was OK. He said he'd take me to dinner and asked me what I'd like to eat. I said whatever's good at the moment. How about abalone and shark's fin? And he really did treat me."

While Lively was eating, he thought of Wufu and me. He wasn't thinking that we'd never eaten it and should try it. Oh no, he just wanted a chance to show off. So when he was eating, he put a third of his food in a plastic bag that he took with him. When he got to the derelict building, he saw the empty bottle of booze and started shouting and swearing that we hadn't left him any. The foreman was putting away the tools we'd dropped outside before he brought me the money, and heard him. So the two of them came to the hospital together.

Wufu started to foam at the mouth, and he kept groaning. He was slipping in and out of consciousness. We couldn't pay twenty thousand yuan for his hospital treatment, that was for sure. I talked it over with Lively. We'd forget the maintenance therapy.

"But without the maintenance therapy, Wufu will die," Lively said.

"The maintenance therapy will only keep him alive for a few more days," I said.

"But at least they'll be looking after him, and then he'll die in the hospital, and I'll leave," Lively said.

"Leave?"

"Well, when someone dies, they give you the corpse to deal with, don't they?"

"And I've got to take his corpse home!" I said, remembering the conversation Wufu and I had had when we were drinking the night before. That was what he'd asked, wasn't it? That made me even more sure it was the right thing to do. I tucked the eight hundred yuan into my pocket.

Lively shouted Wufu's name, so loudly that Wufu actually opened his eyes. "Wufu, Wufu, you fucking didn't tell me you were boozing!"

"What are you talking about? How could we tell you when you weren't there?" I said.

"You never gave me a thought—and I never thought of you either." And he said to Wufu, "Have you ever had abalone and shark's fin?"

Wufu was a bit embarrassed about not having left any *baijiu* for Lively; you could see it in his eyes. "What? What's that?"

"You haven't lived if you don't know what abalone and shark's fin is! I brought some for you. Eat up, it's a delicacy city folk eat!" Lively undid the plastic bag from his belt, but there were no bowls, and no chopsticks either. I went out to look for some, but I couldn't find any. There was a utility room down the corridor, with a bamboo broom in it. I tore off two strips of bamboo, but then I thought, *They're dirty. How can you eat abalone and shark's fin with bits of bamboo from an old broom!* I went outside and pulled a couple of twigs from the tree in the courtyard. Lively picked some shark's fin out of the bag with them.

"Want some, Happy?" he said.

I waved him off. It was the first time I'd seen shark's fin, but I told him, "I've had it before."

Wufu opened his mouth and took some, but then he spat it out. "It's bean noodles. You think I've never eaten bean noodles?"

"You idiot! Those aren't noodles! They cost four hundred yuan a bowl!"

A piece of shark's fin hung in the corner of Wufu's mouth, and he stuck out his tongue and hooked it back in again. He chewed and chewed. He chewed some more, and then he stopped chewing.

"Nice, eh? Have some more, go on! Now you're the first person from your village to eat shark's fin! Happy, you haven't tried any!" Lively said. I ignored him. Wufu was lying still, and his pupils had disappeared again. I waved my hand in front of his eyes, but there was no reaction. I held my hand over his nostrils, but no breath came out.

Wufu was dead.

People always say that you die with a rattle and a gasp, or a jerk of the legs, but Wufu died chewing his food. No last gasp or jerks. There was still a piece of shark's fin in the corner of his mouth. I went to wipe it off, and a clump of shark's fin fell out of his mouth. Both Lively and I panicked. "Wufu's dead, Lively, Wufu's dead!" I said.

Lively felt Wufu's head, then his chest, then his feet. "He's dead!"

We never expected Wufu to die so quickly. I put my arms around him and cried. Just two sobs and I stopped. I wouldn't let Lively cry either. I figured we shouldn't cry, or the hospital staff would find out Wufu was dead and take him to the mortuary. Once he was there, they'd send him to be cremated. I'd promised Wufu to take him back to Freshwind when he died. He'd be buried next to his parents, and his wife and sons would follow custom and do "the Sevens" ceremonies, once a week for seven weeks. And every Winter Solstice and Qingming Festival after that, they'd pay their respects and burn ghost money at his grave. So I had to get him home! I said to Lively, "You can't cry! We have to get out of the hospital quick!"

60.

We put our plan into action.

To be honest, it's all a blur now. I can't remember how we decided what we were going to do.

After it was all over, many people asked me a whole lot of "whys," but I couldn't answer. Why hadn't I called his family? Why hadn't I waited for a death certificate? Why hadn't I hired someone to drive his body home? Why hadn't I gone to see our boss? Or the authorities? And so on. Their questioning flustered me, and I stumbled over my words. That was when I realized that I, Happy Liu, really was still a peasant. I had limited understanding and abilities. Wufu had always relied on me for everything. He thought I was omniscient and omnipotent, and I'd really begun to believe it too. Pah! I spat on my little finger. And again, pah! *Happy Liu, you're worth only this much!* I said to myself. Faced with these questions, I lost all my glibness and wit. I stuttered and stammered, as if Wufu's death was my fault. Only after people had stopped asking me questions did it occur to me that I should have said, *I'm just a trash picker, a migrant worker, who can't even get himself paid, or get together enough money for the fare home, and here I am in a strange city and someone's up and died on me.* It was all way beyond me. What was clear was that Wufu depended on me, I brought him here, and he'd asked me several times to get his corpse home. I'd given him my word, so I was responsible. Whether he was dead or alive, I couldn't let him down. That was my belief; that was the rule in Freshwind. But when it actually happened, it was all so sudden, I panicked. I was completely at a loss; the only thing I knew was that, come what may, I had to get the money to take him home!

When I was caught with his body at the train station, they interrogated me. They thought I'd killed him and was getting rid of the body, or maybe I was selling it for a "hell marriage." Nowadays, when unmarried young people get jobs and die away from home, the parents have to arrange a match with another dead person and bury the other corpse with their dead child, a spouse to keep them company in the next world. That's a "hell marriage." A marriageable corpse goes for anything up to ten thousand yuan, and bodies are often stolen from hospital mortuaries or dug up from graves. I took out my ID card for the police to examine and they struck off that charge, but they kept asking me, "Why didn't you leave his body in the hospital for a few days and wait for the family to come?"

"Because they charge hundreds of yuan a day," I said. "The boss wasn't going to pay, and Wufu's family is dirt-poor. Where would they get the money from?"

"You were worried that they'd run up debts they couldn't pay if the corpse stayed too long in the hospital, is that it?"

"What are you getting at?"

"You still don't understand?"

Oh, I understood all right. The police had finally realized I was honest and aboveboard, but they were worried about Wufu's family. They wanted to put everything in writing so the family wouldn't have any suspicions.

I spelled it out. "Wufu's wife has no money. If she traveled to Xianyang to see his body, she'd have to pay for her fares, food, and accommodation, and I thought that since Wufu was always tight with money when he was alive, he was sure to be a skinflint in death. So I felt I had to keep their costs down and get Wufu home myself."

"Did it ever occur to you, if you'd been in Wufu's place and he'd done that to you, that you might be angry with him?"

"If I were Wufu, I wouldn't be in a position to do anything. I'd just say, 'Thank you.'" I pressed my hand to the small of my back as I said that. It was only when I got to the police station that it really began to hurt. "Wufu should thank me!" I repeated. I meant it too. Wufu's spirit was still around, and he'd see how much trouble I was going to for him.

It hadn't been easy. I decided that Wufu should be carried out of the hospital on someone's back, and fast, but who was going to do it? Lively Shi was certainly strong enough, but I couldn't ask him. So I made up my mind: I'd carry Wufu.

Lively asked me, "Happy, does someone turn into a ghost as soon as they're dead?"

"Of course, and that ghost's right here in this room," I answered.

Lively looked around. "I can't see any ghost, but I'm sure it's looking at me . . . I feel cold."

"Well, even if Wufu's a ghost, why would you be afraid of him?" The thought emboldened me, and I spat on Wufu's face. "You be a good boy, Wufu. Even if you're a spook now, don't be a bad spook!"

I propped Wufu up. His head slid to the side. I tried again, but the same thing happened. His head was like a watermelon.

It was around one in the afternoon, and there was no one in the corridor. A nurse passed us on her way to the WC and glanced through the door. To distract her, Lively bent over and blew his nose with his fingers. "Don't do that in here!" she said.

I wiped the snot away with my shoes and said, "No, of course not." As soon as she was gone, I put Wufu on my back. I weighed a hundred and twenty-four pounds, and Wufu weighed a hundred and fifty or so. Normally, I could carry a hundred and fifty pounds, but Wufu was a deadweight, and he felt much heavier the moment I got him on my back. I tumbled forward, and Lively had to drag him off me. Then we hauled him back to the edge of the bed. Wufu looked as if he had a smile on his face.

"Happy, doesn't he look as if he's smiling?" Lively said.

"He is," I said.

"Do you figure he still thinks he's eating shark's fin?" Lively said.

I was comforted by Wufu's expression, because it showed he wasn't suffering anymore, and that he was perfectly happy I was taking him home.

I hoisted Wufu up again, and Lively put Wufu's arms around my neck, so he looked like a seriously ill patient. I got my hands firmly around Wufu's buttocks. His pants were wet there. Lively went ahead of us, trotting along, crouched down like a thief.

"Lively, hold him up from behind, hold his back up!" I said. We took the elevator, and in no time at all, we went from the fourth floor to the first floor. We couldn't go out of the main gate, so we went around back through the staff quarters. It was half a mile or so to the back gate, and then we'd be safe.

Wufu was getting so heavy that I couldn't carry him anymore. I stopped for a moment, my legs shaking like leaves. A few people passed by, but they just glanced at us. Obviously, they couldn't know I was carrying a corpse. Wufu kept slipping down, and his arms slipped from my shoulders too. I kept having to crouch over and hoist him up. "Don't fall off like that, or people will realize!" I told him. And he stayed put until we'd passed the staff quarters and were out of the hospital.

Lively seemed to have trouble keeping up with us. I figured he was deliberately trying not to get too close in case we were found out. I was furious. "When push comes to shove, you soon find out who your friends are!" I rued the day we'd brought Lively with us. If only we'd come with Eight, Eight would have carried Wufu with no trouble at all. I turned to look at Lively. His mouth was gaping open, and although he wasn't crying, his face was wet with tears.

"If you keep crying, someone will spot there's something wrong," I said in a low voice.

"But my chest hurts, and my heart's going a mile a minute."

As if my own heart wasn't going a mile a minute.

Outside the hospital, I put Lively in a taxi and told him to go pick up our bags at the derelict building. We only had a change of clothes each, but the boss had given us those thin quilts and we couldn't leave those behind. After all, he hadn't paid us our wages, and we needed a quilt to wrap Wufu in.

After he'd gone, I remembered there was something I hadn't told him: all that trash Wufu had collected was still in our place, and he could give it to Comrade Bull, the man doing the groundwork on the construction site, or sell it to the villagers for a few cents. Lively wouldn't think of that. Well, it didn't really matter if he left it.

Lively returned with three cloth bags and one quilt. He even brought my flute and the miniature pagoda too but forgot Wufu's undershorts, which had been drying on the walkway. Wufu had washed them a couple of days ago, and I'd made him hang them over the railings. I asked Lively if he'd seen them.

"No, and what do you want with tatty old undershorts, anyway?"

I wanted them because Wufu had gone out bare-assed yesterday. I didn't want to send him home like that.

Though we'd come to Xianyang in a company truck, the only way back to Xi'an was in a taxi. We wrapped Wufu up in the quilt, and then poured some liquor over him so we could pretend he was passed-out drunk. Then we waited for the taxi. I was so hungry by then that my belly was stuck to my backbone, and I gave Lively three yuan to go buy some *shaobing*.

He came back with the flatbreads and my money. "Why pay for food? I begged them." Then he said, "Happy, do you think if we'd gotten the doctor to try resuscitating Wufu, he'd have come back to life?"

My heart lurched. Was Lively having second thoughts about what we'd done?

"No," I said.

"But just suppose . . . if there was a chance in a million . . . Just suppose?"

"Just don't suppose!" I said.

Lively stared at me.

"We've got no money, so how could we bank on a chance-in-a-million hope?" I said. Then I suddenly felt very afraid. What if Lively was right? What if I should've gotten the doctor to try resuscitating Wufu? Maybe Wufu would still be alive . . .

My eyes stung, and I imagined that I saw the quilt move and heard a voice. *I could be alive, alive . . .* I ripped off the quilt, but Wufu's face was gray, and he was motionless. I covered him up again.

I repeated to Lively, and to myself, that we'd done everything in our power. We did not have twenty thousand yuan to have him admitted to the hospital, and the doctor had written out the fatal illness note, stating that Wufu could not be saved. By the time I'd hoisted him on my back, his legs were cold, and that meant he was dead.

"We didn't carry him out till he was dead," Lively agreed. We ate our *shaobing*, but they tasted of nothing. I flagged down a taxi, and we put Wufu inside.

"What's up with him?" the driver asked.

"Drunk," I said. "We went to a restaurant, won fifty yuan on the lottery scratch card, and he was so happy, he bought two more bottles of liquor and got drunk."

"You get a bit of money, and you spend it on booze?" said the driver.

"You're right, the broker we are, the more we drink. If we didn't, we'd die of depression!" The taxi got going, with Wufu propped between Lively and me in the backseat. Lively muttered that he was afraid, and I told him to look at the scenery outside. In autumn on the northern plains, the skies are blue and the clouds are white. On either side of the road, the trees and flowers and the grass beneath them flashed by in a blur of reds, golds, blues, and purples. Wufu was dead, and we had sneaked his body away and bolted like dogs with our tails between our legs. By rights, the earth and the sky should have been overcast and gloomy instead of being so resplendent with color. I just couldn't take it in. Wufu would never see sights like this again. Lively was staring out the window and didn't turn around. Wufu slumped against him as we rode over the bumps.

"Shift Wufu over on your side a bit, Happy," he said.

"Give him a push for me," I said.

"I'm afraid to," he said.

I wasn't afraid; it almost felt like Wufu was alive, sitting there between us, and I found myself wondering vaguely why he wasn't snoring. Suddenly aware that I had my arms around a corpse, I said to myself, *I'm not afraid of you, Wufu.*

61.

We got to Xi'an Station and carried him into the square. Then I went to buy tickets. We would get the train to Freshwind Township. But the train didn't leave until twenty past eight, so I told Lively I was leaving him in charge of Wufu while I went to buy some food. Lively protested he didn't want to be left in charge, and went off to buy the food himself. He was such a scoundrel that as soon as he was in a crowded place, he started begging, affecting a limp and pleading pathetically with passersby to take pity on a poor cripple. I was livid and yelled at him to come back.

"Why are you worried about my dignity? And you're not exactly doing yourself proud, carrying a corpse home on your back!" he retorted.

He was so two-faced!

Now I was really sorry I'd gotten Lively to help me carry Wufu's corpse. I mean, I'd thought having him along would be helpful, that he'd give me courage, and I could tell him what to do. But he was nothing but trouble. I clapped my hand over his mouth to shut him up. The idiot thought I was going to hit him, so he bared his teeth and bit me. That really made me mad. Straight after that, I went to buy more liquor to sprinkle over Wufu's quilt, then bought the rooster—and the woman selling the bird got the brunt of my bad temper. We got into an argument because she said the rooster was heavier than it was, and that brought the policeman over to see what the argument was about. And then he discovered there was a corpse bundled up in the quilt.

"What have you got in that bundle?"

"What any worker from the countryside has. Baggage."

"Baggage? Wrapped up like that?"

"Yes, baggage wrapped up like that. Really."

The policeman kicked the quilt with his foot, then prodded it with his baton. "Why's it so soft?"

"It's a side of pork," Lively blurted out. But no one was stupid enough to believe that a side of pork could be wrapped up that securely. The policeman certainly wasn't.

"Eh?" He prodded it again. A corner of the quilt came loose and a foot appeared, not a pig's trotter but Wufu's worn-out shoe, stuffed with a bit of dirty cotton wadding. At that, Lively took off, and the policeman pounced on me.

I'd never been in a police station before. I'd always had as little as possible to do with the police. When the officer handcuffed me to the railing in Station Square, I was really scared. So I told him everything, from beginning to end.

"Stupid man!" he shouted at me.

Me? Stupid? No, I wasn't. Legally speaking, I was in the wrong, but my conscience told me I wasn't. The police officer took notes, then brought Wufu and me to the station. More questions followed. Wufu and I got to share an empty cell that night, and the next day, Wufu's corpse was taken to a Xi'an funeral home. The Freshwind Township government was informed, and Wufu's family was told to come arrange the funeral. The police said I could go.

Go? How could I go? With Wufu in a funeral home, how could I leave? I wasn't going anywhere! I said, "Wufu's going to be cremated, isn't he? He insisted he didn't want to be cremated."

"Everyone who dies in the city has to be cremated."

"But Wufu wasn't a city man. I brought him to the city, and I always looked after him. If he's burned up, how am I going to carry a bag of ash back to Freshwind? Everyone gets buried in Freshwind, otherwise they'd turn into unquiet ghosts. And Xi'an's too big. How's his ghost ever going to find its way home?"

The policeman just bellowed at me to get out. I clung to the trunk of a tree in the police compound. There was a bird's nest up in the branches. They couldn't pry my fingers free. They punched me, and the bird's nest fell on my head. "Bird's nest!" I said. At that, they dragged me off and booted me out. The big iron gate clanged behind me.

I had to go back to the train station. Wufu's wife and her brother were on their way to Xi'an, and I was worried they might get lost, so I went to wait for them in the square.

By nightfall, she was still not there, and all the trains from Shangzhou prefecture had arrived. The earliest she'd come now would be the next morning, so I decided to leave.

Besides, I'd had an idea: I wanted to see if I could find someone with a contact at the police station. Could they bend the rules so that Wufu didn't have to be cremated? I had to try one last time. My first thought was Gem Han; he was the only person I knew with that kind of clout. But back in Fishpond, I found Han's door padlocked. I called his cell phone, but he didn't pick up. Maybe it was Wufu's destiny (whatever that meant) to be cremated. Han was normally in Fishpond Village; even if he was out on business during the day, he'd be back in his rooms at night. Now, when we needed him most, he wasn't here. I was angry at Gem Han, but I was also angry at Wufu for having such a rotten destiny. There was nowhere else to go, so I headed back to Leftover House. We were still renting there, and everything was just as we'd left it. Oddly, although we'd been gone only a month, there was a trail of cobwebs going from the top of Wufu's bed to the window. I gathered his stuff together, then tied it all in a bundle. I left the cooking pots and the fan by his bed, and a pair of cloth shoes I found under the bed, their heels worn down unevenly. I didn't think he'd want those. After I'd gone back to my room, I heard a voice in my ear: *My shoes, my shoes!* So I got them and added them to the bundle, and discovered fifty yuan stuffed into the shoe uppers. He liked hiding money there, but he hadn't taken the money with him to Xianyang, nor had he asked me to put it in our hiding place. I was puzzled. Had he hidden money elsewhere? I rooted around in his room, looking under every brick, in cracks in the walls, under the bed mat, but there was nothing. The walls were smeared with bloody, squashed mosquitos, only the blood wasn't theirs, it was Wufu's. There was the slashed car advertisement, with a string of numbers written on it. I pulled it down, folded it, and put that in his bundle too.

I carefully counted Wufu's savings, noting it as I did so. It should have come to four hundred and fifty yuan, but I'd lent some to old Fan before we left for Xianyang. Also, I'd spent some of our communal money in Xianyang. I didn't have enough to total the amount I needed to give to Wufu's missus; how was I going to explain that to her? I ran downstairs to see if I could borrow some from Almond and Goolies, or Eight, but Eight's room was locked, and there was a stranger in the other room.

"Where's Almond?" I asked.

"Who's Almond?"

"Don't you know Almond?"

"Who are you?"

Who was I? "I live upstairs. I've been away for a while," I told him.

"I'm new here. Are you a trash picker too? And you've been away? I've been hearing noises upstairs for the last two nights. I thought it was a ghost."

"It was."

I was standing under our tree, wondering what to do, when Eight came back. He was wearing several outfits layered one on top of the other, so he bulged all over, and he had his hands tucked into his sleeves. "Who's there?" he called out when he saw my shadow under the tree.

"Me."

He bounded over and threw his arms round me, then punched me and complained that Wufu and I had gone off without telling him and had disappeared for a whole month. When he got home at night, there was no one to talk to. How he'd missed us! "Wufu! Wufu!" he shouted upstairs. "You always wanted me with you, in everything you did. You son of a bitch, why'd you go off and leave me?"

"Don't shout," I said. "Wufu's gone."

"What do you mean 'gone'?"

"He's dead."

His beaming smile froze. "What happened? You had a fight?"

I told him the story, and he burst into tears.

The stranger came out of his room when he heard Eight's wails, so I put my arms around Eight and tried to make him stop, and I wiped his eyes with my sleeve.

"Wufu still owes me five yuan," Eight said.

"You're crying over five yuan?" I was furious. I pushed him to the ground, and the stranger came over to calm me down. I pulled Eight upstairs, and pointed to the fan mounted over the bed, the cooking pot, the two bowls, the plastic basin, and the pile of pull-tab cans and plastic piping in the corner. "I'm giving you all these. Will that cover the five yuan? If it's not enough, you can go get his cart from the depot!"

"I wasn't crying because of the five yuan, but if I want to be paid the money back now that he's dead, does that make me a bastard? What a wretched life he had. In this whole city, he was the only one I could talk to. Now that he's gone, who'll be my friend?"

His mouth gaped so wide, you could have put your fist in it, and he started to cry again. I squatted on my haunches and cried too. Suddenly, Eight asked, "Have you burned ghost money for him?"

"No."

"Why not? There are so many toll gates on the road to the underworld, he's going to need money to pay the tolls." Eight ran downstairs and came back with a neat bundle of old newspapers. He stacked them on the floor. "Do you have a hundred-yuan bill?" he asked. I took out two, and he chose the newer, slapping first one side, then the other, on the newspapers. "We're making you an offering, Wufu, sending you money. This bill is worth ten one-hundreds, and ten one-hundreds is a thousand. There are more than a hundred here, so you've got a hundred thousand, Wufu!"

Eight burned the newspaper ghost money in Wufu's room. I knelt down too and helped feed the paper into the flames. The room filled with smoke, but Eight and I knelt there, keeping the fire going. When the whole bundle of newspaper had been consumed, we watched the flames grow smaller, until they turned into little tongues dancing and flickering. The ash lost its redness, glowed one last time, and went completely black.

"Get up," I said to Eight.

"Let me kneel here a bit longer."

"What happened to Almond? Why's someone else in there?"

"This time they really were arrested."

"Was it that murder case? Did they hide the suspect?"

Eight launched into a long story. "No, it wasn't that. He never turned up. They got caught buying stolen goods off some opium smokers. The police tracked them down, and they were arrested five days ago. If you steal a few bicycles, no one cares. If you rip off a few manhole covers, maybe no one will care, but if an opium smoker takes two hundred yards of iron fencing from the side of the highway outside the South Gate in one night, then that's a big deal and the law comes down on you like a ton of bricks. Almond and Goolies were too greedy. They grabbed anything and everything they could get their hands on. I always said they'd come to a bad end."

Eight had no sympathy for Almond and Goolies's plight, and was about to launch into a litany of complaints about what they'd been doing lately, but I was pissed off and cut him short. I had to go to Gem Han's place and see if he was back. Eight hemmed and hawed for a bit, then got a paper bag out from under his bed.

"What's that?"

"It's Wufu's. You can take it to him."

I tore open the paper bag. Inside was a pair of plastic women's shoes with whittled-down heels.

"Wufu was going to give these to his missus. What are you doing with them?"

"He put them on the window ledge, so I took them."

"You stole his things!"

"I didn't steal them. I took them because he owed me money."

"You mean those five yuan?"

"No, something else. See, the landlord came for the rent and you two weren't here, but I couldn't say you weren't here because then I thought he'd kick you out, and I knew you'd be back, so I handed over your rent. It was fifty for you and fifty for Wufu. I was going to tell you, but then Wufu died, so I didn't."

"You paid our rent? Fifty for me and fifty for Wufu?"

"Yup, fifty for you and fifty for Wufu."

My heart thumped. That fifty yuan I'd found stuffed in Wufu's shoe . . . Wufu must have put it aside to pay Eight back for the rent. I got out a hundred and held it out, but Eight wouldn't take it.

"It's for the rent. Take it!" I insisted.

Eight went with me to Gem Han's place, but the door was still padlocked. I was frantic. I thought of my nephew, the Briquette King, but he was no different from Eight; he didn't have any strings to pull. I put that thought out of my head. I knew only one person, just one, who might swing it for us, and that was Mighty. But I rejected him too. If Yichun was around, I would have gritted my teeth and gone looking for him, but she wasn't, and I really had no desire to see him. He'd already raised my hopes and dashed them once; there was no point in doing that again.

What to do? I couldn't think of anything, except to go back to the train station tomorrow morning and wait for Wufu's wife. Eight wanted to go with me so he could say a final good-bye to Wufu at the crematorium, but I wouldn't let him. I said good-bye to him, loaded Wufu's belongings onto our bicycle, and pedaled off on my own. Wufu always was the one who pedaled, with me on the back, but now I had just his bedroll behind me. *Sit tight, Wufu. I'm pedaling you now!*

62.

I reached the city center. It was nighttime, but the streets were brightly lit, and neon illuminations twinkled on all the skyscrapers. In front of the nightclubs, bars, teahouses, and saunas, the streets were jammed with cars. Groups of men and women, arms draped round one another, were singing, laughing, and exchanging jokes. I looked down and pedaled on. I didn't feel like stopping. But after I passed West Avenue, I changed my mind. *Wufu, why don't I take you for a ride around Xi'an and show you some of the nightlife?* And I set off, in no particular direction, down one lane, into another main road, pedaling, pedaling, anywhere that was lit up, wherever the crowds were.

In one street, I saw what I thought was a freestanding light fixture and was cycling over to it, when suddenly a trash picker popped out from one of the lanes, pulling his cart, head down, back bent. I got the fright of my life. It looked just like Wufu! I stopped to look at him, and he looked at me.

"Hey!" I called.

But he scurried off with his cart. It was piled high with trash, and a bundle of something fell off. When I got to the light fixture, I discovered it was the Chain-Bones Bodhisattva Pagoda, festooned with colored lights on each of its eight corners, all the way to the top.

How had I gotten here? Maybe my feet had brought me of their own accord. Or was it Wufu who'd made me come because he was still concerned about me, or was it some telepathic message sent by Yichun? I leaned the bicycle against a tree and hunkered down. I looked at the pagoda. We'd gone to Xianyang for those five thousand yuan, I thought, and Wufu had died there, but he wouldn't hold it against Yichun. Was he trying to tell her that he wouldn't be able to help earn the money? If Yichun's message had brought me here, what should I do next? I lit a cigarette. The wall enclosing the pagoda was overhung by trees and plunged in deep gloom. The tip of my cigarette provided the only light. I stared at it, and the cigarette fell from my fingers.

I found myself taking a cell phone out of my pocket, pressing numbers. A voice answered. "Hello? Who's there?" It was Yichun! Her voice was not at all clear—perhaps I'd woken her up and she'd crawled out from under the quilt to grab the phone—but it drew me like a magnet. I could pick her out of a crowd of a thousand, of ten thousand. I'd be able to hear her if she sighed, even if it was in the middle of a rainstorm.

"It's me, Happy Liu," I said, my voice shaking.

"Happy Liu! Where did you disappear to?"

"I didn't disappear. I wanted to give you a nice surprise. I went to Xianyang for a laboring job. I wanted to earn five thousand yuan . . ." I stopped. Had I managed to earn any money to give Yichun? Where was the money I'd earned? I broke down in tears.

"Happy! Happy!" Yichun shouted into the phone urgently. There was a crash. She must have gotten out of bed and knocked her tea mug off the bedside table.

"I'm here."

"What's up? What's the matter?"

"You have to save Wufu!"

I told her what had happened in Xianyang, about how Wufu's body had been taken to the funeral home. At the other end of the line, she was silent. Here I was, telling her my troubles, when I should be helping her, not adding my own problems to hers. Why was I making her suffer? I was a

coward; a man ought to shelter a woman from the storms of life, but I was
making her hold the umbrella over me!

"Happy! Happy! Calm down! Have you told Mighty?"

"I don't want to talk to him."

"Why not? He's got his fingers in so many pies, you should go talk to
him. What have you got against him?"

"Nothing. He has his life, I have mine."

"You're wrong, we're all in the same boat. Get in touch with him!"

I didn't answer.

"You must! Go to Mighty!"

A white light was shining on me.

I was suddenly wide awake. It really was a white light, a car's headlights, speeding down the lane, so dazzling I couldn't see a thing.

Had I been dreaming? Or daydreaming? Was Yichun's spirit
instructing me to contact Mighty? All right then, I would. For Wufu's
sake. *It's not coming from me, Mighty. This is from Yichun and Wufu.* I got
to my feet and went looking for a public phone, but the stores were all
closed. Dawn was breaking; I had to get to the railway station. I could
phone from there.

As usual, Station Square was brightly lit, and the sleepers on the
steps outside the waiting room were beginning to wake up, open their
puffy eyes, and go to the public toilets. There was a long line outside of
them, and a man was standing in line for the women's restroom. When
it got to his turn, he bellowed for his missus who was some distance
away combing her hair. She came running over, saying, "Paper, paper,
I need toilet paper!" She had long legs, just like Yichun.

In the phone booth, I dialed Mighty's number. It rang, but no one
answered. I was relieved, then felt guilty. I tried again.

This time Mighty answered. "Who is it?"

"Happy Liu. Meng Yichun told me to call you."

"Is she out?"

"No."

"Did you visit her? Did you give her my regards?"

I was speechless.

"Happy? You there? Say something."

"It's you I want to see. Can you come?"

"Me? Where are you?"

I told him.

"Stay where you are. I'll be there," he said.

But he didn't come. An hour later, the first train from Shangzhou arrived early, and I saw Wufu's wife and her younger brother, hurrying out of the station and peering around them. I called to them. Her hair had gone completely white, even though it had been jet-black when we'd left Freshwind. I was astonished. I handed over Wufu's bundle, his bag, and the eight hundred yuan from the site manager at Xianyang, and told her I had another four hundred and fifty that Wufu had saved. I lied. I told her it was in the bank and I'd get it out for her as soon as I could. She licked her finger and counted the bills one by one, then got her brother to count again. He asked me to tell them what had happened. They didn't seem to blame me, though he did say, "It would have been better to let us know right away."

I flushed. Then we went to the police station, and none of us said anything more. I'd thought about letting them go in alone, while I waited for Mighty outside, but I said nothing. The police made Wufu's wife sign lots of documents, using her fingerprint. When I asked if they could get Wufu's corpse sent back to Freshwind, the police said no; the rules said corpses couldn't be taken out of the city. Besides, Wufu was already at the funeral home. Outside the police station, Wufu's wife suddenly went limp and couldn't walk any farther.

"Will they burn him just like that?" she asked me. "He was right as rain when he left with you, and you're fine, and he's going to turn into ashes."

Jia Pingwa

What could I say? Her brother and I each took her by an arm, but she sagged to the ground like a bag of rice, and I practically had to put my arms right around her from behind to pull her upright.

"Didn't he say anything?" she asked.

"No, it was all so sudden."

"The last thing he said to me was, 'I'm going to Xi'an. Give me forty yuan.' He . . ."

Tears ran down her brother's cheeks, and he cried, "Sis! Sis!"

Suddenly, she began to wail, sitting on the ground and pounding her legs with her fists. "You left together. You said you'd bring him home safe and sound. So where is he? Where? Am I going back with a box of ashes?"

My God, if I could have taken out my heart to show her how much I cared, I would have. Where was Lively Shi? Why wasn't he here to back me up? *Wufu, Wufu, where's your spirit?* I had no energy left to try and defend myself, so I didn't. I said, "I let him down. I let you down. I'm ashamed of myself. I'm a disgrace!" and I slapped myself hard on the face.

Finally, she stopped crying. I found them a taxi and told them to go to the funeral home to say their last good-byes to Wufu before he was cremated. I said I'd go to the depot and sell his cart and get the four hundred and fifty out of the bank, then meet them at the funeral home. When I'd seen them off and gotten back to the phone booth in Station Square, Mighty was waiting for me.

There was no point in asking him to try to stop Wufu's cremation. I simply told him I'd been to visit Yichun at the Rehabilitation Center, and that she was doing all right and might get an early release.

"That's excellent news. Did Ms. Meng ask you to tell me?"

I grunted.

"What's up? Why's your face so dark?"

"It's always been dark."

452

"Last time I saw you, I offered you a job in my company. Why didn't you do that instead of trash picking?"

"Wait till Meng Yichun's released. Let's talk about it after that."

"Fine, bring that Wufu with you. It's steady work in a company. Providing it doesn't go bankrupt, you can both stay in the city permanently!"

"Thank you," I said.

Whether or not I went to work for Mighty, I'd stay in the city, forever consumed with regret that Wufu had died and could no longer keep me company. I looked up at the clear sky, then around me at the endless expanse of Station Square, and at the jungle of skyscrapers beyond. Then a new thought occurred to me: Wufu would be staying here too. Not Lively, not Eight, not even Almond and Goolies. Only Wufu, forever an unquiet ghost, hovering above the city streets.

AUTHOR'S NOTE

HAPPY AND ME

One afternoon three years ago, I was at home reading *Journey to the West* and thinking that the monk Xuanzang and his three disciples were really four different aspects of the same person, when suddenly there was a loud rapping at the door. These days, when everyone has telephones, it is rare for a visitor to turn up unannounced. I wondered who it was. I was not expecting anyone. I deliberately waited awhile before opening the door, to indicate my displeasure at this uninvited guest. Knock, knock, knock, the noise came again, getting louder with each rap. Finally, there was a thud as someone kicked the door.

Indignant, I flung the door open. On the doorstep stood Liu Shuzhen.

"Ai-ya! I thought you weren't home!" he said.

"It's you!" I exclaimed. "When did you get to town?"

"I'm a city-liver now!" He never did speak properly.

I smiled and told him to come in and sit down. "Shuzhen, you do have a way with words!"

"Don't call me Liu Shuzhen. I've changed my name to Liu Gaoxing, Happy Liu! Call me Happy Liu."

And that was my first meeting with "Happy Liu," the city dweller.

Anyone who has read my novel *Qinqiang*[1] might remember that the character Shuzheng is modeled on Liu Shuzhen. He and I grew up together. When we were little, I wanted nothing to do with him—his hair was a bit crinkly and his nose was always running with yellow snot—but I idolized his *da*. Where I grew up, we always called our fathers *Da*. Shuzhen's *da* was not one of the Jia family, so to me, he was "Uncle," and since you had to add a name after "Uncle," he was Uncle Wulin. Uncle Wulin was illiterate, but he was a wonderful talker. He could recite operas by heart, and he told us stories from *The Romance of the Three Kingdoms*. Shuzhen's *da* was a tall man, at five foot eleven. He was particularly eloquent when he got angry with his wife: he would sit cross-legged on his mat, and out would come a stream of marvelous curses, a sort of rapid-fire comic monologue. He never lost his cool, but he could be extremely sarcastic. During the Cultural Revolution, our junior secondary school closed down, and Shuzhen and I worked on the commune farm together. Afterward, he went into the army, and I went to college. Time passed, and I used to come home to see my parents at New Year and other festivals. By then, Shuzhen was working in the township government offices as a cook, though he soon got fired for poor hygiene and taking leftovers home to feed his family's pigs. More time passed. I wrote my books; Shuzhen worked as a plasterer, made "hanging noodles," ground up soybeans for bean curd, and had a fried-breadstick stand at country markets. He turned his hand to just about everything, but never with any success. He eked out a wretched existence and was the butt of jokes in the village. But as soon as I arrived, he always got wind of it, and rushed over to see me regardless of the hour, day or night. We talked and laughed at length, never feeling sleepy or tired, until my mother made a meal for us, and we ate, and he smoked one cigarette, with another stuck behind his ear, and finally left.

---

1   The title *Qinqiang* means Qin, or Shaanxi, opera. The novel was published in Chinese in 2005 and won the 2008 Mao Dun Literature Prize.

I enjoyed talking to him. He had so much to tell me.

One summer when I was back visiting, all my other childhood friends dropped by, but there was no sign of him. Where was Shuzhen? I asked. The others said he might be over in the fields on the river's west bank, transplanting rice seedlings. This was long after the wheat harvest, and the new seedlings were into their second round of irrigation, so what was Shuzhen doing still transplanting them? I asked.

"His kids are little, so he's the only one working the land. But it doesn't matter how many hours he puts in, he'll never get ahead!"

At nightfall, I crossed over to the west bank to see him. He was working a narrow strip of land, bent over transplanting long rows of seedlings, a wraithlike figure in the moonlight. He had a radio perched on the bank, and he was listening to the folksinger Song Zuying. I shouted his name, and he splashed over to me, with excited shouts. "Let's go back to my house!"

"You carry on," I told him.

But he said, "I'm already behind. Getting more behind won't make any difference!"

He had recently built himself a house at the edge of a stream, leaving no room in front. New Year's couplets were still pasted on either side of the entrance gate. One read, "The mouth serves not just to eat and drink but also to smile" and the other, "Close your eyes and the darkness will make you sleep sweetly."

"Did you come up with those yourself?" I asked.

"I did, but they don't match." With his finger, he scraped between his teeth, then smoothed back the corner of the left-hand couplet. "I told the whole village, take the tiles off my roof, but if anyone takes my couplets, I'll break their legs!"

Once we'd reached his yard, he shouted to his wife, "Boil some water! City folk are very particular. They won't drink it unboiled, so make sure it comes to a rolling boil." When she brought in the pot of water, he grabbed a handful of sugar to put in the water. "Fry some eggs for us," he told his wife.

She looked startled. "But we don't have any hens; there aren't any eggs!"

"No eggs?"

"It's much too late in the evening to be eating eggs!" I hastily added.

He cackled with laughter. "Useless woman! If you haven't got any eggs, why don't you go borrow some and make yourself scarce, instead of standing there saying, 'We don't have any eggs'!"

That made me laugh too.

"Forget the eggs. We have to give Pingwa something to keep him happy! Get our money chest in here!"

His wife was still not playing along. "Money chest?" she queried.

"Brainless woman! What's our sow if not a money chest?"

So the sow, already penned for the night, was let out. She was driven into the room, belly trailing on the ground, and Shuzhen scratched her hind legs. The sow settled herself comfortably on the ground, all four legs splayed. And a string of twelve chubby little piglets came climbing over the doorstep, one after another.

"Amazing," he said. "Each piglet is worth fifty-eight yuan, fifty-eight! Times twelve, how much does that make?"

We talked late into the evening, and Shuzhen never made it back to the fields to finish his transplanting. I asked about the village. Things were not good, he said. There was less and less land. The road had been upgraded to a grade one highway, and that ate up land. The railroad was built; more land went. Now they were building an expressway, which would also need land. The villagers now had only two-tenths of a mu^2 per capita. It was all very well to have these new roads and railroads, but where were the villagers supposed to plant their crops? The scientists had invented everything else, so why couldn't they invent a way of

---

2   One US acre = six *mu*.

growing crops without land? How many girls and boys had I seen in the village, he asked. None? That was because there weren't any. They'd all left to find factory work. In the old days, your sons went to be cannon fodder for Chiang Kai-Shek, and your daughters were snatched by the local governors. Nowadays, you had kids for the city to take!

"Fucking A went and pulled down his two-room house and sold the rafters over his wife's head, and with his wife so sick too! Was it her or the money he was after?

"B finally gave up his bachelor life and got married, and the woman came with three kids. Her previous husband had fallen out of a tree and ended up paralyzed. She married B on the condition he support her ex-husband[3], and so without an ounce of effort, B got himself three ready-made children!"

Then Shuzhen asked me if I knew a doctor who could treat mental illness.

"Why?"

"It's C. Remember him?"

"No."

"You don't? When we were kids, we stole his apricots, and he chased us into the lotus pond!"

"And he's gone crazy?"

"He and his wife have had a hard life. They make a bit of cash grinding up soybeans for bean curd for a whole year so they could send their son to college, and when the boy graduated, he refused to come home to teach in the County Town. He's just drifting around Xi'an. As if that weren't enough, their daughter left to look for a job, and there's been no word from her in two years. It's not C. It's his wife who went nuts. Can you find a doctor for her? I'm embarrassed to pass their house. She's lost all sense of shame; she runs outside without her

---

3   An old custom called *zhaofuyangfu*, where the new husband gains the children from a previous marriage but must support the ex-husband too.

pants on; I don't know where to look." Listening to Shuzhen, I could only sigh.

"Why are you sighing?" he asked.

"Country life is so hard."

Shuzhen had visited me once before in Xi'an, only finding my house with great difficulty, but I was at a meeting in another province. When I got back, my daughter told me that someone had turned up, covered in dust, saying he was my old classmate. She had offered him some tea, but he didn't drink it; he just wanted some cold water from the faucet. Then he spat a gob of phlegm on the floor and scuffed it in with his foot. She couldn't understand a word he said, and he finally left. It must have been Liu Shuzhen. I scolded her for not treating him with respect. Country folk live a hard life and, like anyone with a hard life, have a lot to worry about. The thing they most hate is being treated rudely by family and friends in the city. If you treat them well, they'll praise you to the skies. They'll say you have a car, live in a Western-style villa, read books as thick as a brick, and even if you eat bean porridge, they'll insist it's really ginseng and bird's nest soup. They'll do everything in their power to look after your old home for you, making sure that not a pear goes missing from the pear tree in your yard, and when they visit their family's graves at the Grave-Sweeping Festival, they'll shovel some dirt on your ancestors' mounds too.

But if you slight them, they'll bear a grudge forever. No matter how momentous your achievements in the outside world, it'll have nothing to do with them, and if someone asks after you, they'll say, "Oh, him! Why d'you want to talk about him?" When you go back to the village, they'll keep their distance, or if they can't avoid you, they'll say only, "You're back . . ." as they walk on by. If you hold any family celebrations or funerals in the village, they won't come even if you lay out food and drink for the villagers, and if they do come, they'll bring a bucket, and for every bowl they finish, they'll tip half a bowl of food into the bucket and take it home for the pigs. So I told my daughter, "Whether I'm at home or not, if anyone turns up from my village, you must welcome them with a big smile and a good meal. Don't make them change their shoes when they come in, don't put the ashtray next to them when you offer them cigarettes, and make sure you look at them and pay attention to whatever they say. They're country folk, without much education, but they have a sense of humor and wisdom that city folk don't have."

I was sure that Liu Shuzhen would never come to the city again after the way my daughter treated him, but he came one more time—as Happy Liu.

This time, he'd come to join his son. His son had been in Xi'an for quite a few years by then, delivering coal for a coal store. His son had not inherited his father's and grandfather's cheery good humor. He was morose and taciturn, with a big chip on his shoulder. He had wanted to leave home and get a job in the city as soon as he finished junior secondary school. His father had let him go. As Shuzhen put it, "Father and son are always at odds, so I figured, let him fucking go, and if he doesn't starve, at least that'll be something!" But when his son came home for Chinese New Year, he was wearing a smart suit. They played poker, and every time he lost a yuan, he pulled a wad of hundred-yuan bills an inch thick out of his jacket pocket before finally extracting a one-yuan bill. He put the wad of notes back and lost one yuan again. And again. He never gave his father any money at all. So Shuzhen decided to come to the city in search of work too. By this time, he was fifty-three years old. He spoke like a much younger man, but his back and legs were no longer as strong as they had been. He couldn't run fast, and the work was wearing him out. He had worked for a month at his son's coal store, and he was sharing his son's shed, thrown together out of plastic sheeting. It was so hot that he splashed water on the ground every night and slept on a bamboo bed mat. He didn't care about that. What really riled him was that he and his son had completely different ideas about things. When he earned money, he saved it. When his son earned money, he spent it. He wanted his son to build him a new house

461

back in the village, but the young man refused. They had a huge fight, and Shuzhen decided to leave and go it alone. The only work he could do on his own was trash picking, so he started picking trash.

Trash picking? I realized I had never given that job a moment's thought. After Shuzhen's visit, I reflected that I had lived in Xi'an for more than thirty years, and I had seen trash pickers pulling their carts or riding their three-wheelers every day. I'd had them collect old books and periodicals from my apartment, but I had never asked myself where these people came from, why they were collecting trash, and whether they could make a living from it. They roamed the streets by day, but where did they go at night? City folk, including me and my family, pride ourselves on our stylish, luxurious bathrooms, regarding them as a sign of progress and civilization, but the city is like its people: what goes in must come out; we excrete as much as we ingest. Then why do we simply not see, or care about, the people who do the job of cleaning up our waste? They're as essential to our lives as breathing, and we don't forget to breathe, do we? I'm constantly telling people we ought to be more grateful, yet what usually moves us are heroic acts of altruism and self-sacrifice. How have we managed to completely forget about the sun in the sky and clean water in the earth?

That day, Shuzhen and I talked about the ins and outs of trash picking. Shuzhen's experience as a trash picker had clearly become the prism through which he observed Xi'an and his life as a migrant laborer in the city. Sitting arms akimbo and cross-legged on the sofa, he exuded self-satisfaction as he looked at my astonished expression. Sucking hard on his cigarette, he took his time explaining it all to me: people came from all over to work as laborers, but the situation in the areas they came from varied. The towns of Dongfu and Xifu in the Guanzhong plain were fairly well-off, and people from there knew what they were doing, finding themselves jobs in big companies in the development zones. The people from Northern Shaanxi were generally tall, and they liked to stick together, working for a labor contractor, doing building or road-construction work, or working as security men in hotels and residential compounds. Of the three districts in the south of Shaanxi Province, the people from Hanzhong and Ankang looked like southern Chinese. They knew how to make themselves agreeable and mainly worked in service industries as sales assistants, or in hotels, teahouses, and foot-massage parlors. As for Shangzhou District, it was the poorest and most remote in the whole area: it did not produce food and nor did it have reserves of coal, oil, or natural gas. The only way for the locals to make money was to open small eateries, but they generally loved art and literature and were eager to see their children educated so that they could escape the mountains as soon as possible. He gave me an example: our county's government, overseeing a population of three hundred thousand people, raised a little more than twenty million yuan annually in revenue. But ordinary people raised a hundred million a year to send their young people to college—every year, every single year, a hundred million. The country folk were like sheaves of corn, pressed and wrung to extract the last drop of moisture from them, until only the husks were left. And hardly any of those students returned home when they graduated. They found temporary work in government offices or private companies in the city, continually changing jobs and business cards. The pitiable resources of the Shangzhou Mountains were leached away, all the money taken by students. The elite, those with education, migrated. It was the single biggest migration in China's history, with people moving en masse to the city. The city was one great maw, slurping every drop of oil from the soup bowl. "They put on new clothes and go!" Happy Liu said. "All they leave behind are tattered old padded jackets. Shangzhou is left destitute. In the end, even those left behind have to go. The prospect of Xi'an dazzles them. In their eyes, its streets are paved with gold and silver. But they leave with no funds, no skills, and there's no one with power and influence to smooth their way when they arrive in the city. The only way they can eke out a living is to take on the hardest, dirtiest, and most exhausting work that requires the least skill—delivering coal or picking trash. And if one person does well, then they draw others after them, first family members, then fellow villagers, one after another, until now, when Shangzhou folk make up most of the trash pickers and coalmen."

After that, Happy Liu paid me frequent visits, whenever it rained. Rainy days were his rest days, "holidays" he called them, and either he came to my house or invited me to his rented room. It was from him that I learned that many of the younger generation of the Jia clan had come to Xi'an as migrant workers. But they had not contacted me, perhaps because I had not been home much and they felt they did not know me, or perhaps because they were not doing well and were embarrassed to admit it. In any case, what could I have done to help them? Although I was a well-known writer, I had no official clout or money. Happy Liu wanted nothing from me; he knew me and he knew my situation. He came because we were almost the same age, and because he needed to talk, and I needed to listen, and so we became close. Whenever I had a family occasion, like a birthday party for my elderly mother or my daughter's wedding, I naturally invited him. He looked and dressed quite differently from the other guests, with his booming voice and his laugh that sounded like the Hong Kong actor Stephen Chow. He stuck out, as if a potato had suddenly appeared in a basket of apples. But he was a cheerful potato. And as soon as the others found out that he was a migrant worker, they were amazed at his calm good humor and thoroughly enjoyed talking to him. He was full of fantastic tales of village life and city trash pickers, which he brought vividly to life. As our guests listened, entranced, his face would suddenly become grave, and his language elegant and classical. He had, he said, "read an uncountable number of books and had an inexhaustible appetite for the strange and marvelous." His listeners, many of them university professors, exclaimed, "Happy Liu! Your imagery is superb, better than Pingwa's!"

"I got better grades in school, but I'm still just a ceramic tile. So is Pingwa, but fate decreed that his is glued to the cooktop and I'm glued to the WC!" And he cackled with laughter, wiped his runny nose, and said, "I'm just Runtu, the hired hand's son!"

I tried to stop him. "Enough of your crazy metaphors. I'm not Lu Xun, and you're not my family's hired hand."

"I don't care whether you're Lu Xun," he insisted, "but I'm definitely Runtu!"

But he was no servant of a long-dead, famous writer; he was Happy Liu, and he stirred in me a strong desire to write about him and his community of trash pickers. In every large city, there are celebrations easily costing tens of millions, splashy parties displaying the kind of ostentatious luxury that the era of prosperity has brought. Perhaps by writing about trash pickers' lives and their thoughts and feelings, I could put my finger on the pulse of otherwise hard-to-reach aspects of city life today. The desire grew in me, and I told a friend about my idea. He disagreed with me: history has always been created by society's elite—in the old days, it was emperors, their commanders and ministers, scholars, and beautiful women; nowadays, it's officials, industrialists, financiers, leaders of fashion, and other powerful people. If you want to write mainstream literary work, you have to write about them, not about trash pickers, he told me. My friend was not wrong, but I had my own reality, circumscribed by the environment in which I lived, and my knowledge and abilities. Other people might write better on my friend's topics, but I wanted to write about what I could, and felt I should, write about.

Over the years, I have given much thought to the following question: as a writer in my fifties, of many years' standing, in a country that reportedly publishes a thousand or so novels annually, what should I be writing about and what significance do my writings have? I have weighed myself in the balance: I may not be a mythical hero, a Houyi, shooting my arrows at extra suns, or a Xingtian, wielding shield and ax, but neither am I a dilettante writer, in the business of producing popular-genre fiction and making myself rich. I'm not setting myself up as high-minded or especially ambitious, and I don't claim to write good work. But then few are capable of writing a classic or seeing the big picture, so why should I not write notes on society that I can bequeath to posterity, I reasoned. I wanted to write about Happy Liu and others like him coming to town from rural areas, about how they get here, how they adapt to city life, their viewpoints, how they feel about the hand that fate has dealt them. And if I can enable my readers to understand these things from my writing, then I will be satisfied.

I was once at a conference where a reporter repeatedly asked me, "What's your next novel about?" I grew impatient and sketched out my plans; what I did not expect was that he would announce it in his newspaper, and other newspapers would republish it, and tell everyone that my next novel was to be about migrant laborers. Then I received an anonymous letter, perhaps from a reader. There was nothing in it, except two slips of paper. On one were the following words: "Before one studies Zen, mountains are mountains and waters are waters; later, mountains are no longer mountains and waters are no longer waters; after enlightenment, mountains are once again mountains and waters, once again waters." The other read, "Every book presents something fresh and new, with unparalleled eloquence." These were both ancient sayings, and I took the fact that a stranger had copied them out and sent them to me as a reminder, a suggestion, an encouragement, and an earnest hope. I was moved by the letter, but also quite anxious. I felt pressured. As I sat down to write, I realized that I understood only Happy Liu, not the whole community of trash pickers. You can't make a meal out of a daikon radish. I had to focus; I had to enter the world of trash pickers.

I began to explore. I asked a literary critic friend, Mr. Sun Jianxi, also from Shangzhou District, to help me, because he'd once told me that almost a third of the population of his home village had come to

Xi'an as trash pickers. My friend Sun was impulsive and enthusiastic; he immediately contacted a relative who was a trash picker—let us call him D—and explained outright that I wanted to see where they lived. The relative initially responded, "Jia Pingwa? You mean the writer?"

"You've heard of him? Yes, that's the one. He wants to meet you," Sun said.

There was silence; then the relative asked, "He wants to see us? Like we're performing monkeys?"

"No, he's not like that."

"Well, if he's coming as a fellow countryman, that's fine. He can come talk anytime. But if he's playing the Empress Dowager playing at harvesting the crops, then tell him no."

Sun relayed his relative's message. I told Sun, "It's true we're going so I can gather source material for my writing, but let's forget that for the moment. And let's not act as if we pity them or have plans to rescue them. Let's just drop in." So we went, and I didn't take a notebook, or tape recorder, or camera. We simply filled our pockets with cigarettes.

That evening, we went looking for the address Sun's relative had given us. I had no idea there were so many satellite villages on the south side of Xi'an. And they all looked pretty much the same. We actually went to a different village, one with dozens of lanes, and two hours later, we still had no idea where he was. We asked a man hunkered down smoking under a lamppost, "Is there someone called D living in this village?"

"The sky is full of stars. How would I know?" he said.

"Do trash pickers live here?" I asked.

"That lane down there is full of them!"

We went down the lane, and sure enough we saw a lot of carts, with women sorting trash into categories, and two men eating their dinner in a doorway under the lamplight. Their bowls were full of corn porridge cooked with potato. The potatoes had not been sliced, and the men opened their eyes wide as they ate them whole.

"Do you know D?" we asked. They shook their heads but said nothing. We went into another yard, surrounded by buildings like watchtowers. There were dozens of doors, each to someone's home and covered with a curtain. They looked like the drawers of a medicine cabinet in a Chinese herbalist's store. Sun raised his voice. "D!"

A woman drew back her curtain and came out to pour away some slops. "Don't shout. Someone's sick in here."

"I'm looking for D," Sun said.

"There's no one called D here."

We never did find D, but that evening, we went into a dozen or so yards on the pretext of looking for our friend from back home. We spoke to fifteen or sixteen trash pickers, saw how they lived and what they ate, got a rough idea of what brought them to town, and when, and what they were earning. They looked at us warily and were not talkative; if pressed to say more, they'd respond, "I couldn't say," and disappear with a laugh. None of them was like Happy Liu, which I was sorry about. Still, in the yard at the end of the lane, there was a lame fellow who was more talkative. He accepted a pack of cigarettes from me, tore it open, and flipped the cigarettes at the people standing in each of the doorways. Every one he tossed was caught midair. They surrounded us then, exclaiming, "Cigarettes are expensive!" The lame man said he'd been trash picking in Xi'an for ten years, and the others in the yard were all people he had subsequently brought from his village. It was like the old call to rise up in revolution, when one person would sign up for the Red Army, then bring along others. The village they were living in was called Trash Village.

Sun told them, "In our village, there was an old man with seven sons and grandsons who joined the army, so the old man was called 'begetter of soldiers.' You're a begetter of trash pickers!"

It was meant as a joke, but then a woman spoke up from another doorway. "He's never begotten anything. He hasn't even got a missus!"

The old man went red with embarrassment and took us into his room. Brushing the dirt off the edge of the bed, he invited us to sit down. "It's not true I haven't been married," he said. "I've been married three times! It's just that we didn't get along, and I split up with each of them before a year was up."

His room was a filthy, cramped, windowless space and stank to high heaven. Sun pulled back the old man's bedding, took the lid off his cooking pot, and peeled apart the *ganmo* sitting on a plank at the head of the bed. "Can you still eat them when they're this moldy?" he asked. Then he found a magazine under the pillow. "You read magazines?"

"Yes."

"You know there's this author . . ."

I hurriedly stopped him and took the magazine. Half the pages were stuck together, and I couldn't pull them apart. "What's sticking them together?" I asked. The old man went scarlet, and muttered something about the fancies he had when he was in bed and how he had to jerk himself off, and he didn't want to dirty the bedding, so he . . . And he snatched the magazine back and pushed it under the pillow again. I didn't blame him, and I didn't make a joke about it either. I asked his name, and he said his family name was Bai and his given name Dianrui. He took pains to explain which characters were used: "Dian" as in "palace." It certainly had an elegant ring to it.

This Bai Dianrui made an impression on me, and I visited him a few times after that. He was very self-assured. When I offered him a cigarette, he offered me an aluminum window frame that he'd found. I refused it. He asked me what I did—was I a reporter? If so, would I take his picture? He'd love to see himself in a big photo in the newspaper. So the next time I went, I took my camera, but he was so ill with diarrhea, he couldn't get out of bed and didn't want his picture taken.

We contacted Sun's relative again and finally figured out which satellite village he was living in. Sun and I went to see him, taking an art teacher friend with us. He had a car and drove us there, because he

Jia Pingwa

wanted to paint some of the trash pickers. When we got to the village, D was watching for us. He was wearing a pair of leather shoes, but his legs looked oddly bowed.

"Did you find those shoes in the trash?" Sun asked.

"Where would I find new leather shoes like this in the trash? I was given them. I thought I'd give them to my son, but I put them on for your visit. Only they're a bit small." Then he whispered to Sun, "Is that Jia Pingwa in the suit?"

"No," Sun said, and pointed at me.

"He's kind of short!"

I still had some cigarettes with me, but when I offered them, he said he'd given up smoking. We walked down the lane and into a yard, at the back of which stood a shabby, six-story tenement. Sun's relative lived under the roof, where there were seven rooms, the other six occupied by members of his extended family. They had just returned from picking trash and were busy lighting fires and making dinner. I was introduced, and they greeted me with smiles. Then we sat in D's room. It was so small, you could barely turn around. It was a hot day, and there was a terrible smell of dirty shoes. The artist could not bear it and excused himself, saying he was going downstairs for a stroll and we should call him when we were ready to leave. He had never lived in the countryside. I had, so I took my shoes off and sat on the bed. I asked him how much they paid in rent and which streets were their patch. I asked how he got there in the early morning and back again in the evening. I found a bowl and poured some hot water from the thermos. He had an expressive face, but he didn't give much away in answer to my questions. For instance, he said the rent was "fine, they could pay it," and that their patch was outside Zhuquemen. He made a decent living, and he had a bicycle. He and his wife rode into town on it in the mornings. They stored the carts overnight in the trash depot, and things were going well, much better than before.

470

"Don't be so proper!" Sun said. "Say whatever you want! Shoot your mouth off!"

"Really, shoot my mouth off?"

"Shoot!" I said, and all three of us laughed. After that, the conversation livened up. D was certainly entertaining. He didn't share Happy Liu's vivid expressions, but he was spot-on with the anecdotes he recounted, and he even remembered when and where they'd happened. I teased him a little to get him going, but after that, I was completely immersed in his trash-picker stories, happy when he was happy, and sad when he was sad. His wife was outside, preparing dinner on the stove. She called, "Why don't you tell them about the defeats? Anyone would think you were like Lord Guan[4] and always won your battles! Come here a minute."

He went out, then came back to say, "The missus wants to know if you've had dinner. If you haven't, you're welcome to eat with us."

"We'll eat with you," I said immediately.

He relayed the message, adding, "Go buy some hung noodles at the village store."

I hurriedly said, "Don't bother buying noodles. We'll have whatever you're having. Tell us more!" He told us three stories: once he'd been beaten up at a construction site; another time, he'd been conned out of three hundred yuan by some thugs when he was trash picking; the third time, he'd been fined by the SCOUT patrol.[5] By that time, the food was ready. It was corn porridge, no vegetables, or vinegar, or chili pepper. He gave me a big bowlful and said they had some salt. He put a paper bag

---

4   General Guan Yu (died 220 CE) is a Chinese historical figure whose stories are found in the much-loved historical novel Romance of the Three Kingdoms.

5   Literally, the City Appearance Management Department (市容), part of the Urban Administrative and Law Enforcement Bureau, or Chengguan (城管), in every large city in China. Called the SCOUT patrol in the novel.

of salt in front of me, and his wife supplied a pair of chopsticks. They were stuck together and I knew they hadn't been washed properly, but I couldn't ask her to wash them again, or wipe them on a bit of paper. If the chopsticks were clean enough for them, they were clean enough for me. So I dug them into my bowl and slurped down the porridge.

D watched me eat. Then he got an electric fan out from under the bed. It emitted only a few puffs of air, and in some places, the cable had cracked and the wiring hadn't even been taped over with insulating tape. I was worried that he would get an electric shock, but he said, "It's nothing." He turned the fan around so the air blew in my direction. When I had finished my bowl of porridge, he double-checked whether I'd had enough.

This relative of Sun's became, if not a friend, certainly a familiar acquaintance. He often dropped in on Sun, and whenever he turned up, Sun would phone me and I'd join them. Sometimes he brought along a curio he had found, for instance, a bamboo flute or an old-fashioned glasses case, and we would give him a hundred yuan for it. He knew I was a collector, and once presented me with a small black pottery jar, which he thought was an antique. I accepted the gift with thanks, but I could tell it had been made only a few years back. I tried to press some money on him, but he refused. "I'd accept if I'd only made ten yuan today, but I made eighteen, and that's enough for me. Actually, I'd like your help." A fellow trash picker had had his cart impounded when he parked it on the side of the road. It was a main road with a sign prohibiting nonmotorized vehicles, but the man was illiterate, and now the SCOUT patrol was demanding five hundred yuan to release it. Could I help him get his cart back?

"I'll get it back for you," I told him.

"If you do, I'll buy you a drink!"

The truth was that neither Sun nor I was in a position to pull strings with the SCOUT patrol. But I had to help, so I called a friend at the TV station, and we concocted a plan. I got him to bring along a video camera, so that if they refused to release the cart, we would threaten to do an exposé of their cruel treatment of a vulnerable section of society. Off we went, full of bravado, but when we got there, to my astonishment, some of the office staff recognized me. They were really excited to see me and treated me like an honored guest. That boded well. After a few pleasantries, I explained the situation, and in no time, the cart was released. D threw his arms around me in excitement and told me I was "cool, really cool!" He asked for my business card and said if anyone tried to bully him again, he'd show them my card and say I was his cousin. "Can I say you're my cousin?"

"You can!" I said.

A few months later, I finally began to write my story of the trash pickers.

It was far more difficult than expected, because I kept thinking that I was about the same age as Happy Liu, Bai Dianrui, and D. Had it not been for my having earned a place in college in 1972 as one of the "worker, peasant, soldier" cohort when classes resumed during the Cultural Revolution, I was sure I'd be a farmer now, and a middle-aged trash picker too. What form would my life have taken? It grieved me to think of the poverty, low status, loneliness, and discrimination they experienced, having left the land to come to the city. Something seemed to weigh down my pen. I would finish a chapter, then tear it up, and start again, and tear it up again.

I asked myself a host of questions: Why had this class of migrant workers appeared in China? Was it an inexorable part of the process of political and economic reform, political expediency, or long-term strategy? Who organized or managed this class? Would they ever be accepted and integrated into the city? Was migrant labor really a way to make the peasants rich? What would happen to villages deprived of labor power? Were city and countryside merging together, or was the gap between rich and poor widening? I am not a politician, and I do not understand much about running a country, nor am I an economist with the skills to direct society. Nevertheless, as a writer, even though I perfectly understood that one's writing should not get mired in controversy, I could not rid myself of an innate sense of anxiety that made writing this book an agonizing process. I was also astonished to discover that although I had lived in the city for decades, and normally prided myself on being a modern man, I still had a peasant's mind-set: deep in my heart, I loathed and resented the city, resented it on behalf of those trash pickers. The more I tried to write, the less I wrote, and eventually I consigned a manuscript a hundred thousand Chinese characters long[6] to the flames.

I stopped. I decided to give it a rest, then start again. As it happened, something major came up, and it was months before I took up my pen again. It involved a couple from the village where Sun's relative lived; in this case, the man, who was actually just a few years older than I, and his wife were working as trash pickers in Xi'an, and their daughter was waiting tables here. Someone offered to find her a better-paying job, but it was a trap. She was kidnapped and trafficked to Shanxi Province. Every time the father saved two thousand yuan, he went off in search of his daughter. He had been doing this for two years, and finally tracked her down in a mountain village in Wutai County, Shanxi. He'd never told anyone what had happened, because he felt so ashamed, but when he was leaving to rescue his daughter, he had no money for the fares, so he came to borrow from Sun and me, and had to tell us what had happened. We were angry with him for never having reported such a major crime to the police, and for not telling us before now. How did he imagine he was going to rescue her single-handedly? we asked. We immediately took him to the police station, but the local police simply ignored him, on the pretext that he was only renting a room there and his permanent residence, his *hukou*, was elsewhere. After a fierce argument, the police were persuaded to register the case,

---

6   Around seventy thousand words in English.

and they confirmed that they could indeed go free the girl, but only if the father could provide the precise address of the household to which she had been sold. They also demanded a minimum of five thousand yuan in expenses for the trip. The father was about to set off for Wutai County again, to get the address. Sun and I warned him not to alarm the family if he visited his daughter. Two weeks or so later, he was back. Weeping, he said, "I'm telling you, Shangzhou's poor, but those Wutai gullies are much, much worse. Our daughter's just a young girl, and they keep her tied up in the house, like a cow. She's had a baby too." As he cried, Sun and I cried too. Then we took the money to the police. But the police said they couldn't spare anyone right then; it would be a month before they could free up an officer. At that point, Sun and I reported the case to the parents' police station in their village, where we had a contact; the chief agreed to make the trip in person and reduced the fee by one-third. After more back-and-forth, a rescue team was assembled and set off. The plan was for them to arrive in the Wutai County mountain village that evening. Sun and I fretted over whether they would find the girl, whether the family and the whole village would let her go, whether a fight would break out, and whether it was safe to drive the mountain road at night. We were on tenterhooks as we sat by the telephone, having arranged that as soon as the girl was freed, they would call us. Nine o'clock passed, and there was no news. Ten o'clock—no news. Eleven o'clock—no news. Sun got out a basket of peanuts. "I'm sure it's fine. The police chief is an experienced man. He's rescued three trafficked women before now." We tried to defuse the tension by eating the peanuts, but we'd soon finished them and crunched the skins to dust in our hands. Midnight arrived, and there was still no phone call. "Is there something wrong with the phone?" I asked. I checked, and it was plugged in. I took out my cell phone and dialed the number. It rang right away. Sun's mother, a woman in her seventies, was sitting with us and was so anxious that she burst into tears. "She's such a bright, beautiful girl!" she said. "How could she have been forced into marrying an ugly forty-year-old and bearing his child? If the rescue attempt fails this time, the family will move her away for sure, and then she'll never come back!" Sun tried to reassure her. "Don't talk like that!" But the old woman would not stop, Sun flared up, and then the pair of them had an argument. Then there was silence in the room, except for the ticktock of the clock on the wall. At 12:21 a.m., the phone rang. Sun and his mother reached out at the same moment, and the phone fell to the floor. It was the police, saying simply, "We've done it! We're leaving the gully now." Sun and I shouted in unison, waking the neighbors, who came and asked what was happening. At one o'clock in the morning, Sun said he felt like eating a bowl of noodles. His mother rolled out some dough, and we had two bowls each.

Sun and I got a great sense of achievement from this rescue, and we couldn't wait to tell the story to all our friends. Until three days later, when the old man came to thank us, and we heard what had actually happened. Then we were no longer so happy. The villagers had formed a mob, pursued the police furiously, and blockaded them in, shouting, "Why shouldn't we have wives? All thirteen women we bought ran away . . . Do you want this village to die?" A fight broke out, and the police chief ended up with a torn uniform and a big bruise on his leg where a stone had struck him. If he had not fired his gun into the sky, the rescuers' lives would have been at risk. The daughter got away, but she was not able to take her son, who was under a year old, with her. This was a real tragedy: father and daughter were reunited, but husband and wife were separated; the father got his daughter back, but she lost her son. When I paid a visit afterward to the old man, he was still picking trash. His daughter refused to see anyone.

I continued to visit the lanes where the trash pickers rented rooms. Every time I went to the south side of the city, I found myself veering that way. If I bumped into any trash pickers on the main street, I would stop and exchange a few words, or simply stand and watch. Nearly a year passed. Not much changed. Most of the trash pickers I had gotten to know were still in Xi'an, and still picking trash. One man had put his child through college, and the child graduated, but the father fell seriously ill with asthma, and had to give up picking trash and return to his village. Another earned enough money to acquire a business partner and open a convenience store in the County Town, and he built a new house in his home village. He was held up as an example of what trash pickers could achieve, and was widely admired. And some, of course, died in Xi'an: one was run over by a car, one died of cirrhosis of the liver, and a third was robbed and killed by a fellow trash picker.

When I read about the robbery and murder in the newspapers, I went to the village where Bai Gongrui was renting a room. Bai was not there, but I met a young man who had been picking trash for two years and, as it turned out, had met the robbery victim. He could not understand why the man had not invested the hundred thousand yuan he had saved over ten years of trash picking in a house in Xi'an. "Are you buying a house as soon as you've got the money?" I asked the young man. "Definitely!" he exclaimed. "Won't you go back home?" I asked. He said, "I made a blood vow at the grain mill at the village entrance never to return!"

Happy Liu was still in Xi'an, of course, and seemed in better health than before. Every six weeks or so, he'd go home to tend his crops, then return to the city. Every time he came back, he either phoned to let me know he was back or turned up on my doorstep. He chatted about this and that, his face full of expression, his laughter joyous.

"Why are you always so happy?" I asked. He paused, then said, "Well, my name's Happy. How could I not be happy?"

What kind of a man was happy even though he was not fortunate? But at that moment, I understood how I had to change my thinking, and how I had to write the novel. At the start, I was writing about a multitude of trash pickers, based on Happy Liu's stories, but delving into so many people's lives had been a dead end. Although that one comment from Happy Liu meant nothing much in itself, strangely it was as if kindling that had hitherto only been smoking suddenly leapt into flames. So I made Happy Liu the subject of my novel. He was, after all, unique. Yet he was also typical. He had turned into the man that he was now because the more life weighed on him, the more he knew how to bear difficulties lightly; the more he suffered, the more enjoyment he got out of life.

"Happy Liu, now I understand you!" I exclaimed.

"Understand what about me?"

"You're a lotus growing out of pond mud!"

"Don't use all that fancy language about me! You know the brick kiln back home? When I came out of the kiln, my face was as black as a pan bottom, so black it made my teeth look white."

That was Happy Liu in a nutshell: a clean life in a filthy place.

He put it much better than I did. I laughed, and he cackled along with me. That day, we had *paomo* mutton soup.

I started the novel again. The original title had been *City Life*, but I changed it to *Happy* (《高兴》).[7] Before, I had drafted it similarly to my novel *Qinqiang*, writing about a city and its many residents, but now, the focus was on Happy Liu and two or three of his buddies. The original structure was like that of *Qinqiang*, layer upon layer of cave homes rising up the mountainside, or a huge patch of thousands of wild chrysanthemums carpeting the gully floor. Now it was a single small pagoda with bricks neatly laid one upon the other, or a single rose blossom with layer upon layer of petals opening out.

It did not take me long to draft the novel this time, and when I finished, I felt a huge sense of relief. Before I did the final revisions, I returned to my home village. Things had changed: when the new highway was built, sections were made to follow the south bank, not the north bank, of the Dan Jiang River. A road I had driven for decades suddenly presented a different aspect. The first thing I did on every trip

7　Re-titled in English, *Happy Dreams.*

home was to visit my father's grave, burn ghost money, and make an offering of liquor. The pain of losing my father never lessened, and this time was no different, even though he had been dead for eighteen years. As soon as I knelt by the grave, my tears began to flow. But this time, for the first time, there were flowers. My younger brother had planted all kinds of shrubs around his grave, but I had never been there at the right time. Now, all kinds of flowers were in bloom, in a variety of shapes, sizes, and colors. As I knelt to burn the paper money, I noted how death and the smell of fresh flowers merged into one. Tears running down my face, I muttered to my father, "With *Qinqiang*, I wrote about how the peasants of our area left the land, and now with *Happy*, I've written about how they live in the city. At least I've written it . . ." Just at that moment, I felt a breath of wind, and the flowers trembled, and the ash from the paper money danced in the breeze. For a long time, I sat there, dazed. Then it occurred to me that there was something wrong with *Happy*. I left the grave, the smell of death and the perfume of flowers still in my nostrils, mulling over the fact that although I had written how Happy Liu enjoyed his life, setting my story against the background of the hardships of a trash picker's life, something essential was still missing. I was unsure what the problem was—perhaps the narrative angle? I got no further in clarifying the problem, but I was absolutely certain that minor adjustments were not the solution. I had to change the angle, and if the narrative changed, the book had to be rewritten.

I abandoned my plan to tour all the Shangzhou District counties and hurried back to Xi'an. I immersed myself in the fifth revision of the work, making major changes to the protagonists, cutting out many details and whole segments of commentary. To the best of my ability, I curbed my tendencies to euphoria, hyperbole, and complexity, and tried to make the story real, and detailed, so that it felt warm and intimate. With the plot and the protagonists so pared down, I frequently broke the rhythm as I wrote, and where it read too smoothly, I deliberately went for awkwardness, making the language abrasive and clumsy, as if

I had not used any skill, as if it were written by someone whose talent had completely run dry.

Happy Liu stopped by a few times during this period. He was such a strange man. He saw me amusing myself with ink painting and calligraphy, and he actually bought some ink and a brush and practiced writing characters on old newspapers at home, hanging each sheet on the walls of his room. I was even more astonished when, after he discovered that I was writing a book in which the main character was based on him, he started writing an article about me, thirty thousand characters[8] long. He had scribbled down stories in a notebook of our shared childhood, using pens of assorted colors. As a piece of writing, it was basically unstructured, and many of the Chinese characters were written incorrectly, but he had brought those long-ago events vividly back to life. I did not know what to say to him. He would certainly never get anything like this published—he had dashed it off in a few free moments—but how could I tell him not to write? I told him, "Happy, if you'd gone to college thirty years ago and stayed in Xi'an, you would definitely be a far better writer than I am. If I had joined the army and returned to the village, and then come to town to pick trash, I wouldn't be half as good at it as you, nor would I have your joyousness and humor."

But when I had rewritten three-quarters of the novel, I got some bad news that almost made me start all over again. I was chatting with a writer friend and enthusiastically reading him the first three chapters, when he suddenly said, "Are you beginning with the peasant carrying his friend's corpse home on his back?"

"Isn't that a good beginning?" I said.

"Where did you get that story from?" he asked.

"I adapted it from a TV news report."

"Have you seen the film *Falling Leaves*?" he asked.

---

8   Around eighteen thousand words in English.

"No, what about it?"

"Well, that film is about a peasant carrying his friend's corpse home on his back."

I was thunderstruck and hardly dared ask what happened in the film. But when he told me the plot, I relaxed. The director may well have seen the same report as I had, but the film was purely about the details of the man's journey home. For me, it was only the opening of the novel. My friend advised me to change it anyway, but I refused. Why would I change it now, when I had written it into my first draft in 2005? The film was the director's, and my book was wholly my own work. A mule and a horse were two different things.

About three weeks later, it was pouring rain, and I was writing the ending of the novel when the phone rang. I was annoyed at the interruption and didn't answer it. But a little while later, it rang again. I picked up the receiver and barked, "Who is it?"

It was Happy Liu. "Why didn't you answer the phone?" he asked.

"I was busy."

"I know you're busy, and I can't burst in on you, but when I phoned, you didn't answer! What are you busy with? Are you still writing about me? When are you going to finish?"

"I've nearly finished, just making a few minor revisions," I said.

"You find it so difficult to write! But I've already finished writing your biography!" And he cackled with laughter over the phone.

He was phoning me from right downstairs. I put down my pen, opened the door, and a very wet Happy Liu came in.

ABOUT THE AUTHOR

Born in 1952 in Dihua Village, Danfeng County, Shaanxi Province, Jia Pingwa went on to graduate from Northwestern University's Chinese department in 1975. He is deputy chair of the China Writers' Association Presidium and chair of Writers' Association Shaanxi branch. Among his best-known works are the novels *Qinquiang (Shaanxi Opera)*, *Ruined City*, *Turbulence*, *Old Kiln Village*, *The Lantern Bearer*, *Master of Songs*, *The Pole Flower*, *White Nights*, *Earth Gate*, *Gao Lao Village*, and *In Memory of Wolves*. He is also the author of several short story collections and novellas.

ABOUT THE TRANSLATOR

Passionate about spreading Chinese literature to English readers, Nicky Harman has translated the works of many renowned Chinese authors into English. They include Anni Baobei's *The Road of Others*, Chan Koon-Chung's *The Unbearable Dreamworld of Champa the Driver*, Chen Xiwo's *Book of Sins*, Han Dong's *A Phone Call from Dalian: Collected Poems*, Jia Pingwa's *Happy Dreams*, Dorothy Tse's *Snow and Shadow*, Xinran's *Letter from an Unknown Chinese Mother*, Xu Xiaobin's *Crystal Wedding*, Xu Zhiyuan's *Paper Tiger*, and Yan Ge's *The Chili Bean Paste Clan*.

Harman has won several awards, including the Mao Tai Cup People's Literature Chinese-English translation prize 2015 and the 2013 China International Translation Contest, Chinese-to-English section. When not translating, she promotes contemporary Chinese fiction to the general English-language reader through literary events, blogs, talks, a short story project on Paper-Republic.org, and with the Writing Chinese project 2014–2016 at Leeds University. She also mentors new translators, teaches summer school, and judges translation competitions. Harman resides in the United Kingdom and tweets as the China Fiction Bookclub @cfbcuk.

TRANSLATOR ACKNOWLEDGMENTS

I have hugely enjoyed translating Jia Pingwa's novel, *Happy Dreams*. It's a story that is both gritty and touching, with a Chaplin-esque hero and imaginative and expressive language—from puns, jokes, and bad language to occasional lyrical flights of fancy—What more could a translator want?

That said, the process of translation was also something of a challenge. For instance, the novel contains large amounts of dialogue, much of it in dialect. Dialogue must read as if someone is actually speaking it. Dialect presents further difficulties, first and foremost to understand it, before rendering it into convincing English. Fortunately, a number of people helped me along the way. First, I would like to thank Jia Pingwa for patiently answering my questions and even sending me two hand-drawn diagrams! Also, my heartfelt thanks go to Liu Jun, who did a great job checking and elucidating dialect expressions and explaining cultural context, and to Gao Gao, Wang Bang, and Yan Ge for the same reason. And last, I thank Amazon Publishing's editors for their careful examination of my translation, and for making useful suggestions that significantly improved it. Between them, they enriched my understanding of the novel and saved me from a few embarrassing mistakes. Any errors that remain are, of course, my own responsibility.